SIR WILLIAM

Sir William

DAVID STACTON

This edition first published in 2014
by Faber & Faber Ltd
Bloomsbury House, 74–77 Great Russell Street
London WC1B 3DA

Printed by Books on Demand GmbH, Norderstedt

All rights reserved
© The Estate of David Derek Stacton, 1963

The right of David Derek Stacton to be identified
as author of this work has been asserted in accordance
with Section 77 of the Copyright, Designs and Patents Act 1988

This book is sold subject to the condition that it shall not, by way of
trade or otherwise, be lent, resold, hired out or otherwise circulated
without the publisher's prior consent in any form of binding or cover other than
that in which it is published and without a similar condition including this
condition being imposed on the subsequent purchaser

A CIP record for this book is available from the British Library

ISBN 978-0-571-32258-9

Our authorised representative in the EU for product safety is
Easy Access System Europe, Mustamäe tee 50, 10621 Tallinn, Estonia
gpsr.requests@easproject.com

for Charles Monteith

NOTE: The third section of almost any *no* drama, or the third piece of any complete cycle, is generally devoted to a woman who describes a journey she has taken, points out the beauty spots along the way, and cries woe. The result is something in the *Sharawadgi* style, though as Hannah More said, "The *Chief Attraction* was to meet the Brahmin and the two Parsees."

Introduction

The Case of David Stacton

Might David Stacton (1923–68) be the most unjustly neglected American novelist of the post-World War II era? There is a case to be made – beginning, perhaps, with a simple inductive process.

In its issue dated 1 February 1963 *Time* magazine offered an article that placed Stacton amid ten writers whom the magazine rated as the best to have emerged in American fiction during the previous decade: the others being Richard Condon, Ralph Ellison, Joseph Heller, H. L. Humes, John Knowles, Bernard Malamud, Walker Percy, Philip Roth, and John Updike. It would be fair to say that, over the intervening fifty years, seven of those ten authors have remained solidly in print and in high-level critical regard. As for the other three: the case of H. L. Humes is complex, since after 1963 he never added to the pair of novels he had already published; while John Knowles, though he continued to publish steadily, was always best known for *A Separate Peace* (1959), which was twice adapted for the screen.

By this accounting, then, I believe we can survey the *Time* list today and conclude that the stand-out figure is David Stacton – a hugely productive, prodigiously gifted, still regrettably little-known talent and, yes, arguably more deserving of revived attention than any US novelist since 1945.

Across a published career of fifteen years or so Stacton put out fourteen novels (under his name, that is – plus a further raft of pseudonymous genre fiction); many short stories; several collections of poetry; and three compendious works of non-fiction. He was first 'discovered' in England, and had to wait several years before making it into print in his homeland. Assessing Stacton's career at the time of what proved to be his last published novel *People of the Book* (1965), Dennis Powers of the *Oakland Tribune* ruefully concluded that Stacton's was very much 'the old story of literary virtue unrewarded'. Three years later Stacton was dead.

The rest has been a prolonged silence punctuated by occasional tributes and testaments in learned journals, by fellow writers, and around the literary blogosphere. But in 2011 New York Review Books reissued Stacton's *The Judges of the Secret Court*, his eleventh novel and the second in what he saw as a trilogy on American themes. (History, and sequences of titles, were Stacton's abiding passions.) In 2012 Faber Finds began reissuing a selection of Stacton's novels.

Readers new to the Stacton *oeuvre* will encounter a novelist of quite phenomenal ambition. The landscapes and epochs into which he transplanted his creative imagination spanned vast distances, and yet the finely wrought Stacton prose style remained fairly distinctive throughout. His deft and delicate gifts of physical description were those of a rare aesthete, but the cumulative effect is both vivid and foursquare. He was, perhaps, less committed to strong narrative through-lines than to erecting a sense of a spiritual universe around his characters; yet he undoubtedly had the power to carry the reader with him from page to page. His protagonists are quite often haunted – if not fixated – figures, temperamentally estranged from their societies. But whether or not we may find elements of Stacton himself within said protagonists, for sure his own presence is in the books – not least by dint of his incorrigible fondness for apercus, epigrams, pontifications of all kinds.

He was born Lionel Kingsley Evans on 27 May 1923, in San Francisco. (His parents had met and married in Dublin then emigrated after the war.) Undoubtedly Northern California shaped his aesthetic sense, though in later years he would disdain the place as an 'overbuilt sump', lamenting what he felt had been lost in tones of wistful conservatism. ('We had founding families, and a few traditions and habits of our own . . . Above all we had our sensuous and then unspoilt landscape, whose loss has made my generation and sort of westerner a race of restless wanderers.') Stacton was certainly an exile, but arguably he made himself so, even before California, in his estimation, went to the dogs. In any case his fiction would range far away from his place of birth, for all that his early novels were much informed by it.

Precociously bright, the young Lionel Evans was composing poetry and short stories by his mid-teens, and entered Stanford University in 1941, his studies interrupted by the war (during which he was a conscientious objector). Tall and good-looking, elegant in person as in prose, Evans had by 1942 begun to call himself David Stacton. Stanford was also the place where, as far as we know, he acknowledged his homosexuality – to himself and, to the degree possible in that time, to his peers. He would complete his tertiary education at UC Berkeley, where he met and moved in with a man who became his long-time companion, John Mann Rucker. By 1950 his stories had begun to appear in print, and he toured Europe (what he called 'the standard year's travel after college').

London (which Stacton considered 'such a touching city') was one of the favoured stops on his itinerary and there he made the acquaintance of Basil 'Sholto' Mackenzie, the second Baron Amulree, a Liberal peer and distinguished physician. In 1953 Amulree introduced Stacton to Charles Monteith, the brilliant Northern Irish-born editor and director at Faber and Faber. The impression made was clearly favourable, for in 1954 Faber published *Dolores*, Stacton's first novel, which *Time and Tide* would describe as 'a charming idyll, set in Hollywood, Paris and Rome'.

A Fox Inside followed in 1955, *The Self-Enchanted* in 1956: *noir*-inflected Californian tales about money, power and influence; and neurotic men and women locked into marriages made for many complex reasons other than love. In retrospect either novel could conceivably have been a Hollywood film in its day, directed by Nicholas Ray, say, or Douglas Sirk. Though neither book sold spectacularly, together they proved Stacton had a voice worth hearing. In their correspondence Charles Monteith urged Stacton to consider himself 'a novelist of contemporary society', and suggested he turn his hand to outright 'thriller writing'. But Stacton had set upon a different course. 'These are the last contemporary books I intend to write for several years', he wrote to Monteith. 'After them I shall dive into the historical . . .'

In 1956 Stacton made good on his intimation by delivering to Monteith a long-promised novel about Ludwig II of Bavaria, entitled *Remember Me*. Monteith had been excited by the prospect of the work, and he admired the ambition of the first draft, but considered it unpublishable at its initial extent. With considerable application Stacton winnowed *Remember Me* down to a polished form that Faber could work with. Monteith duly renewed his campaign to persuade Stacton toward present-day subject matter. There would be much talk of re-jigging and substituting one proposed book for another already-delivered manuscript, of strategies for 'building a career'. Stacton was amenable (to a degree) at first, but in the end he made his position clear to Monteith:

> I just flatly don't intend to write any more contemporary books, for several reasons . . . [M]y talents are melodramatic and a mite grandiose, and this goes down better with historical sauce . . . I just can't write about the present any more, that's all. I haven't the heart . . . [F]or those of conservative stamp, this age is the end of everything we have loved . . . There is nothing to do but hang up more lights. And for me the lights are all in the past.

Monteith, for all his efforts to direct Stacton's *oeuvre*, could see he was dealing with an intractable talent; and in April 1957 he wrote to Stacton affirming Faber's 'deep and unshaken confidence in your own gift and in your future as a novelist'.

The two novels that followed hard upon *Remember Me* were highly impressive proofs of Stacton's intent and accomplishment, which enhanced his reputation both inside Faber and in wider literary-critical circles. *On a Balcony* told of Akhenaten and Nefertiti in the Egypt of the Eighteenth Dynasty, and *Segaki* concerned a monk in fourteenth-century Japan. Stacton took the view that these two and the Ludwig novel were in fact a trilogy ('concerned with various aspects of the religious experience') which by 1958 he was calling 'The Invincible Questions'.

And this was but the dawning of a theme: in the following years, as his body of work expanded, Stacton came to characterise it as 'a series of novels in which history is used to explain the way we live now' – a series with an 'order' and 'pattern', for all that each entry was 'designed to stand independent of the others if need be'. (In 1964 he went so far as to tell Charles Monteith that his entire *oeuvre* was 'really one book'.)

Readers discovering this work today might be less persuaded that the interrelation of the novels is as obviously coherent as Stacton contended. There's an argument that Stacton's claims say more for the way in which his brilliant mind was just temperamentally inclined toward bold patterns and designs. (A small but telling example of same: in 1954 at the very outset of his relationship with Faber Stacton sent the firm a logotype he had drawn, an artful entwining of his initials, and asked that it be included as standard in the prelims of his novels ('Can I be humoured about my colophon as a regular practice?'). Faber did indeed oblige him.)

But perhaps Stacton's most convincing explanation for a connective tissue in his work – given in respect of those first three historical novels but, I think, more broadly applicable – was his admission that the three lives fascinated him on account of his identification with 'their plight':

> Fellow-feeling would be the proper phrase. Such people are comforting, simply because they have gone before us down the same endless road . . . [T]hough these people have an answer for us, it is an answer we can discover only by leading parallel lives. Anyone with a taste for history has found himself doing this from time to time . . .

Perhaps we might say that – just as the celebrated and contemporaneous American acting teacher Lee Strasberg taught students a 'Method' to immerse themselves in the imagined emotional and physical lives of scripted characters – Stacton was engaged in a kind of 'Method writing' that immersed him by turn in the lives of some of recorded history's rarest figures.

*

Stacton was nurtured as a writer by Faber and Faber, and he was glad of the firm's and Charles Monteith's efforts on his behalf, though his concerns were many, perhaps even more so than the usual novelist. Stacton understood he was a special case: not the model of a 'smart popular writer' for as long as he lacked prominent critical support and/or decent sales. He posed Faber other challenges, too – being such a peripatetic but extraordinarily productive writer, the business of submission, acquisition and scheduling of his work was a complicated, near-perpetual issue for Monteith. Stacton had the very common writer's self-delusion that his next project would be relatively 'short' and delivered to schedule, but his ambitions simply didn't tend that way. In January 1956 Monteith mentioned to Stacton's agent Michael Horniman about his author's 'tendency to over-produce'. Faber did not declare an interest in the Western novels Stacton wrote as 'Carse Boyd' or in the somewhat lurid stories of aggressive youth (*The Power Gods, D For Delinquent, Muscle Boy*) for which his *nom de plume* was 'Bud Clifton'. But amazingly, even in the midst of these purely commercial undertakings, Stacton always kept one or more grand and enthralling projects on his horizon simultaneously. (In 1963 he mentioned almost off-handedly to Monteith, 'I thought recently it would be fun to take the Popes on whole, and do a big book about their personal eccentricities . . .')

In 1960 Stacton was awarded a Guggenheim fellowship, which he used to travel to Europe before resettling in the US. In 1963 the *Time* magazine article mentioned above much improved the attention paid to him in his homeland. The books kept coming, each dazzlingly different to what came before, whatever inter-connection Stacton claimed: *A Signal Victory*, *A Dancer in Darkness*, *The Judges of the Secret Court*, *Tom Fool*, *Old Acquaintance*, *The World on the Last Day*, *Kali-Yuga*, *People of the Book*.

By the mid-1960s Stacton had begun what he may well have considered his potential *magnum opus*: *Restless Sleep*, a manuscript that grew to a million words, concerned in part with Samuel Pepys but above all with the life of Charles II from restoration to death. On paper the 'Merrie Monarch' did seem an even better subject for Stacton than the celebrated diarist: as a shrewd and lonely man of complicated emotions holding a seat of contested authority. But this work was never to be truly completed.

In 1966 Stacton's life was beset by crisis. He was in Copenhagen, Denmark, when he discovered that he had colon cancer, and was hospitalised for several months, undergoing a number of gruelling procedures. (He wrote feelingly to Charles Monteith, '[A]fter 48 hours of it (and six weeks of it) I am tired of watching my own intestines on closed circuit TV.') Recuperating, he returned to the US and moved in once more with John Mann Rucker, their relations having broken down in previous years. But he and Rucker were to break again, and in 1968 Stacton returned to Denmark – to Fredensborg, a town beloved of the Danish royal family – there renting a cottage from Helle Bruhn, a magistrate's wife whom he had befriended in 1966. It was Mrs Bruhn who, on 20 January 1968, called at Stacton's cottage after she could get no answer from him by telephone, and there found him dead in his bed. The local medical examiner signed off the opinion that Stacton died of a heart attack – unquestionably young, at forty-four, though he had been a heavy smoker, was on medication to assist sleeping, and had been much debilitated by the treatment for his cancer. His body was cremated in Denmark, and the ashes sent to his mother in California, who had them interred in Woodlawn Cemetery, Colma.

From our vantage today, just as many years have passed since Stacton's untimely death as he enjoyed of life. It is a moment, surely, for a reappraisal that is worthy of the size, scope and attainment of his work. I asked the American novelist, poet and translator David Slavitt – an avowed admirer of Stacton's – how he would evaluate the legacy, and he wrote to me with the following:

> David Stacton is a prime candidate for prominent space in the Tomb of the Unknown Writers. His witty and accomplished novels failed to find an audience even in England, where readers are not put off by dazzle. Had he been British and had he been part of the London literary scene, he might have won some attention for himself and his work in an environment that is more centralised and more coherent than that of the US where it is even

easier to fall through the cracks and where success is much more haphazard. I am delighted by these flickers of attention to the wonderful flora of his hothouse talents.

Richard T. Kelly
Editor, Faber Finds
May 2014

Sources and Acknowledgements

This introduction was prepared with kind assistance from Robert Brown, archivist at Faber and Faber, from Robert Nedelkoff, who has done more than anyone to encourage a renewed appreciation of Stacton, and from David R. Slavitt. It was much aided by reference to a biographical article written about Stacton by Joy Martin, his first cousin.

SIR WILLIAM

I

IT IS A COLD DAY in January, 1782. There is an echo in the air, as though the invisible had snapped its fingers; and the street musicians find their strings drawn taut, so that their fiddles sound an octave higher, with a shrill, emasculate, *castrato* sound not unlike the tone of a glass harmonica. London is white. There is a foundation of dirty snow, reticulated by sleet, upon which stands a burned-out edifice of trees. The sky, a half-formed cataract, shows here and there the blind blue of vision, hardened and rimed over. In Covent Garden the horses blow steam over the vegetables. Down near Blackfriars Bridge, the shores of the Thames are a similitude of asbestos and isinglass, cracked to the edges of water which looks a glossy black.

In Portman Square, Mr. Greville does not mind any of this. Being interested in little except appearances (it is why he has bought the house), Mr. Greville does not mind much of anything except being snubbed. Lacking other qualities, he has made a virtue of *vertu*, which has no need of heat, and is himself an object of *vertu*, so he seldom feels the cold—in the weather, in the world, or in anything. Mr. Greville is pettifogging, pusillanimous, pretentious and pink, but he is also the younger son of the Earl of Warwick (and thus the Honorable Charles Greville), so somehow he hangs on. He is an amateur, a dilettante, a *kleinigkeitskrämer*, a *pococurante*. Call him what you will, he has made the Grand Tour, he is much the same in all languages. He is not ill-favored, despite the affronted eyes of the perpetual diner-out: his mouth is shapely, his voice a sonorous squeak; his manner is adroit; he does have a heart, small, well-regulated, but sufficient to keep his cheeks aglow. If it fits in with his plans, he contrives to be kind; and so he takes in everyone except his betters. And Emily is not among his betters, as he himself would be the first to state.

He is reading a letter, an excellent example of the papermaker's art, since he has provided the paper himself, but the writing, though legible, is a servant's copperplate, too genteel to be correct, too emotive for gentility. He catches a word here and there:

> . . . believe me I am allmost distrackted, I have never hard from Sir H. . . . . . what shall I dow, good God what shall I dow . . . . I think my friends looks cooly on me, I think so. . . . . O dear Grevell write to me . . . Don't tell my mother what distress I am in and dow aford me some comfort.

He is delighted. Things have worked out to plan. He will afford her some comfort, if not much. Though he feels ambition to be vulgar, and no doubt he is right, Greville does have plans. This time they have been successful. At the cost of handing the girl a bundle of franked covers, he is now in a position to have her on the cheap. He is pleased, for though knocking up tuppence tarts in Green Park does well enough for a commoner, it is not prudent; it is not comfortable; it is not sedate; it does not satisfy. And besides, there is always the Peril to Health. So he can afford to be generous. Not only is the girl prepared to be discreet, but her mother will make an excellent *gouvernante* of small economies.

"My dear Emily," he writes, and considers he is being kind, as indeed, for him, he is, and tells her she has been imprudent (she has: she is with child), and extravagant (Sir H. allowed her the use of a carriage). It is best, in emotional matters, to establish the business arrangements in writing. He says he will look after the child. He has no love of children, being one himself—he has no love of rivalry in anything, for there is the risk of failure, the no less embarrassing possibility of success—but these things are sometimes important to women, and besides (*noblesse oblige*) the child may *just* be his. He would not dream of acknowledging it, but he cannot bring himself entirely to reject it, either. He is like this in many things, which no doubt explains why he has just lost his seat in Parliament.

He has not kept his seat, but he wishes to keep Emily. Therefore he encloses money—with an adjuration not to spend it—seals the letter, and settles back to wait. He is content to wait. Indeed, poor man, he will wait his life away, patient, sly, cunning, bland, adroit, not entirely deficient in charm, but doomed always to sit at the wrong mouseholes, for the right ones have been taken up already by larger, quicker, more aggressive cats. Still, in his small way he does know how to manage a catnip mouse, and how is he to know that this time he has a catamount by the tail instead? She scarcely knows it herself.

She is disconsolate in Wales, where she is about to receive his letter; or rather, since it is better in this world to put all pain behind us, and since the only way to do this is to modulate present events to the past tense, endure, and hope for pleasure presently, Wales was where she was.

Indiscretion had brought her there. It was not her fault. In a world which preferred the huffy distinction of immobility, a trait imported from the imagined French, she had had the vulgarity to be born vivacious. As the country daughter of a village blacksmith, and hence trite, she could not help but be. The world was alive to her, not merely a charade, for she had seen it in color; and after you have seen the world in color, the gray ground of the English water-color school does not suffice.

Wales, however, was damned cold. The Reverend Gilpin in his works upon the Picturesque, admired that countryside but spent his winters in a comfortable parsonage, whereas Emily was imbedded in what could scarcely be called a crofter's cot. Icicles bayoneted the eaves, and the thatch was slimy with hoarfrost, which gave it the mucous glitter of elvers in a pail. The chimney smoked. Indeed, it had smoked the owners, so that Granny Morgan looked like some *Frisian* curiosity, freshly extracted from a *Danish* bog.

Had it been any other season, Emily could have gone for pensive strolls in the ivied ruins of the nearby abbey, to be caught up and rescued by a passing nobleman; but paper shoes, which were what she had fled in, cannot withstand the snow. Therefore she had no choice but to sit indoors and wonder which answer she would get to her letter, yes or no; for if one were bad, the other would be worse. Why this misfortune had befallen her, she did not know, for she had meant no harm. She never did.

She had only tried to better her situation, first by taking one with the family of a fat-faced physician named Dr. Budd, and then in other ways. Dr. Budd's house was near Blackfriars Bridge, and Emily had not been happy there, and what was worse, it was the time of the Gordon Riots, which had frightened her.

"Nonsense, my girl, so long as you stay indoors you'll not come to harm," said the cook; but a rock came through one pane of the kitchen window, smash, and something very like a gunny sack smacked into the areaway, but was human, and had its bones cracked, and bled and died.

There was nowhere to run but up to the attics to hide. There is nothing for anyone of common sense to do but that, in any age, with the devil right behind you; but still, if you can get to the top first, by the time he gets up he's winded himself—he's just like you are—so he has to behave himself after that. He hasn't the breath for his original intentions. He can only marvel that he made it to the top at all.

If anything, the Budds were worse than the riots, what with the starched-cambric rustle of intrigue belowstairs, and such sounds as she overheard of the same thing going on with a silken swoop above, among the quality. So what with the giggles and buckteeth of the second parlormaid, a most superior person, and the gravelly eyes of Dr. Budd's lady, who always had a plump arm to interfere—and Lord, how the wicked man did pinch—Emily soon came to regard herself, without complacence, as a pretty creature, though not, though never, with him.

With, as it happened—but she could not quite remember this clearly—a real officer, a lieutenant in the Navy, who had sworn eternal devotion; but unfortunately he had had to sail away, as they so often do, so down she went with a bump again, and how was she to rise? What she had done immediately after that, except that there had been a great deal of it, she neither could nor would remember.

"My child," said an old crone, in cheap night lodgings, "why are you here? You are too young and pretty. You do not belong here for another fifteen years at least." And she peered about the slumside dormitory, where ugly women crept drunkenly from cot to cot, the youngest of them thirty-five.

Since no one had spoken kindly to her for several days, Emily tumbled her story out, among these dank and greasy shadows, and begged for sympathy.

"I saw no harm in it," she said (indeed she had enjoyed herself). "But then the Budds turned me out, so I want employment."

"The harm is in the getting caught," said the old crone. "And as for employment, we women have but one, but in the future you must mind your wage."

Emily was indignant. "I could not go with any man I did not like," she said.

"No woman ever does, but grant, the rich are always likable," said the old crone. "If nothing else, 'tis money makes them so. But never spend your earnings, for as you can see about you, that is a fair cruel thing for any woman to do. And if you are seriously minded to reform, perhaps I can assist you, for I have among my acquaintance a Dr. Graham, a most philanthropic man." And she gave a lopsided, well-intended, but dissembling leer.

So Emily went to work for Dr. Graham's Temple of Health, an establishment in Adelphi Terrace much patronized by the voyeur; and as for the old crone, she spoke privately with the learned proprietor, pocketed her 2/6, and was never seen again.

Two gentlemen at the Temple of Health attracted Emily's attention, the first because he stared at her so, the second because she could not help it; he reminded her of her naval gentleman. They came day after day, to watch her while she impersonated the Goddess of Health and gave old gentlemen their mud baths. She had several weeks to gather her impressions.

Greville had the eyes of an affronted pig, though in actuality pigs have vivacious eyes; and though she liked him well enough, she did not like him very much. She thought him stuck up. "I am not," he seemed to say, "as other men. Tinsel goods are all very well for your present situation, but when you wish quality, as no doubt in time you will, you may have me." What girl of spirit would accept so grand a proposal made upon a scale so small?

The other gentleman, Sir Harry Featherstonehaugh, had eyes of a warmer, softer quality, like soaked raisins. He was handsome, sleek, boisterous and seductive. He knew how to put you at your ease. He made jokes (Greville never made jokes); he never gave lectures (Greville had with him always an invisible podium); he asked her to go to the country with him. He did not seem disappointed when she said, "Not likely." Instead he gave her things, sweetmeats, a shawl, a good dinner or something silly. Then, if she liked it, he asked her again. He was hearty and never vulgar, he knew how to treat you properly, and they became friends.

So what was the harm in it?

What fort would not capitulate upon such terms, in short, everything, and a truce with life. She had been besieged too often. In time one comes to dread manning the same defenses every day, just as many a wary bitch has allowed herself to be taken during the season, merely to litter and have done with it.

Besides, he took her to Up Park, and she had never seen a country house before, let alone driven sensuously between its gates, around the bend so accurately calculated by Capability Brown, and there was the house, an enlarged toybox upon an eminence, and all the retainers out to receive them, cap in hand, except for the housekeeper, who had the prim look of a Presbyterian gratified, but not amazed, by still more evidence of sin.

"Never mind," said Emily, who didn't, not just then, "I am the image of a lady; I would confound Beau Nash," and leaped down tomboy hoyden instead of waiting to be handed out, and went indoors to drawing rooms hung with yellow silk, and everything so fine.

Over the wall of the local grange in Cheshire, where she was born, she had seen big fat blooms of white lilac as a child, and jumped to catch them, but they were too high, and there was no way in. Whereas here there were lilac trees everywhere, though the season was over and they would not bloom again until next year. She would stay.

So for the next six months she lapped luxury not only with appetite but aptitude, the way a child tucks into gooseberry fool; for the decorum of an occasional bonbon may satisfy effete minds, but gooseberry fool is the epitome of porridge, and who can have enough of that? It is only the adult who makes choices. A child or a dog merely goes from dish to dish, whiffling down whatever's there, without comparisons.

It was the same with everything. There were horses, so she rode them, and rode them uncommonly well. There were pier glasses, so she peered into them and never saw any image but her own in them again. But then, women are seldom spontaneous; at most they consent to a plastic pose. Show me as I am, they cry, but what they mean is, give me back that first revelation at the mirror.

She danced; she drank; she gambled. There were amateur theatricals. So, since she had a natural talent for the histrionic, she was the Empress in Kotzebue's *The Mother,* and so felt real emotions for the first time.

In short, she had all but two of the attributes of a courtesan. She lacked passion (but would have liked such things if they occurred at the right time, which they never did. Either she wished to enjoy the comfort of freshly ironed linen and a feather bolster all to herself or to examine her fingernails—and there was Sir Harry instead. Men never understand these things. It is useless to explain. So one must put up with it, though few people look their best with their hair out of place, or unshaven in the morning. He did not seem to realize that). The realization, one morning while he snored, that he was an animal, despite his good manners and bad taste, revolted her. For that was her other limitation: she liked things to be nice. It is part of the secret women hand around among themselves at teatime, like the head of St. John the Baptist on a plate; when all is said and done, they are merely animals. Whereas we, of course, are not.

However, though men are incurably given, for short periods of time, to the primitive pleasures of mere repetition, it is possible to hold their attention in other ways by the use of such ingratiating riddles and spells as "Oh, Harry, not now"; "Please don't"; "Oh you shouldn't! You are so silly," or if all else fails, a simple fact of nature assures us three to five days a month of peace and quiet. So after a while things went better and she became a sort of mascot to Sir Harry's two packs, the Snyder one he used for hunting, and the black, white and tan kind he hunted with. Both the Snyders and the Raeburn Hoppner packs piled up into imperial heaps in the evening, like Roman senators after an orgy; had the same sort of loose skin, raised a cry in the same manner, and wagged their tails. Some of them were nice, agreeable, healthy young men who smelled of leather and oatmeal soap, buckskins and gillyflower water, but she was not to be caught out.

Of Sir Harry she was now a little afraid, as the poor are of their landlords. Besides, she was with child.

"Then you'll have to pack up and get out."

He was behind his desk, in the household offices. Now for the first time she saw the raw cruelty of an amiable man who likes everybody well enough, but whose personal comfort has been endangered. It is the look good hosts have whose guests have stayed too long. Glimpse it once, and you will never dine there with the same ease again.

"But I *live* here . . ." Emily was bewildered.

"The season is over. We are all going away. Christmas is coming. At Christmas we go home to our families. Do you understand?"

Emily didn't.

"Then I will make it plain. I would as soon pay another man's gambling debts as acknowledge a trull's child." Turning to the housekeeper, he added, "See that the girl is packed up and sent off and pay her ticket to wherever she wishes to go. And that's an end to it."

Emily still didn't understand. She wasn't like that.

"Come," said Sir Harry, not unkindly. "You have had an expensive summer. You have hired phaetons at five and a half guineas the day, ridden two Arabs lame, and drunk the cellar dry with the rest of us, at 8/6 the bottle. So now you must pay for it in your own time, for I shall not. I pay only for the summer, and a damned bore most of it was, too. You are very young. You will have other summers, my dear, somewhere."

She now understood. "Oh its my dear, is it?" she shouted.

Sir Harry dreaded scenes almost as much as he dreaded wrinkles in his buckskins. Today's were yellow and, flawlessly tight, as so they should have been, for he had had them wetted and then dried on him, which took hours.

"Get the girl away," he said, "and see she does not write."

The housekeeper got her away. Like the devils in a morality (and life was moral, was it not, if it was anything), she had her pitchfork ready, and wielded it with a will. To few of us is it given to participate in the drama of salvation, but she was lucky in her situation:

she had her chance once a year. Later she married him, by methods based upon what the others had done wrong.

Emily went first to her grandmother's and then to Wales, with nothing to sniffle over but some dresses snipped of their buttons, for Granny had sold those to a passing tinker; and nothing to amuse her but the drama of her own life, which she thereupon enacted with vehemence. Feeling be damned. There's always rhetoric, and even alone, we are at least assured of an audience of one, which is better than nothing. If we can render feeling convincingly, we need never undergo it again. The expression of feeling is nothing but *solfège*.

"Loved, adored, feted, encouraged to dance upon the tabletops, and then cast out, with child—dropped, abandoned, hustled away by the back stairs on a frosty morning. Can any career have been so misfortunate as mine?" she demanded.

Like most audiences, Granny Morgan, though enthrallable, was tough minded. "Oh a good many, I imagine, dearie," she said.

"I truly loved Sir Harry," said Emily with dignity and pathos, besides.

"Nonsense, a man like that ain't nothin' but what he owns. And in my opinion not even that, unless he parts with some of it. If you had loved him, you would not have given in so easily, for a woman in love has nothing to offer but herself, so naturally that is the one thing she refuses to give. Whereas, merely to go to bed for cash—you did get cash, didn't you, dearie?—allows her to hold herself in reserve, put something by, feel respectable, and none of your honeymooning hinghanghow off to Bath in a curricle, and blossoms in the dust in the morning, neither."

"Not a shilling," said Emily.

"Oh, dearie, that's bad."

"But I learned how to ride, across the fields in the morning, and dew on everything, and steam off the horse; it was an h'Arab, a great-great-grandson of Eclipse. He said I reminded him of Rubens; of course that was early on."

"Rubens is all very well for a musty old country house, but means little to the modern connoisseur of taste or beauty," snapped Granny Morgan, holding one of the dresses up. It looked bedraggled. "I'm afraid they don't suit, dear. There is nothing for it but to wait for a new style."

"I wrote him seven times. I exposed my heart."

"Oh that! But did you write the other one, the practical one—about the money and all?"

"Yes," said Emily, brought low. "But I fear he is *very* practical."

That was when the postboy came.

"Well, what does he say?" asked Granny Morgan.

Emily had been frowning. Charles Greville did not write an easy hand, and besides, you had to twist the paper around to follow the sentence, because he would not waste a fresh sheet—not him.

"He holds out promise of reform."

"But will he pay for it?"

"He *says* so."

"Then let him reform as much as he pleases," said Granny Morgan. "Some men are like that, you know. One of my men, now, wouldn't touch goose until it was green. It gave me the shivers, bumping into it in the dark in the pantry, hung high and a-slitherin'."

A log fell in the grate.

"You know, tainted meat," explained Granny Morgan. "And I suppose he wants you to have the child *here?*"

"Well, he says *not* there."

Definitely not there.

Like most humane men, Greville did definitely shrink from the human. To be human is to be smirched. To be humane, requires nothing more intimate than benevolence. The singular success of that bucolic *pasticcio, Love in a Village* (still performed) arose in large measure from its irreality. So Greville moved out toward the villages, where a cottage would be cheaper. He was determined, for he did not overestimate his own charms (he never overestimated *anything*), to keep Emily a virginal distance from town. He found what he wanted in a series of small two-storied builders' huts run up for speculation on Edgware Row, way out in the country, the nearest excitement an occasional hanging at Tyburn Hill, with the town on the horizon and Hyde Park not too far away.

It was a bargain. There would even be room for his mineral specimens. "Nature's jewels," as he would explain to Emily, and, to others who might notice the absence of busts after the antique, "Her sculpture, too." But since Greville was art dealer for his uncle, in a good season there would be *bustos* enough, and what furniture was not worth the selling could be used here when he had gotten rid of the town house in Portman Square, for he planned to combine pleasure with economy—a thought that made the snow outside (he was returning from his solicitors' in a carriage) sparkle to him like ermine in a pantomime.

"Please, dear Greville, tell my poor, distraught mother that I am *saved*, and that I recommend her to my Benefactor," Emily had written. He had done so, and far from finding her distraught, had found her a brisk, practical woman of that class. She would make an excellent housekeeper for little more than the household allowance and a share of Emily's pin money. It did not occur to him to ask why, any more than it occurred to him to ask why she chose to call herself Mrs. Cadogan, when there was no evidence of a husband, and Emily called herself Lyon. He took such things for granted. It did not occur to her to tell him why, either. So did she.

She had received him in the public room of a coaching inn, in dim light, would have preferred to have interviewed him in her own parlor, but at that moment had none. She was a good-humored woman, too experienced to be budged by the mere blandishments of vice, but respectability had, for her, the irresistible appeal of novelty. In her turn she was as impressed as he had been, and in much the same way. When it came to members of the upper orders, she had seen worse.

"He is a fine gentleman," she wrote to her daughter. "A *fine* gentleman. He likes everything proper and sedate, if you catch my meaning. It is a *fine* chance to improve yourself. The other gentleman was not. You have been very giddy, but I was a young girl once myself, and say *nothing*. However, now you have had your lesson, you must be a girl of spirit, and snatch the opportunity. He would prefer you have the child *alone*. My thoughts are with you, if my body is not. Do nothing indelicate."

Being a girl of spirit, Emily tore the letter up. As for the lesson, she had not had it yet; it would be at least another two months until she had it, and she could scarcely wait to get rid of it. She did not like to be seen at a disadvantage. Meanwhile she struck a bargain with herself. She had been a hoyden; now she would be a lady —in Portman Square in March, or not later at the most than April. She had tried the Profession and failed. She did not think she liked young men. They jounced you too much. From now on she would remain content with old ones, for Greville, at thirty-three, had certainly the patina of age, and she did hope that was not a surface, merely.

Greville stood in the drawing room of his unsuccessful mousetrap. He was feeling joyous, but moldy. The joy was caused by anticipation; the mold, by the failure of the mousetrap. It had been built to catch an heiress, but when it came to cases, the girls were nothing but intermediaries between their parents and their fortunes, and Greville did not like to deal with intermediaries. He had dealt with the parents direct, and they, in their turn, had dealt as directly with him.

He was not discouraged. He still had confidence that in time he would discover the right parents. What he did not like, though he had no diffidence about taking commissions as a middleman for his uncle's Italian antiques, was to be put to the indignity of selling his own excess furniture.

Mrs. Cadogan saw what the house was for and that it had failed. She even saw why.

"Oh, sir, you shouldn't be fussing about furniture, that is what a housekeeper is for," she said, and earned his gratitude; not his undying gratitude, for Greville's gratitude was apt to perish unexpectedly from internal injuries, not differing in that respect from most other people's gratitude, but still, it was a beginning.

It had been planned to be. Mrs. Cadogan had early observed that most men in Mr. Greville's station needed not one woman but two; that is, one to keep them running, and one to keep them on the run—or to be blunt, a housekeeper and a whore. Not that it would ever do to be blunt; you could tell that by the way the poor gentleman hemmed and hawed, with yards and yards of padding around an almost invisible meaning, like something too fragile to be jounced.

Like Emily, she had expected to come here. But no, Greville said he had taken a cottage at Paddington. The air was salubrious there; it would be more suitable. A girl such as Emily, fresh, unspoiled (he winced), accustomed to the country, would naturally prefer country air and a quiet existence alone with him. We must assist our little flowers to unfold.

Mrs. Cadogan understood perfectly. He could not afford to keep the house.

"And will there be unsightly marks?" he asked.

Mrs. Cadogan blinked. "Marks?"

"It was my understanding that sometimes in these cases, because of the . . . ah, sudden change in . . . er, weight . . . I suppose you might say, that there were in that case, well . . . ah, marks."

Mrs. Cadogan had once been forced to seek employment of a quack in Mecklenberg Square, but a quack, if he knows nothing else, as indeed he doesn't, at least knows his terminology.

"You mean striae, sir," she said. "Why no, I don't expect so, for I told her not to move about too much. Besides, the birth was premature. It couldn't have weighed that much."

"I should have thought it was the pregnancy that was premature," said Greville with asperity, but only because he had caught sight of a scratch on a Sheraton chair. With his customary acumen in such matters, if in such matters only, he had been one of the first to buy from Mr. Sheraton's workshop, while the price was cheap. How had it gotten there?

To that Mrs. Cadogan had no reply. It had happened before her time.

Emily had voided the miserable object, but had had to give it suck, and though impatient, what with one thing and another, did not want to see it go. But neither, if she could not have it, did she ever want to see it again.

The wet nurse, who had made a long journey to fetch it back to its grandmother—for at least they were sure who the grandmother was—paused in the doorway.

"Now, miss, be sensible."

"I don't want you to take it away."

"You hired me to take it away, and what would I do without the money? And you love your grandmother, don't you? You wouldn't want to deprive your grandmother of its board and keep, would you? The poor old lady has little enough as it is."

"But it's mine."

"And more shame to you," said the wet nurse heartily. "That's what I say, and I've had ten o' me own. Each one of them," she went on, "a shame. For unless they die at once, the lambs, then I have to find a wet nurse for *them,* at very high rates, I assure you, and where it will all end I'm sure I don't know. It's worse than taking in each other's wash, and with wash, you can wash it more than once and you needn't be too particular about the dirt on it, neither."

"Let me keep it at least one more day."

"Indeed, I shall not. I am paid by the day, and, selfish creature, would you starve me? You think of nobody but yourself."

"But it's my baby."

"And it's my livelihood you're trying to rob me of, so you needn't take that tone," said the wet nurse, and waddled away with it toward the door.

"Poor child, condemned never to know a woman's love," shrieked Emily, in a last thespian lurch.

"Now there's where you're wrong," said the wet nurse. "I should say it was the father it would never know." The higher the fee the greater the immorality, as far as she could judge, and since in this case the fee had been minimal, she banged the door twice, for she had small patience with small sins. If one is going to sin at all, one may as well get it over with in a lump and devote one's life to repentance; and Emily, she had seen at once, was a repeater.

Emily wept for days, but beginning to feel lonely and bored, and having somewhere to go, decided to be about her business, which was to search out a father; though Greville was not a father, he might perhaps make a suitable uncle, given the right niece. She wanted to be soothed. Why has life no temperate zone, when the world has one on the other side of the Channel, so they say, but farther south, or in America, among the Indians?

"I want," cried Emily, "to be safe," forgetting that, as Herr Goethe says, the dangers of life are infinite, and that safety is among them. But then, she had not read Herr Goethe yet and not had, so far, his splendid opportunities for no less splendid observation.

Though as much the victim as anybody else of the soul's inflation, Mrs. Cadogan was cubically correct in her estimates, and so met Emily with exactly the right degree of *ballon*. Greville was shy (which for once stood to his advantage) as well as ruthless, and had gone out on a pretense errand to negotiate the sale of a Greek vase of ravishing shape and pornographic design, so that if the one excellence did not sell it, the other would, for art allows us to contemplate that which we would not countenance in life; it allows us to achieve heights of the spirit otherwise denied us, as he never tired of saying, and besides, he knew just the right buyer.

It was April, and therefore spring, the season of gratitude. In such weather chilblains cease to itch and begin to heal; it is by such signs that we know it is spring.

The snow was swept into thawing heaps, exposing here and there an area of green drugget, thinly worn, called grass. And though the fruit trees had come into bloom, the blossoms had the cloudy, frangible look of Murano glass, sedate but foreign. The air had the faintly puzzling but nostalgic odor of partially evaporated scent, too strong, too sweet, hoarded for too long, and dilute in a gust of wind. In Hyde Park, as Emily drove by, a single exploratory squirrel ran across the ground and spiraled up a tree; a white swan had warm breast feathers for the first time in months, and opened its heavy wings, like a pickpocket's coat, to show how the trick was done. The road was muddy, despite some lingering frost, another harbinger.

Emily had spent enough of her life defenseless and on foot, greatly to appreciate the superior elevation and extensive mobility of a carriage. It did feel grand to move along that way, with no more effort than was required to watch the coachman's back and to prevent one's own back from being sprained by an unexpected lurch. She sat there with the equanimity of a parcel, misdirected, but now on its way to the right address; it need do nothing but wait to be unwrapped. For the moment, its time is its own.

The carriage reached Tyburn Hill and went on. To her right, at a distance, stood some houses, like a row of ivory dominoes, waiting to be added to; to her left, open countryside, inhabited by rooks, though while she watched, a cow sat down. The carriage was not moving rapidly. There was time for the cow to sit down. Then the coachman turned into Edgware Row and stopped.

"My goodness, is this mine?"

"If it's not, it soon will be, I expect," said the coachman, with a wink which clapped her back into the lower orders. It was her voice; though silent, she had felt a lady.

He handed her down quite respectful-like, as though perhaps this was her first time at this sort of thing, which required gentleness, and the rudeness could wait until later, when the thing was done.

The front door opened and Mrs. Cadogan came out onto the stoop, chunky and proper, so the coachman had to swallow his grin, hand the trunk down, and believe what he would have preferred to believe, given the chance. They were rich merchants, perhaps, in a small way.

"Emily," cried Mrs. Cadogan, with a glance at her daughter's figure and then relieved smiles.

"Oh, Ma," said Emily, who really was most glad to see her, and ran to her, but was the taller of the two, so she did not snuggle well. It was an affecting scene.

Properly affected, and moreover adequately tipped, the coachman tilted his cap and drove away. There being no neighbors with a curiosity to satisfy, the women went indoors.

Emily was fond of her mother, for the two women had seen little of each other in their lifetimes, and so had not gotten stuck by that emotional taffy-pull between the generations which leaves each side with sticky fingers always—the solicitude of a mother seldom, if ever, being accompanied by anything but a total obliviousness to her children's feelings. However, a discreet system of delegated authority (Emily had been reared by her Grandmother Kidd) had left Emily and Mrs. Cadogan free from bitterness. Indeed, so essential were they the one to the other, that they might have been, if not fellow conspirators, then animal and trainer.

Mrs. Cadogan began training at once, by example, and showed her the house.

Born to the lower classes, and her experience so far limited exclusively to the upper, Emily had never before been in one of those middle-class establishments where everything is new—like the world before the Fall—but God, Eve and Adam. It was like being in a shop in which everything has been bought for one already, so that there is no agony of choice. Not only was the house fresh as paint, but the paint was fresh as well, in colors of clotted cream, with a French scenic wallpaper in the dining room, the carpets untrod, the furniture polished to a sample sheen. In the library, however, the books looked used, though at least the bindings appeared to have been oiled recently.

"Who's Demosthenes?" asked Emily, staring at a set of the *Orations* in tooled calf.

"Somebody valuable I expect," said Mrs. Cadogan proudly. "Mr. Greville is particular."

"Oh dear," said Emily, who had forgotten him for the moment, but felt some reverence for his possessions. "Is he like this, do you suppose?"

"Well, I moved the furniture about a bit and added flowers. He's been fussing. I suspect he's as nervous as you are."

"I'm not nervous."

"Then pretend to be," snapped Mrs. Cadogan. "These worldly gentlemen are always shy, you know. Soft words may butter no parsnips, but they do very well for a gentleman, so unless you want to eat parsnips again, use butter. That's my advice to you. And never show your temper. Mr. Greville does not care for temper. Did you get any jewelry?"

"Granny had to sell it."

"And good riddance. Jewelry is vulgar. He says so, so don't ask for it. He is not rich, therefore he is apt to be fastidious. Drinking is frowned on, and so is cards. Cosmetics is fast, so don't use 'em. And now you'd better see the arrangements upstairs."

There were four rooms upstairs, four rooms down. The four down were library, drawing room, sitting room, dining room. The four up were, on the left of the stairs, Greville's bedroom, and behind it Mrs. Cadogan's bedsitter, containing her few cherished possessions—a cracked Lowestoft plate bearing the arms of the Dukes of Bristol, her marriage lines to Mr. Cadogan (she had found them on a peddler's barrow and taken a fancy to the name), a small trunk, much traveled and always locked, a china statuette of George II—and on the right of the stairs, Emily's sitting room and bedroom. There being no attics, the cook and the parlormaid lived in the basement, behind the kitchen.

The sitting room contained everything necessary to repose and leisure, namely a spinet, or inferior sort of harpsichord with an insufficiency of keys, a music rack, a chair for the as yet unhired music teacher, a chaise longue, a table for sirop glasses and bowls of sweets, a glassed bookcase containing the works of Madame de La Fayette in the original and of Mrs. Barbauld in English, a grammar, an embroidery frame, a box for silks, a large mirror in a severe gold frame, a table for playing patience on, and two chairs on either side of the fireplace, one for him and one for her.

The bedroom, on the other hand, was a cheerful room containing a bed, a chair for breeches and dressing gowns, a small wardrobe (Greville thought of everything, or at any rate, planned to limit expenditure), and on the dressing table a mint copy of Hayley's *Triumphs of Temper*, a work of educative merit superior to all those of Hannah More combined. It was to be her Book of Hours. It taught temper, and at the worst, at least its noble numbers were conducive to sleep.

Across the bed lay, freshly starched, a somewhat peculiar garment, half village milkmaid out of Rousseau, half negligee out of Crébillon *fils*.

"He would like you to wear that. It is a morning costume," explained Mrs. Cadogan, unpacking the remains of Emily's finery. "And as I suspected, he would not like you to wear these. So off to the barrowboy they go."

"But those are my clothes!"

"It is a new life, and therefore there will be new clothes," said Mrs. Cadogan, herself wearing a striped dress, a crisp apron, and a mobcap in which she resembled nothing so much as an amiable toad. "If I can dress the part, you can. So off with your things, and then we'll go downstairs to wait."

The only reassuring thing so far was that in the back garden there was a white lilac tree in early bloom, drowsy with bees, and heavy on the branch. It was an omen. But all the same, the wait seemed very long.

Greville had been detained. He had had no trouble with the vase. "It is a great art in life to know how to sell air," says Gracián, subsection 267, or, since Greville could read Spanish, *"Gran sutileza del vivar saber vender el aire."* But Greville did not know how to sell air. He merely knew how to displace it; in his case an inherited skill for which, nonetheless, he took great credit. The vase had sold itself, rather winningly.

The trouble was Emily. Seduction is an art. The ability is given at birth. We can polish the skill, but we cannot polish what we do not have. And though it was essential to appear the seducer and to chuckle about the little lady tucked away somewhere, and possible to do the tucking, given one had the deposit money, the actual process of performing the rite had left Greville weary and wary to the point where he sometimes wondered if other gentlemen of his acquaintance did not also exaggerate their trophies the better to conceal their wounds. However, go home he must, and so home at last he went, though with his mask on. He was kindly but above these things. That was his mask.

He hoped Emily was comfortable and had recovered from her untimely experience. He had no doubt but that Emily was tired this evening and would require rest. In short, what the devil was he to do with her?

On the second day, Emily and Mrs. Cadogan refrained from discussing what had not happened the first night, which was also what did not happen on the second; on the third evening, Greville was out; on the fourth morning Emily had hysterics; and on the fourth evening Mrs. Cadogan, though gingerly, took the matter into her own hands.

"Em'ly is here only to do your bidding. You have but to say, and she will do what you wish. Em'ly has retired only to await you, sir."

"Has no one ever told you the word is in three syllables?" demanded Greville, irritated both with himself and her.

"What word is that, sir?"

"Em'ly," snapped Greville.

"How else would I address her? She is my daughter."

"Then we must change the name," said Greville firmly.

"I shall think about it and advise you." When she had gone, he sat glumly to the contemplation of his port, alone, for he could not very well show her off to his male acquaintance until he had something to show.

Today is Thursday, he said to himself. I shall approach her on Friday and every Friday thereafter. That will be suitable; and he began to devise lists of names. The Fair Teamaker of Edgware Row was the epithet he had chosen, but what the devil was he to call her?

Port is a heavy drink. Three bottles of it are even heavier. It was all he could do to stumble up to bed.

"Oh dear," said Mrs. Cadogan, who had been hoping for developments, and philosophically blew her candle out. "What is to become of us?"

Emily was asleep and vastly enjoying herself. She infinitely preferred to sleep alone, though such luxuries are seldom possible, short of widowhood. Men are so messy.

Summoned from sleep in some dark part of the night, she felt a body in the bed beside her. It was a smooth, hairless, slim body, adolescent in quality, and breathing liquorous fumes. It was an apologetic body, she decided, as well it might be for disturbing her, so she was not alarmed.

"Feel no fear," said the body. "It is only Greville."

Which was true enough. "Oh, dear, dear Greville," she said, and stroked his hair which, since he did not shave for a wig but had it cut to a stubble, was no more alarming to touch than it would have been to rub a hedgehog the right way.

To her surprise, though naturally revolted (men are beasts), she was not displeased. The sensation was localized, transitory and brief. He did not derange her hair. He did not make ugly noises. There was the added advantage that she could not see him. It could not be denied that the sensation, so long as one was careful not to become aroused, was conducive to repose; and when he was adequately relieved he had the good taste to go away and not to clutter up the bed.

"Very well then," he said, in his own room. "From now on it will be Thursdays."

"Very well then," said Emily, in her own bed. "Really, all things considered, it is not so bad, and later on I suppose he will taper off—most men do."

"Very well then, at least it has led to something, and I suppose in the morning we will find out what," said Mrs. Cadogan, and went to sleep again.

"Damn," said the parlormaid, awakened in her bed by sheer frustration. "It is a suitable employment, but what young man would come this far out of town to see me?" She was an authentic member of the lower orders and would not last long.

It is a rum household, thought the cook, in the midst of slumber. "But that no doubt is because they are members of the gentry, or as near as makes no difference. Tomorrow they shall have overcooked turbot for lunch, with a shriveled lemon, curdled hollandaise sauce and some dead parsley for garniture, and that will take care of them." For she took pride in her work and worried incessantly.

In the morning, Greville came downstairs, descriptions of illicit rapture completed in his head, and halfway down, paused, for Mrs. Cadogan was in the hall, looking up at him.

"I have decided to call her Emma Hart," he said. "Emma is a fashionable name, and as for Hart, it is a pun, for not only does she seem to have one, but she is like a young doe."

He then entered the dining room where he ate two eggs, three grilled kidneys, half a sausage and some kedgeree to keep his strength up; after which he sauntered to town, not only a virile, but a proven man.

Mrs. Cadogan bounced upstairs as fast as short legs could take her.

"You have given satisfaction," she said, bursting in on Emily, who was about to commence "The Jolly Miller" on the spinet, in order to express herself.

"I have made my sacrifice," said Emily.

"He has given you a new name."

"He has given me *what?*" Emily's mind had toyed for the moment with jewelry.

"He wishes you to be called Emma—Emma Hart," said Mrs. Cadogan.

It was not a diamond, but it would do. "I must say I like the sound of it," said Emma, new born, trying it a few times and even playing it on the not quite harpsichord (E, A, A), back and forth, into a little jig. She was in good spirits. He had given her her adolescence back again, quite untarnished, except on Thursdays. She had had no idea these things could be so sedately done.

It was the beginning, not of a passion, which she would have viewed with repugnance—being at bottom a stout English girl—but of affection, which she felt far more. There was something endearing about him after all; he was the runt of an imaginary litter.

"But dear me," she said, "isn't he stingy?"

"The color is back in her cheeks. I have rescued her from the mire. She is like a rose after rain, a briar rose," said Greville.

"And she loves you for it, of course?"

"Passionately," said Greville, determining that Emma should never sleep with any man whose reticence he could not trust, which meant with no man. "She is like a Greek goddess."

"Which one?" asked Towneley.

They were in his atelier. Lest for a moment anyone might believe that Towneley did anything except be Towneley, it must be added that by atelier he meant the room in which he kept his sculpture, not the room in which he did it. Lady Di Beauclerc might so far forget herself as to deign to draw a little, but Towneley never forgot himself. Being well-bred, he admired only. What he admired most was mostly Roman sculpture, for he liked a sure thing, and usually a copy of a sure thing at that, which is what the Romans had admired. However, as did the Romans, he called it Greek.

"A Hebe," said Greville, catching sight of one.

"Come now," said Towneley, "if that is the case, you may as well have a Ganymede instead. But I do not think that is *quite* your taste. An Athene perhaps?"

"She is untutored."

"A Thetis? Perhaps she has had naval connections?"

She had. Greville blushed.

Towneley was satisfied. He had rather thought so. "Of course we will come to see her. What does your uncle have to say, by the way?"

Greville had several uncles, but Sir William was always the one referred to. For he was more than famous: he was also a connoisseur, and had already sent back from Naples more Etruscan vases than any other living Englishman.

"Not only is he the power behind the throne," Towneley had once said, in his not unkindly—but if we wish to be witty we cannot have qualms—way, "he is also the chair the nephew sits in." It was true enough. Greville cut a fine figure, what with that idyllic face, but without his uncle he would scarcely have been competent to cut ice.

This kind of bickering, since it was the only kind he knew, seemed to Greville both warm and congenial. It was the great world of little gossip, and he knew no other. Indeed it was easier to gossip about the great than actually to endure them, for any show of vigor, except in the matter of bric-a-brac and chitchat, would have been detected at once and despised. In this world one exerted oneself only to inherit money or to conceal the fact that one had not. Since Greville did both, he qualified; his position was secure. But as one must provide the occasion for gossip as well as the gossip itself, he had come to ask his cronies to Edgware Row.

So Emma, who did not, in the presence of her mother, find the absence of other women distressing, but was bored, soon had a host of distinguished gentlemen, all pink, all plump and all benign, to entertain her. There was Towneley himself, the first epicene man she had met, though apt to pinch in the dark to prove his manhood; there was Mr. Hayley, almost as dull as his verse, but just as distinguished and far nicer. And there was Lord Bristol, the Bishop of Derry, rosy cheeked as a law lord and just as spiritual; a lovably wicked old man (he was fifty-two) who told her God must have been in a romantic mood the day He created her. He had pudgy hands and a wholesome laugh, and she liked him best.

Each one, as he left, said to the others: "Now how do you suppose he managed *that?*" Greville was pleased and proud of her. She had conducted herself well. But must she conduct herself in *that* voice?

"It is her native Doric," explained the Bishop of Derry. "Her wood-note wild." To Emma he said, "My dear child, speak more softly, enunciate, and if you cannot put the 'h's' back where they belong, do not be impatient on that account to shove them in where they most certainly don't. Never grow excited; and practice aspirating into a candle flame each night—that will soon take care of everything."

"Asp, eat, oat, Ute," said Emma, obediently. "Heat, heart, hot, hut." And soon she had it in the proper order, unless she did get excited, and with the exception of "a."

"Hate, hat, hard, Harold," prompted the Bishop amiably. "And then there is the problem of such things as honor. Their derivation is usually French, and that is why we do not pronounce them properly. They are not quite a part of the English tongue, you see."

"Yes, I see," said Emma, and for a wonder she did. "It is one of your jokes."

"It is one of God's jokes," he corrected her. "But we do the best we can."

"What are Utes?"

"American Indians," said the Bishop. "Have you never read your Voltaire? A pity. He is one of the few pleasures of which the Cloth is capable. Because it is naughty, you know. I shall send you a copy, for while you are at it, you may just as well learn French."

"There seems a great deal to learn."

"Not as much as you might think. Consider Charles."

Emma was shocked. "Greville is truly learned," she

said, and meant it. It was no more than he said himself.

"I know. It is a great waste. However, you must not mind my little ironies."

"I don't," said Emma, who didn't.

The Bishop of Derry went away, sighing for true, as opposed to technical, innocence, and wondered how Greville *did* manage it.

He managed it, among other things, by rigging thimbles and saving string, and all those other stratagems to which those who would have the world think well of them are put. The house was to be run on £100 a year. He insisted on it. He also insisted Emma keep accounts, writing down such sums as apples, 2½ pence; mangle, 5 pence; coach, a shilling; and poorman, ½ pence. For five poormen, you could buy more apples. For five coaches, muslin by the yard. So she wore muslin by the yard. It was not merely economy. It was discipline. For dress, charity and entertainment, she had £30 pin money per annum. The housemaid was paid £8, and the cook £9. Therefore the cook did very little cooking, but did sometimes dust; and when she was not dusting, Mrs. Cadogan did most of the cooking. She was an excellent cook. It was an excellent arrangement.

His sherry, port and portraits he paid for himself, as also the rent of the house. That was his contribution, and as for entertainment, it need not prove too dear, for in the absence of any other, they had him.

Mrs. Cadogan, who had no allowance, did not happen to find Greville that amusing, but since Emma did, it could not be helped. Greville, who dressed, if not in the height, at least in the hand-me-downs and foothills of fashion, had an arrangement with his tailor. But what did he do with the other three hundred pounds a year he surely had? It was a mystery. He neither gilded the cage nor left it open. He neither forbade a trip to town, nor provided a carriage. So they could not find out. In the evenings, sometimes, if there were candles enough, he read them *La Nouvelle Héloïse*. His French was like the rest of him: he did not stumble, he never lost his place, but he had no lilt. It was in truth a bore.

But Emma found *La Nouvelle Héloïse* affecting.

"To think a simple love could live so simply," she said.

"My dear, that's why," said Mrs. Cadogan, gathered up her darning (cotton and needles: 9 pence), and went to bed.

Greville now came spontaneously every Tuesday, as well as according to his system, on Thursdays. Emma did not mind. She was meek and submissive and grateful and still young enough to believe that everything went on forever, instead of grinding, as it did sometimes, to a halt. What was to be done? Not that Mrs. Cadogan longed for livelier scenes; she had had quite enough of those in her younger days, thank you, but since she happened to be a very good plain cook indeed, she did hanker after a slightly larger allowance and a nip or two on the bottle in the afternoons. Unfortunately Greville marked his bottles.

Then, to relieve the tedium, came the visit to Ranelagh. Either somebody had suggested the idea to him, or else it was to be their Annual Outing. They were eating, at the time the visit was proposed, one of Greville's celebrated imaginary meals.

The phrase was the Bishop of Derry's. "Go dine at his house; yes do, but come on to dine with me afterward," he said. "Or better still, take along a Sandwich in your greatcoat pocket, lest you feel faint on your way back. Greville is the best creature in the world. Or the second best. But he serves imaginary meals. You are asked to dine. You are told the menu in advance. It is an excellent menu. The wine is superb. The dining room is elegantly appointed. The service is everything that service should be. You are even allowed to discuss the meal, a thing allowed in no other English household, for though we worship at the throne of Gastronomy, we do so ashamed, alone, and after fasting. However, to what I was saying: his meals are famous. His dishes are fine. His cutlery is impeccable. But *there is no food*. None whatever. A solitary pea upon a plate, an inch of flounder drowned in a sea of sauce, a scruple of savory imposed upon a merely ideal lozenge of toast. The man is not only mad, but thin."

He was quite right: there was none. Only the knowledge that there was a carrot pudding steaming in the basement, and loads of lovely jam, sustained Emma and Mrs. Cadogan through these singularly absent feasts.

"To Ranelagh," said Emma.

Greville sat there, the image of foppish benevolence.

"And would you like that, my child?"

"Oh yes, I should like that very much."

"Then there is no difficulty," said Greville. "We will go tonight, after the smoked salmon and the cottage pudding."

The salmon would be sliced thin, to look like horn windows at sunset. As for the pudding, it was remarkable how such a man could live so long on starch, though true that he dined out frequently and sometimes brought the menu home to show it to them.

To Ranelagh they went. Of London's pleasure gardens —there were once as many as five—it was the most famous and the most sedate. That is why he had chosen it. There are a limited number of places to which a kept woman of the demimonde may go. And he did not, for reasons of jealousy, wish her to go anywhere that the demimonde itself went. That left Ranelagh.

The building had been refurbished last year. It was a rotunda of vast dimensions, supported by a central column. Music was played there while you walked around and around. When you were tired of walking around and around, there were the gardens, which were the sacred precincts of the fribble and the fop, for the shrubbery had grown to a sufficient height to permit of privacy in diversion, so that sometimes a startled shriek was allowed to mingle with the mellifluous cadences of Performed Song.

> "On Thames's fair bank a gentle youth
> For Lucy sighed with matchless truth
>   Ev'n when he sighed in rhyme.

> The lov'ly maid his flame return'd
> And would with equal warmth have burn'd
> > But that she had not time...."

Emma hummed, and God knew how she had learned it, but then women are as sensitive to the latest airs as savages are to tribal drums, and seem to learn just as much in the same way, even at a distance.

An outing demands a new dress. There was one. The two women had managed to smuggle one or two *Repositories of Fashion and Mode* into the sitting room upstairs, paid for out of the apple money. The result was not an *entirely* new dress, but an old white one, fitted with a transparent pelisse of scrounged tulle, dyed smoky in the basement, surreptitiously, with lampblack. With a blue sash, a transformed bonnet, some blue morocco pumps filched from the embers of Sir Harry's wrath, and a muff to keep her hands warm—for it was summer—the outfit did well enough. So well that Greville wanted to ask where it had come from, but thought better of doing so, lest he be told. So instead he did an unusual thing: he smiled.

Emma smiled back. She was still too trustful. Since she was unconscious of her beauty as yet, she believed that people liked her for herself rather than merely for her appearance, and she felt very much herself this evening.

It was a quarter to nine by the clock on the library mantel. Above the clock hung the only small Paulus Potter in England, a portrait of a cow. Facing it, from the opposite wall, the Honourable Emily Bertie impersonated, though with delicacy, Thais. Since this had been touched up by the artist himself, to conform to the purity and exactitude—particularly to the exactitude—of Greville's celebrated taste, the Honourable Emily Bertie looked smudged, but was large enough to balance the small Paulus Potter. Greville looked at her fondly. He had got her on the cheap, yet she was indisputably a Reynolds. She lent the room tone.

He was in a good humor. Emma and he made a handsome couple, he thought, nor was he wrong, for he was a handsome man, at least from the neck up, despite that look of a baby which has not been given what it wants for some time.

He had address. He was well-bred. It was merely that he could never understand why no one liked him better, since he was always careful to do everything the right way, from little compliments to even smaller gifts; from the procurement, on commission, of an urn, to agreeing with everyone when they told him to. He looked, in other words, like an Eton portrait, a presentation piece you give away as you leave, available always as a fourteenth at dinner if one had forgotten to ask him before, and as last man into the Cabinet.

Now where, everyone asked, when everything was made up, shall we put Greville?

"In his place," said Lord North, the then First Minister.

"Well, he won't do for the Cabinet. A gentleman in waiting, perhaps? I doubt if the King would mind."

"The King has no mind. He has gone barmy again, so they say," said North with a chuckle (or perhaps it was Pitt).

As indeed he had. Father George was toppled down with tares, mostly of his own sowing, and all burdensome. He was having one of his rest periods. And as for Charlotte of Mecklenburg-Strelitz, who had had a cool hoyden charm when young, she now looked like a dropsical mouse. But Greville had long ago given up trying to explain to Emma the nature of politics. She would not listen. The scramble for place did not interest her. As far as she was concerned, she had found hers, and high time, too, for she was seventeen.

Meanwhile here was the carriage, the horses stomping methodically, like prisoners taking their exercise; into the carriage they got, and "Ranelagh, my man," said Greville, in a youthful, manly tone, and off they went across Paddington Green, down Park Lane and over the fields to Chelsea. The trees in Hyde Park were pools of black, like ink blots by the Brothers Cozens, of no artistic merit, but a curiosity; and the shrubbery was fragrant, indeterminate and blobby. The night was clear with a shimmer to it, the sky a miniscus, and here and there a star danced —all of them Emma's, all of them musical. Inside her muff her hands met with cosy delight. He was not a dull old stick. Things would go better now.

The dull old stick sat with face averted, waiting. He was a town man. He preferred scenery where it belonged, at Drury Lane.

The Thames was a black mirror, reflecting the firefly lanterns of wherries, for since it was possible to arrive at Ranelagh by both carriage and boat, no matter which side one entered from or with whom, one never knew who might be there. Above the trees rose the Central Edifice, a large, purring dome. Before the carriage, rose the gates.

So they entered the gardens, a perfect Gainsborough couple, resembling that connubial self-portrait "The Walk," in which, before feathery foliage which looks as though it had been taken from a hatbox rather than from nature, the painter, dressed as a gentleman, conducts his wife—who has a certain charm independent of assumed station—toward the spectator.

Greville took Emma's arm; it was the expected thing.

Emma was disappointed. The trouble with respectability, even if perilously achieved, is that inevitably, since it consists in doing only the expected thing, it lacks spontaneity. It has no spirits. It does not run; it perambulates. They perambulated.

"My God," she said, "is there nothing else to do but this?"

"What else would there be to do?" asked Greville indulgently, who was himself bored but found the sensation familiar and therefore congenial. Even the music was congenial.

"But does nobody sing?"

"Not during the symphony, no," said Greville, and blinked like a barn owl. He had just seen some people he knew. He bowed.

"Who was that?"

"Nobody in particular," said Greville, glossing over an

actress, a member of Parliament and two disreputable duchesses, and for once he was right.

They were on their third lap around the Rotunda. Having deduced that she would be introduced to no one, Emma demanded to go outdoors. Greville was willing, for the third time around was never a novelty.

Emma could hear the jagged sounds of song.

"Oh let's hurry, Greville, do," she said, but Greville would not. He had heard Mrs. Bottarelli sing that moral *aria da capo*, "The Chaste Nymph Surprised," before, and to judge by the pitch, she was up to the third, final, bitter resignation bit where she repines, tears her hair, slaps her bosom, rolls her eyes, creaks in her corsets, and never a fold or wrinkle out of place. Mrs. Bottarelli was getting on, and her enunciation was not correct, for how a dramatic soprano can sing with plumpers in her cheeks, he did not know. The only person he knew who might know was Towneley, who had a fine soprano shriek when surprised or when roistering upon the Continent, a thing he was fastidious enough never to do at home, except sometimes in the evenings; a little rouge for warmth, but you were not supposed to notice it.

Mrs. Bottarelli was succeeded by a Mr. Hudson, who sang "Content," a largo jig by a Mr. Goodwin—a curious melody to be likened only to the effect of a fat man falling through glue.

Greville suggested an inspection of the ornamental water, but the lower ornamental water being bordered by far from ornamental members of the lower orders, turned back. Emma was again disappointed. She was willing to accept Greville as a model of deportment. He was the only model of deportment she had seen. But they seemed to be enjoying themselves down there, and she would have liked to watch.

"Greville, I am excited. May we dance?"

"It is not done unless there is a ball."

"They were dancing by the ornamental water."

Greville was shocked. His face recomposed itself and emitted a silent, peremptory hiss, which is what an owl does—hoot when it knows something, and hiss when it doesn't—and he was *very like an owl*. "Those were the lower orders," he said, and from his wrists shook back impatiently his bands, for in these moods he was a High Church clergyman too, not particularly devout, but way up in the thing, that was clear, and in regular attendance at Easter and at the marriage of his fortune-hunting friends—the last of the beagle pack, but there—whether it be St. George's, Hanover Square, or over the hills and away as far as Wimbledon.

They were now back to Mr. Hudson, still dispelling "Content," or the last few lingering notes of it anyhow, with becoming diffidence.

"I can sing better than that, and what is more, I shall," shrieked Emma, and was away before she could be stopped, and up upon the podium. She was delighted with her own daring. So were the musicians. So was the audience. And as for Mr. Hudson, he had tired of "Content" years ago.

It was her first audience. She forgot about Greville. An audience was an enthralling thing. She had not known. She had been given a few private lessons, to while away the tedium of those hours she could not spend with Greville, so she sang.

"Hither Nymphs and Swains repair,
    Quit the baleful scenes of strife,
  Leave the rugged paths of care,
    And taste the joys that sweeten life..."

she trilled, accompanying herself with a few experimental, but since she was eager to please, explicit gestures. The audience whistled, applauded and catcalled for more. She was a saucy lass.

What these songs said was true. The way she sang them did show that she believed that. As an encore, because she could not bear to leave yet, and as a tribute to Greville, she sang something more recent—Dr. Downman's "To Thespia." She could not see Greville in the crowd in front of her, but raising her arms toward where he had been, she warbled:

> "Oh come my fair one! I have thatch'd above
> And whiten'd all around my little cot,
> Shorn are the hedges leading to the grove,
> Nor is the seat and willow bow'r forgot,"

and made it a joyous invitation, like the "Song of Solomon" in the version you are allowed to read, but Greville in a good mood had explained some of the naughtier bits, and my, she had had no idea it was such a racy thing.

Emma's gestures, though she had never before so deliberately made one, were those of a village Siddons. They had a mesmeric effect. As slowly she raised her arms toward Him, the audience turned to see to Whom. They found her most affecting.

Greville, who never forgot himself, lost his nerve and jumped nimbly behind a tree.

There was more applause. "Oh thank you," said Emma. "But I can sing no more. I have exhausted my repertoire."

"Indeed you cannot and have," snapped Greville, rearing up out of nowhere. He grabbed her down and made off with her, followed by jeers, catcalls, admirative noises, empty gin bottles and derisory shrieks.

There would never, never, never be an end to it. He shook like the most expensive lap dog from Peru, shivering not for warmth, but as far away from her as he could get, with the rage of a baby most devilishly betrayed, let down, exposed, unmasked, traduced, made common sport of, should have known better than to take up with a common trull, I do not doubt Sir Harry's taste, he has married his housekeeper, that explains his taste, but though he flung you out into the ungrateful grass after a mere six months, I wonder at his patience, even so; in other words, hate hath no synonym and rage no end to simile. Apart from that he would not speak.

"Why, whatever 'as 'appened?" demanded Mrs. Cadogan, surprised into the vernacular.

"Madam, you are her mother. Need you ask? She has shown her upbringing, lapsed into her native vulgarity, and made a fool of me," snapped Greville, going into the library and slamming the door so hard that he set in motion both the small chandelier in the library and the large one in the dining room, whose vitreous derision lasted for a minute and a half by the clock—to Mrs. Cadogan, for an eternity.

The life here may not have been much, but as she had feared, it had been much too good to last. Wearily she trudged up the stairs, as far as she was concerned, just twenty-four hours before the removers, and already mentally bending with them to remove. If you cannot afford the theatre, you can always read the sonnets at home instead.

But Emma's thespian talents, so freshly awakened only to be trampled underfoot, carried her through. Ripping off her ludicrous finery, a task not difficult—it had been basted merely; unstringing her corset, her dearest, most secret grownup possession so far, and he had not even noticed it; letting down her auburn hair; slipping into a simple cottage dress (which suited her to perfection, as she well knew); and pausing only for an instant before her mirror to make sure her wild, disheveled and grief-stricken locks were disheveled to the best possible advantage;—a Fair Penitent, a Magdalen, A Woman Undone and Utterly Given Up to Shame (it was at this point that she collided with Mrs. Cadogan on the stairs), a Village Milkmaid, La Penserosa with good cause, a Wailing and Abandoned Woman (taken from an engraving after Poussin's "Massacre of the Innocents"), an Andromache, both Marys at the Tomb, Niobe Humbled utterly, Penelope perhaps—she dashed down the stairs, giggled out of nervousness, remembered to cry, and burst in upon him, weeping bitterly.

He was seated in a Greek chair, calming himself by the examination of a few choice rocks from his collection, two pieces of branch coral and a sea sponge of rare and intricate design. He looked annoyed.

"Forgive, forgive poor repentant Emma," cried Emma, raising her hands clasped in the gesture of the old Hellenistic Beggar he admired so much—the wrong sex, but of that no matter. "Forgive"—she said, and paused—"an Errant Soul. Or, if you are ashamed of me, Dismiss me, Abandon Me, and I shall disappear as Poor and Miserable as when you found me—in fact, more miserable, for never again to see my Dear, Devoted Greville."

From real emotion Greville shrank. But in this tirade he seemed to detect the authentic notes of a comfortable, conformable and convincing insincerity. Laying aside his branch coral, he consented to look at her, his pale blue eyes full for the moment of a responsive and therefore insincere tenderness, while at the same time having a blinding image of himself as he must have looked leaping behind that tree. But he decided to forgive. He was mollified.

"Free from ambitious pride and envious care,
  to love and to be loved is all *my* prayer,"

Emma recited, adapting freely from Hayley, the house poet, and drying her tears—since he would not dry them for her—she abandoned the one attitude to take up another, head on his hand, sitting on the floor to be more comfortable.

"Come, it is too late in the evening for Greek attitudes," said Greville. "Go to bed."

At these kind words she scrambled up and went away. Her dress was thin. It could not be gainsaid, she had pink and delightful thighs.

Nonetheless the girl needed discipline, so he decided to abandon his spontaneous Tuesdays for the time being. When Thursday came around, he omitted Thursdays as well, and since Thursdays were a part of that system by which he regulated his life, this was the more serious omission. It was all very touch and go.

Emma kept to her room, too weak with shame to take any nourishment other than a custard at noon and a very large tea, three oranges, a bowl of apples, a bunch of grapes, half a pound cake, two bowls of Devonshire cream, a basket of strawberries, half a saddle of mutton, thirteen haws, to keep her hands busy, and two Anjou pears. Grief, she found, had made her hungry.

"What have I done?" she wailed. "What have I done?"

"You've been yourself, and it won't do," said Mrs. Cadogan. "Not in this household, anyway. From now on you must emulate others. There is no other way to please them."

But it was Towneley who saved them.

"Of course I have heard about it," he said, wagging a modish tasseled slipper. "It's all over town. Which do you suggest, that I stuff my ears with loyalty, or cotton wool?"

Towneley was fond of Charles. If not his own sort of man, he was at least the next best thing—a fussy, prissy, predestinated bachelor, manly of course, but given to gossip in the right congenial way.

Someday the boy might marry. There are heiresses in Cumberland who will put up with anything. He had no desire to diddle him out of £10,000 a year. On the other hand, he had no desire to lose his company, either. Therefore he must be induced to keep Emma on. Besides, Towneley liked Emma, mildly. He judged people by his own evoked images—all of them artistic—and when he thought of Emma he saw first of all the Borghese hermaphrodite, and second, "St. Cecilia," also in Rome, huddled up under her altar like Andromache in the snow. Since both these statues were among his favored female works (his favored male work was Georghetti's "St. Sebastian" on the Palatine. Ah, if we had Georghetti's "St. Sebastian" we should all be happy, if, as usual, bored), he had a soft spot in his heart for her. She was as sexless and as *séduisant* as a boy.

Towneley had a discursive mind. He returned abruptly to the point.

"My dear Charles," he said. "You have mistaken your vocation. No wonder you are tired. You are minute in particulars, and have no principles whatsoever. Therefore you are either a scoundrel or a pedant. Since you live on unearned income, are precise in your accounts, and related to almost everybody, clearly you cannot be a scoundrel. Therefore a pedant you must be. You want employment, you relish the antique, you have an eye for sculpture—at any rate you seem to have an eye for mine—nature has supplied you with a Galatea, so chip away. Fashion her into one of the hetaerae. And then, if you really cannot abide her, sell her, for by that time she will fetch a better price."

"Sell her?"

"Oh come now, Charles, what else is there to do with her? Think of the future. Every man has two chances at a good match: when he is young and seems romantic, and when he is older and seems a good catch. There are many women eager to marry a minister, should you become one, with or without portfolio. Meanwhile enjoy yourself: instruct the girl."

"It is true that I have much to teach," said Greville, with the obliviousness of true humility.

"My dear boy, of course you have," said Towneley, with a cockatoo prance. "So why not get it out of your system now, while there is still time?"

So Emily was saved, in the best Hannah More style, by education. Greville commenced at once, though he would need advice.

The most notable exponent of education, excepting always Hannah More, was Mr. Day, the friend of Erasmus Darwin, the friend of Anna Seward, the friend of Johnson, who in his turn was the friend of Mrs. Thrale, who had married a merchant, so none of them was exactly respectable. Nor would the Bishop of Derry do. He was an admirable sedentary old rip whom eminence had rendered plummy, who admired erudition, could pull odds and ends of Horace out of a hat with the best of them, read the worst parts of Procopius in his cabinet, and had no use for education whatsoever. He preferred, he said, learning, for you can educate a rabbit, but nothing will make him learned unless he wants to be, in which case he is not a rabbit, so why stuff the memory with forcemeat, like a Michaelmas goose? It is a waste of time.

There was Rousseau. ...

Looking up at the Paulus Potter, Greville uttered an ungulate groan: should he begin with Taste or Tacitus? Or would his own moral apothegms be better? He had already instituted a course of instruction in those.

"If you give compliments solely in order to give pleasure, you will get what you want," he had said when she was trying to butter up Mr. Hayley. "If you give them solely to get what you want, you will merely displease. You have not the art to dissimulate, dear Emma."

"And it must be said, you do not seem to need it," said Hayley, about whom everything was pleasant but his verse. "If you wish me to inscribe the *Triumphs of Temper*, why of course I shall."

"I do not like the girl to appear pert," said Greville. "She is at times."

"You must come to the country more often. So is my climbing rose," said Hayley. "She is Serena to the life."

"Reading it is one of her few diversions."

"She seems to wish to improve herself, at any rate," said Hayley, Serena being the heroine of the above-mentioned work.

Indeed she did.

"Being ignorant of Taste, her only thought, upon seeing the sculpture around her, is to ask the subject of the scene, and so, to feed her curiosity, I have thought it best to instruct her in the elements of Classic Greek Myth," wrote Greville to his uncle.

As for the celestial tittle-tattle of Greek myth, Emma had seldom heard such disgusting carryings on in her life, but into the memory box it went, and down went the lid, while Hope droned around the room with all the random diligence of a mosquito.

"The gnats in this part of Delaware are as large as sparrows. I have armed myself against them by wearing trousers," wrote the Earl of Carlisle. In it went. Had she not been so pretty, Emma would have qualified as a bluestocking tomorrow. She had the erudition of a magpie; that is, she did not care what it was, what it meant or where it came from, but if it sparkled, into that jackdaw's nest of a memory of hers it went. The worst was French.

"On peut comparer la société à une salle de spectacle: on n'y était aux loges que parce qu'on payait d'avantage," mouthed Emma.

"And what is this ubiquitous caterwauling, pray?"

"It is French."

"Child," said Mrs. Cadogan, who lived in terror of foreign travel, for parsnips were not procurable abroad, "why?"

"It is a polite accomplishment and contains no 'h's,'" said Emma, holding out the book. "You see. There is an haitch. But you pay it no mind. That's the beauty of it."

"She is teachable. She shall vie with Mrs. Delaney," said Greville.

"Ah, Charles," said the Bishop of Derry, "you are a willful man. You would curdle cream. Have you not yet learned that artless prattle is superior to the artful kind?"

"Not twenty-four hours a day."

"Ah well, perhaps not," agreed the Bishop, and taking her hand, led Emma out into the garden, to name the flowers and plants and any animals therein at that time residing.

"Must I really read Dr. Johnson?" asked Emma.

"No, my child," said the Bishop, who had been contemplating a zinnia, a most rare flower, and did not want his pleasure spoiled. "If an elephant could have written verse, he would have written much in the style of Johnson. It is not easy; it does not convince; but it is full of ponderous felicities. There is even here and there the gleam of a tusk. But though it is quotable, it cannot be read."

"Not even the *Dictionary?*"

"The *Dictionary* is different. Here and there the *Dictionary* is amusing. As good as a novel, but with the words in their proper order, so I am told."

"You are making fun of me."

"No, I am only making fun with you. If Charles must

convert you into that horrid grownup thing, a gentlewoman, he is going about it the wrong way. Even he should know a gentlewoman never reads, except, of course, the 'Court Gazette.'"

"There is little other diversion here, except to sing and play the spinet and sew."

The Bishop of Derry was shocked. "How sad," he said, "to be so serious so young."

"I am not sad. I find it paradise."

"A strange Methodistic paradise, all gray. Now had you read the *Alcoran,* you would know that true paradise consists of nothing but your pretty self and milk and honey. My dear, you *are* diversion." And the Bishop went back to contemplation of his copper zinnia, a plant from the New World, but in England, a novelty.

It was Mr. Hayley who provided the diversion, not the Bishop of Derry, and most certainly not Greville. Mr. Hayley had gone to see his friend Romney, the painter, who though he had been living in London for some years, had only recently arrived, and was at the moment fashionable. "Romney's pictures are hard, dry and tasteless, and such as you would not like in the least. And I am enough secure that he will never make a first-rate painter," wrote Northcote to his brother. That showed you how well established Romney had become. In these matters, a word from Northcote was enough.

Mr. Romney was a paranoiac of great charm, which is to say, in his own day, an original. His studio in Cavendish Square was vast. It was not England; it was not Italy; it was not anywhere. Freed for a moment from his vanities, his insanities and his own innate inabilities, he shut his eyes and life came flooding in, sepia wave after sepia wave of women who writhed and turned and were waves and not women, badly drawn, not drawn at all, merely fixed in the act of being either that bright turbulence the nearly blind see by daylight, or else the promise of something unknowable.

What I am I am, and that's a pity, thought Mr. Romney. But what I draw for myself is quite another thing. For he had long ago given up hope that those half-understood and barely attended-to visions of his would ever find a model through whom he could express them.

He did not enjoy being a fashionable painter, for since all women of fashion desire to have the same face, he was forced to draw the same face always, which was not even the face of any particular woman, but only the face of fashion, and no relief in sight, but a change of style, which would merely be the same thing all over again with different eyebrows. Where is the woman with the courage to look like herself? Where, for that matter, the man? These do not exist. We are all afraid of something. Besides, he could not but hanker after the history or fancy piece, for since he had no talent for composition, that, of course, was what he longed to do.

In short, he was in the dumps. His talent was limited, in so far as he could draw accurately only what he saw. And who could get a woman to sit still long enough to show her character? She knows better. As soon as you begin to get close, she begins to fidget. As for sharing the canvas with anyone less undifferentiated than a child, that was out of the question, so there went composition. Even Reynolds had been constrained to draw the Waldegrave sisters separately.

Hayley wanted a portrait of Serena, engravable for a new edition of the *Triumphs of Temper,* and therefore an excellent advertisement for them both. The *Triumphs of Temper* is a poem of ideas. Where another poet would match words, therefore, Hayley matched wool. "He is a *workbasket* poet," said Farrington, just as catty as Northcote and every inch the R.A. "His verses are upon every girl's sofa." And so they were, laid face down. A fresh edition appeared every year, at Confirmation time.

"But can she sit still?" asked Romney. "I am slow to compose."

"I fear she sits still for quite long periods of time," said Hayley. "She is a sweet thing, and has little else to do. Greville keeps her, you see."

"Oh Greville," said Romney, with a contemptuous

snort. He, too, had had to deal with the purity and exactitude of Greville's taste. "Very well, bring her along, and we'll take a look at her." It was Greville who had told him he was not quite *ready* yet. He decided to up his price, should a commission be forthcoming.

And so the second lesson began, with the first one as yet unlearned.

Though amoral in important matters, Greville was strict in trifles, and insisted upon a duenna, so Mrs. Cadogan went along.

As the sittings progressed, and there were to be more than three hundred of them, she spent most of her time reorganizing the kitchen. Romney came from their own part of the world. The three of them understood each other at once. No matter what their vices, they were all innocent in a most venal town, and if Mrs. Cadogan was perhaps less innocent than they were, why that only improved her cooking, which was a blessing, considering what Romney generally ate. Within the confines of the studio they were quite gay, like prisoners in Bedlam, who do not care where they are.

"And where is your wife, Mr. Romney?" asked Mrs. Cadogan, a woman's first question to any seemingly single man.

"At home where she belongs, I trust." Romney liked women well enough. It was only their company he could not abide. Their company fell short of the ideal. And answering a woman's second question before it was put, with a glance at the stack of portraits in the corner, waiting for delivery, he added: "She is well provided for."

"And your children?" Mrs. Cadogan persisted.

"With my wife. I would prefer that in their younger

years they had some experience of the country, which is wholesome, so I am told." Though it was all very well for Reynolds to do the Honourable This or That as the Infant Samuel, that was by no means the same as having the pudgy things pewling about underfoot. No doubt Reynolds loved children, but Reynolds was a bachelor, and so could well afford the sentiment. Sentiment is not the same as rocks in one's best asphaltum, and three pounds' worth of chrome yellow expended upon the funeral of a dead cat.

"Sir, you need a woman's care," said Mrs. Cadogan, unimpressed.

"The char comes in every second Wednesday. I also need peace and quiet."

Neither one of them had won. It was therefore necessary, as it is after inconclusive battles, to declare an *entente cordiale*. Mrs. Cadogan sailed off to the kitchen. He was, she confided afterward, a dear old gentleman.

He was nothing of the sort. He was merely a boy tortured by a vision he could not even see, who drew very badly, and who was forty-eight; in short, as lonely as a genius, even if he was not one.

"Ah," he said, "the music of the spheres," for he had heard a kettle boiling. Inside of two weeks the studio reeked of boiled cabbage, shepherd's pie, jam tarts, Yorkshire pudding, brown Windsor soup, baked widgeon, jugged hare, blood pudding, venison patty, suet roly-poly, and all those other treats of the commonalty which in Edgware Row could be served only on the sly.

"She is a wonder," Romney said to Hayley. "She can sit for hours immovable, and yet her face is never still. In the face she can be anything. In short, she is so vivacious that, tell me, what does Greville see in her?"

"He reads to her."

Which he did. He hoped, by example, to rid her of her native Doric, or failing that, of those tones in it which made the Boston Stump sound like a dance. He instructed her as one would address oneself to the elocution of a parrot, but his voice was a drone, and do what she would, Emma could not drone. She was too happy. Mr. Romney had asked her to come back again.

"It is useless," said Greville. "But her French is not too bad."

It was better than his own, since the proper English always speak that tongue as though groping around in a hip tub for the soap they cannot find but on which they have no desire to slip when they get out to dry themselves with their native tongue.

Serena was disposed of, but Greville had commissioned a three-quarter portrait (that being the cheapest size). Romney proposed to paint her in a poke bonnet, with a toy spaniel in her lap.

"What are you looking for, dear child?"

"The spaniel," said Emma, with a disappointed air.

"The spaniel is hypothetical," he assured her gravely. She was the most entrancing personage, the ideal daughter, and he had produced mostly far from ideal, and solemn, if reverend, sons.

"You mean it isn't here?"

"It isn't here," said Romney.

"It never is, is it?" said Emma, and gave him a quizzical look.

So the next Thursday there was a toy spaniel which yapped and barked and relieved itself against a fulllength portrait of Lord North.

"The dear thing. How I wish I could take it home."

"You may if you wish."

"Oh no, I mayn't. Greville has a rooted horror of the animate; he has never explained why. But it is part of his system, I expect."

So the spaniel stayed in the studio, to its own vast relief, with a soft-boiled egg in the morning and kitchen scraps, until Emma forgot the pretty thing and he could give it away. Romney did not mind. It was a happy time for him, his only one.

It was a very happy time.

I am an old man, he thought, with a few cronies. The only part I play in their lives is the part I play when I am asking to visit them. I sit inside the dungeon of myself, a room as large as this studio and just as empty. I paint portraits the way a prisoner cards jute, and sometimes, if it is not always winter, there is a ray of pallid sunlight for a few minutes in the morning, before I cloud over again; though all the sun does is show the rings and shackles in the opposite wall, and the dust. I have waited in vain for the jailer's pretty daughter to unbolt the door with a metallic clang, and open it. I was a young man once, but now my only visions are a purely physiological phenomenon occasioned by pressure when I blink in the dark, when the inchoate roils; the only light, the dead cells in the eye, for the inchoate is uncreatable, for I do not know where to begin.

But now the jailer's pretty daughter comes regularly on Tuesdays and Thursdays, and would come every day if she or I were free, and so the dark is light enough. I do not mind carding my jute.

She had become an obsession. He saw her everywhere, most clearly perhaps, because surrounded by a nimbus, where she was not.

Emma, too, seemed happier, more like her portrait, fresh painted, which had joined Paulus Potter and Thais in the library, with another ordered to balance it—Emma as Spinstress, half cottage ornée, half Graeae. But except for basking in the improved temperature, Greville scarcely noticed. Like Romney, he had been overwhelmed by a ray of hope. His uncle's wife was dead.

"Good news, what, Charles?" said Towneley, in his best poke-a-stick-at-a-hedgehog way.

Greville curled into himself.

"I mean, since you are the favored nephew, no doubt you will inherit his wife's estates, given he does not marry again and produce young." Sir William was not only a doting uncle, he was also a childless man.

Greville did not consider this remark well-bred. It smacked of the frank.

"He is coming to England."

"In that case you will be making a trip to Wales, I

expect," said Towneley. "Lady Hamilton's estates are in Wales, are they not?"

Greville curled tighter than ever. Towneley was amused. When he was a boy, a gamekeeper had once given him a hedgehog which he had fed sweet milk from a tube, and in time it, too, had uncurled and eventually died. Towneley, who like most eunuchs, was afflicted with immortality, poured the sherry—a plump, complacent Jupiter, with money of his own.

"He is bringing, I believe, a vase."

Greville was alarmed. "That is not a matter to be spoken of."

"Like what song the Sirens sang, and what name Hercules took among women? Alcmene, I expect; he was a mother's boy and stuck with the heel of memory, like a crust of old bread. But I would like to see the vase."

He saw the vase. He always saw everything, for his principles were sound; when you cannot wheedle, threaten and—if possible—do both, for the best doors are not only closed, but have two locks.

So one day Emma saw from her window a tall, lean gentleman who looked very like Greville, but a Greville made out of some more durable material—say bronze—accompanied by Greville and a packing case, descend from a carriage in front of her door. Since she had been told not to come downstairs until summoned, all she knew about him for the time being was that the two men went into the library and closed the door.

She was late for Mr. Romney, and had no desire to linger; if that was Sir William, she already had heard enough about him to be terrified. He was, said Greville, a very grand personage: a Knight of the Bath, a Minister Plenipotentiary, a man of impeccable taste, a member of the Royal Society, an Intimate of Royalty, an expert alike upon Correggio and Vesuvius. He played the flute and ate young women raw, and what on earth was she to say to him, and should she curtsy?

"Oh, George, George, I do get so tired of nothing but ladies and gentlemen!" she said. If it was not a *cri de coeur*, it was most certainly a *cri de cour*. If one does not know French properly, one can form these puns.

"The expression is perfect; don't budge," said Romney, and sketched rapidly. He had discovered that the knowledge that she could hold a pose made it easier for him to work fast.

"And what am I to be this time, George?"

Romney looked at his canvas. "Cassandra," he decided, "for no one would listen to her then, and I have not the time to listen to you now."

It was a circular portrait, to fit Hayley's wainscoting, and one of the best things he had ever done. And what was more, here he was right now, in front of the easel, doing it spontaneously, without the need to plan it in advance. It was a Cassandra, however, eager, dubious, young; without one prophecy as yet fulfilled; hurt by childhood perhaps, but not as yet, thank goodness, by life.

"Emma, may the Gods keep you as you are," he said, brushing busily.

She seemed puzzled. She did not understand. It was just that added nuance needed to show Cassandra when young, for the young are always puzzled. He set it down.

Jumping from the dais, she came to watch.

"Why, George, that's how I used to look. Now how did you ever guess that?"

He felt a pang, for it was true. She was growing up. She would never again look the way she used to look. He must hurry to catch it.

"And how do you think you look now?" he asked. "Look around and show me." He waved a marl stick at the studio.

In thirty different attitudes, not counting sketches, which were littered everywhere, there she was, as a Bacchante, as Miranda, as Nature, as St. Cecilia, as Euphrosyne, as Cassandra again, as Sensibility, as Alope, as Circe, as Allegro, as every dream he'd ever had, and all the same imaginary woman, with a chaste body, and everything an attitude.

"As Ariadne, I think," she said. "It does look so respectable, as though I'd never come from anywhere, as though I just was."

He was disappointed. It was merely a pretty portrait. "My dear, you transcend the respectable. You are the thing itself." he said. "And like the real, you can imitate anything."

She giggled. "Did you know I was the goddess Hygeia once?"

He blinked. Warren Hastings had sent home from India some extracts from the 'Bhagavad-Gita,' with notes, and reincarnation had struck him as a wistful notion.

"Well, I was," said Emma, and looked stubborn. "At Dr. Graham's Temple of Health in Adelphi Terrace. It was ever so funny. I posed before old gentlemen up to their necks in hot mud—like this." She struck an attitude. "I wore a real Greek costume, too."

"You did what?"

"After I got tired of being pinched by Dr. Budd and selling apples, which wasn't much better, and falling in love with Captain Knight . . ." She had forgotten about that. Love was not the same as gratitude or affection or security. Indeed it had been quite terrible, as she remembered. Then she forgot it again and laughed. At Mr. Romney's she was allowed to laugh. Greville did not like it. So she did an imitation of one of Greville's taut little smiles instead. The effect was startling. For a moment Greville flitted across her face, and then he was gone, as though he had never been, and the face was as placid as before.

"It was either sink or swim," said Emma, "and they paid me a shilling a day. I left because he wanted me to demonstrate the Celestial Bed upstairs as well, and that was going too far. But he said he was sorry I did not find the work to my taste, which was nice of him."

Romney found her better than a magic-lantern show, a hundred expressions, all different, all luminous. But he knew better than to ask what they meant. Besides, probably she did not know.

"Do you think," he asked, "that you could manage a Grief?"

She was not sure. She ransacked mythology. "Who was Grief?" she asked.

Romney did not know mythology well, but had been commissioned by Alderman Boydell to do a fancy piece for the Shakespeare Gallery, and if that was successful, perhaps more than one. "Cordelia," he said.

"Oh yes, of course," said Emma, and without hesitation—now that she knew who had felt it—did Grief perfectly.

But when Romney was alone and Emma was gone and the fashionable or at any rate rich sitters had gone, and his work was done for the day, or after he had come home by himself after dinner at a tavern with friends, he lit a lamp in the echoing silence of the studio and went from picture to picture; and sometimes, instead of going to his narrow bed, would doze in a chair in the studio. When he woke, at foggy dawn, in the flannel light, there she was still, his niece, his inspiration, his company, his better self. For George Romney was an ugly, disappointed man. He could only draw beauty. And here, at last, after years of the most impeccable drudgery, was beauty to draw. Even those shapeless, desperate, blobby nightmares in sepia were now made bearable by taking on Emma's gestures and Emma's face.

He wept for joy. He had at last become a painter. She had transubstantiated him. Even his paid portraits now came to resemble Emma, in gesture, in expression, so that hers not theirs became the fashionable look and was bearable, since now she was the fashion. So when Alderman Boydell's Shakespeare Gallery opened and the "Cordelia" was shown, she performed that highest creative act of which woman is capable, and the only one she ever has any use for: she launched a new fad. You saw the Emma look everywhere.

Greville was annoyed.

"I told her to dress simply, and now simplicity has become the fashion, however am I to get her to return to her senses and dress plain?" he demanded, certain, in a woman's world, of but one thing—that cheap muslin

would rise in price and the cost of ribbon soar enormously.
Nor was he wrong.

Emma had come home to find Sir William standing before the mantelpiece, and had not been frightened one bit, for he had gone out of his way—which was not far—to please her. He seemed to know exactly what to say to a person, as though to give pleasure gave him pleasure and had nothing to do with the proprieties. She could romp with him when she chose, and called him Pliny the Elder, for fun; the Younger being Greville, though the Younger Pliny was an astute, pushy, contrived young man, far too concerned with the family properties at Stabiae.

They were in the garden, under the lilac tree, where the late summer sunlight was like pale tea not steeped long enough. Sir William was making invidious comparisons.

". . . whereas in Naples the sun shines every day, and if there is a cloud, it is out of Tiepolo," he said.

Emma did not know who Tiepolo was.

"Like Canaletto, except that he paints well," explained Sir William. "You must see one. You have the Tiepolo look." He was wrong. One cannot have the Tiepolo look without a *cicisbèo*, which requires maturity of outlook, and Emma was not yet eighteen.

The sky lacking Neapolitan consistency, they went indoors to open the packing cases, from one of which Sir William extracted the Barberini, the Byres, the Hamilton, and he hoped what was to be next, the Portland, vase, a squat, ugly jar of indeterminate color, cluttered with shrubbery and figures of white glass in cameo.

"Not only is it unique, but it may well have contained the ashes of Alexander the Great," said Sir William firmly. "We may expect eighteen hundred guineas, at the least."

"But where shall we put it?" wailed Emma, who did not altogether feel at her ease in a house where everything was beautiful but nothing ever stayed put for long, except the furniture, though she always put Mrs. Cadogan's gin bottle in a good safe place, in case the sideboard should be moved in the night.

"In a good collection, I hope," said Sir William. "We have saved it for England, and no doubt at a tidy profit, too. But Greville must see to that." He was in a good mood. He had taken the death of his wife Catherine with equanimity, for not only was he gracious to others, but—a man who lived up to his own principles—he saw no point in causing himself undue pain.

With Emma he was pleased and agreeably surprised, since he was slightly deaf in the right—or woman's side at any table—ear. She was a living statue. He was not without his human side, but then, he did not happen to find statuary inhuman. No matter what incongruous instrument she might be at, Emma fell into marmoreal poses naturally, as though Niobe had been pushed before a harpsichord; her breath had the soft cool freshness of marble, and all in all, she was a creature worthy the approbation of Winckelmann or Mengs. He went away delighted.

"My nephew," he said next day at the Royal Society, to Sir Joseph Banks, "has got himself a pretty miss."

"My God, how?"

Sir William looked put out. He was fond of his nephew. Charles was one of his hobbies, and one gets fond of any toy. Unfortunately he was also fond of the truth, so long as that deity could be kept at a distance, discreetly draped. Truth he saw always as a garden statue —the best procurable copy, maybe even an original, something at any rate with a pedigree dating back to Lord Arundel's collection—at the end of an allée, backed by box, to improve the view. It had to be there, but on the other hand, one seldom went down that way. Sir Joseph and he, however, were old cronies.

"I do not know," he said. "She is naïve. She has yet to learn ingratitude."

"Some of us don't, you know," said Sir Joseph.

"Perhaps not. But they throw scenes." He was thinking of his wife, a conformable heiress whose career of discreet invalidism had so recently been rounded off by the appropriate distinction of death. She had played the harpsichord well (he had played the flute), and sometimes he looked around to say something to her, in the late afternoon, and found she was not there. She had not thrown scenes, but she had made her presence palpable. Greville's toy had made him lonely.

"She is called the Fair Teamaker of Edgware Row," he explained, aware that that mincing, sneering tone proper to the *ton* did not always convey one's true feelings.

"You must take me to meet her. At times one tires of botany," said Sir Joseph.

"If I go, I shall."

"You will go," said Sir Joseph, grunted, and swiveling around to a large folio volume on a lectern, began to display something that interested him: a series of engravings of landfalls, all similar, all different, meticulously drawn by the cartographer. He would never travel himself. He was too happy at his club. He was too happy with the Royal Society. But he would very much have liked to see a landfall one day from the sea; and when he looked at dried botanic specimens, he did so as a modern man would wistfully examine travel brochures. These are the places I shall never go. They are the more beautiful for that.

As for Sir William, no matter how he might ape the *pococurante*, he was only waiting to be interested in something, for there was something wild, hurt and congenial about him. Though distant, he was a good man to drink with, and no fool.

"The Little Teamaker of Edgware Row," said Sir Joseph. "It sounds like one of Michael Kelley's songs."

"It is like that, and when the performance flags, they actually wave real flags, to perk you up, like street buskers."

"Who, Charles and his doxy?"

"She is not a doxy," said Sir William, determining to take a carriage to Edgware Row. His curiosity was piqued, as it would have been by any odd animal in a raree show. One goes because it is a novelty, but puts up with it for ten years because it is a pet. He looked out the window at nothing in particular and fidgeted to get back to Naples. I am an Englishman. I find England congenial. Nothing else is quite so congenial. And yet I miss the sun. I miss the bay. I miss the inconsequence of their quarrels. I miss the fruit.

"And what is that one?" he asked, pointing to one of Sir Joseph's series of almost indistinguishable coasts.

"They have yet to be lettered, but I believe it is Mooréa. An island in the South Seas. She is an English beauty, all peaches and cream, and speaks her native Doric still, so they say."

"Oh her native Doric," said Sir William. "It is strange, we get these phrases from Greece and Rome, and yet I have never been to either. As a matter of fact, it is a light and coarse voice, but singularly pleasing."

"Charles would destroy the world, out of the foible that he is competent to save it," said Sir Joseph. "But fortunately he does not know how to begin. I have imported some breadfruit trees."

"Breadfruit trees?" Sir William had been thinking.

"Oh, they do not bear loaves, like something out of Sir John Mandeville, but their fruit is edible, and the leaf beautiful. No matter what we do to harm them, there are still a few harmless creatures in this world. Why not go to see her?"

"She belongs to Charles."

"Nothing belongs to Charles but a few pieces of pinchbeck, and nothing ever will," said Sir Joseph. "He is himself pinchbeck, and besides, if she pours tea and you drink it and it is good tea, what's the harm in it?"

"You must come to Italy; the strawberries are delicious. Small, and feral and bitter. The trouble is, I like her. It is much more dangerous than a passion, for a passion soon ends."

"In that case, I shall travel with my own sugar," said Sir Joseph, "in a castor." And he shut up his portfolio of landfalls. "I doubt if she gets much female company, poor dear, so perhaps the male will do. Take me along."

Sir William took him along.

It occurred to Greville that he had seldom seen so many pawky gentlemen in such congenial circumstances. The Teamaker of Edgware Row was invaluable. But though he had told her to flirt with his uncle, he had not told her to flirt with him that much. The girl was forward. She presumed. One tires of every toy in time. A rest from each other would do them both good, but it must be an inexpensive rest. And what is cheaper than home? She should go to Park Gate, where her grandmother kept the child. Sir William and he were off to inspect the family property in Wales.

Emma burst in upon Romney, her eyes sparkling with fright. He always marveled at her eyes. Only when sleepless did they have that poached-cod look inevitable to the lower classes from which she had sprung.

"I am to be cast out. Abandoned!" she cried. "I need your help."

"What you mean is, you need to talk," he said. Her emotions were too fluid. For this he would need water color. Where the hell was a pliable brush?

It was what always happened. As soon as you settled comfortably in, once the nasty part was over, to be the hoyden younger sister, the favorite niece, even at last the wife, once you had relaxed, they flung you out. But that was not something she wanted to say to George.

"I am to be sent to Chester while they go to Wales."

"In that case you can visit your daughter."

She had forgotten she had told him about that. She wished she had not.

"And your grandmother, too. You are fond of your grandmother."

"Oh that was a world away, and I shall never be allowed to come back," cried Emma, and sobbed away with a will.

"Of course you shall," said George, but wondered, with panic, if she might not be right. He had hundreds of sketches of her. He could work from those. But that was by no means the same thing as being able to work with Emma there.

He proposed a game of blindman's buff, for he was a selfless man, so what with sticking his left foot through the hands of Mrs. Hope Devis (due Thursday) and one thing and another, he soon made her forget her woes, which was just as well, for she would be left alone with them soon enough.

As so would he. Mrs. Hope Devis was too much the parvenu to put up with patching, and so the whole thing would have to be fresh done tonight.

Emma took a look around the studio, as though for the last time, which is what she always did in any house, surprised, if she came back, not to find that it was still there but that she was, and went to Chester.

"The chief peculiarity of Wales," said Greville, stumbling on a piece, "is the prevalence of igneous rock."

"When you have conquered Vesuvius with a hired guide, Cadr Idris is an inferior peak, though Wilson, except for his portraits, is a wrongly neglected painter," said Sir William. "There is his view of Tivoli. There is his view of this. Though it is a pity," he added, peering round at the fog, "that this so seldom has a view."

"If you put money into the property instead of taking money out, we could make Milford Haven a port and double the revenue."

"No doubt," said Sir William. "But for whom, lad, for whom?"

Greville blushed.

"By the way, my niece Mary has sold the vase," said Sir William mildly. "You are a good boy, Charles, but you dawdle overmuch."

"Mary gossips."

"And what does she say?"

"That you have been seen too much with Emma and have taken her to Reynolds to have her portrait done."

"Well, so I have. So where's the gossip now?"

"She is as perfect a thing as can be found in all nature. I will not have her traduced."

"She is better than anything in nature; in her particular way she is finer than anything to be found in antique art. So why should I not have her portrait by Reynolds if I wish? In his own way, he, too, transcends art. Indeed, he has very little to do with it. In those circumstances I consider the painter and the subject felicitously matched."

"Then you do like her?"

"I like her appearance," Sir William said cautiously. "Just what was it you and Mary had in mind?"

"Her voice is shrill."

"Her voice, fiddlesticks. There's nothing wrong with her voice. She's a country girl, that's all. The world is not Middlesex, Charles, even though the world, for some inscrutable reason, chooses to live there. It is all very well for Towneley to speak of prunes and prisms, but a large, generous mouth is worth it all."

"Then you do like her."

"I was speaking of your cousin Mary," said Sir William, with dignity, "who has not only accomplished the matter of the vase with her customary combination of finesse and dispatch, but has deposited eighteen hundred guineas in Coutts' bank, *sans peur, sans reproche* and *sans* fee. I think we will now descend."

So down into the mizzling clouds beneath their feet they went. In Wales, as usual, it was cold.

In Cheshire it was no warmer. Emma was in seaside lodgings, left to contemplate that ocean which Fanny Burney informs us is cold but pleasant, but which as far as she could see, was merely wet and damnably dull. Fanny Burney, however, had had a bathing attendant to divert her, whereas here the only human creature was an old winklewoman with a large basket and a very small catch, all grumble, beard and scratch.

"Mama?" asked Emma Carew—for so the child had been named—aged two, but nagging happily, for children are as impervious to the weather as to most things.

Emma seized it with a mixture of maternity and revulsion, for the child was damp.

"Poor motherless lamb," she said evasively, and cursed them all. It would be necessary to seat the child upon a horse to be certain of its paternity: Sir Harry had a most individual seat, whereas Greville resembled nothing so much, up there, as a pedestrian grown weary.

She bent down, all Ariadne, to inspect the child. Two years ago she had wept inconsolably to give it up, and here it was, a stranger. Tentatively, she leaned over and made noises at it.

Overhung by such generous glamor, the child smiled. Contact had been established. The terms of the treaty had been signed, including the secret clause. Whatever else happened, they would know each other *now*, which was harmless, delightful and no more innocent than snakes and ladders, skip the stone, Troytown, or any other game.

Forlornly, she took the child away from the beach, through the late, low sun. There had not been any letter from Greville as yet.

Once she had gone, the sandpipers rushed their invisible prayer rug up the beach, and just as incontinently, rushed it back down again. It was the hour of muezzin.

In bed that night, Emma heard no familiar sound, whereas in Edgware Row there was at least the bell-ringer who gathered people together at late hours, in order to conduct them through Hyde Park at sixpence the head, so they might not encounter footpads, shrub-lurkers and common highwaymen. That we should sleep young and alone is so shameful a waste of a perfectly good body, that despite all resolution—in the absence of any cuddly animal—she took the child to bed with her.

"Would you think it, Greville," she wrote in the morning, "Emma—the wild, unthinking Emma—is a grave, thoughtful phylosopher. For endead, I have thought so much of your amiable goodness, when you have been tried to the utmost, that I will, endead I will, manege myself and try to be . . ."

Greville always skipped those bits.

"And how is she?"

"Abergale is too expensive, two and a half guineas a week; Hoylake has but three houses, not one of them fit for a Christian; they are now at Parkgate, fed by a lady whose husband is at sea, for a guinea, ten and six a week," said Greville.

Sir William had inquired after her emotional condition, but then, Charles would not know that.

"She adds, 'Give my dear kind love and compliments to Pliney and tell him I put you under his care and he must be answerable for you to me wen I see him. I hope he has not fell in love with any raw boned Scotch whoman.'"

Sir William smiled. "Yes," he said. "She would add that."

"I have had no letter from you yett, which makes me unhappy . . . My dear Greville, dont be angry but I gave my Granmother 5 guines, but Emma shall pay you," wrote Emma. And again went out to confront the empty sea.

Mrs. Cadogan had struck up a raillery with the winklewoman, condescension in every line, but Emma preferred not. She was too disconsolate. She watched the child. She did not think she had ever been in so large and bleak and lonely a place before. Even the slight surf was surreptitious here, as though not to disturb the silence, and nowhere could she glimpse so much as the green sign of a tree. The beach was a dirty gray receding plane across which the child crawled like a white grub. In all that desolation, only the winklewoman turned around and around.

Oh God, abandoned, thought Emma. He has abandoned me.

This was unfair to Greville. Though he had thought of doing so, he had taken no action yet. Whether it was a matter of screwing his courage up, or his emotions down, Greville was always slow to act.

"If you are in bad case, you must marry; or if not marry, stand for Parliament; or failing that, do both," said Sir William. "In any event, you must do something. You have been eligible too long. Why, at your age I had already married this." With a wave of his hand, he indicated three flooded collieries, the family farms, Milford Haven and £5,000 a year, all he had left of a kind and loving wife's tender solicitude, but no doubt in time it could be made to pay better.

He felt sad. Life's larger emotions are so destructive that it is better to restrict oneself to the smaller ones. With a little effort and discipline this can be done, and they are far pleasanter. It may be submitted, however, that those restricted to the reticences of mere feeling perhaps ache the longer for it. And Sir William ached. He was tired of going home to an empty hall, and though a kept woman does well enough, she seldom knows how to keep house.

"I must say, your young woman keeps an excellent house," he said.

"It's the mother does that."

"I see."

"They are inseparable. That's why I shall ask them to return before we do, to get the house in order."

Sir William turned on him a look of blinding benevolence, slightly more searching than the Eddystone Light. "Charles, you plan."

After all, I am his favorite nephew, thought Greville, gratified. He wished to manage his uncle's estates, but how to ask?

Sir William, it appeared, was willing to hand over some, if not all. In the matter of ready cash, however, though doting, he was no fool, and would do no more than to go surety for a loan—enough to disinherit him, should he be unable to repay it promptly, but still, a loan.

"It is the best I can do. Marry, Charles. At least we know it will not be a runaway match, unless the hostler has learned how to harness a snail; but marry, do. My father married twice, and the family is none the poorer for it."

"I would have to be unencumbered." Athene, the goddess of wisdom, was, as we know, born full-grown from the forehead of Jove, but being a dutiful daughter, may be presumed to fly back home again when needed. Greville had just been visited by an idea.

His uncle did not appear to have heard him.

"I have always believed that Milford will rival Portsmouth and Plymouth in its time," said Sir William, contemplating with affection two stranded dories—one with a staved-in bottom, a bit of broken rope twisted in a rusted ring—tidal ooze in the estuary, two broken-down tenements, a grogshop, half a barn, and a horse whose Creator, though an excellent colorist, had clearly had no knowledge of anatomy.

"It would be necessary to suborn the Members for Pembroke," said Greville. Just as a painter keeps certain works by him, so was he most unwilling to part with Emma. She was not merely the best, she was also the only thing he had ever done. Nonetheless, with a little prodding here and there, the idea had been born.

He decided to be kind. He wrote to her.

She was holding her elbows in warm salt water to cure a rash she got when she was nervous. The letter was kindly and asked after the child. Greville's prose was based upon the absence of concrete nouns, but by repeatedly avoiding his subject, he did in time succeed in making his meaning plain. Whatever he did not say was what he was talking about.

Emma, who had hoped to take the child back to Edgware Row, answered at once. No one, he had said, must know that it existed. But he would pay for it, all the same.

You dont know, my Dearest Greville, what a pleasure I have to think that poor Emma will be comfortable & happy. Now Emma will never expect what she never had, so I hope she will be very good, mild & attentive & we may have a deal of comfort. All my happiness is now Greville & to think that he loves me makes a recompense for all ...

Emma prepared to leave, if sadly. It was better to give the child up.

And yet ... and yet. ...

"A very proper sentiment, too," said Greville, putting the letter aside.

"As for the *form* of this surety," said Sir William, who was not only a shrewd Scots bargainer, but also at times a tease. "It shall consist of a lien against my estates, collectable only after my decease. So unless you wish to feel the pinch, manage the properties well."

At Parkgate it was the end of the season, so the weather had at last turned fine. But the beach, voided of its happy families, now contained no one but the winklewoman, with here and there the soft, sudsy suspiration of a living winkle—for she was not so sharp-sighted as she used to be—and in the distance one dirty vagrant King Charles spaniel, joyously on the prowl.

Emma, though sprung from the people, did not happen to be trapped in the cages of their philosophy. There is something to be done, not nothing, so one need not put up with it. Nothing will turn out for the best unless we give it a good shove in the right direction. Though things will turn out for the best in time, it would be much better if they did their turning now. And though clouds may contain a silver lining, that is not where a silver lining belongs; a silver lining belongs in an opera bag.

At Cavendish Square she watched the Duchess of Argyll, with a cramp in one elbow and a strained, painted look, descend to her waiting carriage, and then herself ran up the steps.

"I'm back, George," she cried. *"I'm back!"*

George came out of the shadows and took a look at her. There was nothing to see but beauty. She was a resilient girl. The rash on her elbows had disappeared.

"I missed you," he said, and sounded as though he had, which made her look serious, for so far he was the only person in her life who ever did.

"The Duchess of Argyll has a most inconstant nose,"

he said, feeling happy. "No matter where you put it, it is always either too high or too low."

"I saw her leaving. You gave her a cramp, George, in the arm."

"I also gave her a pleasant expression, which she did not have before. Have you time to pose? If so, whom shall you be?"

Yes, she had time to pose. To read, to sing, to pose for Romney were her only recreation. "Helen," she said, "brought home again."

"Cheshire is not Troy. No, today you shall be Miranda." Humming, he set a fresh canvas up, for it had been one of his Caliban days, and Prospero was not one to prefer Ariel to his own daughter.

> *And these, our revels,*
> *Shall vanish into air, into thin air.*

Greville was writing to Sir William: "Emma is very grateful for your remembrances. Her picture shall be sent by the first ship. I wish Romney yet to mend the dog." He hoped negotiations would not be protracted.

But they were.

Sir William's existence had been made agreeable by two excellent decisions: one within his control, the other not. He had married a woman afflicted by both fortune and delicate health. He had been made ambassador to the unimportant Court of the Two Sicilies by George III, who understood him to be a connoisseur, so no doubt he would be happier in *virtuland*.

He was, and had been now for twenty years. One thing that kept him there was a most un-English aptitude for eating fruit; not the woodchuck delights of apples, medlars and those austere Kentish cherries with the texture of nipples and the taste of warm blood sausage, but enormous mounds of melons, oceans of oranges, pyramids of Sicilian lemons stuffed with sherbet and then chilled, and the Arabic intensity of coarse green limes. Another was the climate. And most important was that only there could he afford to live as a Hamilton, if only a collateral Hamilton, should.

So he had managed to retain his post, by what means was unknown. Sir William preferred the strings he pulled to be invisible, an illusion at which he was vastly skilled, since the only thing he had brought with him from childhood—a condition from which he had escaped as quickly as possible—was the art of being the puppet-master of himself. He was of course unmistakably an Englishman of the better sort, which is to say, a Scotsman. He never forgot that. But still, every time he returned to Naples he felt as though a curtain had gone up. The stage was bathed in light, the figures ranted on, the music was agreeable.

He was delighted with the Romney. It would match the Reynolds he had already, and true, she was a Greek statue to the life, but he did not particularly care for sculpture in the round. He preferred his art restricted, like his life, to two dimensions, and those to be seen from in front. In these emotional matters, it cannot be denied, distance brings relief.

But neither could it be denied that he was lonely, and the mother both knew her place and how to cook a decent meal in it.

But why hurry?

Now everything was as it was before. Emma had gotten over her scare and was content. Sometimes Greville was there. Sometimes he was not. When she was bored, she could visit George.

But Mrs. Cadogan smelled something in the wind, and stuck her little nose up, like a groundhog at its burrow, and listened for reverberations and watched shadows. She did not like what she saw.

"Lazy girl, you have had two offers of marriage and one to be set up, on more liberal terms than here, from Greville's friends already," she grumbled.

"They are not friends. They come to gawk." She would not leave Greville. It was useless to argue.

"But why? He does not even sleep with you any more."

"Ah I know," said Emma, snuggling farther down into

the enormous bed, incurably virginal. "He is considerate even in that."

"But have you no desire to better yourself?"

"Myself, yes; my position, no," said Emma, and after her mother had gone, jumped up to examine herself in the mirror—all that lovely flesh, and every inch of it untouched by anyone since goodness only could remember when. She wondered what she could wear today that would please dear Greville. Something old, she supposed, for there was very little that was new.

"I cannot endure the poor creature. She is always there," said Greville.

"Ah, then your uncle did take a fancy to her," said Towneley.

"I must marry or burn, he says."

"If I may venture to add a textual commentary, what he means is that if you marry your debts will be burned. It looks similar, but it is by no means the same thing. I know this, and yet, as you can see, I am by no means a Bible man."

"There is the younger daughter of Lord Middleton," mused Greville. "But I shall need thirty thousand pounds at least."

"If you take the advice of an experienced man, you will ask for more and settle for less. It is amazing, on the whole, what you can acquire in that way, and the other way round is seldom possible."

Should I marry [Greville wrote to Sir William], she shall never want, & if I decide sooner than I am forced to stop by necessity, it will be that I may give her part of my pittance, & if I do so it must be by sudden resolution & putting it out of her power to refuse it . . . I should not write to you thus if I did not think you seem'd as partial as I am to her. [Of course he liked her. Did they not have the same taste?] She would not hear at once of any change, & from no one that was not liked by her [it made no sense, but like Shakespeare, Greville could write and never blot]. I think I could secure on her near £100 a year [and would his uncle do the same, please?]. And I think you would be as comfortable as I have been and am ...

In Cavendish Square, George groaned, stirred, and woke into an atmosphere of roiling darkness, linseed oil and turpentine. The walls were lined with faces he could not even see. His night vision was nonexistent. A sound was what had waked him. It was the constant purring irregular motion of a spinning wheel, wettened fingers, and bobbin and thread. There was a quick, brisk, metallic snip.

"I have cut the thread," said a voice in the dark.
"The thread is too short," the old woman whined.
"It is always short," said the voice in the dark.
"The next is his," the old woman whined.
"It is long but short," said the voice in the dark.
"Aye, it always is," said the old woman's whine.

Out of the darkness came a wave of breasts and arms and thighs and heads and draperies, crashed down on him, and ebbed and sobbed away again. It would be back. It always came back, and each time more featureless than before. It had already caught its only light.

George put the pillow over his head, but the spinning wheel whirred on anyway.

In Edgware Row, Emma smiled, stretched, snuggled into the comforter, and went to sleep again.

Not everyone matures; some have maturity thrust upon them, like a package no one else will carry. Greville, in the library downstairs, was writing letters again, for he had heard an alarming thing. Sir William was seen much these days in the company of Lady Craven, a woman apt to marry almost anyone (eventually she married the Margrave of Brandenburg-Anspach, who, whatever else might be said for him, was certainly not an Englishman), and who was still fecund. "If you did not choose a wife, I wish the Teamaker of Edgware Row was yours," he suggested. He had been flushed. The question with Lady Craven was not whom she should marry, but who would take her. She was a dangerous, fortune-hunting woman.

Well, thought Sir William, why not? I am fifty-four, my position is secure, so why should I not? I need not remarry. I am a widower, and a widower is acceptable in all those places where a bachelor is not, and so need not go to the inconvenience of a wife. I do not need money. And besides, it would be agreeable to have the house well run.

Though garish in England, in this climate the Romney lacked color. However, as he remembered, its subject did not. He smiled.

Greville did not care for the terms. If she was merely to be packed off, where went his bargaining? He wrote Sir William:

> If things remain as they are, I shall, to be sure, be much straitened in finances. I shall be so whether she remains or not, literally her expences are trifling ... At your age a clean & comfortable woman is not superfluous but I should rather purchase than acquire it. ... Your brother spoke openly to me, that he thought the wisest thing you could do would be to buy Love ready made, & that it was not from any interested wish, as he was perfectly satisfied with the fortune he had, & that he should be very glad to hear you declare openly your successor, & particularly so if you named me; I write without affectation or disguise.

My brother does, my nephew does not, thought Sir William. And which brother, by the way, Charles, or the Archdeacon of Raphoe? He wrote right back:

> It would be fine for the young English travellers to endeavour to cuckold the old gentleman their Ambassador. I should like better to live with you

both here & see you happy, than to have her all to myself, for I am sensible I am not a match for so much youth and beauty.

In half of that suggestion, Greville saw a solution, a way to get her out there without scenes. How pleasant of his uncle to have thought of it. He was now down to the fine work of bargaining, which is best done in the darkness of privacy, so he packed Emma off to the seaside again.

She found it much the same in Cornwall as it had been at Parkgate, except that this time there was not even a winklewoman to disrupt the view. The only grumbling here was done by the sea itself, in the motion of the tides against the pebbles, and her elbows itched again.

"I told you in my letter of thanks for the signed bond, that sealing and signing was nothing without a witness's name; you will, therefore, be so good as to send it back with that addition," wrote Greville, but raised the figures on the bond. Emma's traveling expenses would be thirty guineas, payable in advance, and "If Lord Middleton was made sure that I was your heir, then my proposal for his daughter might meet with more favourable a reception than," concluded Greville lamely, "if not."

"Very well, have done with it," snapped Sir William, and sent fifty pounds and signed the bond as well. Greville was too particular in his terms, as well as stingy.

"You must tell her," said Greville to Mrs. Cadogan, "that all she is asked to do is to spend six months with my uncle, with yourself as chaperone." And went to the country for the weekend. He hated scenes.

"George, I am to be sent to Italy for six months. It is a holiday. And Greville is to join us later."

George broke his brush. He would have believed it if she had not said it all at once, but a woman with a joyous secret is a cautious animal and only shows you a bit of it at a time, hints at it, nags at it, brings it into the conversation, and drives you crazy until at last she consents to wear the new dress and show it to you. He heard the spinning wheel.

"We shall come back very different, I expect," she said, with a slight quaver at the mouth.

George did not look at her, but at his easel. That was how she had looked six weeks ago.

"You have been to Italy," she said.

"To Rome. You will see Raphael. He is a very great painter, Raphael."

"And he will paint me too?"

"He is dead."

"I am sorry. I forgot. There is so much to remember." She could not sit still. "Oh, George, I am distracted. Please hold on to me."

He held on to her.

Towneley stretched lazily his immaculate and silken legs, and his eyes were soft with a kind but contemptuous glow.

"You have brought it off," he said, as though to say, Now you are locked in with me.

With a glance at the door, which was open to an empty room beyond, Greville reached for the decanter, which was half full.

George sat alone and wrote:

> Sir, that portrait which you commissioned, of Emma Hart, as a Spinstress, has now long been finished and dry. It has recently been seen by a Mr. Christian Curwen, who has shown great interest in it. I remain, sir, yours respectfully,
>
> George Romney

Certainly Greville did not want it; as certainly, he did

not wish to let it go. It was the same with everything. He replied:

> There are circumstances which force the natural bias of character and render it prudent to change the scene of action to train them to the necessary sacrifices. The separation from the original of the Spinstress has not been indifferent to me [on the contrary, it had forced him to go away for the weekend], and I am but just reconciled to it [it was now Tuesday] from knowing that the beneficial consequences of acquirements will be obtained, and that the aberration from the plan I intended will be for her benefit. I therefore can have no reason to value the Spinstress less than I have done, on the contrary the just estimation of its merits is ascertained by the offer from a person who does not know the original [though our conduct needs no justification, the world is unjust, so it behooves us not only to cover our tracks, but to explain: it was his apologia], yet I find myself daily so much poorer, that I do not foresee when I can pay for it, and I am already too much obliged to you to avail myself in any degree of your kindness to me—perhaps Mr. Christian might accept my resignation of it and pay for it, and give me the option of repurchasing if the improbable event of my increase of means [a most improbable event, for though he had quite civilly informed Lord Middleton that he thought the family amiable and the daughter interesting, his politeness had not been returned] shall enable me to recover what I now lose with regret [and so on] . . . I shall thus multiply the objects of expectation from better times by keeping hold of the Spinstress without postponing the payment.

As indeed he had.
But then, if we are not so fortunate as to be born of tempered steel, why then we must do the next best thing and temporize.

Indubitably he would die a bachelor.

They were upon the Continent. Emma had been at her most superbly theatrical. If the heart stops, beat the breast and it will soon start up again, like a turnip watch. They sat in a coach with Gavin Hamilton, the painter, a connection of Sir William's, up on the box for company as far as Rome, though so far they were only in Dijon, opposite a *charcuterie*.

"Just look at the lovely sausages!" cried Mrs. Cadogan. "Pray stop."

"My heart is broken. How can you be so cruel? I am oblivious to scenery. I am indifferent to the picturesque."

"Ah, ducks, how can you say so?" asked Mrs. Cadogan, leering out the window with the pursy eyelids of a born cook, and she banged on the roof until the coach stopped, and then scuttled into the *charcuterie,* though she was back soon enough, empty-handed.

"An écu for a Polish sausage," she said indignantly. "It is not to be borne. It is too much."

Gavin Hamilton leaned down obligingly from the box. "Indeed, madam, it is," he said. "Nothing is cheap in France except the people."

So on they drove, past Avignon, past Arles, past Marseilles, Nice, Savoy, Milan, and finally Rome, where Hamilton left them and they were turned over to a Mr. Graffer, who had been sent out to Naples to install an English garden there. But he was delayed, so they continued alone until at dusk they reached Gaeta, where the air shimmers and is all overture until the babble and chatter cease, and the first arioso is there to be listened to.

It was a simple lesson in pedagogy: if the child cannot learn the lesson, supply it with an easier, more agreeable one, and thus—learning that learning is not to be feared —it may be guided through the most intricate curriculum, insulated by its ignorance, and so escape unscathed, not having learned a thing at all.

But before that it must sleep while its elders make the

classroom agreeable by erasing traces of imminent toil, removing advanced pieces from the piano, and pinning funny animals on the walls.

It is the gateway to Naples, Gaeta.

III

ADAGIO, sings one of the competing singers in Mozart's *Impresario,* and makes something quite pretty out of it, too. But then the Impresario is a very wise man.

From nowhere, but they have an incipiently Italian look, cherubim assemble in vast quantity—for the plush folds of night are rich and heavy—to kick themselves into position with pink rudder toes; the orchestra of dawn chirps up again, now a rooster, now a flute; and with a flumpy heave, aside the curtains go upon the loveliest of painted scenes. The dawn floods up like a chorus from Glück, and there it is, the harmony of the world, wet and dripping, in a tonal net. And there is the great globe itself, the loveliest piece in the Cosmic Opera House, for if it does not contain everything, everything may be seen from there, or from the boxes.

Signor Pomposo, otherwise Ferdinand of the Two Sicilies, enters on a white horse. No matter what the opera, it is always written into his contract that he be allowed to do this. Nobody knows why. Signora del Largo, Maria Carolina herself, in other words the Queen, but no match for the *castrati,* putters about and beats the scenery. The arrangement is frontal, after Metastasio. Demofoönte steps forward and accosts the Principessa Arethusa, who should be in Syracuse where she belongs, but of that no matter. She is a short, Levantine, bad-tempered creature.

"Who is this woman?"

"I do not know. Perhaps she is *hors de Syrie*," replied Sir William, with full orchestra; he never stoops to a pun, but he cannot resist this one.

It is a comedy by Paisiello. It is called *Timante*, or *The Kingdom of the Two Sicilies*. It is not one of the maestro's better efforts, but it cannot be denied the scenery is superb. Hackert, the King's painter, always puts in a lot of sky, but then, at Naples there always is a lot of sky, all of it blue, and every shade of blue, for it shifts, it alters, it rustles like a peacock's tail; at night it has a thousand eyes. The sea, which has no tide to be taken at the flood, though sometimes it turns stormy, is green to purple at the deeps, and celadon elsewhere. It is layered with minnows, though farther out there are San Pietro and even pike, all beautiful, though the taste is muddy.

"Lady Hamilton has been laid up with a fever, and I was obliged to undertake her cure, which I completed in five days," wrote Sir William once. "Luckily there was a lake close by and I amused myself with catching pike." The Bay of Naples is very like a lake, and Sir William likes very much to fish. He is, after all, a diplomat. So does the King. He is a glutton.

Sir William has decided that Emma, who has learned manners, must now learn that quite different subject, the manners of the world. That should keep her occupied for some time, since the manners of the world are not seen through in a day.

He has been up since dawn, and is at the moment eating breakfast on his terrace and admiring the view, an unnecessary but pleasant occupation, since the view is already admirable. Dawn, in his case, is an event put ahead to eight o'clock, for though he rises earlier, his time until then is taken up by such chthonic exercises as answering dispatches and dispatching answers, so that he may have the day free for such diplomatic chores as hunting with the King and dining with him afterward; which is something like hunting with the hounds and running with the fox, but necessary. Today, however, is to be different. Today Graffer is to arrive, at last, with plants selected by Sir Joseph. And so is Emma.

Graffer has been delayed. To Sir William's left, Vesuvius rocks like a moored ship, its funnel smoking, a visible symbol of latent industry.

Who could not be happy here?

The answer is, Emma. She has been here four days, and all she does is write to Greville.

> I try to appear chearful before Sir William as I could, but am sure to cry the moment I think of you. For I feel more and more unhappy at being separated from you, and, if my fatal ruin depends on seeing you, I will and must at the end of summer. . . .

That is when he said he would come out.

> I find it is not either a fine horse, or a fine coach, or a pack of servants, or plays, or operas can make me happy. Sir William . . . can never be anything nearer to me than your uncle and my sincere friend.

Nonetheless, she was to have them all. Unlike his nephew, Sir William did not find generosity incompatible with thrift, and to do him justice, was exactly the same, even when he had less money.

"I know, from the small specimen during your absence from London, that I shall have at times many tears to wipe from those charming eyes," he told Greville. Graffer had arrived. If he had not Emma, he had at least the English garden to divert him.

"I have a very good apartment of 4 rooms, very pleasant-looking to the sea," wrote Emma. Why would he not answer?

He had not the time. He had turned to commerce and was busy with a scheme to settle a colony of American fishermen at Milford, to carry the whale fishery from thence to the South of Falkland Islands. Americans in those days being a practical people, the fishermen had gone to the Falkland Islands direct, but the scheme was none the worse for that, so it engrossed him and he engrossed it. Let her wait.

Emma opened the *Triumphs of Temper*. A leaf fell out. She had picked it that last afternoon at Edgware Row, but now it was dead. Also, this far south, the *Triumphs of Temper* did not read well, so she put both away.

It was the fifth day.

> I have had a conversation this morning with Sir Wm. which has made me mad. He speaks half I do not know what to make of it.

On the contrary, she knew exactly what to make of it. It was a siege.

"Mother, help me," she demanded.

"Daughter, help yourself," said Mrs. Cadogan, who liked the look and scale of things here, had never liked Greville, and certainly did not care to see her daughter behaving like a willful fool.

"There seems a great deal," she added kindly, "to help yourself to." She had two cooks, a housekeeper, three housemaids, an equerry, a butler, a coachman and six tweenies under her already, and since they did not understand her and she could not understand them, the household was functioning smoothly. So long as she kept them down, she might pilfer from the household accounts as she liked.

> You do not know how good Sr. Wm. is to me, he is doing everything he can to make me happy, he as never dined out since I came hear & endead to spake the truth he is never out of my sight, he breakfastes, dines, and supes, & is constantly by me, look-

> ing in my face [Emma wrote] & I do try to make myself as agreable as I can to him, but I belong to you, Greville & to you onely will I belong & nobody shall be your heir apearant.

By God, he was the "heir apearant," not she. Would she ruin everything?

> You do not know how glad I was to arrive the day I did, as it was my Birthday & I was very low spirited. Oh God, that day that you used to smile on me & stay at home & be kind to me, that that day I should be at such a distance, but my comfort is I rely on your promise & september or october I shall see you, but I am quite unhappy at not hearing from you, no letter for me yet Greville, but I must wait with patience.

The thoughts of children on their birthdays are sometimes bitter ones, but at least there were gifts: a carriage fresh-painted, a coachman, a footman, a boat and sea bathing from it, a cashmere shawl, some of Lady Hamilton's summer jewelry, new muslin dresses and Alençon lace to trim them with. There were concerts at home, and for the first time in two years Sir William had accompaniment for his flute. There were walks in the insect clatter of the Via Reale at night.

> . . . and I have generally two princes, two or 3 nobles, the English minister & the King, with a crowd behind us. He [the King] as eyes, he as a heart, & I have made an impression on his heart.

The Queen she had not met. No matter what their own morals, queens are not permitted to receive kept women.

There was even a visit to Pompeii.

"Shovel some pretty little trinket in," said Sir William, "so the girl can grub it out. I want to please her."

But though he pleased her, he was not Greville. Why did she take that attitude? Did she want to ruin him?

Did she not realize she was a gift, a premium upon a signed bond, an anything, but most assuredly not his?

"I won't, I won't, I won't," said Emma.

"You have a true friend in Sir William," wrote Greville, months away. "Go to bed."

"The girl is pretty, stubborn, foolish and desperate," advised Sir William. "She proposes to return to England to persuade you, and I have thought it best to say that in that event I would pay her passage there." And in that event . . .

> Onely I never will be his mistress. If you affront me, I will make him marry me.

An inoperative threat, for who was she to make any man marry her? Greville did not reply.

> If she behaves herself, we may be friends, but she may not return here [he wrote Sir William]. Without any other plan, she must wait events, and the difficulty will be to reject improper offers; and if a journey homewards should give a favourable one, it should not be lost; but, at any rate, she will have the good sense not to expose herself with any boy of family, she must look to from 25 to 35, and one who is his own master.

Since he wished not love but complicity, and so was no rival for her affections, Sir William merely handed this epistle to Emma and went to Caserta to inspect the beginnings of the English garden. He now knew the outcome he might expect, but though he had broken horses in his time, this had taken longer and was more difficult and left him as sad.

For the afternoon, he diverted himself with Graffer's gardening plans; as one passion begins to fail, it is necessary to form another, since the whole art of going through life tolerably is to keep eager about something. The moment one is indifferent, *on s'ennuie*.

This evening, perhaps.

> "Why should I not, if so I choose,
> Amend my morals to my views,
> As Nature herself, the wench, imbues
>   her lips with coral?
> And looks at the world in stark amaze,
> Her victory won, her brow a maze
>   of bayes and laurel . . ."

sang Emma, banging away at that latest thing, a pianoforte, which having a hard touch, could most satisfactorily be banged.

"What is that caterwauling?" demanded Mrs. Cadogan, who had heard it three rooms—and what was worse, four servants—away, and did not care for the sound of it.

"It is not caterwauling. It is an impromptu," said Emma. "I have reached a decision: I have given in."

It had not been so bad. Besides, afterward he had soothed her when despite herself she had burst into tears. He was almost as good as George. Poor George; these last few months life had been so disturbed, she had not thought to write to him.

"Apart from that, I do not care a *fig* for Greville!" she shouted.

Mrs. Cadogan had never before seen her in this mood. It was a new mood. She had changed in the night. She was not what formerly she had been. She would now impersonate herself and ape sincerity. From now on not even her mother should know some things.

Undressed, Sir William had looked like a badly peeled banana.

"I shall marry Sir William. Wait and see. I shall be safe. I shall be secure. I shall be untouchable. And I shall have a nephew."

Mrs. Cadogan, though not regular in her attendance at church, recognized sacrilege when she saw it. "Well, I never," she snapped. "What an idea!"

"It is not an idea. It is a plan. It is *le plan Hamilton!*" shouted Emma. "Since it is all he cares about, I shall disinherit him."

"You could certainly do far worse," said Mrs. Cadogan. "But you will have to keep your temper."

She kept her temper.

"Delphiniums won't hardly grow in this soil," said Graffer. "Neither will 'olly'ocks. And me kids don't much care for it, either."

A beautiful plant called Emma has been transplanted from England, and at least has not lost any of its beauty [Sir William Hamilton wrote Sir Joseph]. But they have now discovered that nature does enough here, and that all assistance is quite unnecessary. Graffer is not happy. Our dear Em. goes on now quite as I could wish, improves daily, & is universally beloved. She is wonderful, considering her youth and beauty, so that I see my every wish fulfilled.

She was indeed wonderful. She did not lose her temper once, not even when tempted to do so by its constant tugging at the leash. *Le plan Hamilton* took five years.

Emma's passion is admiration [Greville advised his uncle] & it is not troublesome, because she is satisfied with a limited sphere, but is capable of aspiring to any line . . . & it would be indifferent, when on that key, whether she was Lucretia or Sappho or Scaevola or Regulus; anything grand, masculine, or feminine, she could take up.

And had. But the more we do the quicker it ages us, and just as we think we're catching up with ourselves, we find we've lost what we were; we are now only the things we do, and so we grow worldly instead. Though to grow worldly, you must first have entree to it, and that would not be possible until she was married. She had made an agreeable discovery: it is possible to be a tart at night and a silly girl by day, both Thais and niece and a young matron too, for if we no longer care, we may be plural and so all things to all men—except what they really want, and when they get it, throw it away.

"You have a lovely voice, my dear," said Sir William. "We must train it." He would have said the same thing to a canary.

She went to two retired *castrati* singing masters. At any rate, they were retired from the stage; to retire from one's own condition is more difficult. One was called Giuseppe Aprile, the other Giuseppe Millico, but she called them Tweedledum and Tweedledee. They taught her much. Aprile could sound like a bell up to E above the treble stave, and had a warm and sympathetic character.

"In Germany," he said, for he had been a success in Stuttgart, *"rouladen* is a kind of rolled meat, but here it is the following." And he showed her how. He was the jollier of the two, a man of the most impeccable dishonesty. Millico was apt to be dour, for he had sciatica.

"You are an English miss, in which case I suppose it must be Handel," said Aprile, "but in Italian, *please*. No, not that way. It is an aristocratic work. Sex is the entertainment of the poor, but it is the recreation of the rich, so toy with it."

"It is," added Millico, "considered vulgar to show abandonment or pleasure."

"Simulate, but never feel. It is the only way to achieve a pure tone," said Aprile.

"My child," said Millico, his eyes glistening with tears, "you are a very beautiful woman. And besides, you do not sing so very bad. Almost as good as Monticelli," he added, naming the singer he hated most.

"That on the wall?" asked Aprile. "It is a Caravaggio. And no, I cannot tell you which sex it is. Indeed, which sex it is would be difficult to determine."

"I only asked to know."

"Dear lady, we can never know. In this life, nothing is certain."

Since she had no curiosity, nothing ever impressed her as being odd. By and large, she took it as it was, because it was there. But all the same, they were funny gentlemen; they cheered her up.

So did the painters.

Though by no means a snob, in fact, not a snob at all, Sir William, far from holding the mirror up to nature, held Nature up to the Mirror, to see what it was like. So painters were in spate. Sir William Beechey drew her, very badly. Cousin Gavin, whose forte was ancient Romans, made the attempt and failed. Marchant cut her head in cameo, for a finger ring. One man worked in wax, another in clay. The King's tame Germans did their level best, with somewhat flat results. A Mr. Hudson painted her for the lid of a snuffbox. There were so many of them that a room was set aside for their use. Emma sat on a dais, both to watch and to pose. It was exhilarating to see herself set forth in so many forms, but she missed George.

If all other entertainment failed, there was always the King, the Queen, the Opera and Vesuvius, each with a separate establishment. Sir William was interested in all four of these diversions: the King, professionally; the Queen, if needs be; the Opera, when unavoidable; and Vesuvius for recreation.

Vesuvius was in eruption, a sight not to be missed. They went by carriage to Portici; from there they would proceed by ass.

The carriage rolled along the waterfront where there was a crowd in the midst of which a tall, sulky, big-nosed, pasty-faced, dribbly lipped man was keening away like an auctioneer.

"Whatever is he doing?" asked Emma.

"It is the King," said Sir William, and waved. "He is selling fish. It is his hobby to sell fish. It is quite harmless, for he always gives them their money back afterward."

The crowd roared, and obligingly the King tossed it a fish.

"And what does the Queen do?"

"The Queen," said Sir William, "is more difficult, if less fatiguing. She plots."

The carriage rolled on. Sir William was nervous, for he had not shared his volcano with a woman before. Vesuvius was his hobby, and a hobby is a spiritual exercise, a selfless activity. Vesuvius was his answer to himself. Whenever he climbed it, he felt justified, even if he did need a guide to help him over the rough spots. That did not bother him; if we are really intelligent in this life, we always need a guide, for the guide is a limited being, so we make use of what he knows, intensively, to extend our own general sense of well-being. There is a purely physical wisdom in this world which the wise have not, for wisdom is disembodied, and so, if they are wise, they hire it.

None of which he could explain to Emma, but from Emma he wanted only a beauteous enthusiasm. He had long ago discovered the giddy freedom of saying witty things to a pretty woman who cannot understand them; at most they catch the shimmer and the hook, but never the joy of trawling in the void, so you may be as philosophical as you wish, with impunity.

At Portici they left the carriage and clambered aboard the donkeys—gray velvet creatures all rubbed the wrong way—while two miles off, the lava steamed like the world on the last day. Emma, who had once, as a child, worked with pit ponies, was reminded of that, but did not say so. They began to climb.

The night came on, cool from the sea, but warm from the volcano. Out to sea the islands seemed to move about as the air shifted in temperature, and the lights of fishing boats flared up like hissing embers. The lava flow, which had been all steam, was now all light.

At a hermitage halfway up the mountain they stopped to drink the local wine, ashy, resinous and bitter as the best Burgundy. The hermitage had a terrace from which one could admire a cascade of fire falling down a precipice, like a basilisk fleeing up a chimney, incandescent in its element. As the hot stuff fell it set fire to trees and brushwood, every one a burning bush, every one an Isaac.

Emma was properly enraptured. "I could stay all night," she said. "I shall never be in charity with the moon again, for it looks so pale and sickly; and it is the lava that lights up the moon, for the moon is nothing to the lava."

Sir William was touched. He had come merely to show off an enthusiasm; he had not hoped to share it.

The lava parted around a hermit's hut and usurped a chapel, icons or no. It was most Protestant lava, for there are no religious preservatives against the fury of nature; the fury of nature is in itself the preservative. A badly painted madonna bobbled on the surface, hissed, bubbled, cracked, burst into flame and was sucked under.

Emma, in white and with her hair unbound, flitted gracefully on the balcony. "If I had a tambourine, I would dance!" she cried.

The hired help was touched. He was a Milord. She was, if not Milady, something less solemn and more vulnerable, the favorite of the hour.

"Why must we go so soon?" asked Emma. "Sir William, you must bring me again."

Sir William was moved. His wife had been a mousy creature, but now she was a dead mouse, and one must not speak ill of the dead. But she had never liked Vesuvius in this way, and never looked so intangible by moonlight as did Emma, dancing.

On the way down they met a company which had not dared to climb so far as they. The silly cowards. It made her laugh.

Sir William had his oddities. That could not be denied. She did not care for some of them.

Standing in one of the drawing rooms was an upright open chest. It sparkled in the candlelight, for it was rimmed with gold, though its interior was black as pitch.

"It is from Pompeii," said Sir William, and sent the

servants away. This was a moment he had arranged for himself.

"Stand in it, my dear."

She did not want to. She was afraid to face the dark. She backed into it, and it fitted her exactly. The wood was old and smelled of earth, potato bugs and the root cellar.

He opened a casket and took out a necklace and a pair of earrings and told her to put them on. She put them on. He told her to raise her right hand to her throat. She raised her right hand to her throat. Lifting up a candelabrum, he held it over his head so that the light played over her. Since the windows were open, the light flickered. She closed her eyes.

"That was how they found her," he said.

"Found who?"

"Fulvia Octavia Porsena," he said. "It was an old Etruscan family. When the air touched her, she fell to dust." He moved around to the other side, the flames of the candles darting after their wicks in the sudden draft. "That is her jewelry. It was found with her. She, too, was beautiful."

"Sir William," she said. "I feel cold."

"You may keep the jewels. They suit you to perfection." Seeing she was frightened, he hesitated, and then added, "Emma . . ."

"Yes?"

"In privacy it does not matter. Say 'William,' if you will," he said. And with the sad smile of someone who cannot quite touch anything but is moved all the same, he added, "Thank you, my dear. Since you are yourself so beautiful, you must allow me the beauty of my whims."

He then went off to arrange a treaty so that in exchange for hides, beef, tin, lead, copper and textiles—of which she had plenty—England might receive figs, licorice, goatskins, sulphur, salt, marble, almonds, currants and raisins, which she would not know what to do with, though the salt would be useful to preserve the beef, and no pudding was ever the poorer for a raisin or two.

She wrote him love letters, in her new, worldly style, while he was away. "I am a pretty woman, and one can't be everything else, but now I have my wisdom teeth, I will try to be ansome and reasonable."

But wisdom teeth ache like the devil coming in.

Mrs. Cadogan was amiable. "A gentleman of his age, you cannot expect the world for breakfast."

"I shall get it served again in the evening, hotted up, if I don't eat it now," said Emma.

"To think my Emma would want diversion."

"Well, the more interesting the world is, the more bored you get," said Emma, who was learning. "Which language do we study next?"

It was quite remarkable, her aptitude for languages. A philologist might have been slowed down by interest, but not she. Words were like money—a series of counters with which you got what you wanted—and varied from country to country, like the coinage. These were blue, these were yellow, these were transparent, like beads. You strung them into sentences and with them bartered for company, conversation, a new shawl, the gossip of the day. Italian, French, a smattering of German—it was all the same to her.

"Sir William's mistress is an interesting woman, is she not?" asked the Queen.

"Interesting to look at," said the Spanish Ambassadress.

"It is all, I assure you, that I wish to do. Tell the Ambassador I shall call on him. If I am curious about her, think how infinitely more curious she must be about me." And with some complacency, Maria Carolina displayed her skirt.

"Sir William was up early this morning," said Mrs. Cadogan.

"He did the necessary and then he left."

But Emma was in an excellent mood. Things were coming on.

Sir William took her to the opera. "There they are," he said, pointing to the Royal Box.

Emma was disappointed. The King looked like a Nesselrode pudding well enforced with lady-finger fat, his cherry slipped down to make his mouth, his face a mass of imperfectly whipped cream. Maria Carolina, made maternal less by childbearing than by some glandular imbalance, was a regal, overdressed, portable shriek. The sons had the waiting look of heirs; the daughters the desperate one of unmatched heiresses. The Queen belonged to the age of intermarriage, not diplomatic relations, and regarded her subjects stolidly. Ferdinand smiled, waved, and did other things.

" 'He gropes his breeches with a monarch's air,' " said Sir William. "That's Johnson. We shall watch the stage instead. It will be more seemly."

Sir William, who was fond of music and so did not much care for opera, confronted the stage. Virtuosity did not appeal to him; he preferred his own flute and someone to play *continuo*. If we are to rise above ourselves, someone must play *continuo*, though now it seemed to be he who played it, for Emma was beginning to find vanity in art, though thank God she was not yet swollen to the proportions of signora Brigida Bandi, the eminent contralto. Hers was still a modest drawing-room vanity, and may it remain that way.

The orchestra was drowned out by a volley of trumpets. A gentleman suddenly galloped down out of the wings on a white barb fourteen hands high, the plumes on his helmet three feet tall. He drew rein beside the soprano, also, alas, beside the chandelier. The plumes caught fire and burned down to his helmet, but he was a professional. The show must go on; he ignored the conflagration. *"Mia speranza, io pur vorrei,"* he sang, though his visor had stuck.

"But I thought the opera was *Romulus*," said Emma.
"So it is, but that's Marchesi. Both the horse and the

aria are written into his contract, otherwise he will not sing."

With an angry glance at the chandelier, Marchesi cast his helmet aside, and taking out his snuffbox, walked to the footlights. He was wearing oxtongue shoes with paste buckles, flowered stockings, green knee britches and a cuirass. At the rear of the stage, the soprano crossed to her mother, who was seated there, to use a gargle and a looking glass. The swill was deposited in a tumbler.

"Fire the cannon," said Marchesi, and disappeared. The cannon were fired. The auditorium filled with smoke. The King looked apprehensive.

From backstage came sounds of celebration, and on marched the chorus, pulling a chariot, preceded by lictors and followed by the people. The supers carried ancestral portraits, each looking like Marchesi. In the chariot, Marchesi, with a new set of plumes, his hands and feet shackled and chained, raised his arms with a rattle and burst passionately forth into a paean of joy.

"But I thought this was the triumph of Romulus?"

"And so it is, my dear."

"Why then the chains? Is it perversion or vice?"

"It is neither. These people love a mad scene, a sacrifice or a scene in chains. They have not the polish to deal with ordinary things, so they put drama where drama is not. Hence the chains."

Marchesi clanked and rattled away and went on as maddeningly as a water closet with an interminable run. You wanted to jiggle him.

"As you see," said Sir William, "Opera has much to teach."

At Posilipo there was a late evening party with torches in the shrubbery, garlands on the herms, and a regatta. The King went by in a barge, as tall as Caligula, accompanied by a solemn music—or at any rate, Neapolitan boat songs—but he was much too fat to recline properly. He was not too fat to chase a woman. With a painful alacrity, he turned his torso and ogled her with his vast yellow bloodshot eyes. The passage of his barge set their own wherry awash.

"Tell milady I am only sorry I cannot speak English," he said.

"Indeed," said Emma, "it is a blessing he cannot."

"Lovely like marble, but like marble, a cold race," said the King, who was merely habitually acquisitive and had meant no harm.

"I have not wrote this ten days as we have been on a visit to the Countess Mahoney at Ische 9 days and are just returned from their," Emma informed Greville. They had gone in a hired galley, in stable weather, with a harpsichord on deck, a semicircle of musicians, and the Countess down to the shore to meet them. "Though I was in undress, onely having on a muslin chemise very thin, yet the admiration I met with was surprising."

Like many almost sexless creatures, Emma was attractive to women of a certain taste. It made her life much smoother, since they never told her why. Ischia was a volcano once, too.

"When we came awhay the Countess cried & I am setting for a picture for her in a turkish dress, very pretty." She enjoyed writing to Greville these days. It is not given to every woman to love two generations of the same man, and, to tell the truth, she now preferred him in the older version. In London, she had been locked away in a box; here she sat in one.

"There has been a Prince paying us a visit. He is sixty years of age, one of the first families here, and as allways lived at Naples & when I told him I had been to Caprea he asked me if I went their by land; onely think what ignorance. I staired at him and asked who was his tutor."

At Caserta, the English garden was not going well.

"The Queen has dropped it," said Graffer, "and what is worse, His Majesty has taken it up. He wants a maze. I am a gardener, not an antiquarian. There has been no maze in England since Fair Rosamund's bow-er."

"You could make a little one of box," said Sir William.

"Box grows slowly. By the time the box is up, we'll be down to his grandson, at the earliest. He wants it now. It's one of his pranks; to confuse the courtiers, he says. I'll not please his pranks, for he's no king to me."

Sir William had one of his happier solutions.

"Lay it out as a knot garden, tell him it will grow, and once he's forgotten it, you can dig it up again and turf it over," he said.

Notions are one thing. Any woman can have notions, but it is harder to be visited by an idea. Nonetheless, Emma had just received one.

She was sitting in Sir William's gallery of statues, surrounded by Castor, Pollux, a dubious Vespasian, a Mourning Woman, a Crouching Venus (it was a pair), a Hellenistic Prince in gilt bronze, and two Senators, one of them lacking a head. She felt rebellious. What did he see in them anyway? And he moved her about as though she were an art object. Very well then. She would be an art object.

Getting up, she rang for a shawl and a full-length mirror. Then she arranged herself, a Crouching Venus first, then the Mourning Woman. She was reminded of George. What with George and the Opera and a dash of mythology besides, she found that Grief, Joy, Surprise, Awakened Conscience, Noble Resignation, An Orphan's Curse, Herself Surprised, they came quite easily; they were easy to do, so long as you watched the mirror. A portrait was all very well, but a mirror was better.

For Cornelia, however, she would need two children. It was Sir William's birthday. This was to be her surprise.

Sir William galloped home from Caserta, past the poorhouse. It was a very long poorhouse, for Naples was a very large town, and though the King was generous, he could not be generous every day, so the rest of the time there was precious little to do but spend money and corrupt the taxgatherer.

As sometimes happened in the evening, Sir William did not feel so immortal as was his wont. No doubt on their birthdays the Gods occasionally feel the same way, conscious perhaps of Christianity in the future, waiting patiently, with an undertaker's air.

A great many things could be counted in Sir William's head at any given moment, for though he was not restless, his thoughts were often so. Ideas to him were like fruit: one does not grow them oneself; one merely touches them to see if they are ripe, before plucking them. Did a horse ever take all of its feet off the ground at one time? Would there be a war, and if so, with whom? At any rate it would not affect them: they were too far south. What about the English garden? It would have to be finished; it was a matter of national prestige. If Oliver Cromwell could have his portrait behind a door in the Pitti Palace, surely His Britannic Majesty might be allowed to plant a garden here. What was to be done about Greville? It seemed he could succeed at nothing unless it hung on Sir William's affairs. At what age did a healthy man have his first heart attack? No doubt she was sometimes shrill, but she was a grateful creature, and at least she was always there when one came back. Since she never asked for anything, it was a pleasure to give her gifts. She had natural breeding and referred to him by his first name only when taken unaware.

At dinner she seemed nervous. Afterward she excused herself. He kept his birthday privately, but even so, that was unlike her. He took coffee in the large salon, where the sculpture was. It was bitter coffee. He let it stand. When he heard a rustle, he paid no mind to it, for it was only the evening shadows closing in.

"Who's there?" he asked, catching another sound. It was a footman, squeaking across the parquet with a candelabrum, to open the gold-and-white doors leading to a farther room.

In the darkness beyond the doors the candelabrum

caught a weaving figure in long Roman garments, gathering flowers in a meadow. The walls were blue. Space was blue. In the Elysian Fields one sees a good deal of blue. The flowers were yellow. So was the dress. The figure looked this way and that, now stooping, now plucking, and in the candlelight, space seemed infinite. It was like that scene in Swift, at Glubbdubdrib, where the past is shown, too real to be touched.

"William, is it not that fresco we saw underground at Herculaneum, to the life?"

Sir William dropped his coffee cup. He had been dreaming.

"Don't be cross. Perhaps I have not got it quite right yet, but there are more."

There were more. It was the beginning of what were to be called her Attitudes. He was entranced. It was not so much that she moved, as that she was so moving. She could make the past move.

"No, not quite that way," he said, dismissing the footman, and from then on it was he who held the candelabrum up.

"My dear, Herr Goethe is coming. He is a great man. And though I know that concept to be repugnant to the female temperament, yet to men such do exist, so entertain him. We will do the Attitudes."

The Attitudes had become famous.

He was a great man. He was almost as good as Kotzebue, and had written a novel sufficiently illusory to make women cry. There was the added advantage that when he traveled he left his native language, that is most of it, at home, and spoke French. He was not alone. Some people, in moments of self-doubt, produce a mirror; Goethe produced Tischbein, a young artist brought along to sketch the Master when told to. Goethe, so they said, had a universal mind, and if he found that restricting, did not show it. He was no more frightening than any other young man of good family.

Though without affectation, he was not without mannerisms and had a tendency to sit about in rooms as modestly as a public statue patiently waiting to be unveiled, and when he spoke, spoke as a priest does through the mouth of the oracle. Sir William could not help but notice that his chair was an exact two inches in front of Tischbein's chair, no matter where they might find themselves.

Sir William was amused. Like all well-bred people, he demanded of others only that they play their role. If they asked you backstage, he did not like it. He clouded up at once. But since Goethe could be seen only from out front, he found him, though German and hence irrelevant, congenial.

Emma was up to her star turn.

So this is hate, she realized, with some surprise (it was a Medea). It is certainly a most sustaining emotion, I had forgotten it; but, afraid to linger, hurried on to a Psyche Abandoned (after Thorwaldsen). It was marvelous really. The emotions could be not only shown but felt, merely with the aid of two shawls, a chair, a candle and an urn. It was possible to express them all; Sir William had shown her how. For Joy, however, one needed a tambourine (with fitments from Pompeii. Joy was authentic, though the wood hoop itself was new).

"*Schöne,*" said Goethe.

"*Schöne,*" said Tischbein, though he did not altogether approve, for in Winckelmann he had read that Expression is an unfortunate necessity which arises from the fact that human beings are always in some emotional state, and Tischbein, who was a learned painter, had found this to be true from his own experience, and not only true, but deplorable.

"*Wunderschöne,*" said Goethe sharply.

"*Wunderschöne,*" repeated Tischbein.

As the two men said it, they seemed to bend over invisible oars, while behind them the minor members of the Neapolitan German colony followed them (the oars were locked) in expressing admiration with the same most audible hiss, in unison. *Vogue la galère.*

There are geese in the Forum, thought Sir William.

They will rouse the guard. And so Rome cannot be taken, after all; the relevant anecdote may be found, with some labor, in Livy.

Emma was up to Lucretia now, in the opulent manner of Giulio Romano, also to be found in Livy, with a bare bodkin. Goethe admired, though what he remembered was a large portfolio he had seen recently in which the physiognomy of the horse, by means of the eyes mostly, was utilized to show the entire range of the emotions, from Startled Joy to Woe. Ox-eyed Juno is one thing, but the English are noted for their addiction to and emulation of the horse.

"Tischbein, is it not so?"

"*Ja*," said Tischbein, without listening. He was a paid companion. It was always so, though later he hoped to have disciples of his own.

Emma was beginning to tire, but Vivacity came next, so she was not worried. She was enjoying herself. There was so much to feel—whole continents of emotion of whose existence she had been ignorant. She beckoned to the footman. It was time to bring the children in, for she planned to conclude with a Cornelia and Her Jewels, to be followed by a Hope, a 19th century emotion perhaps, but then, artists are always a generation ahead of their time.

"Standing, kneeling, seated, reclining, grave, sad, sportive, teasing, abandoned, penitent, alluring, threatening, agonized . . . one manifestation follows another, and indeed grows out of it," said Goethe. For that is the way life is: one thing leads to another. We need merely follow, being careful only that of any two roads, we take the right one, lest we be left. "Her elderly knight holds the torch for her performance and is absorbed in his mind's desire," he added.

Perhaps he was, at that. For Sir William had never been given to the passions; he was cerebral. At any rate, he would not have mentioned them, for English is the language of the affections, not of the passions. Anything else fortunately remains a lexicographical impossibility.

Nonetheless, it was true; it was his mind's desire.

After the performance, he took Goethe down to the cellars. The lantern made little holes of light in the surrounding darkness. Bronzes, *bustos,* and sarcophagi cast muddled silhouettes against the ceiling and the walls. Standing in the middle of the floor was a chest with a gold rim, upended.

"She stood there once," said Sir William, "in a Pompeiian dress. The effect was striking."

Goethe stared at the chest. It looked very like Pandora's box, without the lid. Hope, no doubt, was fluttering about upstairs, or else waiting quietly in her bed, her wings invisible, a hope realized.

Had Sir William been a fellow German, Goethe would have said, "You are to be congratulated, sir."

Had he been English, and therefore truly clubbable, Sir William might perhaps have permitted him to say so.

As it was, with a last look at the chest, which was a shrine of some kind, the two men went back upstairs, sobered by the thought that under different circumstances they might each have found somebody they could talk to, at last.

Emma's letters were too long, so Greville did not read them. In order to have our letters read, we must insert in them something the lector wishes to know, and there was no longer anything about Emma that Greville wished to know. But he answered them because in that way he could bring things to Sir William's attention indirectly. She should be a go-between. He had found her proper use.

He was concerned with the improvement of Milford Haven. Instead of taking money out, Sir William should put money in.

> I dare say [wrote Sir William] all you propose, such as an Act of Parliament and buildings and exchanges, would be greatly to the advantage of the Estate in process of time, but it is by no means convenient to me to run myself into debt and difficulties

for a prospect of future advantages to be enjoy'd—
by whom?

The man is ungrateful. I am only acting in his best
interest, thought Greville, had the Act of Parliament
passed anyway (it would allow him to pour money into
Milford Haven Harbor), and drew a draft upon his
uncle's bankers, which he cashed with some pleasure.

At an official reception to which all the world and his
wife came, Emma could not appear. Like a child, she was
to be allowed downstairs only in the presence of the
more indulgent members of the family. And since she was
a child, she did not relish that.

The King and Queen were to make a call, much as they
would have gone to the bank, for such was the political
situation that England seemed their one security.

Since formal calls can scarcely be made impromptu,
Emma had already seen the carpet rolled out to the
street, and was well aware of an anticipatory bustle
among the chambermaids and footmen. So when, at her
singing lesson (she had put back the regular hour), she
heard coach horns in the street and the clatter of a stage
carriage, a natural curiosity impelled her—forgetful that
she was not to be seen—to the landing at the top of the
main hall, to see who it could be. The clustered columns
of the landing made her indiscretion discreet without in
any way concealing her.

Below her Sir William was receiving first the King,
then the Queen.

"Caro cavaliere!" yelled the King. Since he refused to
speak anything but Italian, and the Queen—except for
an occasional guttural curse—restricted herself to French,
the conversation had a worldly air.

"There are disturbances," said the Queen, "in France."
To entertain royalty is not easy, for their attention tends
to wander. Maria Carolina's wandered.

Looking down, Emma saw a massy woman of about
forty, with a long face, lovely arms, and a poached look
about the eyes. In one hand she held a long white glove

negligently, as Pharaoh would hold a gold-and-lapis flail, the symbol of his office, though to use it, you flick the power itself, not its embodiment.

Looking up, the Queen saw a mobile creature who had the look of someone worth knowing, were she but knowable.

Sir William followed her glance. Emma ducked out of sight. The Queen and Sir William progressed to the salon, where they talked of France, to an obbligato from Ferdinand, who never talked of anything but hunting. He did not mean to be discordant, but having no other subject, he played always the same tune.

They stayed an hour.

"So that is Miss Hart," said the Queen, leaving. "I should like to talk to her. It is a pity I cannot." She needed a new confidante, for a new favorite is cheaper than an old one, if only because accounts have not been struck yet, and besides, she has the unique merit no old favorite can have, of being new.

Their carriage rolled sonorously away (because of the horns). Sir William went upstairs, where Emma was at her singing again.

"My dear child," he said, noticing she was flushed. "You must never look down on royalty. They are not designed to be seen from above. It is they who belong on the balcony, not you."

"Indeed I meant no harm," said Emma carefully, but with a forgive-me look. It was a new attitude.

"I'm sure you didn't." She was a little minx. She was a most amusing creature.

At dawn, when he could get away, Sir William went out to fish in the bay alone, in a longboat. That is, he had two boys row him out, sent them back in the dory, and told them to return when he should wave.

Hot sun is good for old bones, and he was fifty-nine. However, since each good comes accompanied by its own evil, he had come prepared, and wore a large, floppy, disreputable hat.

He got nary a nibble, but there is a truth locked up in

every platitude—crisp as an almond none the worse for a frazzled shell—and one does not go fishing to catch fish.

The hobby is praised in Theophrastus, who also informs us that love is the passion of an idle mind, as no doubt it is. But Sir William did not have an idle mind. At most, he allowed it to idle at times in order to let it rest. Theophrastus further quotes the tragic poet Charaemon to the effect that Eros is variable, like wine; that when he comes in moderation, he is gracious, but when he comes too intensely and puts men in utter confusion, he is hard to bear.

Passion is ludicrous and vulgar (here there was a bite, but it turned out to be an orange grown drowsy with its own weight). To the English, vulgarity is an all-embracing concept that includes all living matter and most inanimate, with the exception only of themselves. Sir William did not except himself. He was quite willing to laugh at his own passions, given he might do so reminiscently (here he threw the orange at a pelican, who did not want it either).

"It is usually agreeable, all the same, to have her here," said Sir William, himself a downy old bird, as becomes a diplomat. "I shall do nothing, but if she does, I shall not interfere." And he went on fishing for no fish, contentedly.

North of Brescia, Goethe confronted the foothills with equanimity. They looked at him. He looked at them. Then, twisting in the saddle, he turned his face upward, for a last dose of the sun, and rode on with relief. It is necessary to make the Grand Tour, no doubt, but he was not sorry to be going home. He had gathered his impressions and made, on the whole, an excellent one on his late hosts. It was time to create.

Nonetheless, when the shadows began to fall and he drew rein for the night at Como, he found to his annoyance that he was humming *"Mein' junges leben hat' ein End',"* so he stopped. It was an old German pietistic parlor song from past time, written by the Norns.

Kennst du das land....

"You are growing up, my child," said Mrs. Cadogan, doing Emma's hair, which gave her pleasure. It was such an occupation as Fafnir would have enjoyed. It was like carding red gold. "Pray why?"

"It cannot be helped."

"Of course it can be helped. It is certainly no reason to ruin your appearance."

"No," said Sir William, still out at sea. "It cannot be helped. But all the same it is a great shame."

He was almost aware, these days, of the drawing about him of an invisible net. It was a silken net. Since he had tarried too long, he found himself being rowed to shore through the fishing fleet, which was putting to sea to cast out theirs.

It was New Year's Eve of 1789; and then, just as suddenly, of 1790.

In 1789, there was a gala at Ranelagh, to celebrate the recovery from madness of His Most Gracious Majesty George III. That was how he solved his problems. When he became bored, he went away. When his interest was aroused again, he came back, to find everything much the same, except for the increasing difficulty each time of getting back. The orchestra played "Rule Britannia" (by the author of "Sally in Our Alley") and the national anthem. We can all recover from madness in time; here was proof. At Posilipo, Sir William gave a dinner to celebrate the same event.

There was an earthquake in Calabria. Angelica Kauffmann painted Emma as the Comic Muse. Sir John Acton became the Neapolitan Prime Minister.

"Sir John Acton," Sir William explained, "is a man of great character, most of it bad. But though of an *émigré* family, he is an Englishman. He is competent, which is the next best thing to ability, and far rarer. He plans to reorganize the fleet."

Ferdinand assisted at the birth of a new age by founding a silk factory. There was a revolution in France, and refugees began to arrive, among them Madame Vigée-Lebrun, the painter, who painted Emma, not very well.

Torn from her native Paris (it had seemed prudent to remove—she had no taste for painting commoners), Madame Lebrun did not care for much of anything. Indeed, even at home she had sometimes felt much the same way. She drew Emma as a bacchante. "As a bacchante," she said tartly, "she is perfect." The Queen, whom she also drew, did not speak *quite* flawless French, but was at least noble. Breeding counts. These things show, no matter what we do.

Emma decided to hurry things a little. Opposite her, Sir William was peeling a banana. She giggled reminiscently. Dressed and undressed, they are so different, which provides a key, but a key to a midnight lock only. To come and go freely by day, you need a skeleton key, and for this the best procedure is to take that wax impression called gossip, the one all-purpose key for all social occasions. The time and tide had come. It was to be taken at the flood.

It was indeed a flood. It beached the most amazing mail—for the net was now visible—in handwriting which ranged from the flaccid to an angry scrawl knotted with rage.

His family heard the gossip first, which is to say his uncles, cousins and aunts. There were several disapproving screeds from his favorite niece Mrs. Dickenson, Mary Hamilton that was. What did this talk signify? Did he mean to disgrace them all? Let him disavow the rumor at once.

"I am sorry," said Sir William. "She is necessary to my happiness, and the handsomest, loveliest, cleverest and best creature in the world."

"I confess I doat on him," wrote Emma to England, feeding the flames. "Nor I never can love any other person but him." She was not lying. She believed it.

As for the gossip, that was another thing. "I fear,"

wrote Sir William, dipping his pen in cold water, to douse them, "that her views are beyond what I can bring myself to execute, and that when her hopes on this point are over she will make herself and me unhappy. Hitherto her conduct is irreproachable."

"It is said he has married her," said Towneley.

"I was most happy to hear that he was *not* married," wrote Heneage Legge, a friend of Greville's then passing through Naples, a man with a modest talent for social espionage. "However, he flung out some hints of doing justice to her good behaviour, if his public situation did not forbid him to consider himself an independent man. She gives everybody to understand that he is now going to England to solicit the King's consent to marry her. She is much visited here by ladies of the highest rank, but wants a little refinement of manners."

"You need not be afraid for me in England. We come for a short time, to take our last leave," Emma informed Greville.

"*They* say they shall be in London by the latter end of May," wrote Legge.

The Duchess of Argyll, a relative by marriage, her first husband having been a Hamilton—the woman Emma had watched leaving George's door—had come to Naples. She was one of the Gunning sisters, who had gone to London years before to make a good match, and besides, the Anglo-Irish are not so strict in particulars as their English cousins.

"After all, William," she said, "why not? She's a likable creature, she does very well here, and we are not *there*."

Unfortunately the Duchess of Argyll died.

"You may think of my afflictions when I heard of the Duchess of Argyll's death. I never had such a friend as her, and that you will know, when I see you," Emma wrote Greville.

"Was I in a private station," Sir William told Sir Joseph—that eminent botanist having asked, like everybody else—"I should have no objection that Emma should share with me *le petit bout de vie qui me reste* under the solemn convenant you allude to. I have more fairly delivered you my confession than is usually done in this country, of which you may make any use you please. Those who ask out of mere curiosity, I would wish to remain in the dark."

In chains, on very thin gruel, preferably. It was the devil of a business, and how had it grown up round him so suddenly?

"I shall allways esteem you for your relationship to Sir William, and having been the means of my knowing him," Emma wrote Greville, with what was quite a pretty wit, though veiled.

As a countermove, Mr. Legge persuaded Mrs. Legge to cut Emma dead, and sent the good news to Greville at once. (Now that the Duchess of Argyll was no more, the social maneuvers of Mrs. Legge might be assumed to loom large.)

> Mrs. L is not over scrupulous in her manners or sentiments beyond the usual forms established by the rules of society in her own country, but, as she was not particularly informed of any change in Mrs. H's situation, she had no reason to think her present different from her former line of life, & therefore could not quite reconcile it to her feelings to accept those offers of friendship & service, though there was no doubt of their being kindly intended.

Greville was gratified. "Mrs. L. has done the right thing," he said.

"No doubt she has, but it does not seem to have been enough to raise her from the obscurity of middle-class life," said Towneley. "Pray, who *is* Mrs. L.?"

"Mrs. Legge, of course."

Towneley did not ask who Mr. Legge was. To establish *his* credentials, he felt sure, would have meant a rummage at least three generations back, and he had not the time.

The wife of the Spanish Ambassador paid a public call at the British Embassy, with as many *contessas* as she could assemble. Honor was at stake, and nobody much liked the British colony anyway, except for Sir William, of course, who was a dear.

"I was staggered to hear them speak always in the plural, as we, us and ours," wrote Legge.

The Bishop of Derry, who was in Ireland for one of his rare ecclesiastical visitations, asked them to come there for a breather if they found the English air too thin. "Take her as anything but Mrs. Hart, and she is a superior being," he said privately. "As for herself, she is always vulgar." But he meant to back them up.

"As I have experienced that of all women in the world, the English are the most difficult to deal with abroad," wrote Sir William to his niece Mary, "I fear eternal *tracasseries*, was she to be placed above them here, and which must be the case, as a Minister's wife in every country takes place of every rank of nobility."

He was thinking it over.

As to our separating houses, we cant do it or why should we, you cant think 2 people that as lived five years in all the domestic happiness that is possible, can separate & those 2 persons that knows no other comfort but in one anothers company, which is the case I assure you with ous, tho you Bachelers don't understand it, but you cant imagjine 2 houses must separate ous, no, it cant be, that you will be a judge of when you see us [wrote Emma to Greville, that most unhappy man].

Like all expatriates, Sir William found it necessary to go home from time to time, in order to re-establish the validity of his reasons for staying away. And Greville was making a mash of the Welsh estates. So since they were now inseparable, they both went.

* * *

"Are you going to marry her?" demanded Sir William's sister-in-law, point blank.

"As a public character at Naples, I do not think it right to marry Mrs. Hart—from respect to my King."

His sister-in-law gave him a sensible-matron look. They had known each other too long for that sort of evasion. "Very proper. But I hope you think there is something owing to *yourself*."

"As to that, the first object is to be happy."

"It is," said his sister-in-law, "*not*." She had never before heard a doctrine so shocking.

Mary Dickenson, having met Emma, felt otherwise.

"I have always liked what you have written on a certain delicate subject, and you and I think very much alike," said Sir William gratefully.

Emma had not much cared for the look of the cliffs at Dover. Like the English temperament, they may not be pure white, but they look white, and they have a cold and decided hauteur which does not welcome the invader. In Italy, she was what she was. Here she was only what she had come from. And besides, Italy was warmer.

Sir William was annoyed. "Why should I not please her? She has pleased me. Besides, I do not exist solely that Charles may have his inheritance. That does not seem to have occurred to him."

Indeed it had not. For to Charles, everything in this world must have its reason, and in this matter he saw none.

"She does not know," said Mary Dickenson, who had asked Sir William and Emma to the country for the weekend, but spoke mostly to her uncle.

"Doesn't know what?"

"Anything. She is innocent. But there is hope. Her left hand has been busy recently, and when it needs help, I suppose the right will have to know. So why not ask for it, when the time comes, and see?"

"Mary!"

"Why not? It is what you want to do, whether you know it or not. And I must confess that when I think how much it will displease Cousin Charles, I almost condone it."

In the young, impatience is merely anticipation; in the old, the knowledge that there is not much time left; in the world, both. But having enunciated this apothegm, Sir William found himself unwilling to be hustled along, though it was late to tarry. The first is done for us, and the second by us. Perhaps he merely wished to retain for as long as possible the illusion of choice.

"I hope," said Mary's husband to Emma, "that Sir William will find Emma and Lady H. *the same.*" For Mary's husband was no fool either.

"I am very glad you have seen Sir W. Hamilton comfortably and had time for conversation, tho' probably the *Lady* was in the way," said Lady Frances Harper in a loud, shrill voice. "I believe it likely she may be our aunt. My mother seemed to fear it. Do you think it likely? *I own I think not;* for making a *shew* of her *Graces and Person to all his acquaintance in Town* does not appear a *preliminary for marriage.*"

Whatever else one may say for it, this is not the tone in which one dissuades a distinguished, independent and famous relative from doing as he pleases.

Emma had gone off to see Romney, who felt less delighted than he had hoped to. She was not quite the same Emma, that was why.

The English lack—their culture is based upon its absence—the bump of admiration. But she was the latest sensation, which is something else again. A sensation is permitted to wax warm, for it will pass. Her attitudes were unique. Her contralto was the correct oratorio rumble and left the stemware intact. The secret of her success was in request.

"A particular friend of mine," wrote Sir Thomas Lawrence, "promised to get me introduced to Sir. W. H.'s to see this wonderful woman you have doubtless heard of —Mrs. Hart." He had been in London five years earlier when she was there, but apparently he had not heard of her then, or if he had, had not listened, the name then being as hard to catch as it was now impossible not to drop.

"George, you may paint me as 'The Ambassadress,'" said Emma, and preened.

"I expect Sir Thomas will be doing that." The only thing a really creative person has to teach is himself, and she had outgrown him; although it was very gratifying to have her call, and he would do the portrait, of course.

"However did you guess? He has particularly demanded to take my likeness next week."

Lawrence, using an old canvas, daubed her in over an allegory of Liberality guided by Sagacity, a work by Reynolds. He was not without a sense of humor, and as he had supplanted Reynolds in other things, why not in this, as well?

"Her acting was simple, grand, terrible and pathetic," said Romney. But why, oh why must she act now, here in the studio, where once they had been content to play?

Or maybe she could no longer help it.

Even Horace Walpole approved, that man who approbated only the Artificial and the Misses Berry. "I make *amende honorable* to Mrs. Hart," he said. "Her Attitudes are a whole theatre of grace and various expressions."

"Everything she did was just and beautiful," said the Duchess of Devonshire, "but her conversation, though perfectly good-natured and unaffected, was uninteresting, and her pronunciation very vulgar."

Who would think so much could come of a mere Attitude? Things were indeed coming on. And even George had cheered up, the silly old thing, and was painting her again as everything—as Joan of Arc, as Magdalen, as Constance. Only the King remained to be consulted.

Hamilton waited upon him at Windsor. The result was a compromise. If the Queen would not receive her, the King would not object; if the King did not object, the Queen would not receive her. Thus whim and honor both were satisfied. A devoted couple, the Royal Pair were astute at compromise.

"Sir William," said Emma, "has proposed."

"To think that I should see the day," said Mrs. Cadogan. She had not interfered. She had not hoped. She had been sure.

"Oh the good, good man," she added perfunctorily, and blew her nose.

"And had I not something to do with it?" Emma was indignant.

"Indeed you had, but that is not something a woman confesses to, if she be wise," said Mrs. Cadogan.

"I am glad," said Lord Bristol, all Bishop of Derry again, and so appropriately benign, "that you have secured your own happiness."

"Sir William has actually married his gallery of statues. They are set out on their return to Naples," wrote Horace Walpole, elaborating, even while he purified, his style. It was one of his celebrated letters, he had not as yet decided to whom.

And so he had, at Marylebone Church, in the presence of Lord Abercorn and the secretary to the British Minister to the Court of Savoy. Greville did not attend.

If we do these things at all, we may just as well do them in church. But still, her sense of accomplishment, though concealed, diverted him, and since no man rushed into the church to show just cause, he went on with it and it was soon done. He had only wanted to give pleasure; therefore, the quicker out of England the better.

With unusual prudence, Emma had signed the register with her name by birth. She wished to be sure.

She had brought it off. It felt much the same as not being married, only with something left out, but she was now secure. On the last day before they left, she posed for George once more.

"Tell Hayley I am always reading his *Triumphs of Temper*. It was that that made me Lady H., for God knows I have had five years to try my temper," she said. "I am afraid if it had not been for the good example Serena taught me, my girdle would have burst. If it had, I had been undone, for Sir W. minds temper more than beauty."

"Emma," said George, painting a stranger. "The Gods have been kind to you. You have never been in love."

"I dote on Sir William," said Emma indignantly, whom this one small point had perhaps been bothering.

"Ah, that's not loving," said George. "That's not the same thing at all. That only comes afterward, or without, or never."

He wanted to lay his brushes down. Spoiled by success? he thought. Nonsense, I was spoiled by my failure. We lose our talents when we lose heart, that's all. It's merely a matter of character. For most of us there comes a time, not when we wish to make little legends—we're wiser than that—not to push away the bad things, but to soften their edges, to make an idyll out of pain, to show what it could have been, even to pretend that was the way it was. Or is. We enter into illusion the way a condemned man takes up residence in the death row. For who can paint against a spinning wheel?

At least she was still loving. "George," she said, "you shall come to Naples and paint me as often as you like. Would you enjoy that? It will be like old times."

"Yes, I should like that," said George, and never saw her again.

On the last night of their stay, Sir William and she went to the theatre, where everyone ogled them and there was even a play for them to ogle. The leading actress was Jane Powell. Emma did not tell Sir William who Jane Powell was, but went backstage after the performance, by herself, to meet her; and then the congratulations were truly meaningful, or at any rate their meaning was underlined, overscored, kept private and enhanced, for they had been fellow servants at Dr. Budd's in the old days, Jane Powell and she. Tears, joy, accomplishment, were all their conversation.

"I always said you did not lack ability," said Jane

Powell, speaking as one woman to another, which is to say as a professional actress.

"And I, that you were then my ideal," said Emma, relaxed and therefore plainly lying.

"I *knew*," said Jane Powell, simply.

"Your rise, though rapid, even to the callow eye of youth, was yet predictable," said Emma.

So since Jane *knew* and Emma had risen, they corresponded for a year or two, in the moistest of terms. It does not do to lose touch with old friends, and besides, the acting profession is uncertain.

IV

Usually during an interregnum, it is the King who leaves, the people who stay behind. But in France, it was the people who had flocked out of the capital to hiss and boo and gouge each other's eyes out; the King and Queen who had been left stranded.

Through the streets of Paris, His Britannic Majesty's Ambassador to the Court of the Two Sicilies clattered over the cobbles toward modern times. The King and Queen had tried to flee, but had been hauled back from Varennes to promulgate the Constitution; a symbolic scene, which is to say, the Constitution was handed to the King, the King handed the Constitution to the members of the National Assembly, and the National Assembly kept it. As for the people themselves, they were not present, but off somewhere looting houses, rioting for bread, and shouting *Liberté, Égalité, Fraternité*: *Liberté*, because it belongs in a straitjacket, or at any rate a lot of people who did were clearly at liberty; *Égalité*, because it does not exist, for we are not born equal—a few of us are born with brains; *Fraternité*, because though it is an amiable notion, no one practices it, least of all the French. Give them a fine phrase, and the people will die for it, whereas no one will fight for a good dinner, and if he has one, is too comfortable to do so.

"I will tell you what the French have done, they have

made me weep for a King of France, which I never thought to do; and they have made me sick of the very name of Liberty, which I never thought to be," said the poet Cowper, who was gently mad, saw God in the garden, was fond of playing with hares—though not of starting them—and could usually be returned to sanity by his companion, Mrs. Unwin.

Sir William and Emma were quite acceptable to what was left of the French Court, for the snobs had been the first to leave, and those left behind, needing British aid, could scarcely afford to be snobbish. But Emma was disappointed.

This large-jawed foolish woman with the inane blue eyes could look regal when she wished. Such was her childhood training. At the moment she was trying to impress upon Maria Carolina, her sister, by means of her sister's envoy, that she, too, could sway whole empires if she chose, no matter what went on outside the window. If she had learned to tremble, she did not show it, for it is France is the plum, not the Two Sicilies. She presented a letter, her last, to her sister, and a jewel or two, and went away.

Besides, nothing was wrong. It was only that the gardeners had been overworked recently, and underpaid. There had been a famine somewhere. And chambermaids who do not come are merely feckless creatures, not amazons who storm the barricades and, once they have lost their looks, put their daughters out for hire. If trees were chopped down in Versailles park, the weather was cold, it was done for kindling wood, because they knew no better. One did what one could to help. One encouraged industry. One ordered a new necklace from one's jeweler and tried to show that one was not afraid. One did one's duty.

"Did you notice their stockings?" asked Sir William as they came away. His face in repose did not look reposed.

"Whose stockings?"

"Everybody's. They had runs and they stank. There is

either something wrong with the laundresses, or else they have at last learned that the Sun King is dead, and the sooner out of France, the better."

He directed the coach to Naples as fast as they could get there, for Naples is backward and out of date, and so life is still pleasant there, forgetful that even those notoriously indifferent travelers, the French, may also leave France, if they so choose, in that latest and most convenient of conveyances, the world's first modern conscription army.

However, when Gaeta came in view, he cheered up. Nothing had changed. The farther south you go, the less it does. It might even be wise to plan a visit to Sicily.

"But why were they shut up like that, like prisoners?" asked Emma.

"Because they were caught," said Sir William, and looked out the window at the lustrous shores of what might very well be the last large private kingdom in the world, run down perhaps, but still in the possession of the original owners; not farmed for profit, not a pantisocracy, not anything really, except what it was.

"I wonder how Graffer and the English garden are coming," he said, for you cannot explain politics to a woman. She merely looks sympathetic and tells you what to do. She will not listen.

The English garden was doing excellently. Not only was it suddenly popular—for with France gone we will need allies—but it had taken root.

"After knowing Naples, it is impossible not to wish to *live* in order that one may return to it," Sir William had said, in bed in England with a cold. "If I were compelled to be a king, I would choose it for my kingdom. The storms which desolate Europe pass over his head without injury."

Though there certainly seemed to be more English visitors about than usual.

"It appears to me that education in England does not improve. They lead here exactly the same life they lead at home. But since they are here, I suppose they must be given dinner."

"Yes, Hamilton" said Emma, addressing her husband for the first time with the form suitable to her new station. In her lap was a silver bowl full to the brim with cards left on the Embassy. The more elegant among them had engraved on them in purple or black ink small views of their owners' estates, which was the current fashion and so much taken up by the swollen fop, the lesser gentry and nobodies, if rich. She was still wearing the gown in which she had been presented at Court.

"My dear," said Maria Carolina, stretching out both hands, "you made it. I am so proud of you. And my congratulations, by the way, on the clever skill with which you brought it off."

Emma curtsied. But of course it had not been like that. That was just a fantasy. What the Queen had actually said was, "How pretty. My dear, you must come to see me soon, and we will talk."

It had been a levee. Levees are impersonal. She and Sir William moved away, but Emma carried herself with quite a different air now. In England, either one was defiant or else one stooped. But to enter Naples again was to enter the world from a tunnel—a little higher in France than England, but not much—and at last to see the sun ahead and then stand upright in it.

The Queen wished a new alliance, as did Acton, so of course Emma would be made much of. To the Queen, politics was still an intimate affair, akin to recreation, but with the enhanced annoyance of dealing with people when what you needed were pawns.

Greville had sent Sir William a letter, sending in the bill for the upkeep of Emma's child. It came to £65/6/8. He had promised Emma to see that it was taken care of.

> I have taken a liberty with you, and I communicate it to you instead of Lady H. because I know it would give her some embarrassment and she might imagine it unkind in me so soon to trouble you about her protégée . . . I do not mean this necessary step to be concealed from Ly. H. . . . I know

> Lady H. will consider your attention on this subject as additional proof of your kindness.

"I think," said Sir William, "you had best read this, my dear." And watched her while she did.

"Is it true?"

"Yes."

"Is it yours?"

Emma hesitated. "Yes."

"Is it his?"

She shook her head. In some cases it is better to lie with the head, and the Lord grant it was no lie.

"Then there is some hope for it," said Sir William, paid the bill, and dropped the letter into the wastepaper basket. "However, since we must pay for our mistakes in this world, the sum will be deducted from your pin money. To which," he added, with a crinkle of amusement, "I will now compound the yearly sum of sixty-five pounds, six shillings and eightpence."

But he made no break with Greville. He merely became more observant.

Emma decided to make Greville her commission agent. "Sir William has asked me that you buy five yards of the new grosgrain ribbon for a hat." "Dear Greville, will you send out, please, a hip tub, for Sir William's bath?" Greville detested errands, but as a dutiful nephew, would feel compelled to run them.

Sir William watched these commissions pile up with some awe. "My dear, what will you think of next?" he asked mildly.

"Oh I don't know. Something impractical to deliver, difficult to carry, and wellnigh impossible to procure, I expect," said Emma, whose pin money was now five times the household expenses at Edgware Row, and her private apartments the size of the house.

"I see," said Sir William, thoughtfully. It was a new Attitude, but as usual, she forgot it. You never saw any of these facets for long. Who cares whether it be forgetting or forgiving, so long as the subject is not brought up?

The Chevalier de Seingalt came through, his sleeves a mass of dirty lace, already accumulating his memoirs. "A clever man marrying a young woman clever enough to bewitch him," he noted. "Such a fate often overtakes a man of intelligence when he grows old. It is always a mistake to marry, but when a man's physical and mental forces are declining, it is a calamity." The first part of this dictum was taken out of any comedy by Gozzi, the second was the current wisdom of the day and therefore his own apothegm. It had to be owned, however, that the physical and mental forces did not seem to have declined much. Unlike his nephew, Sir William had not the art of running dry. He hoped to die a mortal, not bleached wood.

He was assembling the catalogue of his new Etruscan vases. In the morning, he looked at the vases; in the afternoon, he received the engravers; in the evening, those who would provide the letter press. "I do not mean to write a book, but to furnish matter for many," he said. What he did plan to do, in time, was to sell the collection, for if you have a real enjoyment of such things, it is best to explain that you indulge the interest only for commercial reasons, so that, thinking you tasteless, the connoisseur will leave you free to enjoy your tastes instead of trying to overwhelm you with his own, which are, of course, superior.

Nothing must be allowed to impinge upon taste, though the King was an exception, since he arrived only to take Sir William away. The impingement took the form of a *grand battu*. Hunting alone interested him. And hunting wants taste. "Those acts and functions which are never mentioned in England, here are openly performed," Sir William reported in a dispatch home.

Ferdinand shot from the safety of a pavilion toward which the game was driven, so the only exercise he got was butchering the meat, a chore he relished and therefore one at which he was competent.

To the left stood a pile of bowels and offal, high as a man, and constantly added to. It was made up of the innards of on the average a thousand deer, a hundred wild boar, two or three wolves and as many foxes. At a trestle table stood the King, stark naked except for a brown-leather butcher's apron, his white skin splattered with blood. Two lackeys slung a carcass on the table. The King slit open its guts, flung the viscera to the offal heap, disjointed the corpse and called for another one. The Queen, who was sometimes forced to attend at these rituals, did her best to ignore them, but had no lady in waiting to talk to. No lady in waiting could stand it. *Flop* down on the trestle table went the next corpse. Over the offal pile hovered a buzzing corona of bluebottles. From time to time, finding his hands too slippery to hold the knife, Ferdinand would wash them in a bowl and call for a towel. This entertainment went on from dawn till dusk, unless he went fishing instead. He was an enormous man with a powerful chest.

At intimate dinners, which Sir William had to attend three or four times a week, the conversation was of the day's hunt. But Ferdinand was a most popular sovereign. Among the people his nickname was *il Nasone*. And it must be confessed that though a frightful coward, he meant no harm.

The Queen's sport was Government. If the King objected, Maria Carolina put on her white kid gloves. They were the means to power. Ferdinand was a fetishist. No one knew why. The condition had merely arisen. She had only to don elbow-length gloves, and he would slobber, grow affectionate, and do as she wished. If he seemed reluctant, she slapped him with them, and that invariably made him behave.

She marveled at this singular weapon sometimes. She would have liked to know the cause of it. It is often wise to know on what foundations the power we wield rests. But possibly he did not know himself. Needless to say, the wearing of white kid gloves at Court was the prerogative of the Queen. The possession of a pair, particularly on the part of any current mistress, was tantamount to treason.

Usually she had the gloves sent from Vienna, paid for out of the Secret Fund. "Never forget," Maria Theresa had told her, "that you are a German." She never had. She did not cheat in an Italian way. An English alliance seeming advisable, she sent for Emma daily.

"The Queen," said Sir William, "receives her most kindly. Emma very naturally told her the whole story and that all her desire was by her future conduct to show her gratitude to me, and to prove to the world that a young, beautiful woman, though of obscure birth, could have noble sentiments and act properly in the great world." One's best suit is the truth, so long as one does not lay down all of it.

> I have been with the Queen the night before alone *en famille* laughing and singing, but at the drawing-room I kept my distance, and payd the Queen as much respect as tho' I had never seen her before, which pleased her very much. The English garden is going on very fast.

My God, thought Greville, whose eye had caught the word Queen, I have given shelter to a fiend, but since Sir William could not live forever, pushed on with improvements at Milford Haven and told him as little as possible, except that cash would be short this year.

The revolution in France, which did not concern any of them, continued to revolve.

"Lady Hamilton has nothing to do with my public character," Sir William reassured the Foreign Office. "She knows that beauty fades & therefore applies herself daily to the improvement of her mind."

" '. . . trimmed with three rows of black lace, interspersed with rosebuds,' " read Mrs. Cadogan. " 'Dresses this coming season will have a simpler, purer line, and the bodice, to use so indelicate a term, will rise almost to the armpits. A wide sash of *peau de soie,* completely plain, tied below the bust, forms the only adornment. Its colors may be Cornish pink, *vert de nez,*' whatever that is, 'and cerulean.' Shall I go on?"

"Yes, but first hand me the skin cream. And I shall need another jar of rain water if I am to make myself proper."

And looking in the mirror, Emma thought, I am twenty-six, whoever would believe it? Certainly not Sir William, who is sixty-two.

"'... in the new Grecian mode,'" Mrs. Cadogan continued. "'Ladies of the *ton* will be delighted to learn that Mr. Humphreys, the fashionable fanmaker, has received an assortment of light Kashmiri shawls, fresh shipped from India, both handsome and suitable to our crisp, early English autumn.'"

"I am the happiest woman in the world," said Emma. "We must ask Greville to send out some. Take note of the address."

It was true enough. Not only did she have the world in her grasp, she had grasped it.

But there was serious study, too. They had worked their way to Volume IV of Dr. Burney's *History of Music:*

> It may be asked, what entertainment is there for the mind in a *concerto, sonata,* or *solo?* They are mere objects of gratification to the ear, in which, however, imagination may divert itself with the idea that a fine *adagio* is a tragical story; an *andante* or *grazioso* an elegant narrative of some tranquil event; and an *allegro,* a tale of merriment.

Imagination diverted itself, though not with Dr. Burney. It was what she had observed herself. He was an author admired perhaps more for his truth than his felicity.

As Goethe said, the dangers of life are infinite. It almost slipped her grasp.

Sir William was ill, at Caserta.

"Oh my God!" shrieked Emma, and had she not instantly fallen into the role of loyal and faithful nurse, would have thought herself as instantly undone, cast out, rejected and a widow. "You must come with me. I shall need you to make possets."

She was a good nurse: she could act out anything. And Mrs. Cadogan had a flair for fortifying jellies, beef broth, sliced cucumber rind on the forehead during fevers, and enough common sense to damn the doctor. Though no substitute for it, these things sometimes assist Grace.

Undeniably he was ill. Looking at him, Emma felt that "chastity of silent woe" first phrased by Falconer. For long periods of time he stared only at the ceiling, which was a high one.

"He does not know poor Emma," said poor Emma.

Nor did he. In so far as he was conscious of anything, it was of being on his back like a turtle, unable to make his body move, a posture demeaning to a man of active habit. As the fog cleared he could see the clouds on the ceiling. They parted to show eternity. Out of that space appeared a fly which, circling, grew and became a bustard, and gyred and grew red in the wattles, and was a vulture sloping over a parched plain. At all costs it must not get into the Tiepolo, for that meant death.

Sir William heaved at his shell, but could not budge it. He could scarcely make it rock. He could only look deep down into the ceiling.

The doctor came and went, a gossip and a busybody at the pinnacle of his profession.

"After knowing Naples, it is impossible not to wish to *live*, in order that one may return to it."

The doctor made his inspection, and the good word went around. The man was immortal. He still had his own teeth, so he must be.

"He will live," said the doctor to Emma. "But if you like, you may call in a second opinion."

"My God, why?" asked Emma. "Is not certitude enough?"

"Ah, dear dear lady. Ah, *bellissima signorina,*" said the doctor. It was enough.

Mrs. Cadogan sniffed at the bottle he had left behind. "Elm tea," she said, "with laudanum," and poured it out.

The crisis passed in eight days. The vulture began to recede. In ten, it was no more than the Host, hovering in the approved manner over the approved Tiepolo crowd, a white dove.

"I have been as ill as him with anxiety, apprehension and fatige; the last, indeed, the least of what I have felt," reported Emma. Her world had pulled through. It was enough of a miracle to turn one Catholic, and a candle would do no harm.

Sir William, who had been wandering and had almost reached the sulphur shades—for the odor of which he did not care—began to rearrange himself and became aware that he was weak. Next he felt himself being fed. Then he smelled an arm. His hearing was restored. At the end of the garden was a stout iron door. With some effort, he got it open and stepped out into the garden beyond and heard a bird again. Also footsteps. Also that familiar sound, the turning of a page. Since the sun was on his eyes, he opened them, dazzled to be alive.

"God's masterpiece, a silly woman," he muttered indistinctly, the end of a thought he could no longer trace back to its source.

"He knows me. He lives!" shouted Emma. "Sir William lives!" Taken up by the echoes, the cry went around the corridors and down the stairs. He lived.

It is reliably reported that goslings fix their affections upon the first object they see that moves. Sir William opened his eyes and smiled at Emma. As why not? She had nursed him. Whatever else she was, that astounded him. In the polite world, when we fall ill, we lie alone upstairs until either we are fit again to receive those visitors, our friends, or have been removed in a wicker basket by the back door. At the very most, those who are courageous enough to risk contagion leave their cards downstairs. For the rest, the elephant must find his own way to the boneyard, or stop inconveniencing the world and get well, for one more canceled dinner at short notice and he will be dropped. Illness is in the worst of taste.

Nonetheless, they seemed delighted to have him back. The King gratulated him upon his recovery. The Queen sent word that she was pleased. Graffer, though begrudging each one of them, as is a gardener's way, sent eight perfect roses.

Sir William was once more, now that Horace Mann was dead, the oldest living continuous Minister, and so a rarity worth visiting, though true, he had put many people to the cost of black silk, who must now store it away against the next occasion.

"The fundamental trouble was a liver complaint, long threatening," explained Emma. Like Sir William, she, too, had fallen into the convention of writing to Greville as to a friend.

Sir William, alienated by illness, looked around him, with the curiosity of a poor cousin, at the possessions of that now defunct personage, his recent self. He had never before seen them as a stranger would. Here they were, the rational possessions of a gentleman of limited though extensive means who had lived in this house for twenty-eight years. Not the richest tomb in Roman Nola contained so much. If I cannot be buried with it, I can be buried from it, he thought, so in that sense it comes under the head of funeral furniture.

The most finished of these possessions was of course —as it had always been—the view, the bay, the city, and Vesuvius beyond. That, too, must be left behind, but not yet.

"I wonder if all of us who could not bear to leave the world behind are not somehow still here," said Sir William aloud, and began to cheer up; foolish fancies always cheered him up. On the desk was a Roman phallic flute on which he found he could still lip a note or two. The notes sounded dusty and faraway. He put the flute down.

A bust of Marcus Aurelius, vulgar but sumptuous, the tunic porphyry, the neck and face white marble, stared at him with inlaid eyes. He preaches resignation in his works, but in person looks buffeted, assured and smug. If a little learning is a dangerous thing, what then are we to say of too much?

He picked up a theatre mask from Herculaneum and held it to his face. Peering through the eyeholes, he was in truth a noble ancient Roman, his only view, to look out through the eyes, his only air, two breathing holes, and the whole thing musty. He laid it down. It was a tragic mask. It did not suit him. Though we all come to it in time, who would choose to see the world with dead men's eyes? Yet he did agree with Lady Holland, a woman experienced in the emotions in every way and so an authority upon this subject, in wishing that it were sometimes possible to indulge in a serious mood.

Nor had he realized before (it was all he had been able to see through the mask) how cluttered up these walls had grown with Emma. She was everywhere: by Reynolds, consonant with the best interiors, so that did no harm; by Romney, all innocence and bad drawing, so that was no harm either; by Beechey; by Angelica Kauffmann (in a spindrift huddle against a wall); by Masquerier, a *portrait d'apparat*, since, though Sir William was not shown, Vesuvius in the background hinted at his existence; by Westall, R.A. (looking rather cross), as St. Cecilia; as an analphabetic but obliging sibyl by Vigée-Lebrun; by W. Bennet (*pénible*); and dancing, by Lock (rather fetching). All in all it was too much Emma, and more to come, since he had commissioned Rethberg to pencil the Attitudes. And never the same look twice, although among so many—if one could be sure of none of them—one could at least choose the mien that one preferred.

He was too old. From now on she must be his youth. He could observe youth by observing her, and that way perhaps somehow enjoy it.

Looking out the window at Vesuvius, he was himself again. "I shall climb you once more," he said. "Then twice. Then a hundred times." It would be good to feel solid, if smoking, ground beneath one's feet again. The old man is not, after all, so very old.

Rather civilly, Vesuvius erupted in his favor, like a

playful captive whale that spouts, or a prize child, performing for the Board of Governors. They were old friends, he and she, and she had been dormant for too long. He felt restored. Like his friend Walpole (who also found it impossible to indulge in a serious mood), he had a partiality for professed nonsense.

Meanwhile, there was the mail to read.

"The French National Assembly," he said, "has declared war against Bohemia, Hungary and Sardinia. It is a large island, somewhat to the north of here."

Emma looked distressed.

"There is no need for alarm. We have ships. And so, for the matter of that, have they," he said, looking out at the harbor, where some rotten Neapolitan brigantines were soaking at anchor.

"The Queen is back from Austria," reported Emma, "and has asked us to a ball."

Sir William had rather thought she might.

The chief architectural felicity of the palace at Naples was a double staircase—which is to say one flight poured suavely down from one end, the other from the other—meeting a few feet apart in a landing elevated a few steps above the marble flooring. One led to the King's apartments, the other, to the Queen's. Not only did they maintain separate establishments, they maintained separate doors. Though they lived with pomp, neither one of them was precisely formal.

The stair hall itself was vast and drafty and never lit with candles enough. What candles there were had flames which blew all one way, like willis in a ballet. The wall opposite the stairs was mirrored.

"And did Your Highness enjoy your stay in Vienna?" Emma asked the Queen.

"It was heavenly. I made two marriages."

The doors were opened, not an inch too soon, by a most dilatory footman who had misgauged the royal trajectory.

"I am struck by your *tournure*," said the Queen, without flinching.

"Oh, do you admire it?"

"I admire what there is of it," said the Queen, who was apt, having bad shoulders, to be a prude; though having good arms, never a puritan. Out onto the *piano nòbile* landing they went.

The King appeared on the other one, with Hamilton and Acton.

"It is a considerable source of pleasure to me," said Acton, "as Prime Minister, to discover that as Minister for War, I had improved the troops, and that as Minister of the Marine, constructed a navy against just such an emergency as—as Prime Minister—I found myself confronted with. But of what use are the Army and the Fleet, you have seen for yourself. And though Admiral Caraccioli, my successor, is an excellent man, it does not seem to me that he has the knowledge to continue those reforms which, as his predecessor, I could always count on myself, so to speak, to push through."

"Most certainly," said Sir William, who had been confused not so much by the multiplicity of office, as by the rapidity of succession to it.

". . . an enormous boar, five feet six in length, confronting me," said the King, "ambushed behind a rather large statue of Ptolemaeus IV Philopater, which my curator had relegated to that remote spot, hoping to weather it into some semblance of antiquity, for it had been an injudicious purchase . . ."

"To think," said Lady Dunmore, surveying in the far distance Emma and the Queen across the gulf that separated them, "that I knew her when she was a mere nobody."

"Nonsense," snapped Lady Webster, who was not Lady Holland yet, and did not know her either, "you knew her when you thought she was a mere nobody. She herself has never had any illusions of any kind."

"My husband feels," said the Queen smoothly, "that we might best send our fleet to blockade the French at Toulon," and looked down at the roses on her dress, which were made of pink satin and were full-blown. She had achieved maturity. It was a time of national crisis. It was too late for rosebuds now.

". . . charged, with gleaming tusks," said the King. "Leaning toward my musket, which stood in a prepared position, I pulled the trigger which my gamekeeper had cocked for me—my heavens, there's a pretty creature."

It was only Lady Plymouth, seen from behind.

"Lady Hamilton seems to have been taken up recently by the Queen," said Lady Plymouth. "I wonder why."

"That is an assumption which I can only regard as deriving from defective observation," said Sir William. He and Acton were now discussing the new Guido Reni in the Cathedral.

"And what, Sire, was the outcome?"

"The outcome?" asked Ferdinand suspiciously. "Why, the same as usual, a little butchery and an excellent dinner. Pray, sir, do you fish?" It was always his second topic with a stranger. If they did not hunt, they must surely fish, otherwise what else was there to do in life?

"We will now," said the Queen, in her easy German way, "turn to lighter things." It was an order.

There was wenching, of course.

Lady Plymouth drew herself up rather sharply, but then—remembering that these were troublous times, that royalty had its problems like the rest of us, and that any incident, no matter how trivial (The War of Jenkins's Ear was in her mind: she seemed to remember that Jenkins had been a Fowey boy), might lead to serious consequences—patriotically ignored the pinch and continued down the stairs.

The company reached the ground floor and processed to the ballroom, which was the theatre refurbished.

"There is no precedence observed here," said Lady Anne Miller, disapprovingly. She had complained too soon, for the Queen, who these days left no Englishman unturned, for the aid that might be under him, made for her at once.

The musicians were seated in a pyramid, with the kettledrummer on top, riding out the noise like King Mausolus in his chariot, or more appropriately (he was a

German) Thor, thumping away on the Last Day of His Wrath. Since it was suppertime, there were no tables. Royalty is supposed to dine alone at table—it is an unbearable rule of etiquette—so the Queen, who hated to eat alone, had solved her dilemma by removing the tables. Food was lapped.

Lady Anne, who had dished herself a saucer of tay, found it difficult to rise at the Queen's approach without spilling her tay as she did so.

"Pray sit down," said the Queen benevolently. Down went Lady Anne again, saucer aquiver.

The Queen, a woman of intellectual capacity, seeing the tay about to spill, with her usual resource pretended to avert her glance until Lady Anne was once more safely seated. Could our own dear Queen have managed the matter more graciously? Lady Anne became a partisan.

"Ferdinand," said the Queen. "I think the time has come to display approval of the English garden."

The King, whose only motion was to allow himself to be pushed by contraries, had taken it up as soon as she had dropped it.

"We have approved," he said, "daily."

"The times are bad. It is necessary to make a show of force. We will approve together," she told him. "Tomorrow."

Inspired by a second marriage, and at last uninhibited, Graffer had done well. Some Botany Bay plants, despite the stubbornness of Captain Bligh, had beached here and shot up to forty feet, mangling the culverts with tenacious roots. In summer, the camphor tree spread over the groves a most colonial fragrance. No horticultural cliché had been neglected. Green lawns constructed the sloping scene and guided the sparkling rill. The trees were tufted; some lofty towers were imbosomed; the roof of the cottage *ornée* was covered over with weeds. No gaudy flowers were permitted to bloom around the artificial cave, and the adjacent waters had a pearly gleam. Not only was Graffer well-read, he had a large, roomy and extensive budget. It was not merely a garden; it was a green anthology.

Unfortunately, to enjoy an English garden requires some previous education, and no one can be sensible of the beauties of Homer when coming to them direct from a reading of Tom Thumb and Jack the Giant Killer.

"Where is the English garden?" asked the King.

He was in it.

"Lord," he said, "there is nothing here but grass, and trees that bear no fruit."

"Send our compliments to Sir Joseph Banks," the Queen said graciously to Graffer, who was a hireling, nothing more, whereas Sir Joseph had patronized the piece. "And tell him we will reward his efforts suitably, though not, I fear, soon. We are not," she explained, "*immediately* pleased."

What he got, during a lull in life's incipient battles, boxed, crated and sent the long way around, to avoid Napoleon, was a set of Capodimonte dinnerware, a most suitable gift; as she pointed out, even a philosopher must dine.

Sir William had had some of Emma's portraits taken down. At first she did not notice. She was a narcist: mirrors were what she used. But then at last she did.

"I'm gone," she said, dismayed.

"Only for restretching," said Sir William uneasily. "And who could miss them in the presence of their bright original? They were but cold copies." "The Ambassadress," by Romney, he had left in a tactfully obvious position. It was the one she would have preferred, he thought. It showed her now.

He was wrong. "Even George's other Cassandra?" she asked.

"Cassandra is not, perhaps, tactful to the times."

"But that was such a happy day," she wailed obscurely.

He restored the Cassandra. It was a Cassandra young and doubly burdened with a gift of tongues. Emma spoke Italian better after five years than he did after twenty.

She could think of only one reason for her banishment.

"Is the war going that badly?" she asked. "Must we pack so soon?"

"It is not going well," said Sir William, and went off to fish in troubled waters.

It had not occurred to him before that a mistress may have charms anterior to those of a wife—a state of affairs not only unique, but in this case, it seemed, unavoidable.

* * *

Aware, though not consciously, of a certain coolth in the air, Emma, in order to share her pleasures with Sir William, went to the trouble of having her songs arranged for viola and piano, so that they might be musical together. A flute would have been too like in tone to her voice, and the viola was his only other instrument.

Sometimes she sang duets with the King. "It was but bad," she said, *"as he sings like a King."*

Her newly gained assurance, or the show of it, was too recent as yet for her to be as unaware of it as Sir William was of a good suit of clothes.

"She cannot be totally indifferent to the facts of life," said the Queen, exasperated, "for from all accounts she seems to have lived one." And went graciously in to visit Emma.

"Do you and Sir William never discuss politics?" she asked cooingly.

"He prefers not."

"A pity. It is the proper vocation of princes," said the Queen, "but sometimes an expert opinion does no harm."

"It is the very thing he says himself!" cried Emma, radiant with compliance. "I will speak to him."

"Pray," said Maria Carolina, and took the creature's paw in a jeweled hand, "do. You will gratify thereby"—and here she attempted to totter, but alas, her iron stays were too rigid; no matter how she tried, they kept her upright—"an old woman's whim [she was a healthy, bouncy forty-three] and do yourself no harm."

"Send me some news," Emma wrote Greville, scarcely daring to disturb Sir William with her prattle, "political and private, for against my will, *owing to my situation here* I am got into politics and wish to have news for our dear much-loved Queen."

"You neglect your handwriting rather too much, but as what you write is good sense, everybody will forgive the scrawl," said Sir William approvingly, over her shoulder.

"Since we have formed an alliance with Great Britain," said Lord Acton, "I see no reason why we should not now recognize the French Republic, promulgate the British alliance, and receive thereby a somewhat smaller contingent of the French Fleet for a shorter period than we had expected to do."

"Never!" shouted Maria Carolina.

Being the son of an émigré, Acton had developed a most Italian shrug of the shoulders. "Oh well," he said, "perhaps for a little while. First we entertain them, then we let the English chase them away."

But the French ships were already in the bay.

"They have come to overawe Us," said Maria Carolina, quivering. "We are not overawed."

"We are your friends, good people," shouted the French. "We are your friends. Destroy your King and Queen. Turn out your priests, listen to our legate, and accept liberty." They spoke in French, for they had been given to understand that tongue was everywhere understood, as it must be, for it had always been the language spoken anywhere they had been.

"Long live the King!" shouted the oppressed populace.

The French Legate, Citizen Hugou de Bassville, though the Queen refused to receive him, was not discouraged. He had the escutcheon on the French Embassy repainted. What he had in mind was a beauteous Minerva with a lance in one hand and a cap of liberty in the other. No, the cap of liberty should be upon her head, for Liberty should have at least one hand free.

It was beautiful escutcheon. Looking out the window

the next morning, he was pleased to see a peasant kneeling before it in the street. One had only to show the ignorant the image of enlightenment and they revised their ways at once.

"Bring that man to me," he said.

The man, picturesque as a *sans culotte* but a lot cleaner, was hustled upstairs. He seemed frightened, or perhaps what he felt was awe—for the two are similar —and having heard of awe only by hearsay, Hugou de Bassville could not be accurate in his diagnosis.

"Ask him if he knows the name of the goddess he is worshiping," he told the interpreter.

"He says, 'Why were you down on your knees down there?'" explained the interpreter.

"It was such a beautiful madonna," said the *lazzarone*. "Such a pretty hat."

"Madre mia!" said the interpreter.

"Minerva, by whom we mean Athene, the Goddess of Wisdom, was the daughter of Zeus, by whom we mean Jupiter. She had no children," said Bassville, struck by the implications of what he had just said, but only lightly, as in passing.

"The French are very funny," said the *lazzarone*. "The Virgin Mary was the daughter of St. Anne, everybody knows that."

"Do you mean to tell me," roared Bassville, who had begun to catch the drift of this, "that the man thought he was worshiping the *Madonna?* What ignorance. What impiety."

"No, I didn't," said the interpreter, "but, sir, I couldn't think of anything."

"Throw them out," said Bassville. It was a thankless task. You asked for a stone, and they gave you bread. So often the downtrodden could be liberated only by calling in reinforcements. It would mean war.

Everything means war, but for the moment there were no reinforcements, so Bassville went on to Rome and the more congenial boyish task of burning the Pope in effigy.

The King buried the silver and gave up three hundred and ninety-two of his dogs. He had the menagerie killed.

He had the chandeliers taken down. If the Queen wished to scribble, she could do so by the light of a storm lantern. He had made his preparations and went off to hunt and fish with his customary courage. Acton could take care of the rest.

Lady Elizabeth Foster arrived.

"Lady Elizabeth has expressed an interest in Vesuvius," said Sir William.

"Oh the good kind lady," said Emma, whose temper was not always quite perfect. There were many English ladies to present to the Queen these days. Had Emma not been of so forgiving a disposition, this duty would have given her a singular and exquisite pleasure. Here she was their only entry, whereas in England they would not have let her in at all. She was beginning to discover the joys of being affable from a superior position. Her standards were improving. She began to hold opinions, a task not difficult, for they weighed light and were soon gotten rid of. One had merely to pass them on.

In August, the King of France was executed. This made the King of Naples conciliatory. He agreed to receive the French delegates.

"To avoid war, we caress the serpent which will poison us," said Maria Carolina, returning, unopened, the gift of a basket of fruit.

"He would have danced a minuet upon the mole, had the French requested it," said Acton.

Apart from that, the sun shone and there was nothing wrong. Nonetheless, into each life a little rain must fall, though not much.

"His Britannic Majesty's government," said Sir William, "has been pleased to declare war against France." His face, which was generally marble, was for the moment blancmange.

"I suppose that means we may not travel, that the mails will be delayed, and that the Bishop of Derry may not come out to us," said Emma, grasping the consequences with her usual sagacity.

"Not even as Lord Bristol. They have pulled down the

pillars of society. They respect neither the Ermine nor the Cloth. So it would not be safe."

"Still, we need not delay this Thursday's dinner, need we?"

"I fear it is too late now to delay anything."

Greville, too, had sent stirring news. With his customary pertinacity and financial flair, he had managed to cut the revenue of the Welsh estates by half.

They both considered this. It could not be denied: Greville was a remarkable man, astute, perspicacious and easily defeated. There are times when even banter fails.

"Truly they are vile creatures," said Sir William.

"The French?"

"Estate managers of all sorts," said Sir William. "You had better dress. The Queen has sent for us."

As so she had. She was a commanding woman, restless, peremptory and prompt. Though she abhorred to meddle, when there was a decision to be made, she made it. This habit of mind showed in her face, for had she not been a Queen and therefore a beauty, people would have found her *jolie laide*. Her religious beliefs never wavered, her convictions were firm: the former, that the survival of herself, the House of Hapsburg and the Neapolitan Throne were essential to Him; the second, that this could be done. A scale model of decorum, but able in everything, she believed in enlightened self-interest, employed her own spies, and literate to a fault, had read both the "Social Contract" and the Manual of Arms. Though not a snob, she insisted on her own precedence as a matter of principle, and in any other time or place would either have implemented a new age or have been struck down by it. Her husband, who had begun by loving her, would nowadays as soon accost the Sphinx.

"I have had shocking news. Truly shocking news. I have only just learned," she said, "that my sister has had her head chopped off." The light was merciless. She blinked.

Sir William could think of nothing to say, or rather,

since as a diplomat he was full of little nothings, could not bring himself to say it, for it would be improper to condole upon an event so novel. The mind cannot grasp it, so the heart has no response. The shock is too great.

The Queen spread her muscled arms in a gesture more suitable to Madame Georges than to royalty.

"Oh where is there a roomy hell big enough to hold the French!" she cried. "She was my sister. How *dare* they?"

She was in that rarest of states, a royal rage—not a tantrum, which is common enough, but a rage—authentic, vulnerable and dangerous.

It made her movements jerky. Sir William was unpleasantly reminded of a clock he had once seen somewhere in Germany, on which the monarchs of the hours, life size, had each come out on their hour, brandished their weapons, and when their hour had struck had departed just as jerkily. It had not before occurred to him that the world he had known for a lifetime was a transitory phenomenon, for he had loved it almost entirely because it was there.

"They shall not cut off mine," said the Queen, in her incisive way. "I shall have theirs."

Emma's eyes sparkled, as they always did at the theatre, with an emphatic radiance. Looking beyond the Queen's shoulder, Sir William found himself face to face with a herm of the god Terminus.

"Si Son Altesse Royale," began the Marchesi Solari soothingly.

"Never speak to me in that tongue again," said Maria Carolina magnificently. "It is the language of the criminous. *Je poursuiverai ma vengeance jusqu'au tombeau.*" She had lost her head. "Address me in Italian or German, if you please."

In December, she gave birth prematurely to a new princess. "May God," she said when they brought it to her, "chastise the French." It was on her mind. "If he won't, I will." God, in these matters, was much like the King. He might mean well, but He needed prodding.

It was a period of indecision and unrest, the King devoting himself to the former, his subjects to the latter. A manifesto was found placarded up in the streets. WE PREFER DEATH TO THE FALSE FRIENDSHIP OF A NATION WHICH IS ONLY PROUD BECAUSE OF THE WEAK RESISTANCE IT HAS ENCOUNTERED SO FAR, it read. However, when it came to recruiting, enthusiasm, if it did not disappear, at least dodged nimbly out of sight.

Sir William was hard-worked. True, the work was cut out for him, but still, tailoring it together into reports was skilled labor—no easy task for a man new come to it. He would rather have cut them from the whole cloth. Politics, though a parallel study, has not the charm of volcanology, nor the aesthetic satisfaction of an antique vase. Even the most vivid of police reports lack the immediacy of portraiture, and political attitudinizing had none of the vivacity of Emma's Attitudes.

In July, he and Acton signed a secret treaty of alliance between England and Naples, for with so much *Liberté, Égalité,* and *Fraternité* abroad in the world, and most of it preparing to march South, the King of the Two Sicilies did not feel at liberty to act openly. An advance contingent of the English fleet arrived the 11th of September.

"My dear," said Sir William, "I have met the most extraordinary young man. He has come to ask for two thousand Neapolitan troops to help defend Toulon, and what is more, he has gotten them. I think one day he will astonish the world. So though it is not my policy to allow officers in the house, I have asked him to stay with us. Tell Mrs. Cadogan to have Prince Augustus' old room made ready."

"As astonishing as that?" asked Emma. When she met him, she saw only a tired man of thirty-five, not handsome and in no way astonishing. What is more, he had brought his stepson, a priggish young gentleman. Sir William's preferences were sometimes devious to identify. Captain Nelson did not look the man to have an interest in either bibelots or botany.

"I am to take him off to the King's banquet," said Sir William. "We must dazzle him a little, and since he has had no experience of royalty as yet, perhaps that will do it. Will you amuse the son?"

Young Josiah Nisbet was unamusable. He did not sing. He would not dance. He watched. He was a proper little sneak. He looked out the window, saw the view was not English, and never looked again. His opinion of himself was high, and apparently he saw no reason to alter a judgment so painfully formed, to such universal satisfaction. He drank too much.

"My stepgrandfather," he said, "is a clergyman. You must excuse me if I cannot admire your Attitudes. My tastes have been formed in another school."

"In a jelly mold, more likely," said Mrs. Cadogan when she heard of it.

Nor was he any more obliging about the evening concert.

"Is not the song, at least, lovely?" asked Emma. She was old enough to be his mother, and very glad she wasn't.

"I cannot judge. I am no connoisseur. Besides, it is an *Italian* song, is it not?"

"The father is better," said Emma.

"*Ummmmm,*" said Mrs. Cadogan, like a short, companionable Norn.

"I am now only a captain; but I will, if I live, be at the top of the tree. I was not born to blow birds' eggs and dig in a garden," said Nelson to Sir William, with a burst of irritation, for these blood sports were those his wife found seemly and she knew no others. "Lady Hamilton has been most good to young Nisbet. It cannot be easy."

This touch was one that always made Sir William purr. In any conversation what he admired best were the sparks.

"Just so," he said.

"What do you think of my captain?" asked Sir William.

"I like him well enough," said Emma, who was always cautious to praise no man other than Sir William much, unless she truly did not like him.

Sir William laughed. "You will like him better as an admiral, I expect."

"Is he to be an admiral?"

"I should imagine so. A war brings men of ability to the top, out of the general drowning. If they know how to stay afloat, we haul them aboard from the shipwreck and give them a title. If they do not know how to stay afloat, they sink, and so need bother us no more."

Emma decided to show her charm. Say what you will, a uniform, unless bloodstained, is most flattering. With a uniform beside you, you do not have to worry about the color of your dress or what waistcoat it will go with.

"Lady Hamilton," Nelson wrote home, "has been wonderfully kind and good to Josiah. She is a young woman of amiable manners, and who does honor to the station to which she is raised."

He had sailed.

"What do you mean, gone?" asked Emma. "We were to have luncheon with him aboard the *Agamemnon*."

"He heard of a French corvette worth capturing, so he went to capture it. One cannot blame him. He is not rich and must live off prize money."

"But he has taken our best butter dish," wailed Emma, as indeed he had. The *Agamemnon* lacked a butter dish, so he had borrowed one. "I hope he sends it back, for we have not another so commodious."

He sent it back. They did not see him again for five years. But since he was so clearly a coming man, it did no harm to correspond.

As usual, there were other guests to entertain. Lady Webster was an exacting one, for boredom demands to be fed.

"I hope you will find everything quite comfortable," said Emma, surveying with pride the large, ample bedroom.

"Quite, thank you," said Lady Webster, and as soon as the trull was gone, made a dart for the writing desk, as for a planchette, though from the other side of silence.

"The Hamiltons are as tiresome as ever; he as amorous, she as vulgar," she wrote, and went to bed satisfied. In proper circles, malice is always an acceptable substitute for wit, and in general regarded as superior to it. She had a reputation to maintain.

Lady Webster was succeeded by William Beckford, the wealthy *cause célèbre*, and a Hamilton cousin. He had, they understood, been staying with some footmen in Portugal, but it could not be denied he did know how to praise a lady.

"The poor old woman who mistook you at dawn for a statue of the Holy Virgin need not have been ashamed to have renewed her homage in open daylight," he said, and quite made Emma blush, not for herself alone.

"There is a letter from Nelson," said Sir William happily. "I must say he is very civil."

"What does he say?"

"Why nothing," said Sir William, interrupted in the midst of a fond but purely private approval. "As I told you, he writes an excellent note."

She had a rival. When men grow old and are childless, it sometimes happens so. Willy-nilly, they search out a son.

In February, the Neapolitan fleet arrived back from Toulon, its only trophies some four hundred French refugees, its only victory that it was still afloat. Nelson's news continued good, however. He had lost an eye in Corsica. Sir William seemed deeply affected.

"Let us hope that, like Odin, he exchanged it for wisdom," he said, forgetting Ragnarök. We have surrogate families and surrogate sons, and are ourselves leading surrogate lives, though whether we are delegated or relegated to lead them, and by Him or whom, is open to question.

But taking her cue, Emma admired him loudly. That Greville had been made Vice-Chamberlain to the King seemed to impress Sir William less. He had other interests now.

In Naples, there was a Jacobin plot against the Queen, nurtured until it budded, and then nipped. Politics was like gardening, really: you cut them back to get a bigger bush and more flowers.

"I go nowhere without wondering if I shall return alive," said Maria Carolina, who slept in a different bedroom every night and sometimes did not sleep at all. She spoke much of death, to Sir William's annoyance, for though he believed in nothing too much, he was just as firm a devotee of nothing final.

However, survival is like any other game: with skill, aptitude and concentration, we may do much. It resembles maneuvers. So long as we hang back and never surrender, we cannot be wounded or captured. Only a coward goes over to the other side. Discretion, proper diet, an astute choice of winter quarters and a little looting may be depended upon to pull us through. As a Scotsman, Sir William took pride in hanging on. He was sixty-four and ill in bed.

Vesuvius soon brought him around. There was an eruption preceded by an earthquake. The earthquake was so violent that, at Caserta, all the servants' bells began to ring of their own accord. The palace was surrounded by armed bands, the citizens thinking the grinding of the earth an attack by the French, cannonading from the sea.

Sir William got out of bed and soon had watch, telescope, thermometer, pencil and notebook ready. As he watched, there was a loud report, a canopy of black smoke, and a fountain of fire. He moved his household to Posilipo and went to investigate. It was her thirty-third eruption. She was, as usual, diligent in the production of antiques, good wine, rich soil and the best spectacle.

The summit of the peak was invisible, but there was lightning aplenty, fireballs floated about like bright incandescent cabbages, the air was sulphurous, the electric fire resembled serpents, and the sound reminded him that he had once made a tour of the Carron iron foundry in Scotland.

Lava poured down Torre del Greco to the sea and there turned to steam, its thirst slaked. The countryside was covered with wet ash. A gentleman at the English factory filled a plate with ashes, popped in a few peas, and on the third day they came up and put forth leaves. Not even a war can halt, though sometimes it may occasion, the forced marches of science.

"Aimez-vous donc les beautés de la nature?" demanded a Frenchman with a smudged face, standing hot-footed beside Sir William. *"Pour moi, je les abhorre!"*

Sir William ignored him and decided to take a boat to Torre del Greco. The eruption was great good luck. He was already drafting a possible report to the Royal Society. He saw his career crowned, as he would wish it to be, by Minerva, the Goddess of Tact.

But at Torre del Greco, when he put his hand in to test the water, it was scalding hot, and the pitch between the planks of the boat began to dissolve, so he turned back, having no desire to be a boiled ambassador.

The air began to clear. He could see that the old crater had fallen in, and determined to climb the peak, which he did, taking his usual guide, Bartolomeo Pumo. It was his sixty-eighth climb.

Someone had gone before them. They could see the footprints in the hot ash. A fox, some lizards and some insects had also been there. They could not get to the top. Metallic deposits made the lava resemble a field of irises growing in a desert. There were seven new craters and two whirlwinds. It was most stimulating. He went back.

"I am grieved," said Emma, "that pressing domestic duties prevented my joining you." And she managed to look both wistful and grieved. She professed, as every sensible woman does, to encourage the hobbies of her husband, and since she was his hobby, had not hitherto found this difficult. But now she had a hobby of her own—the Queen.

Those who had conspired to murder her were to be hanged. "It is an affront to the cause of Liberty," said the French Consul, the French having so far guillotined 2,625, whereas the Queen demanded only 3. But a hanging is different. A hanging shocks the sensibilities.

"This infamous revolution has made me cruel," said Maria Carolina, hovering over a death warrant with a wistful expression.

There was suspicion everywhere; society had gone for good; cliques were the rule. Emma saw the Queen every day, and as a result was almost sick of grandeur. Nonetheless, she brought herself to gulp it down.

"Greville has redoubled his efforts. From half the income we could expect from Milford Haven, he has so built upon the thing that now we may expect none. No doubt he has my best interests at heart, but thank God he cannot touch my capital. Nelson has lost an arm and been made a Rear Admiral of the Blue. I told you he was the coming man."

Sir William looked as pleased as though he had achieved that goal himself. "He will be out to us soon, I expect, for Bonaparte is in Nice."

"There is but one course open to us," said the Queen when she heard that. "We must prepare for war and sue for peace."

The Bishop of Derry arrived, on his way to Milan.
"Now, William," he said, "how do you come on?"
"We jog along."
"It is not the pace I would have chosen for you."
"I choose my own pace," said Sir William. "I do not intend to creep my way down to death."
"Cannot you see how she has seized control? She has grown into a managing wife."
"Well, she is a wife, and someone must manage," said Sir William.
"I own I liked her better as a mistress than a wife."

"Ah well, so did I. I must own, for the matter of that, that I liked myself much better as a lover."

"You are not a husband; you are only a bachelor with a wife," chided Derry admiringly.

Sir William did not care for this. "I must congratulate you," he said, "upon your turn of phrase. You still put things very well."

"I do not criticize. I commiserate," said the Bishop. "Taken as herself, she is all very well, as I once noted. Take her as anything else, and she is vulgar. It seems to me that I took note of that before, too."

"Ah well, if you commiserate. That is different. But I have never taken her as anything but herself, and very seldom then."

"She will not go down in England."

"I daresay not. She is remarkably resilient," said Sir William.

"Moreover," said the Bishop, "she is getting fat."

"Fat?"

"Buxom."

Sir William was appalled. He saw her every day. He had not noticed, for she had still the same airs and graces, and in the evening the lights were sometimes bad.

"Diet," said the Bishop benevolently, as though to say, Go, my child, and sin no more.

Emma was struggling with a new dress and cursing the dressmaker.

"It is not the dressmaker," said Mrs. Cadogan, speaking out at last. "I fear, poor Em, it is you."

"I am a married woman. I shall eat what I like," snapped Emma. "A body has to eat."

"Not night and day, and most certainly not everything in sight," said Mrs. Cadogan.

"Oh leave me. Leave me!" shrieked Emma, and when she had been left, consulted her image. Juno was plump. Aspasia was plump. Venus was plump. The world itself was plump enough to fall. So what was the harm in it? Though it cannot be denied that ripeness weakens the stem. Current royalty, though not detached as yet, was manifestly globular.

Emma, seeing a triple fold between her breast and armpit, burst into tears, but after some thought, got over it.

Mrs. Cadogan returned to find her munching sweetmeats, and made a dart to snatch them from the burning.

"You have filched my reward," said Emma. "I have consented to maturity."

"Oh well, in that case," said Mrs. Cadogan, "perhaps just one. You have been both brave and sensible. I knew you would be."

Napoleon invaded Italy.

"The Queen says," reported Emma, "that we must admire ability where we find it, and were he any other man, she would admire him."

"Admire, yes, but there is no need to seek it out," said Sir William. "As you can see by the dispatches, it comes to us."

"But he is only twenty-seven," said Emma, from her new and older podium.

"Nonetheless, he means to sack us. We must get the King to act."

They got the King to act. A new uniform was designed for the Royal Corps of Nobles, and a service was held in the Cathedral. He had decided to ask for aid.

"I can answer for the King and the Ministry and of course for myself, but the country makes me tremble," said Maria Carolina.

"Napoleon has spared Rome, for thirty million French francs and the Apollo Belvedere," said Sir William, and looked bleakly at his art collection. Napoleon, like his uncle the Cardinal, was a collector. In his collection a man shows his taste, and Napoleon, being a universal genius, had a taste for almost everything. Perugino or Perugia, it was all the same to him.

The portraits of Emma in her prime were safe, at any rate. English art is not popular upon the Continent. My heavens, in her prime, thought Sir William, and looked guiltily across the table, but there she was, a drowsy cabbage rose, full and beguiling. If one had not seen her first in the bud, one would never have known.

"The Queen says that the late French King's aunts are at Caserta, having had to flee Rome, and that they are dreadful. Is it true?"

Fresh arrived from dingy lodgings in Caput Mundi, they had had everybody turned out and kept the same pomp at Caserta as they had once done at Versailles, though, if the truth be known, on a larger scale.

"Improbable, I should have said myself. They treat inconvenience as though it were a historical event." And he paused, like a dog with one paw up, to indicate a change of statement. "Nelson has been made a Knight Commander of the Bath. That makes him technically my superior."

"How nice for you," chanted Emma. "You always said the man would rise."

"Yes," agreed Sir William, "but not above me. It shows a want of tact."

"You mean that pleasant young man," said Emma, who had been keeping Nelson's various distinctions in an old drawer, and it was amazing, if you put them away one at a time, how rapidly they began to add up. For fame is very like thrift: it may not make one rich, but at least it makes it possible when the time comes to gamble or invest, or both, depending upon one's skill, and of course the outcome.

"On the part of George Third," said Sir William, who in the last decade had scanned the yearly honors' list with mounting chagrin. Though a title may be an expense, it adds that final embellishment to a tombstone which catches the eye of the future epigrapher. It confers a nominal renown, and a nominal renown is much. If one is to have no other, that is all that counts. There is much to be said for a name.

From whichever end you sighted down it, 1798 was not a good year. Acton talked of retiring to England. Worse than that, he had had the Queen's favorite banished to Vienna.

"Is it true?" asked Emma of the Queen, who by some whim had dressed in violet.

"You see me in mourning. My youth has flown. At any rate," she added, with her passion for accuracy, "he has been sent."

Emma was shocked. She had regarded the Queen as a pillar, true, a stout pillar with a pronounced miniscus, of rectitude.

"My dear," said the Queen, quick to sniff an audience and pressing the condoling hand, "think of me, forced to marry at sixteen, against my wishes, without love, as is indeed only proper; the years of emptiness, with no diversion but the King. Cannot you find it in your experience, *somewhere,* to pardon me? Some little transgression of your own, perhaps, in early youth?" Her eyes were beady. She could not abide criticism.

"Surely there were others," said Emma meditatively.

The Queen misunderstood. "What is memory," she said, "if there are to be no more! The King has been most annoyed. I do not worry about that. He has only two moods—the annoyed and the annoying. It is his customary mood. But Acton!"

They could hear the creak of a wooden merry-go-round in the park outside the window. It was one of those days when the public was let into the grounds.

"He was a simple, harmless diversion, nothing more," said Maria Carolina. "He did not even want to hold office—at least, only a little one. So what was the harm in him? Even Josephine Bonaparte has her favorites, and does her husband throw them out? He does not. He is above such things. He asks them in."

From now on, Acton was her enemy.

"Napoleon is in Egypt," said Sir William. "Nelson, they say, is to bottle him up. And high time, too, for he is a man much in need of bottling. The French have gone too far."

It was their fashions. He had been to a dinner for the French Envoy. Madame Canclaux had worn a chemise with nothing under it, and her arms bare. Mademoiselle Canclaux had dined with a blue silk bonnet on her head. Monsieur Canclaux had worn a dark blue coat buttoned to the chin, black leather buskins laced with gold, a broad black leather belt and a scimitar down to his toes; it had clanked every time he sat back from sipping his wine. They had looked disgusting.

"Perhaps," said Emma indecisively, but with her mind made up, "with a flesh-colored underslip . . ." The bonnet she would have liked to have seen.

"I told you they would not last long in those clothes," said Sir William. "We are to have a new envoy. They were going to send Gasse, but discovered he had been Acton's cook. Canclaux told them, so he must now go home to face charges of snobbery, which is the new high treason. It is to be a man called Trouvé.

"But if Nelson can destroy the French Fleet, we may all hold our heads up again. And so, I dare say, will he—higher than the rest of us."

In common with his favorite mountain, Sir William was apt, from time to time, to send up little puffs of steam, and the Knight Commander of the Bath, though it no longer rankled, still itched.

Like all Europe, he held his breath.

V

THE NEWS TOOK LONGER to travel than did the cause of it. He was lost; he was dead; he was missed; he had won; he had failed; he was at Syracuse; no one knew where he was.

Emma was on the terrace of the Palazzo Sesso, looking out over the bay, which she did not notice. Like most beautiful people, she had no eye for beauty unless it be edible, wearable, or capable of being viewed in a mirror. Memory sometimes lends a grace to past scenes, which develop a pretty vignette quality, but here she was in the eternal present, which suited her, and the eternal present had no scenery. She sighed.

Miss Cornelia Knight—to whom Sir William had given house room—an arch and pained poetess, in flight from Napoleonic Rome, the orphaned daughter of Rear Admiral Knight, who traveled nowhere without her telescope, was the first to see a sloop grow larger on the other side of Procida. It was flying Our Flag. The flag grew larger. The sloop grew larger. It halted, put down a longboat, and two gentlemen dressed as captains prepared to come ashore.

In dumb show the sailors, feeling the eyes, or at any rate the telescope, of Rear Admiral Knight upon them, acted out the pantomime of something being blown up and going down for the last time. They were uncouth and unshaven, but from a distance their whites looked white, and their ill-bred gestures adequately conveyed the news.

"The Battle of the Nile has been fought and won," said Sir William. "He has accomplished it." And whisked Captain Capel (Captain Hoste was too hearty an English sea dog to be quite so presentable) to the palace.

Emma went too. After the anxiety of the times and the ho-hum of marriage, this excitement made a pleasant change, and she intended to make the most of it. She had discovered a new Attitude: she would Support the Fleet. What Englishman would see a moral flaw in an enthusiasm so essentially patriotic? Were they not all in Naples themselves these days, eager to catch the next boat out, and every one of them baying for the Navy?

It was the beginning of the Romantic Age. The neo-classical was *fade*. Coleridge was at that moment engaged in adjusting the albatross. Large, dirty, white, and hanging beak down, he had seen it once, in passing, in the window of a bird-stuffer, and ever since had longed to hang it somewhere. It haunted him. Erasmus Darwin had had his day. Wordsworth was the fashion now, alternately swooning over a daffodil and beating the pantheistic bushes with his cane, when he was able, which is to say when he was unobserved, for the impiety of bearing—without first posting the marriage bans—seed. Emma did not propose to lag behind.

The King and Queen were at dinner with their children, for since they expected daily to be crucified, they dined early. Each supper was their last. Waiting, as was only courteous, until Sir William had finished his preamble, the King, spontaneously and without prompting, rose from his seat and embraced the Queen, the Princes, the Princesses and Captain Capel, in an affecting, if perhaps affected, scene.

"Oh, my children, you are now safe!" he cried. "The throne"—and here he sat down once more in a chair that ominously creaked—"is secure."

The Queen fell into one of the new fashionable *faints*, and Emma, not to be outdone, swooned away to such effect that she badly bruised her side. The Queen then brought herself to kiss her husband, whereupon both women burst into tears. Then, since fashions may come and fashions may go but the same things are always expected of royalty, she sent Captain Hoste a diamond ring from her own finger (she had put it on in order to take it off; it was one of the gift rings), six butts of wine, and to every man on board a guinea each, from an anonymous donor, since though France was not yet at war with Naples and the British Fleet could be counted on, armies unfortunately approach by land.

The populace, as usual unpredictable, or rather that nine-tenths of it which in French opinion represented a tyrannous minority, applauded the event. Captain Capel did not care for that. To date he was acquainted only with a small, self-regulating joy—an emotion as carefully to be kept in order as a repeating watch or any other expensive and exquisite gewgaw. He was an Englishman. Scenes of excessive public joy are not well-bred.

In Naples, however, the concept of breeding seemed chiefly restricted to the bloodline of a horse that comes in first. The gazettes were incandescent with sonnets, and the streets with gas. The city was illuminated for three days, the candles filched even from the altars, for surely, under the circumstances, the Virgin would not begrudge the loan. Was she not Our Lady of Victory?

Sir William and Emma received well-wishers at the Embassy door, like officiants at a rediscovered shrine. It was better than the liquefaction of St. Januarius; it meant the liquidation of the French.

"Come here, for God's sake, my dear friend," wrote Sir William to Nelson, "as soon as the service will permit you. A pleasant apartment is ready for you in my house, and Emma is looking out for the softest pillows to repose the few wearied limbs you have left [that is, one eye, one arm, two legs, a torso and a head, and all of it Stalky Jack]."

"My dress is from head to foot alla Nelson. Ask Hoste. Even my shawl is Blue with gold anchors all over. My earrings are Nelson's anchors; in short, we are be-Nelsoned all over," urged Emma.

A resourceful woman, she had flung herself upon her dressmaker instantly, for rank and file are all very well, but first things come first. Not only did she intend to call the tune (she was at the moment humming it), she would orchestrate it too. This was to be her long-awaited apotheosis. She had no time to think of any but practical things. Angels attended her, carried her muff and corrected the lines of her shawl.

As for Sir William, not only did he look ten years younger, but he had shaved.

Nelson, however, was reluctant. He was ill and little inclined toward ovation. A patent of nobility (indeed it was patent to everyone), delivered by mail, to please his wife, would suffice. He had no longing for processions. Nor did he wish to stay with Sir William, for the finances of sudden eminence confused him, and he was out of pocket as it was. He could not make the proper gestures (tipping the servants and such), for he had but one arm and very small pay. Also, he had been wounded on the forehead, had a fever, and was not a pretty sight. He would rather have appeared in public from the safety of an engraving or in a platonizing portrait, Government House style.

Nonetheless, he had to go. It was his duty. The populace seemed stirred, but just as clearly the King needed stirring up, for he seemed more apt to sulk than fight the foe.

In short, Nelson was shy. He had never been made much of. It made him feel as though he had done something wrong; the neglected child must ever be suspicious of a sudden adulation.

On the 22nd of September the *Vanguard* lurched into Naples Harbor, in bad repair and with a list. For the Neapolitans, it had been a long wait; for Nelson, too short a voyage. The bay shimmered like a blue sun, radiant with small boats. In the distance he could see small white images cavorting on the shore, and when the wind blew right, hear an immense banging of tubs, boatswains' whistles and a faint hooray.

"It is like the shark come home," he said. "Here are the pilot fish, and here is the family," and looked alongside where some rusty seaweed did certainly eddy, almost like blood.

Mrs. Cadogan entered Emma's dressing room without knocking. It was well past curtain time. She saw Emma and recoiled. Emma, who had been dressing for days, was pinning a small diamond, sapphire and ruby Union Jack to a kerchief tied around her neck in a naval manner. Where now was Attic simplicity? It had flown and left the gauds behind.

"Even for a snuffbox cover," said Mrs. Cadogan, removing the brooch, "it would be excessive."

Emma, who had managed the Lady superbly, had needlessly elaborated the simplicity of a Sailor's Girl. On this subject Mrs. Cadogan felt herself competent to say little, while removing much.

"But now I look much as I looked before," wailed Emma, whose enthusiasm had at last transgressed the boundaries of taste.

"Indeed, that is just what a sailor looks for," said Mrs. Cadogan tactfully. "There must be no hint that anything has occurred in the interim."

"Emma," called Sir William from the hall below. He was resigned that ladies were dilatory to dress, but not when matters pressed.

However, Emma was at last ready, half Grecian urn, half Jolly Polly on a Toby jug, mature, wise, understanding, sympathetic, motherly—or anyhow sisterly—but with something perennially youthful about her too, and sincere, for sincerity was easiest of all; sincerity was but the work of a moment. Down to the harbor they went; the small boats parted from the prow of their barge, for England took precedence now, since she had won it back again, and therefore, so did they.

"How pretty are the boats," said Emma, who had encouraged local industry. What with wreaths and garlands and freshly painted Madonnas and ex-votos without number, it looked more like Xochimilco at festival than their dear familiar Bay. "Will he be disfigured?"

"Dismembered," said Sir William automatically, and leaned forward eagerly as they drew alongside the *Vanguard*, but sent Emma up the ladder ahead of him, as was only civil.

"Oh God. Is it Possible?" cried Emma, singling Nelson out. In the full-dress uniform of a Vice-Admiral, the effect of the pinned sleeve was not bad; she fell into his arms, or rather arm, and fainted away. Nelson staggered back. Arms lifted her. She was restored. As always happened when she was acting, her affectations fell away; she had no time for them—she was taken up by the thing itself. From being more dead than alive, she became on the instant more alive than dead. Pink-cheeked, rosy, nubile and none the worse for a little sun, she was a perfect Sailor's Lass.

Sir William beamed approval. They made, he thought, a truly effective couple.

To get the King aboard was more difficult, for there was so very much more of him. It took an hour. But once aboard, he was his expansive, genial self. Out of several to choose from, that had seemed the most suitable. He could not have been more paternal, more benign.

"*Nostro liberatore!*" he boomed. Three cheers, hip and hooray.

"What, are there to be only three?" inquired the King, anxious that the thing be done properly, and then stooped, shattered by a grapeshot of applause. He received it, though it was not for him, with folded hands, before continuing.

"Oh had I been able to serve under you at the Battle of the Nile. But I, too, had my duty. I, too, stood at the helm of state."

"What does he say?" asked Nelson, and looked nonplussed when he was told. Why, the great clumsy man would scarcely have been of service in the galley.

Since he could not refuse with grace, he consented without it, and was carted off to the city.

"*Viva* Nelson! *Viva* Hamilton!" the crowds shouted, pressing forward for a glimpse of him, and then, at the second carriage's approach, in a less festive because more familiar tone, *"Viva il Re!"* For never before had so many lion tamers derived such heartfelt applause from the tousled appearance of one solitary, shabby lion.

"Sit down, Emma, pray do."

"Rather stand up," said Emma, "and be seen. For they demand it."

Sir William would not. He was mistrustful of the plaudits of crowds, for they cannot last forever. A mere murmur of private admiration is far easier to sustain. He noticed a curious thing. Nelson, like Emma, never looked the same part twice. Like her, his only stable feature was his will. He could admirably reflect other men's fires. In complexion, too, he was similar, white skinned, but with a variable pink flush—not strawberries and cream exactly, but the very best butter when he was feeling jaundiced.

Since this observation did not match the usual range of his experience, Sir William, with his customary horror of nonconformity, put it away.

"I do not care for the Neapolitans," said Nelson. "It is a country of fiddlers and poets and scoundrels."

"You have struck upon the very reasons we prefer them," said Sir William delightedly. "Though from the other side. It is like two men digging one tunnel: one may blow cold and the other hot, but in the nature of the task, they are bound—if you view the thing in cross section—to meet. We may at any rate be the first to shake hands through the conjunctive hole."

Nelson, who never felt the compulsion to hold his telescope the wrong way around, found this sort of chatter disconcerting. Still, for near seventy, Sir William was undoubtedly remarkable, a plain straightforward fellow after his own heart—as long as you attended only to every other word. Nelson felt at home here.

"I am sitting opposite Lady Hamilton as I write," he informed his wife. As he was. She came in just as you began to miss her, and sometimes, frequently, before.

"Are you writing dispatches?" she asked.

"Only to my wife. It does not matter."

"And what is she like, your wife?"

He could not immediately say. She was a little colorless; she resembled no one. He could not hit upon a comparison. "Oh, she is a young lady much like yourself, much concerned with country affairs, gossip and peach bottling in the proper season."

"I do not gossip," said Emma, "though I have, it is true, occasioned much, and besides, you are wrong—I have never bottled a peach, in or out of season. Though spiced, with meat, they are often served here."

"I am devoted to my wife," said Nelson, whom young ladies made nervous, particularly the older ones. "Indeed, if I had more time . . ."

"You would be about your devotions," said Emma.

Nelson blushed. When he thought of Fanny, it was to see her always fully clothed and far away. She was a distant woman.

As for Emma, had she been a lady, he would not have thought her one, but as she was not, he did. His view of the aristocracy was highly colored. So was she, and Fanny's views of eminence were so discreetly washed out as to seem unreal and colorless. He must say he liked the upper classes better colored in. King Parrot has more to say than King Sparrow, a wider range of vocables, says please and thank you, and is less monotonous. He does not peep.

Fanny peeped. So did her letters. Mr. Ramsey was ill. Mr. Squire was ill of a thorough scouring, after a stoppage of two days and a night. Mr. Bolton had sent fine lobsters and a hare, but the fish and poultry were deplorable. The other four pages were about the advancement of her son Josiah. She did not seem to realize he had stepped into a larger room. It was all most muddling.

Emma bent over him, uncorseted, solicitous, high-bosomed and warm.

"It is evening," she said. "I thought perhaps you would care to admire the lights."

"What lights?"

"Why, the lights of the evening," she said, and led him to the balcony, which overlooked the main façade of the Palazzo Sesso. Three thousand self-feeding lamps spelled out his name across the front of the building. Sometimes their flames blew all one way, sometimes another, according as the breeze blew. They were like stars put in their proper order. It was the fame for which he had burned, and now it burned for him. He was moved.

She had been watching his face with the wary amusement of a good cook watching a guest test a pie. She is so sure of the outcome that she does not require to be thanked.

In the city, a rocket arched, broke, and descended into nothingness. It was followed by another, even more abundant; its color jostled in the air, like dew on an invisible leaf, and then bounced off into darkness. Squibs went off like cannon, the rockets in volleys.

Turning to look over the bay, he saw his name there, reflected backward from a set piece—anchors, wreaths and stars, in white, red, green, and yellow—writ in water, twenty feet across, and there was no tide. He shivered, gooseflesh all over, and backed away.

"There will be more," she said as the rockets faded, thinking him disappointed. "Nelson's name is now eternal."

The sky, empty for the moment, reminded him of the lull in any night battle, with the sea full of jetsam and burning, and here and there a scream, a curse, a burst of light.

"You must forgive me," he said, startled not to anger but to sadness. He felt as a man feels who has gotten with difficulty to the head of the stairs only to discover there is yet another flight to the attic above. "I have not been famous long. I must get used to it."

"You will," she said, with a confidence which startled him even more. No patient is soothed by being told he has a common ailment. He looked down. The street was full of people, waiting down there in the earthy obscurity, like bulbs. When he smiled, they burst noisily into bloom. They applauded.

"Emma," Sir William had said once, "you must never look down on royalty. They are not meant to be seen from above." But she had forgotten it. She bowed. Nelson bowed. What else was he to do? To retreat, rigid, would have been discourteous. And having bowed once, he must do so again. So he did so again.

Emma was delighted. To play Britannia suited her so well that you could almost hear the ophidian slither of her corselet when she did not so much move as shift her trident for a little while and gather in her shield.

"Poor man, he looks undernourished. He wants a fortifying jelly," said Mrs. Cadogan.

"Bring one and I will take it to him." Emma was trembling.

"That I can do myself. He's scarcely fit to be seen."

"What is all the noise downstairs?"

"That Miss Knight," said Mrs. Cadogan, without pleasure. "Not only has she moved in kit and caboodle, but now it seems she has written an ode. She is reciting it."

Emma had isolated her astonishment. "You know, I do not mind the stump one bit."

"Ah well, he's famous now. It's not his fault, poor lamb," said Mrs. Cadogan, and since she loved a hero even more than a gentleman, went off happily to the kitchens to supervise the exact perfections of a mutton broth and skim the scum.

"The British Nelson rivals Caesar's fame," declaimed Miss Knight, in her best leno, looking somber, as a sibyl should.

> "Like him he came, he saw, he overcame.
> In conquest modest, as in action brave,
> To God the glory pious Nelson gave.

> From Gallia, Bonaparte sailed,
> Nelson from Albion's sea.
> Chains were our lot if one prevail,
> The other [and here she paused] sets us free."

If no good at Attitudes, she could at least make the proper gestures, and did. There was applause, and even Sir William favored her with a smile. She was content. She had done well. She was a poetess and an admiral's daughter. For the rest, she could do no more than Pope and lisp in numbers till the numbers came.

"Lady Hamilton has been an angel," said Nelson.

"She has her moods," said Sir William easily, and because his leg was tapping, crossed it the other way.

"A ministering angel."

"The mother has much to do with it. She is an excellent plain cook," said Sir William, echoing, without knowing it, the Greville of fifteen years before. He liked the boy exceedingly.

"She is really delightful."

Not wishing to see too much, Sir William looked away, and sure enough, when he looked back again the expression had gone. Sensing itself to be unwelcome, it had vanished utterly. It would have been foolish to notice it when the boy, he was sure, was unaware of it himself. So many things vanish if we do not notice them. However, here and there Sir William had managed to save a few, for he saved appearances from habit, like bits of old string. You never knew when they might come in handy.

The 29th was Nelson's birthday. Emma, in a mood of austerity suitable to war, had formerly restricted herself to small intimate dinners for eighty, but this time decided to do the thing properly. She enjoyed to play hostess and did it well, and would have asked the world to dine had she been able to procure so large a table, or borrow enough plates. While she arranged the guest lists, Nelson, propped up in bed, was posing for his portrait, which had been commissioned by the Queen. The artist was one of a corps which did the royal children in relays, a man called Guzzardi.

"It is not necessary to rise," said Guzzardi. "The body, I can make up from stock."

Nelson felt irritably the absence of an arm. The best that could be said for the fellow was that he worked rapidly. The result was a flounder in uniform.

Sir William was displeased. "It will do very well, but it should not be given the currency of an engraving."

"My wife has had my portrait of Lemuel Abbott," said Nelson. "I own it is a better likeness." Abbott had shown him—if not as a member of the aristocracy, as an aristocrat—a most clubbable portrait, when the fleet engaged in battle at the rear.

"Abbott?"

"Some English painter."

"The only English painter was Reynolds, but he is dead and so beyond compare. Lawrence will do in a pinch. If you were County, it would be different. There a certain stiffness in the modeling does no harm."

Nelson felt graveled. In this house, where everything was what it seemed to be, except the people, he began to perceive that appearances were not only everything, but had nothing in common with Fanny's perpetual keeping up of them. To reach fame we must move rapidly and travel light. We grow oppressed by boiled pudding and turnip tops, for they retard us. There can be no butterfly without a metamorphosis, and the butterfly is the emblem of the soul. We must pupate into immortality, rest, exchrysalate, move on, and all on a diet of mulberry leaves and water, and leave each dish untasted, merely to touch them all.

"I like Sir William much," he wrote his wife. It was what a schoolboy would have said of a master who did not whip him, explained the logarithmic tables of society, and told one frankly why one was not popular; it was because one was unique. One could move easily and be welcome, therefore, only among one's peers, of which there are not many, and those not always Peers.

"When people say they want something new, what they

mean is that they want the same old thing, only different. To something new, they are inevitably hostile until it has had the edge taken off it by being imitated at least twice. This is why we admire equally the old genius and the young fop, and prefer, naturally enough, the latter," said Sir William. "So Sir Thomas Lawrence, I think, would do very well." And he looked around proudly at his vases, which had been imitated at least twice by Mr. Wedgwood at Etruria, so their value had soared enormously. The best place to achieve novelty is to rummage in an old closet or down a stopped-up well.

"We must be going," he added, for they were to visit the Royal Porcelain factory that afternoon.

"The King might better," said Nelson, who found all this dilatory when there was fighting to be done, "visit the armory."

"Ah well," said Sir William. "Did you know that one of the designers has had made a porcelain cannon, provided with a caoutchouc breech, which shoots hard candy a distance of six feet? For a while he diverted himself with that. He is concerned with ends, not means. He is ugly and likes to be flattered. Talk up victory to him until he can see it as a self-portrait, all apotheosis and very little blood, and he will soon enough gallop off to pose, once he has chosen the right uniform."

"Battles are not conducted that way."

"No, but they may be composed so, after the event."

"He likes to hunt, so I hear. Why can he not like to hunt the enemy?"

"You have not attended a royal hunt," explained Sir William. "It is not here a tallyho over hedges after hounds. He is a large man, difficult to move. It is three hundred years since anyone in Italy has had the skill to run with the fox and hunt with the hounds. Now they sit motionless in a tent, the game is paraded before them, and then they fire. They like to be sure of their trophies, you see. I assure you, for I have often tried, it is no easy thing to flush a King. They may seem mad, but now and again they lapse into sanity. Besides, he has a most extensive warren."

"Warren is the word for it."

"Nelson," said Sir William, "you have seen too much water. You are indifferent to wool. I have been here thirty years, and have yet to tire of it."

The boy had his limitations, he feared: he had ability. That blinkered him.

At the China manufactory, where Nelson wished to buy the similicra of the King and Queen, hard-glazed, as a gesture, the King prevented it. His own image was within his gift. He might bestow it where he would.

"Let him bestow it upon Rome," said Nelson as they came away, his eye caught by the rustle of the trees which met above their heads, a species he had never seen before. "What trees are these?"

"Mulberry," said Sir William. "There is a manufactory for silk, too. We are fair to rival China, though not in bulk."

"Nelson," said Emma, titivating, "is curiously attractive."

"Oh, Em," said Mrs. Cadogan—who had eyes in her head, though it is difficult to be Argus with but two, and those drowsy—"can you never leave well enough alone?"

"I only meant a title will suit him. Why does it not come?"

"A picture must dry before it is varnished," said Mrs. Cadogan. "Such things take always a year. Besides, he has a wife."

"So had Sir William," said Emma idly, meaning no harm.

"Em, you are wicked."

"If Sir William is a father to him, it is only natural I should be motherly," said Emma, and for the instant had an image of her unacknowledged daughter, wandering bleakly along the northern coast in a sea fog, rattling the shale underfoot and doing—what? There had been a letter from her, too painful to answer, which she had mentioned to no one. "It might have been happy for me to have forgotten the past and to have begun a new life with new ideas; but for my misfortune, my memory traces back circumstances which have taught me too much, yet not quite all I could have wished to have known," the poor thing had said.

It is neither true nor fair to say that women have no memory. What they do have is a series of bulkheads and watertight compartments by means of which they manage to stay afloat. The image of Emma Carew gurgled and went under; despite this collision with fact, what Emma did not remember kept her afloat. In the gorgeous staterooms of dream and illusion above deck, there was no awareness—except for a slight shudder along the frame—that anything untoward had occurred.

Acknowledge her, never; but help to get her settled, yes.

"You will be adding Jocasta to the Attitudes next, I expect," said Mrs. Cadogan, far from pleased. Having not much employment these days, she too, like the rest of them, now read a lot.

It was the day of the birthday party.

Over a drink beforehand in the green room, so to speak, Sir William gave the private toast, *Tria juncta in uno,* in allusion to both the motto of the Order of the Bath and that total immersion called Christianity. He did not mind. Besides, a mild flirtation at thirty-four, what was the harm in that? He should be uncle to both of them—husband to the one, and intimate with the other. Why not?

"I wonder you could live here so long and so seldom go back," said Nelson, exacerbated by so much light, who, when he was at sea, had usually the comfort of a British ship.

"My friends drop off from life, like satiated leeches, and my parents are long dead," said Sir William. "I would as soon return to an orphanage." He had been plagued recently by a pestilence of childhood images, gray fields, stone walls and green summer rain. Since to be so is a symptom of old age, he refused to accept his own diagnosis. If we cannot deny the disease, we can at least conceal the symptoms.

Emma, her life until now singularly sheltered on the leeside of a variable but solid male rock, and by the absence of any female friend, from those little gusts of affection which presage the usual jealous storm, had foolishly taken up Miss Knight as a protégée, who had as foolishly, her life hitherto sheltered from the great world by exclusion from it, allowed herself to be taken up. If someone admires our little effusions, it would be tactless of us to question their probity, so Miss Knight added her small stone to the mound of Emma's adulation both willingly and well, and waited now only to hear her own praises.

The British Embassy, like any church, had been better designed for the extraordinary crush than for the occasional visitor, so this time Emma had asked everyone. They sat down eighty to dine, and when they rose there were a thousand more.

In the ballroom, in a costume militant in intent but millinery in detail, she stood waiting while the national anthem played. The guests fingering, if males, their Nelson buttons, if females, their Nelson ribbons, awaited the entertainment. The anthem had additional verses by Miss Knight:

> Join we great Nelson's fame
>   First on the roll of fame,
>   Him let us sing.
> Spread we his praise around,
>   Honour of British ground,
>   Who made Nile's shores resound,
>   God save the King.

Miss Knight looked about her. Whose were these new words? They had been written by a talented young lady, a Miss Knight, the daughter of Admiral Knight (known as *good* Admiral Knight, actually). She was over there.

"I know you will sing it with pleasure," Nelson wrote his wife. "I cannot move on foot or in a carriage for the kindness of the populace, but good Lady Hamilton preserves all the papers as the highest treat for you."

And out fell the disgusting things, in *her* handwriting, when the letter arrived.

A curtain parted before the rostrum.

Lady Hamilton, a Boadicea in white muslin, Greek sandals, a tinsel corselet, a helmet borrowed from the Household Cavalry, and a light blue shawl embossed with gold anchors—carrying in one hand a trident (an exact copy of one found at the Gladiatorial School at Pompeii)—was discovered sitting on a pasteboard rock. Her right elbow was languid to the edge of a replica, in papier-mâché, of the shield of Achilles, the rim surrounded by the motto *Honi soit qui mal y pense* picked out in glitter. She held the pose, rose majestically (it was her new Attitude) and drew apart an inner curtain to reveal a rostral column, beneath a canopy, emblazoned with the words *Veni, Vidi, Vici* (a translation, also by Miss Knight, was available) and inscribed with the names of Nelson's captains.

It was never to come down while they were there, Lady Hamilton said, and went offstage to change, though not much.

"What precious moments the Courts of Naples and Vienna are losing. Three months would liberate Italy," said Nelson.

At the supper given immediately after the performance, they sat eight hundred.

"If the Queen would receive me," complained Nelson, "one could perhaps accomplish much. They say she can make the King do as she wishes, and surely she, at least, wants war. But they say she is ill."

"She is not ill," said Sir William. "She is pregnant. She will get over it. Emma, my dear, it is time for you to intercede."

Like a goddess of victory, Emma went off to oblige, wreath in hand and at the ready.

"I know," said the Queen. "But he will not budge. It is not so much that he is unwilling as that he is inert. However, I will try. If he cannot follow, he can at least be led. But it is not an effort I look forward to, my dear. It calls for kid gloves."

And, ringing, she called for the longest procurable, and, like a surgeon, pulled them on and set to the revolting task.

"It is done," she said afterward. "He slobbered more than usual, but it is done." And stripping off the wetted things, she flung them away into a basket set beside the table, and granted an interview to Nelson, who though a foreigner, impressed her favorably.

However was it managed? Nelson wondered.

But royalty is a trade, like any other, and like any other has its guild secrets. The Queen would not say, and even Sir William did not seem to know.

"She must handle him with gloves," he said. Oedipus with the Sphinx could have said no more.

"The King, I hear, has ordered a set of china with all my battles painted upon it," snapped Nelson. "I will not speak of the impropriety of the *Vanguard* upon a gravy boat, but what battles will he have to set forth when he comes to order his own, or do I have to fight them for him? Or should I suspect him of a taste so simple as to prefer his dishes plain?"

Impatient with Naples, he sailed off to Malta, his departure all Dido and Aeneas at the dock. Lady Hamilton said she would write frequently.

She was annoyed he had not yet gotten his title. "If I were King of England, I would make you the Most Noble Puissant Duke Nelson, Viscount Pyramid and Baron Crocodile," she wrote Nelson. And to his wife: "Sir William is in a rage with the ministry for not having made Lord Nelson a Viscount, for sure, this great and glorious action ought to have been recognized more. Hang them, I say."

Nelson's brother William was also displeased. Though the title had been granted, he had written with an anxiety fresh minted, to ask who might—for Nelson was childless—inherit this honor next. "I have no doubt but Parliament will settle the same pension upon yourself and the two next possessors of your title which they have done upon Lord Vincent," he wrote, for if he were to inherit the loaf, he wished it buttered.

They are in love with each other, I suppose, thought Sir William, driving back from the dock, and himself affected by the parting. I wonder if they know it?

No, they did not. For though Nelson was a good husband, and Emma an excellent wife, fond, affectionate and scrupulous, to love is quite another thing. Since neither of them ever had, they had not the means to make comparisons and so identify the feeling.

I wonder if I should know it? Sir William further inquired of himself, and decided, with some relief, the answer was no. There is a limit to the number of things a man may reasonably be expected to know, and in this matter, at any rate, he had no desire to play the pedant. Grateful that the oracle had spoken, he shut his eyes and basked, a lizard, in the sun.

"I am glad, my dear, that you have had this diversion," he said to Emma, out of his voluntary darkness. "It has improved your appearance tenfold."

As so it had, for appearance and attitudes, if not everything, are all we have left, so it behooves us to take care of them.

"It is wonderful how the old man keeps up," said someone in the crowd as their carriage rolled by.

Aware that he was also called *"verde antico,"* Sir William opened his eyes and gave the woman who had spoken a look to wither stone.

On the plain at San Germano, the Queen, in a blue riding habit with gold fleurs-de-lis at the neck, was reviewing both the troops and Ferdinand previous to the promised invasion—which is to say, relief—of Rome.

On the 22nd of November, the army marched out, its progress interrupted only by a river—the existence of which it had not been informed—and by the seasonal rains which had come down all at once. A declaration of war against France (then occupying Rome) was not thought necessary. Ferdinand was a liberator, not an aggressor, and intended that his action should be considered as well meant.

It went on raining. Sir William had gone to bed, but not to sleep, for downstairs Emma was singing, and the sound buzzed about like a fly in an acoustical trap. It was a piece called "The Maniac."

"When thirst and hunger griev'd her most,
   If any food she took,
It was the berry from the thorn [trill]
   The water from the brook.
From every hedge a flower she pluck'd,
   And moss from every stone,
To make a garland for her Love,
   Yet left it still undone.
Still as she rambled was she wont
   To trill a plaintive song [gurgle].
'Twas wild, and full of fancies vain,
   Yet suited well her wrong.
Oft too a smile, but not of joy [ah, the last stanza]
   Play'd on her brow o'ercast;
It was the faint cold smile of spring
   Ere winter [triumphantly] is past."

Repeat ten times. It was her preferred piece these days. No doubt she found it fraught with meaning, though he wondered how. Eventually the sound ceased. The rain did not. It was a fluid portcullis beyond the window, caught and sparkling in the rays of his lamp. He did not extinguish the lamp. He liked one these days, for company.

When he woke, the rain had momentarily ceased. The room was motionless, the lamp low. He lay just beneath the surface of consciousness, as though under a wet sheet, unable as yet to move. The lamp cast bizarre reflections. At home in Scotland, as a child, he had at this point always demanded a glass of water, because there were funny animals on the walls. And though Lady Archibald had never been there herself, the nanny had always provided one and never denied the existence of the animals; it was an old house—of course they were there. With a charm against dragons, human company and a glass of water, we may achieve much.

"When you grow up," his nanny had said, "you may ride them to Jerusalem."

Curious, she was so pleasant, though of course no gruff and nonsense, that he had forgotten her until now. Though he had been riding to Jerusalem ever since, through pleasant enough country, except for high jinks in the 3rd Guards, and a few moments early on in both his marriages. Now he was in a single bed, in an empty room—as he preferred—with no one to tuck him in, but with a jug of water and a tantalus of brandy near his reach.

Sitting up, he poured himself a jigger, neat.

In the country house of a great-aunt, he had once asked what the rings in the wall were for, along the stairs. Were they for prisoners? Where was the dungeon?

"Your aunt is old and infirm. They are to pull herself to the top of the stairs by."

"And what is at the top of the stairs?"

"All sorts of good things, but there was never a dungeon here, you silly boy. This is quite a recent house."

Since his aunt had died—or as they said, gone to Heaven—shortly afterward, it had always seemed to him that that was where Heaven was, at the top of the stairs. Himself he hauled along by another method, by certain crampons driven in the rock walls of time, called appointments and events. He had the route marked out for him well in advance, in his agenda. If he had not, he might well have lost his way or taken a turning downward.

"Oh well," he said, "there is nothing to be done about it." He listened to the silence meditatively for a moment or two, and brandy being a soporific, dropped back into sleep.

To dress in the morning was more difficult, for to dress marble is an art and requires both strength *and* skill.

"I wish you would not sing that song again," he said.

"Why ever not?" asked Emma, astonished, after so long without one, to be handed an order, even if tied up quite prettily as a request.

"Because I do not like it," said Sir William.

She gave it up. She had still the will to please, if not any longer the constraint.

I do believe she is still quite attached to me, thought Sir William kindly—who up to this moment had never doubted it, but liked to believe the best of everyone, though his thoughts were his own—and gave her money for the household accounts. If we stay on long enough, we all become our own paying guests in time. Besides, he had no real desire to move on.

What he did have was a very real desire for male company. There is this to be said for vases: they do not change their shape.

On the 29th of November came the momentous news that Ferdinand had entered Rome to the pealing of bells and the plaudits of the populace. Two weeks later came the no less momentous news that he was scampering back. Though he had not declared war against France, he had at least provided the French with an excellent excuse to invade him. Nelson returned two days before he did, bearing starch.

"Let the people arm; let them succor the Faith; let them defend their King and father who risks his life, ready to sacrifice it in order to preserve the altars, possessions, domestic honor and freedom of his subjects," proclaimed the King. "Let them remember their ancient valor."

Surprisingly enough, they did, with the exception of a few Jacobins—too busy planning a republic to attend to the collapse of the kingdom—and such of the nobility as were off in the Augean stables, to curry favor. The people rose.

The King cowered and sank. From now on, white gloves or no, he would run no risk. He was a reflective man, even though in his case the trick was done with mirrors. He knew very well what faith to put in the unpredictability of crowds.

It was a hubbub.

VI

"I SHALL AWAIT THE FRENCH surrounded by my loyal subjects!" roared Ferdinand, a royal boom, by now hysterical.

"Of course you shall," said Sir William reassuringly—who had known the King for thirty years—and then himself went home to pack. Or rather, since he had never tied so much as a parcel in his life, sat anguished in a chair while around him his entire life so far was wrapped up and hustled away. Even Emma in fifty versions came down from the walls, was crated and jostled off through the midnight streets in a cart, to be flung into the hold with who knew what indifference.

"We must save your collections at all costs," she had said, but since she supervised the packing herself, naturally made her own choice of what must go first. Nelson had given them the use of two bottoms, one bound for England, the other for wherever they were to go. Though he did not value such things, he valued Sir William. He had been most civil.

Emma, twenty years younger, as Impudence, was carried out past Sir William. He did not notice. Vase after vase went into crates. Even the six over-door panels by Brill, depicting the four seasons and then two more, had been stripped from his rooms.

Emma when young was being carted away. The whole

world when young was being carted away, down to the napery and the silverware. He felt sacked. Even if he got it back, it could never be put up again the same way. In a few days nothing would be left of him except what was left to him, which would not be much: a small Hellenistic bronze for the ship's cabin; a code of honor, a willingness to oblige, and a worn suppleness at how to do it; a hand, some ink, a pen; and what was left of Emma; and Nelson, now and again, he supposed. With his old friends dead or in England, he had forgotten how pleasant it was to make a new one. Even the Bishop of Derry had been impounded in Milan, by the French, and the devil knew how he would get out again.

Nelson, though deficient in manners, was what Greville should have been, who had too many but was compounded of nothing else.

Indubitably sacked, but no massacre is ever complete. Somewhere in the dust and rubble there is always someone to stir and struggle to his feet again, dazed perhaps, but not dead. Odd that it is more often an old woman than an old man, an old either than a child or a youth, but there it is: if you have survived so far, you can survive more.

"Hamilton," he said, "don't be a fool. Get up." Obediently Sir William rose to this, as to most occasions. He had come to depend upon it. An autocrat is the puppet of himself: he obeys, as why not, for it is he who gives the orders. If there is nobody else to love, we look around, make our only choice, and love ourselves. Sir William had no emotions of that comfortable sort. What Sir William loved was order. So rather than sit about like a numbskull, that is what he set himself to achieve.

But Emma had been invaluable. A country girl, she had laid her hands to everything, in a manner in which the aristocrat, socially constrained from birth to pretend he was born without any, cannot. For that he was grateful; it excused much.

Nelson's new coat of arms had come, properly inscribed at the top of letters patent.

"Is it not pretty?" she asked, having scarcely time to look at it herself.

Sir William saw a shield with a Maltese cross, surrounded by the *Tria juncta in uno* of the Order of the Bath, surmounted by an open helmet, a bar, and a man of war seen from the captain's cabin end. The motto was *Faith and Works*. The supporters were, over *Works*, a Lion with a pennant in its mouth, the staff of which stuck into space like a secretary's pen; and over *Faith*, a comely, clean and graceful sailor boy.

"All too appropriate," he said, and handed it back.

A message arrived from the Queen. She sent one whenever she was depressed, so these days they arrived almost hourly.

"She is worried about her head," said Emma. "Whatever will it be next?"

"Her head?"

"Of having it cut off."

"It is too long and square in the face," said Sir William. "Give her my compliments and say I doubt that it would roll."

He was snappish these days.

"I can't say that. I suppose I shall have to fit her in somewhere," said Emma, who had risen not only superior to events, but to the cause of them.

When she returned, she felt no better. The palace had had a boarded-up look, and since the Court was in mourning, you saw black figures at the end of empty corridors, standing about like frightened nuns, or with the naked look of defrocked priests. The Queen talked of death as though it were an experience she had just been through, and the King, though he was taller than six feet, ran back and forth like a little dog already left behind.

"I am making ready for the eternity for which I long," shrieked the Queen, supervising two ladies in waiting who were packing a trunk. "Take only summer dresses," she said, and supervised the jewelry herself. "The King decides to stay. The King decides to leave. If we stay, we shall need nothing; if we are leaving, we shall be packed. You see, I prepare."

But she did not know how. Removing, tactfully, a tiara from a dress hoop, Emma took charge. These movables, when crated, were stenciled HIS BRITANNIC MAJESTY'S SERVICE, NAVAL STORES, BISCUIT AND BULLY BEEF, smuggled to the British Embassy, and then taken aboard Nelson's ships at night. The *Vanguard* was being repainted and refitted for the royal refugees. The smell of white lead was strong.

"The King has had the Minister for War arrested," said Sir William.
"Good Lord, why?"
"For treason. It is ever the fault of the losing side."
"The poor King," said Emma feelingly.
"It cannot be denied that he cuts a very poor figure."

"No time should be lost," urged Acton, "if the wind does not blow too hard." Inclined to be seasick, he would have preferred an overland journey, but, alas, Sicily cannot be reached that way. Yet the King, who had had a toy altar as a child—as well as toy soldiers—could not make up his mind, and still hoped for Divine intervention, though they were running low on candles.

In the end, it was made up for him.

Defense of the Realm, to the *lazzaroni*, meant slitting the throats of Jacobins up an alley, disemboweling a Frenchman, and the looting of an unprotected store. Undeniably they were picturesque, but to combine irregularity into the picturesque—as the Reverend Gilpin says—requires taste, and they had none. They had surrounded the palace. The King was their father, who dwelt in Caserta, a man exactly like themselves who sold fish in the market and when he went hunting did his own butchery. He was tall, virile and ugly. They worshiped him in their own image. But they would not let him go.

"If I run away, they will think I have abandoned them," said the King. "I will never abandon them. They are my people. Besides, how can we get away?"

He had to present himself daily on the balcony, to prevent their storming the palace.

"Give us arms," they shouted, "to defend ourselves and you!" Alas, there were no arms. They had been flung into ditches to rust, by the fleeing army.

"Death to the Jacobin!" they screamed.

"Now what?" said the King, and though afraid, could control neither his legs nor his curiosity, and crept back to the balcony again.

The crowd was tearing apart one of his own messengers, mistaking, or pretending to mistake, him for the enemy. The man had time for one scream before his hands and face were booted to a pulp, his clothes ripped off, his penis and testicles knifed out like spilt, his belly slit, his intestines allowed to dangle and his corpse held up in the air—an offering still smoking because it was still warm.

The King himself, after the hunt, could have done the job no better and had done it a hundred thousand times just as well. It took no time. It was highly enjoyable. And it did not matter what the carcass was.

He went back indoors.

"His Majesty," said Maria Carolina in a hand note to Emma, "has graciously consented to flee."

"I am disappointed in him. He has been inconsistent. One would have expected him to have waited until too late," said Sir William. "But how the devil is it to be done?"

"There is a tunnel," said Emma.

Ferdinand had at last remembered it, a bugaboo from childhood, the family escape hatch, to be opened only in case of dire peril, like Joanna Southcote's chest, which was packed providentially with pistols, rather than advice; for even the wildest and most hysteric dreamer is practical about his nightmares. His father, the King of Spain, had once told him it was there, and he had workmen in the cellars for a week, searching the chthonic dark till at last they found it. It was the way out of the labyrinth. After they had marked it with rags, he had them securely locked up. He was indeed a minotaur. Even the horns had come with time.

It had been a disagreeable afternoon, with Miss Knight and her mother practicing hysterics like scales, until let into the secret. Even Emma was at a loss for words, though she had had the finesse, in the cardplaying sense, to order a cold supper laid out against their return from a visit to the Turkish Embassy, since no public event could be canceled lest public confidence be alarmed. She then dismissed the servants, a reassuring act in itself; Rome is always burning to have a holiday, and no one dismissed for good is ever given the evening off first.

The streets were sullen, except for the chanting of invisible priests and a shriek now and then up a dark lane.

"Why must they wail both before and after the event?"

"They are a histrionic people. If one feels nothing, one must show much," said Sir William, huddled in the carriage.

Out in the bay the lights of Nelson's hurriedly gathered fleet twinkled and receded although at anchor, desolate as a carnival in the rain.

The King and Queen arrived at the Embassy together.

"Consistent in everything, ignoble to the last," said Sir William, but only because he was sad. It was too much like a play on the last night; it may not have been good, but the actors will never act in it again and we will never again see it this way. And yet the action was the same as any other night, the scenery the same, the lights the same, the lines the same.

The Ambassador presented the chelengkh, a frost of diamonds, a plume of honor taken from the turban of the Grand Signor himself, a star surrounded by thirteen sprays of the same adamantine material. It was to honor Nelson.

"It is watchwork," said Kelim Effendi carefully. "You wind it up. Then when you press this"—and he did so—"the star revolves. It is amusing, no?"

It was a whirligig. It ran down.

A little man rose up at Emma's elbow. It was Aprile.

"It is the dawn of a new age, my friends say. But do not vex yourself. I shall neither give you away nor get away. I was adapted to the old one. I only want to say that it was a pleasure once more to hear you sing. The effect is not good, but you do it so well. Whereas with us, it is the other way," he said, and before Emma could stop him, with a twitch, he had wriggled away.

The King and Queen returned to the palace. Emma and Sir William drove to the quay, where a launch awaited them.

Sir William had to be lifted down, and what was more, did not seem satisfied with his seat. The boat rocked. The gunwales were but two inches from the water.

"Be still, William, do," snapped Emma, for it was only a city she was leaving. Sir William these days, to tell the truth, was difficult to manage.

"I must sit in the prow," he said. "I must sit in the prow." And like a blind man, he groped his way there and sat there alone, an hour's journey to the ships, while the lamps of the festive city burned low, and unreplenished, went out, his eyes steady, watching Vesuvius, a dark hulk, moored against the sky.

It was not for some time that he realized she was not with him.

She had gone to the palace. If she had snapped at him, she had cause. In order not to alarm the servants, they had taken only the best things, the vases and pictures, and so been forced to abandon three houses elegantly furnished, all their horses and seven carriages.

There was no reason for William to sit there unique. She had loved Naples, too. But Palermo (it must be kept a secret that that was their destination) was said to be a fine city, and she had never seen it. Sir William had often spoken of Sicily with approbation, as of a place full of interest. Therefore why sit so glum?

Nelson, standing alone on the marble floor of the grand staircase, waited in the almost dark. The palace when empty gave him the shudders. It was too much like going into St. Paul's of a weekday, when God is not there but the thing we are really afraid of is, and skulks in the walls.

The stairs went up into infinity. "Nelson," he said, to reassure himself, and from every undusted corridor came the hollow answer back.

A white figure swirled out of the shadows.

"Emma," he said, astonished.

"I could not desert the dear Queen," she said, and squeezed his hand.

There was a snuffle on the stairs, and a fox fire on the other one, of candles. A sconce moved toward them, and a great boar's head appeared out of nowhere. It was Ferdinand. The snuffling materialized into the Queen, a hatbox and all eight children, one of them in arms.

Somewhere above them a chair fell, a glass smashed.

Ferdinand giggled. "We have left only the heavy things. Heavy things will be difficult to loot," he said, and followed Nelson, Emma and the Queen down a landscape of empty picture frames, moving through rooms he had never known existed, kitchens, storerooms, wine bins, cellars, vaults, and down stairs that were damp and dripped, and no one anywhere. On the walls the shadow of his own enormous nose marched on ahead of him. He followed it.

The air turned warm. They were underground. A rat's eyes gleamed. A spider ran across the dirt floor. A white rag formed up out of darkness. And there was the tunnel, so well concealed there had been no need to hide its opening. It was just a tunnel. It led to the underworld. It was not frequented.

The King held back. The Queen pushed on, with no one to aid her, stumbled, and was angry with everything. The darkness closed behind them against an animal rush of fetid air. Though it had a main gorge, it was not just one tunnel but a maze of bronchial passages through which the sluggish wind breathed itself in and out. There was nothing to see ahead but a small white rag, and then another, until at last there was a bend and ahead of them an alternating glitter, as from off the points of spears.

The passage, which was not paved, became muddy and slippery, and there, two steps down, lay the water. They had been fortunate that the tide was at its ebb. It was, so Nelson said, the Vittoria landing stage.

When he flashed his lantern, a longboat appeared out of the low mist which now clung to the waters. Two hours later, for they had to move cautiously, they reached the *Vanguard,* where Sir William was reading Epictetus in bed:

> As a true balance is neither set right by a true one, nor judged false by a false one; so likewise a just person has neither to be set right by just persons, nor to be judged by unjust ones. As it is pleasant to view the sea from the shore, so it is pleasant to one who has escaped, to remember his past labors.

Quite so.
But Emma had left him.
In the bay, little dark shapes everywhere along the fringes of the city put out into the bay.

"Before we reach Palermo," said Sir William to Emma as she came in, "we must remember to hoist a white sail. As usual, your Theseus has done well."

"My Theseus?"

"Horatio, but the legend is confused," said Sir William, who would rather have rescued himself, and went to sleep.

Others had to wait longer for their dormitive. Lady Knight and her daughter drew alongside.

"I am sorry, but we are already full. There is no room," said Captain Hardy. "You must go to the Portuguese man-of-war."

"My mother is the widow of Admiral Sir Joseph

Knight," said Miss Cornelia, the poetess, her nerves frayed to the point of a beseeching ostentation.

"I am sorry, but there really *is* no room," said Hardy, "but the Portuguese man-of-war has an English captain." He meant it kindly.

So off into the dark they went, all Virgil and Dante and no room at the inn.

In the large, airy and freshly painted state cabin— the smallest, most wretched chamber she had ever seen —the Queen peeled off her own stockings and looked at her first pair of dirty feet. Also it was unpleasant to discover that rumor was no invention: Ferdinand snored. Not even in the Temple had her sister known such squalor or suffered such indignity, of that she was sure. Lady Hamilton was asleep, and as for water, she knew not whom to ask for it. It was intolerable.

"It is disgusting," said Maria Carolina, "to sleep in the same squalid chamber with a man, and that one your husband. It is too promiscuous."

Having had to linger at Naples for two days because of contrary winds, they were now at sea, or rather up to their waists in it, for they had encountered the worst storm in Nelson's experience. There was nowhere to lie down. A Russian gentlewoman, known to none of them, had with the blunt but polite intransigence of that singularly mysterious race commandeered the only bed available below deck, and lay there, clutching an icon, while ladies in waiting no doubt better born than she slithered and sloshed about on soggy mattresses. She was heavily bejeweled. If sink she must, she meant to sink well.

Sir William, in whom age had suddenly revealed the Scot, with a Calvinistic cunning both atavistic and autochthonous, stirred nowhere without two pistols at his belt, determined to shoot rather than drown. He did not intend to die with a *guggle, guggle, guggle* in his throat, he said.

Every time you called a cabin boy, he had been swept overboard; it was another one. Every bowl in the boat had been puked in, but to look on the cheerful side of things, since no one had appetite, there was little chance of their running short on stores. The mainmast had already gone, the mizzenmast could scarcely wait, and "wild to the blast flew the skull and the bones."

Emma, however, who had had to master her stomach quite early on in life's woes, felt no affliction, and was everywhere to tend to those who did. Nelson was proud of her. And she of him. They spoke companionably when they met. The barriers were down. In that weather, they could not long have stayed up.

Count Esterhazy, the Austrian Ambassador, in a religious fit had tossed his snuffbox overboard, for it had his mistress painted nude on the lid and would not look well in Heaven. Prince Carlo Alberto had convulsions and died in Emma's arms, though that was no great loss. He was only six, he could scarcely be considered a personage as yet, and there were royal heirs aplenty still remaining.

The wind changed to a *tramontana*. The King, quickly recovered and excellently well, condescended to say that there would be plenty of woodcocks in Sicily—this wind always brought them—and that he and Sir William might therefore look forward to splendid sport.

"Well," said Mrs. Cadogan, that sensible deity, "why not? The dear man only looks upon the good side of things. I would not myself object to a woodcock pie."

"*Entombez-moi,*" said the Russian lady, in desperate French, "*à Odesse. C'est une petite jolie ville en Crimée, le pays de ma naissance, òu sont situées nos domaines hérèditaires. Tcheripnin doit faire la gisante. C'est mon désir.*"

"*Elle pousse un cri,*" said the ladies in waiting, wringing out their mattresses. It was Christmas day. At two in the morning they dropped anchor in Palermo Harbor.

The Queen insisted upon going ashore at once.

"I have lived long enough," she said gloomily, "even two or three years too long," and disappeared into the darkness, bound for the Colli Palace, where nothing had been aired for sixty years, nobody expected her, and everything was uninhabitable.

"My God," she said at dawn, her fate made visible, "it is *Africa*. Am I to be plagued by the blackamoor as well?" She needed laudanum.

But the King refused to budge until he had slept, risen, been shaved, and consumed a lengthy breakfast. Then, calling his favorite dogs to him (they had slept in the cabin, though refusing to go near the Queen), he ambled out into the cold but southern sun, determined to make the best of it. If he had not burned his boats behind him, he had at least left orders that they should be burned lest they fall into the hands of the French, so he did not fear pursuit. He was King of the Two Sicilies, and if he had lost one, here was the other, and one would do.

"Viva il Re!" shout the populace. *"Viva il Re!"* It was all quite customary.

"The King," wrote Emma admiringly, "is a philosopher." So he was, but Pliny the Elder was laid up with a bilious fever, the Queen had near died, and lodgings were exceedingly hard come by.

The Knights, with that heroic skill to which the incompetent sometimes unimaginatively rise, had seized the only habitable apartment on the *Marina*.

"It was the most tremendous good fortune," said Cornelia, but it was not a good fortune she was prepared to share. She and her mother were quite civil; they even nodded to Captain Hardy, *but there was no room*. Poor Sir William, accustomed as he was to palaces, must feel quite cast out.

"Accustomed as I had been to the lovely and magnificent scenery of Italy," wrote Miss Knight, "I was not less surprised than delighted at the picturesque beauty of the Sicilian Coast. Then, when the prospect of the city opened upon us with the regal elegance of its marble palaces and the fanciful singularity of its remaining specimens of Saracenic architecture, it was like a fairy scene." And, dipping unobserved a wedge of *panettone* into her morning coffee, she giggled like a girl. In the general gallop and galumph ashore, she had for once come out first. She admired the beauties of nature and drank her slops.

But it was cold. It was bitter cold. The stark trees and naked twigs were rimed and icicled, and stuck up all over the landscape like bleached coral on a surfaced barrier reef.

"Light a fire," said the Queen.

"But why? It is only winter. There is no wood. It is always like this."

"I demand fire!" shouted the Queen.

"Let her go to the devil, then," said the King when he heard of it. He would not see her. He blamed her for everything. He ordered a *chinoiserie* casino built on the seashore, and moved into that. He wanted no more of her.

Deprived not only of her creature comforts but of her creatures as well, there was nothing for Maria Carolina to do but shiver, shake, tremble, freeze, steal wood, eat cold porridge, and write letters, with a small oil lamp on the table over which to thaw her fingers every time they froze. Death, suicide, shame, decline, woe, weeping and despair—it was all the same to her. She had a facile pen. She made them vivid.

"The King," she wrote to Vienna, "feels nothing but self-love, and he hardly feels that."

On the contrary, though insensible to cold, he was keenly aware of the pleasures of the chase, as always, and went daily through the Breughel woods. "Do come, Sir William," he said.

Lese majesty is not a crime with which to charm any but complacent princes. As soon as he could move, Sir William went. Emma and Nelson could manage between them, though what was between them, he knew not.

Emma, without sleep for twelve days, was plainly hysterical; but soon enough, brushing the cobwebs away, she was herself again and able the more articulately to lament.

"We miss our dear, dear Naples," she said, thinking

of wardrobes adequately hung, a row of surrogate selves, all swaying, all waiting to be put on.

Nelson, together with the Hamiltons, for want of any other where and to save money, had set up mutual housekeeping in the Palazzo Palagonia. One splendid chamber opened out into another, and the wind blew through and dusted everything. As for the chambermaids, all they did was track in the snow.

Emma enjoyed herself. It was like Cheshire in the winter, but with palm trees.

"On the contrary," said Sir William, "it is worse than Kent, damned cold, damned damp and damned dull."

The King kept their larders stocked with venison, woodcock, partridge, boar and rabbit, but there was a shortage of sallets. Finances were difficult. Greville had triumphantly reduced the income of Milford Haven to nothing and was now endeavoring to borrow against the capital. His efforts might be unremitting, but he himself would remit nothing. Their Naples incomes were confiscate. Sir William had to borrow £2000 from Nelson, and what man likes to borrow money from his own protégé? It was demeaning.

Emma made him marvel. Sentimental people are like volcanic springs: they merely gush, close up, and open for business unimpaired some otherwhere. She seemed to miss Naples not at all. Yet he had to admit that when she had the time she took as good care of him as ever. Only she had not often the time. They none of them had. All naval business was conducted from the house, which meant Emma must act interpreter, since Nelson eschewed Italian and refused French, out of a towering patriotic incompetence. Worst of all, that pewling, mewling heap of diffident disapproval, Josiah Nisbet, was back, soliciting his stepfather's interest.

"He has his nice side," said Emma, about whom he gossiped day and night. She believed in being kind.

"Like the dark side of the moon, no doubt, but we can scarcely expect in our lifetime to see it. Apparently no effort has been spared to bring him here. I would prefer no stone were left unturned to send him back."

"But where can he go?"

"Constantinople," snapped Sir William. "It is the farthest place. He should do well there; he has already manners to rival the Terrible Turk. He will blend."

"You must pardon me, Father, if I speak out," said Josiah to Nelson, "but though never one to impugn your motives or to question your matter, in manner it has been said your attentions to Lady Hamilton approach more nearly those appropriate to our mother than to another man's wife. And though I shall not myself speak of it, I feel it my duty to inform you that I have frequently heard it spoken of."

To Constantinople he went.

What people say, what people say, thought Nelson angrily. She is as pure as the driven snow.

Though perhaps a little more driven. Like Paolo and Francesca, she was caught up into the whirlwind. Emma found the movement exhilarating and Palermo a rumtumtiddle sort of place. Given both men were close by, she was content.

At Kendal, for he had gone home to his wife, Romney —having first retreated to an echoing studio in Hampstead and then here—sat alone in a room, throwing ink blots at a piece of paper, a method he had despised in the Brothers Cozens when younger, but his fingers could find no shapes any more; he had to wait for the shapes to emerge.

The ink spread, the shapes emerged in roaring waves, in clouds, in intangibles, twisted and turned, and before he could catch them, ebbed away again. Each wave crested into Emma before it broke and fragmented into its disparate selves and receded with a hiss, before he could capture it. He was alone on a gray beach, with no other figure in view but an old winklewoman, turning around and around as she bent over blowholes in the sand. Then even she was no longer there. Unlike his monarch, Romney did not retreat into insanity to rest, but managed to get out of it from time to time, for the same purpose. From the next room, as always, came the hum and treadle of the spinning wheel, except that nowadays it was really there; it was his wife's employment.

Then it stopped.

Where is youth? For the matter of that, who was youth? When he was shown the newspapers, his mind clouded with a clawing crowd, baying silent down stuccoed corridors. They had been invaded. They had been forced to flee.

"So are we all," he said, and drew upon a sheet of paper the same incessant fading face. For a few years it had had specific features. Now it had none. As before, so afterward, though what it is we never quite know.

Across the fields, from somewhere, a church bell tolled. It is a great burden to believe and never to know in what. A small boy vanished down a remembered lane on a remembered day, but who was the boy, and where was the lane? He could not see them. The man walking toward you is the man walking away.

"It was a wonder to the lower orders throughout all parts of England to see the avenues to the churches filled with carriages," he read in the *Annual Register*. "This novel appearance prompted the simple country people to enquire what was the matter." The column adjacent stated that at Paris, luxury had at last attained to absolute pitch and was *recherché* in dress as well.

But what is absolute pitch? If we cannot hear it, we shall never have it. So better, though wistful, never to see her again.

"So this is my life," said George, looking around at it. "What went wrong?"

He was their dear Nelson. He never questioned that. Neither did they. He was also their palladium. This pillared hall was very like a temple, but he had never been in a temple. Being narrowly devout, he questioned no gods but his own. Being inaesthetic, he took no comfort from the mere design of the plinth.

But Emma was an attitude, and that he could admire. She was a lady, one who knew how to keep the conversation mild, address a duchess properly, deal with precedence, and jollify a bishop in a manner that his brother William, that sacerdotal climber, had not, nor had his brother William's wife. As for deportment, should that not always be easy and natural? Here he saw it so.

They were at Sir William's table. Sir William sat propped at the head of it. Emma cut up Nelson's meat for him. She wrote his letters. They had grown intimate.

Yet he was always relieved when Sir William came back into any room in which the two of them had just been left. When Sir William came back, something that had been lacking was again complete. Alone with either of them, he waited for the other. That should not have puzzled him. He should have been used to triads: when he had married his wife, she had already had a son.

At Naples, on the 8th of January, the Neapolitan Fleet was burned, like Cortez' at Vera Cruz, with this difference: the actual torch had been applied by an Englishman, and yet the English Fleet could be seen in the harbor, out the window of the breakfast room at Palermo, complete and waiting. The English Fleet cannot burn.

Sir William was distressed to be parted from his collections. "I am desirous of returning home by the first ship that Lord Nelson sends down to Gibraltar, as I am worn out and want repose," he said. "And as the house wants chimneys." He was beginning to feel the chill.

Nelson kept Emma by him constantly. "My public correspondence," he explained irritably to his wife, "besides the business of sixteen sail of the line and all our commerce, is with Petersburg, Constantinople, the Consulate at Smyrna, Egypt, the Turkish and Russian admirals, Trieste, Vienna, Tuscany, Minorca, Earl St. Vincent and Lord Spencer. This over, what time can I have for any private correspondence?" He was devoted to her. From time to time he took out her miniature, in an effort to recall what she looked like.

There was said to be fighting in the streets of Naples. The *lazzaroni* were rioting. The painter Tischbein reported that he had seen a crucifix with the body shot away so that only the legs and arms hung from the nails, like washing. He had been able to indulge the German passion for the beauties of a young, handsome and freshly shot military corpse. They have their poetry, and as models, the advantage that they cannot move. The Royal Palace had been looted, for why should the French have everything? The mob smashed what it could not carry off, as is its way.

"I wonder," said Emma, "whatever became of that strange Russian gentlewoman on the ship. The one who said she was from Odessa."

"No doubt she went home to wait upon events," said Sir William.

On the 22nd, so they heard, the Parthenopean Republic was declared at Naples, while Eleonora Pimentel, another poetess, but more *au courant* than Miss Knight, declaimed an "Ode to Liberty." The blood of St. Januarius had been induced to liquefy for the event.

"He is a saint," Sir William explained. "He is indifferent to political changes. And as for the Republic, what could be more natural, for the locusts have no king."

"What does Parthenopean mean?"

"It is the name of a siren who lured men to their doom in these parts. She is in Virgil. Afterward, her body was found on the seashore."

But Emma neither knew Latin nor was listening. She was reading the *Gazette*.

"They have renamed the San Carlo and put on *Nicaboro in Jucatan*. Why, we saw that on the King's birthday, exactly a year ago. Only here they say it was to celebrate the expulsion of the tyrant."

"They will rename everything," said Sir William. "It is their way." But yes, it was exactly a year ago, so here it was, the King's birthday again. The city twinkled with lamps which glittered, as lamps do on a frosty night, not with hospitality but a marshfire absence. Since there is nothing to hunt at night but owls and mice, the King attended the opera. Afterward there was a gala reception at court, for even in extreme cold, if you huddle together, you can keep a little warm.

The machinery of government had begun to whirl again, like a spinning jenny in an empty room, with a vast grinding of gears, for want of wool. Treaties were signed with both the Turk and Russian, though Nelson trusted neither, for the one was an infidel and the other as certainly not British. Sir William smoothed him down.

"Though we are on an island, this is not the time to be insular," he said, and looked at the mountains without affection. Etna was not only invisible from here, but had nothing to offer but hiccups and Empedocles. It was a second-class mountain. He missed Vesuvius. He missed his peace and quiet.

Greville wrote to say that Emma's heroic conduct during the voyage was on the lips of all, like jam tomorrow. "Tell her that all her friends love her more than ever, and those who did not know her, admire her."

Ah fortunate few, thought Sir William, but handed the message on.

He was not the only courtier who did not care for Palermo much. Admiral Caracciolo, his fleet burned to the water line, asked permission to return to Naples to save his personal property at least. This was granted him. In February, there were food riots; and Cardinal Ruffo, the former director of the Royal Silk Factory at San Leucio, stepped forward with a velvet *swoosh* to ask permission to cross to Calabria and raise a rebellion.

"I know the Calabrians. They sleep with a crucifix on one side of the bed and a gun on the other. We shall use both," he said.

"What does he propose, that we should bombard them with mulberry leaves from a rowboat?" demanded Nelson, but the King allowed him to go.

Surprisingly, by the middle of February he had raised an army of 17,000 men, banded together as the Christian Army of the Holy Faith.

"All very well," sniffed Nelson, who had been brought up to regard Catholicism as neither holy nor a faith, and so mistrusted both camp followers *and* the Whore of Babylon. "But how do you reload a crucifix, pray tell me that? I would as soon fight cannon with an arquebus."

But the King, who as a hunter knew all about the legend of St. Hubertus, and therefore saw nothing incongruous in a crucifix mounted between fighting antlers, began to hum to himself and to lift the carpets to look on the brighter side of things, for he proceeded always by parallels. Not only was that what Frederick Hohenstaufen had done, it was what Cardinal Ruffo was doing.

It continued to snow.

"Still und blendend lag der Schnee," said the Austrian Ambassador. "Isn't it curious that both the English and the French should have such an ugly word for such a lovely thing?"

In the courtyard of the Palazzo Palagonia, orange trees stood set in tubs. From the room in which they were working, Nelson and Emma could see the snow whirling outside, dissolving from the leaves, for the day was not as cold as it looked, and therefore the sun must be shining somewhere. They watched.

"Such a pretty word, snow," said Emma. "And the snow is pretty too, on the oranges."

Nelson considered. "When I was quite young, I made a polar voyage and shot a polar bear. We were almost crushed in the ice. My father used the polar bear as a hearth rug. Our boat was called the *Carcass*. And Northern Canada, too, for that matter, Quebec and Newfoundland . . ." His voice trailed away. He had become infatuated with an American young lady in Quebec, and had almost jumped ship to marry her. It was the only infatuation he had ever suffered. He had forgotten, until now, both her and the feeling.

"But there were no oranges," he said disapprovingly, and went back to work.

Emma, who had caught a glimpse of icebergs if not of the American lady, dipped her pen in ink somewhat guiltily, as though she had evoked a crime. Icebergs were outside her experience. She did not care for the sound of them. Nelson, she thought, was too closely married to his work; but then, everyone she knew was married, even dear Greville, to his inefficiency.

"Why do you never speak of your wife?" she asked, having come out into the verbal estuary of her meander.

"There is not much to say," said Nelson. She saw that her question had been a mistake.

On the mainland, Cardinal Ruffo was remitting taxes to pay his army. In Naples, the French were levying them to accomplish the same end. "We tax opinions," the tax collector said to a Royalist lady. "If you have your own, you must pay double. If you share ours, you need only pay half."

Everything movable had been shipped to France. "*Liberté, Égalité, Fraternité*," caroled the Republic, with Eleonora Pimentel to lead the chorus.

"*Tu rubbi a me, io rubbo a te*," said the people. The liberated did not seem to understand their liberators; it was necessary to translate.

In Palermo, the King went about like a scarecrow, for his income had shrunk. The Prince Royal had opened a dairy. Apart from consuming vast quantities of the best butter, Ferdinand had grown stingy and would not grant so much as the purchase of a new mattress.

"I like neither to see nor be seen," said the Queen. "Circumstances are too painful." So was her mattress. "I see Acton very seldom, to avoid his ill-humor," she told the Hamiltons.

"She has hit upon the very reason," cried Acton, "why I do not see her."

"What is a *cicisbèo*?" Nelson asked Sir William.

"Why do you ask?" inquired Sir William, whom the question, coming from this source, had startled.

"It is what they call me here, so I am told."

"It is a local institution," said Sir William. "You see, they have taken you to their hearts, just as we have." And he smiled benignly at Emma, who smiled, very rapidly, back.

"Though I am almost blind and worn out," wrote Nelson to his wife, "I am quite revived by Sir William's wit and inexhaustible pleasantry and Lady Hamilton's affectionate care." He would have said more, but checked his pen.

"What is a *cicisbèo,* Hardy?" he asked.

"A local institution," said Hardy promptly.

"Ah, but what institution? Or must I ask Troubridge?"

"A man who is seen everywhere with another man's wife," said Hardy. "And what they do in private, God alone knows. But," he added, seeing the expression on Nelson's face, "it is quite harmless. It is the recognized thing."

"Apparently," said Nelson, "and damn."

"Sir?"

"I have broken my pen."

"He seems infatuated with her."

"Good, then he will stay here," said the Queen, whose fondness for dear Emma, though not essential to her politics, hinged upon them. Let them play as they would, so long as the fleet stayed here. About Sir William she did not vex herself one particle; he was her own kind of man. He would survive.

Cardinal Ruffo had swept as far north as Salerno. He was so clearly the stuff out of which heroes are made that there had been attempts to assassinate him already.

"Cardinal Ruffo," said Sir William, quite in his old style, "has taken all the provinces for his knowledge."

If he felt better, Nelson felt worse. His wife had asked if she might join him. "Sir William and Lady Hamilton and I are the mainspring by which the whole machinery of government turns," he explained. And as for coming out, she would not like it and he would not have it. The mere thought made him ill, and when ill he was not altogether agreeable, for far worse than a hypochondriac is a hypochondriac with real complaints, and of these he had many.

Emma nursed him. Poor Fanny, he doubted if she would understand a man's having a female friend, for she herself had none. Yet Emma was a friend. A squeeze of the hand, by way of gratitude, in those circumstances was only civil. Besides, Sir William was always, and better, there.

"I must say that there was *at that time*, certainly no impropriety in living under Lady Hamilton's roof," wrote Miss Knight. (If nothing in particular has happened to us, we can always fill up our autobiography with other people's lives, and hers now made a considerable pile.) "Her house was the resort of the best company of all nations, and the attentions paid to Lord Nelson appeared perfectly natural." As indeed they had, but looking at the manuscript a little later, she could not but marvel at how time flies.

There was trouble with Charles Lock, the new British Consul. Neither Nelson nor Sir William would recognize his right to provide the navy with dried beef at a profit merely marginal, and a consul has to live somehow. He took it ill. Besides, the middle classes never approve of those either above or below them, for does the meat in a sandwich, when it has been bitten, approve of the bread?

At dinner a Turk, in graphic French, entertained Lady Hamilton with an account of his atrocities, dismemberment, mutilation and such, mostly. "With this weapon," he said, and drew his *shabola,* the better to explain with the English of his body, "I cut off the heads of twenty. There is the blood."

"Oh let me see the sword that did the glorious deed!" cried Emma, and clapping up the *shabola,* she kissed it and handed it to the Hero of the Nile.

Mrs. Charles Lock, who was far gone in pregnancy, produced a faint and had to be removed from the room.

"She is either affected or a Jacobin," said Emma. "She wore green ribbons."

"Shame," said the Lock relations.

"Bravo!" shouted the mere cousins-german.

"Oh God," said Sir William. "She is Lord Edward Fitzgerald's sister, and besides, he is distracted about the beef."

"Well, she is affected, and green does not suit her at all." A statement not only true, but like most truths, beside the point.

Emma had discovered the top-heavy joys of gambling. It was what the local aristocracy did—all Sicily was one lottery—and never fainted when they lost, but stepped away like gentlemen to blow their brains out. It was exactly like Carlton House, except that the rooms were bigger. One had merely to play one's hopes and hunches, and no nonsense about remembering complicated things like cards.

She was so proud when she won, and when she lost, only a little sorry, for that meant that Nelson had to go fetch more money, and it was a pity to make him walk —he did limp so.

Gambling sucked her in.

In Naples, General MacDonald, head of the occupying forces, issued a proclamation to the effect that cardinals, archbishops, abbots, parish priests and all ministers of public worship should be held responsible for rebellion in the places where they resided and be punished with death if rebellion there occurred; and that every accomplice, whether lay or clerical, should be treated as a rebel.

"Cardinal Ruffo is a remarkable man," said Sir William. "He was wasted making silk."

"But if they are going to hang him . . ."

"It is precisely because they cannot catch him that they say they will. A proclamation is like a diplomatic protest: it means that nothing can be done, but says what we would do if it could. It is the beginning of the end."

In March, Nelson sent Troubridge to blockade Naples. He could not go himself. His duty, he said, lay here.

That's all very well, so long as he does not himself lie with it, thought Troubridge, but was loyal enough not to listen when others said the same thing. On the third of April he had the royal colors hoisted over a recaptured, which is to say, a liberated, Procida.

"Send me some flour and an honest judge," he wrote

to Palermo. "The people are calling for justice, so eight or ten of them must hang."

"Send me word some proper heads are taken off; this alone will comfort me," said Nelson, who had quite taken up the royal cause.

But Troubridge, who had that morning received a man's head in a basket of grapes—the grapes fresh, the head not—sent the grapes only. The weather was too hot to keep heads.

If the thoughts of the loyal ran to grapes, the King's ran to cheeses—to be precise, to *càciocavalli,* the local cheeses which were always strung up by the neck to dry.

"Democracy and true liberty render people gentle, indulgent, generous and magnanimous," wrote Eleonora Pimentel, the Egeria of the Republic, and then said what she thought of the King and Queen. She did not mince words. She did wish to mince *them.* Since it was time for extreme measures, she decided to rename the streets, perhaps in the hope of confusing Cardinal Ruffo's advancing troops. They were to be called Fortune, Success, Triumph, Victory, Hope, Fertility, Pleasure, Fecundity, Hilarity, Security, Felicity, Valor, Glory, Honor, Prudence, Faith, Concord, Modesty, Silence, Peace, Vigilance, Grace, Love, Hospitality, Innocence and Frugality. The people, who could not tell the difference between Philip V and Neptune, must find their way home as best they could.

"It sounds like a list of your Attitudes," said Sir William, "but without the neoclassical trimmings. I notice they say nothing of Fortitude. We must add a Stratonice to the repertoire, my dear."

It was some time since they had done the Attitudes; life had been too rushed.

"Caracciolo must go first," said the Queen. "He has turned traitor and heads their navy."

He had made an injudicious choice, therefore he should be punished, not judged. Choice is beyond the law.

At Naples, the doors of the theatre were walled up after a performance of Monti's *Aristodemo,* because it portrayed a dethroned monarch recovering his crown. The Republic was taking no chances.

"They are putting on Alfieri at the San Carlo," said Emma, who had the fashion, birth, death and cultural pages of the newspaper Sir William was reading. "Only it is called the National Theatre now, and nobody goes."

"Alfieri is a very fine writer," said Sir William.

"All the same, you didn't have to sit through him when we were there."

We, Sir William had noted now for some time, no longer meant Emma and himself, but Emma and the Queen. He was amused. For of course when Maria Carolina said We she meant only herself. Like a ship in dry dock, she needed these human props only until she was mended and could float in her natural element again. Indeed, to knock them away would be necessary, were she to be relaunched. But he saw no reason to explain that to Emma.

Besides, Alfieri was dull. He had set out to revolutionize the stage, and now the revolution had staged him. Sir William found these small games of tit for tat entertaining, but never explained them, for your born raconteur can be amused only by his own private jokes; they are the only ones he ever listens to.

Nelson, alone and staring at the ceiling, was listening to his conscience, a small voice that would not be still, speaking—plainly, but from far away—in the tones of the American lady from Quebec.

"Naturally I show affection. It is merely gratitude, but more intimate, for after all, we know each other well," said Nelson.

The image of Lady Nelson, crossing his mind as she would cross the front parlor at Round Wood, where she was staying with his father (she was good about staying with the ill, though that diminished her acquaintance), said nothing.

"Oh God, I cannot go back to that existence," he

groaned. "The rooms are too small. The ceilings are too low."

Lady Nelson looked singularly like Sir William's first and dead wife. She was a sick-room and small-gossip wife. She had no other interests. Her face disdained vivacity, which she felt, instinctively, either to be ill-bred or beyond her, and in either event, no concern of hers. Speak of Mrs. Fitzherbert, and she merely said gently, "Yes, but after all, he *is* a prince," hushed the discussion, and went on to talk placidly of the new mangle and St. Vincent's disease. St. Vincent was precious to Nelson, being an elder man who had admired him. His diseases were equally precious to Fanny. Their symptoms were all her contacts with the great.

St. Vincent liked Emma extraordinarily well.

It was intolerable.

"Besides, we are above all that," he said. "For I am *Lord* Nelson now."

Lady Nelson was called suddenly away (a neighbor had croup), stopped to tie her bonnet strings before the hall mirror, made a small cautious Christian smile at her own image, and all neat and tidy, went out. The room was, thank heavens, empty. Empty it looked much the same as before her departure. The ceiling was too low.

"And where is Lord Nelson?"

"In his room, resting."

"He looks worn out these days," said Mrs. Cadogan approvingly. Whatever they did among themselves was their own affair. She was too astute ever to risk a quarrel. Criticism was not among her pleasures. She preferred Sir William, but Sir William was failing. If no one else could see that, she could. She did not wish to discuss the matter with Emma, ever.

"You may judge, my dear Charles, what it is to keep a table for all the poor British emigrants from Naples, who have none, & for the officers of the fleet, as Lord Nelson lives in the house with us, & all business, which is immense, is transacted here," Sir William wrote to Greville. It was time to chase down his finances, which Charles seemed to have scattered like paper through the woods. The King had granted him leave to go back to England sufficiently long to do that. He would come as soon as possible.

Alas, to go was not possible.

On the 17th of April, the French abandoned Naples.

"The Republic is now established," said the *Monitore,* "and to her enemies nothing remains but jealousy, desperation and death."

The blood of St. Januarius refused to liquefy.

The President of the Republic walked up to the Cardinal Archbishop and cocked a pistol. "Unless a miracle takes place, you are a dead man," he said.

The Cardinal Archbishop could see this for himself. "Warm it," he said, handing it to an assistant. The miracle took place, but never before had it been greeted with catcalls and public booing. It was necessary to remove the tax on flour and fish.

> *"S'è levata la gabella alla farina,*
> *Eviva Ferdinando e Carolina ..."*

the *lazzaroni* shouted, which was not the effect intended, though there seemed no way to put the tax back on again.

Nelson finally brought himself to put to sea, in order to pursue a part of the French Fleet which had been reported in the Mediterranean again. He did not catch it.

"To tell you how dreary and uncomfortable the *Vanguard* appears, is only telling you what it is to go from the pleasantest society to a solitary cell, or from the dearest friends to no friends," he wrote Emma. "I am now perfectly the *great man*—not a creature near me. From my heart I wish myself the little man again. I love Mrs. Cadogan. You cannot conceive what I feel when I call you all to my remembrance."

"He loves you," said Emma to her mother.

"Let us hope it stops there," said Mrs. Cadogan.

"Whatever are you talking about?"

"If you don't know, then my heart is at rest," said Mrs. Cadogan, who was prone to regard innocence as nothing more than the absence of evil. And who is to say she was wrong? In self-knowledge there is certainly much evil.

"I can assure you that neither Emma nor I knew how much we loved you until this separation, and we are convinced your Lordship feels the same as we do," wrote Sir William.

"I give and bequeath to my dear friend, Emma Hamilton, wife of the Right Hon. Sir William Hamilton, a nearly round box set with diamonds, said to have been sent me by the mother of the Grand Signor, which I request she will accept (and never part from) as a token of regard and respect for her very eminent virtues (for she, the said Emma Hamilton, possesses them all to such a degree that it would be doing her an injustice was any particular one to be mentioned), from her faithful and affectionate friend," wrote Nelson, adding a codicil both to his current last testament and his latest letter. He had begun to banter wills.

"Isn't that sweet?" asked Emma.

"No one has ever said anything against your virtues," said Mrs. Cadogan. "But then, it is the vices people like to gab about these days."

Sir William had discovered that to feel weary is not the same as to feel tired. One can be quite restored and energetic, and yet feel weary. However, with Nelson gone, the house had settled down so that it was possible to hear Emma singing from the center of silence, rather than merely as the upper stave of any general uproar.

"What is it, my dear?" he asked.

"I don't know. I just opened the score in the middle."

Sir William leafed to the frontispiece. " *'Il Matrimonio Segreto,'* by Cimarosa," he said. "Why yes, that's rather what I thought it was."

"Don't you care for it?"

"Oh it's an extremely amusing work," he said. "Pray continue." An inability to give way to those sudden irritable bursts of steam which others call deep feeling —a mere superficial eruption upon the surface of things —does much to make life bearable. If we do not itch, we need not scratch. The deeper emotions are motionless, though currents eddy through them seventy fathoms down. Since there is no light down there, fortunately for us, we cannot see them. But they are there and they do sustain us. The facile emotions must be very like the feeding grounds in Baron Humboldt's current, off the coasts of South America, where sea life teems so numerous it eats itself up, or else the surface is startled by the hurtling eruption of giant squid, eager to feed and then sink down again to digest its memories. Though living, these grunion and sea scavenge are not the source of life. Their source of life is the depth that sustains them, whose currents run cold below, to keep them warm above.

What sustains them, thought Sir William, is me.

He did not mind that. But he did hope they had at least done something guilty enough to excuse the look on their faces, though knowing Nelson, and Emma too, for that matter, he suspected not.

That Nelson would take the plunge (swift like the eagle from yon lofty tow'r), he did not doubt, for he was a man plagued merely by conscience, which is no substitute for a sense of responsibility, alas.

I must remember, he told himself, that this is something I know *nothing* about, and went to bed, and anticipated no trouble. To give her credit, it was remarkable how little she neglected him.

On the 29th, Nelson returned to Palermo, and Cardinal Ruffo reached Melfi, carrying a banner embroidered by the Queen herself, with her own arms on one side and God's on the other so no matter how the wind blew, one of them would be on the winning side. God may not be there, but it is wise to keep on the good side of where

He once was, for though nobody has seen Him for years, He *may* be there.

At Naples, a *Te Deum* was sung in San Lorenzo, to celebrate the possibility of victory, and a priest was arrested for shouting "Long Live the King." He pleaded drunkenness as his excuse.

"*In vino veritas*," said the judge, and nodded to the shooting squad. "You may fire."

"It would be better to have prayers said for our own safety," said the diarist de Nicola.

The Cardinal entered the city, and the Republicans walled themselves up in the Castelli d'Uovo and Nuovo. That is, the glorious liberators—which is to say the traitors—went there to protect themselves from the reactionary oppressor—which is to say, the liberator. They returned to the egg, while the mob—which is to say, the loyal *lazzaroni*—held carnival out of season, roasted human flesh on spits, played football with the heads, posed women nude as Liberty, had their liberty of them, dragged their victims to the Cardinal, and when he would not slaughter them, they did.

The Cardinal wrote asking the King to return, and granted a truce to the Republicans in the castles. "What is the use of punishing?" he asked. "How is it possible to punish so many persons without an indelible imputation of cruelty?"

The King explained how. "As a Christian, I pardon everybody, but as he whom God appointed, I must be a strict avenger of the offenses committed against Him and of the injury done to the State."

"Hang them all," said Nelson. We need discipline to keep afloat. We must trim the sails and calk the seams if we are to have calm seas and a prosperous voyage.

If there was to be liberty, the Queen wished it supervised.

"The Queen is miserable and says that although the people of Naples are for them in general, yet things will not be brought to that state of quietness and subordination till the fleet of Lord Nelson appears *off*

Naples. She therefore begs, intreats, and conjures you, my dear Lord, if it is possible, to arrange matters so as to be able to go to Naples.

"Sir William is writing for General Acton's *answer*.

"For God's sake consider it, and do! We will go with you, if you will come and fetch us.

"Sir William is ill; I am ill; it will do us good," wrote Emma.

Nelson consented to go. Emma was overjoyed. "We shall see Naples again—our dear old unchanged Naples," she said.

"Will we?" Sir William had his doubts. Though it was his duty, as it is the duty of every man, to see justice done, that is not the same as being compelled to watch it being done. This excursion smacked too much of an outing to Tyburn Hill.

He liked the prospect even less when Nelson took him below and showed him a warrant the King had issued for the arrest of Cardinal Ruffo, who had become too popular. (Is there not always something treasonable about another man's success?) It was to be used *if needed*.

"Lock it up and tell no one," said Sir William, who preferred Blackstone to Chief Justice Coke, and had no love of the Star Chamber.

Nelson locked it up, but they both knew it was there.

"Look," said Emma, who had been trying to read Lessing's *School for Honour, or the Chance of War*, which she found dull. "A dolphin has followed us from port. It is like an opera."

Glancing at the casement, Sir William noticed that it had once been struck by a bullet and that the wood was newly joined around a patch. That is the trouble with a restoration: it may look the same, but it is not.

It would not be like an opera. It would not even be like an *opera buffa*. He went into the cabin to wash his hands.

It was the dawn of June 24, 1799. There were woodwinds in the rigging, and the creak of a piccolo in the timbers. The whole orchestra was starting up: it was becoming day. There was no curtain to be drawn this time, no cherubs, but merely a scrim through which it would be possible to perceive that comedy called Justice. The pumiced decks were swabbed down. As the first light hit them they began to steam. An aureole of sea gulls came out to meet the boats, wailed, and whirled back again. The ship's bell rang for the chorus to come in and take its places. That excellent piece, Monti's *Aristodemo,* or *The Monarchy Restored,* was about to be put on again, though Ferdinand was still in Palermo, pulling at his lower lip and starting hares.

Emma had risen early. In a shovel bonnet *alla marinara,* trimmed with daisies made of cockleshells, a white princess dress *à la Régence* with an exceptionally high bodice, and yellow slippers patterned after a man's evening pumps, she had given some thought to her *tournure,* and so had no doubts, but drew about her in flattering folds an expansive cashmere shawl. The shawl was designed to suggest Mercy. She knew what Justice was.

In the fifth act, the King, struck by a dramatic change of heart, a *deus ex muchina,* ascends his throne, casts out the Grand Vizier, unites the lovers—one of whom always turns out to be his long-lost son or daughter—strips the villain, enriches the rest, and it doesn't matter, because afterward everybody comes out to accept the general applause. Since you have seen it all a hundred times before, there is no need to worry. There is time to bow to one's friends and drink hot chocolate. It will come out right in the end. Or, if the performance is English, and therefore *The Beggar's Opera,* it is only play-acting; at the last moment, the King's messenger will arrive with a pardon. She had seen that, too.

She had known they would see Naples again. That's why she had been so impatient at Palermo, for some operas are a *little* long.

Just the same, they had lost their houses, she had been cast out, so let them hang; it was such a dreadful thing to have done to Sir William at his age.

She stood at the rail and watched the waves, so small they might have been theatrical rollers, the sun a magnesium flare, and the splendid spectacle of eighteen ship of the line, gun hatches open, moving through silence with implacable certainty as they began to enfilade the gap between Capri and Ischia, in order to invest the city.

It was not scenery. It was décor. There were shadows on the sea. The scrim became transparent. Vesuvius became visible, and all the villages along the shore sprang up like footlights.

Nelson stood watching her. On board ship, he was the great man. Anywhere else, he was all at sea. Rather shyly—like a boy at his first ball—he went forward to say good morning, a thin, pale, jaundiced, bilious, one-eyed, one-armed, balding little man with a limp.

Emma, turning, saw neither this puny creature, a mere human, nor the genius inside, but instead that more imposing object, the Hero of the Nile, the friend of the Duke of Clarence, Admiral Nelson, *their* Nelson, Baron Nelson, and who knew what further distinctions were to come.

"Isn't it exciting!" she said.

He thought she meant the deployment of the ships. "Oh yes, it always is." She had a feeling for these things. She understood him.

He felt at his ease, a thing he seldom felt with women. "Dear Emma," he said. He had himself become plummy. He was ripe to fall.

"For a moment you startled me," she said, putting him at a distance and watching Mother Carey's chickens come home to roost.

She had become a mistress of the forms. For harmless boyish moments when they were together, she called him Horatio; for public scenes, Lord Nelson; for intimate dinners, My dear Lord Nelson; when he seemed dangerous, Our dear Lord Nelson, which reminded him of Sir William.

Poor Nelson, thought Sir William, who had just come topside. He has not the sophistication for Emma's simplicity, overlooking that these vain creatures can do anything with mirrors, whether they realize it or not.

It was Emma, first, who spotted the white flags flying on the castles.

"Haul down that flag of truce!" she shouted. "There can be no truce with rebels!" It was her military mood, borrowed from Maria Carolina, who, though she had all Maria Theresa's habits of mind, lacked the mind itself. Maria Theresa, like most commanding women, had produced a nursery of noddles and sticklebacks. Impotence, neglect and a foolish husband had left Maria Carolina with an insatiable craving for glitter and revenge. So Emma must have these things, too.

Sir William and Nelson looked glumly at the flags. They must send a messenger to Cardinal Ruffo.

It was two in the afternoon before the fleet could drop anchor, in battle formation, before the city. "Forty-three fathoms!" shouted the boy with the lead, yet it looked as though they were in deeper than that. The bay was a litter of small boats, for everyone had come out to pay his respects, fling garlands, and cuddle up to the winning side, though until the forts fell the city had not yet fallen. Through a telescope, Sir William could see that the statue of a giant opposite the palace had a large red-flannel liberty cap on its head.

A cutter came alongside with the mail pouch, containing news from both England and Sicily.

"The *Colossus* is foundered," said Sir William, got up, looked dazed, and lurched below.

"It is the heat," said Emma.

But Nelson had paused in his own correspondence. The *Colossus* had indeed foundered, off the Scilly Roads, when almost home.

"It was the transport ship," he explained, "with his antiques and pictures."

"Oh well," said Emma, as though to say, Is that all? "He can buy more. They dig more up every day." She was absorbed in the dear Queen's letters, and some gazettes had come with the new French fashions in them. She did want to look at those.

"Perhaps I should go down to him," said Nelson.

Emma said she would go herself.

Sir William was standing in the wardroom, alone.

"I am so sorry, William," she said.

"It doesn't matter. It could not be helped." His eyes seemed out of focus.

"When we are settled again, you can collect more. There does always seem to be more," said Emma. "The French cannot have taken everything."

"Damn the French!" snapped William, who looked pasty. Poor old gentleman, apparently it was a shock. "Damn them I say."

It seemed so much emotion from so peripheral a cause. "Shall I stay?" she asked.

"No, I'd rather be alone."

"Are you sure?"

"Quite sure," said Sir William bitterly.

She went away. He would be better after a while. And really, there was so much to do.

That night the city, or those parts of it not still in

rebel hands, burned with thousands of lanterns, which made almost enough light to have supper by.

"Where is Sir William?" asked Emma. She wanted to cheer him up.

Nobody knew.

She half rose, but Nelson, with an odd look, said that he would go instead. She was much relieved. What was going on was far beyond her, though to be sure, it had no doubt been a very hard blow. Sir William was quite right: damn the French. But it was not an irreparable loss.

He was still sitting in the wardroom. Someone had lit a lamp, but he seemed not to notice it.

"Greville has been able to salvage only a box with the body of Admiral Lord Sheldam in it. What business had he there? He was not a vase. Why should he be shipped as a vase?" demanded Sir William.

"Sailors are superstitious about bodies aboard ship. He died in Lisbon and had to be sent home."

"Nonetheless, he was not a vase," said Sir William idiotically. He had loved the world. To him there was only one tragedy: that one day very soon—no matter how long from now, it will be very soon—we shall be dead and unable to see it any more. But that is a slow tragedy, and this news was sudden. A man of almost seventy can do nothing suddenly.

"I do not understand," said Nelson, coming closer. "But sir, I am sorry. Truly sorry."

Sir William shot an angry, defensive look at him, and then saw that, by God, he was. This so startled his natural reserve, that despite himself, he leaned up against this most unexpected present male friend and wept.

What can be worse than an old man's tears? They are so beyond the hour uncorked; the wine is vinegar, no matter what the year.

With that almost female sensibility with which he could sometimes smooth life's rougher moments, Nelson reached over and blew the lantern out, and while he waited for Sir William to take hold of himself again, thought most oddly of the Reverend Edmund, his father, at Round Hill, who must be almost eighty now.

"Is he all right?"

"Of course he's all right," said Nelson irritably, totally unaware that he had just earned carte blanche, for there was nothing he wished to do.

Emma, who had noticed a look in his eyes which she had sometimes caught in Sir William's when she knew she had done nothing wrong, looked at the lights in the bay and said, "Oh dear"—and after a while—"but he wants no supper?"

"No, he wants no supper," said Nelson, perplexed, he did not know by what. He did not like this bay. It was too sensuous. It had ghosts in it.

Aware of Emma waiting for him to speak again, he turned to look at the headlands instead.

The next day Sir William was himself again in so far as appearances go, which are perhaps intents. The tyrant Dionysius of Syracuse, so we are told, wrote history as well as tragedy, and besides, his tragedies won no prizes. So Sir William sensibly sat in the sun and wrote dispatches home.

Nelson countermanded the armistice by signal. He would give no quarter to the French. They were a greedy, mangy, vainglorious and more than usually time-serving self-seeking race. There are races which cannot help their not being English. He understood that and could even sympathize. But the French seemed not to care. In short, he did not like them.

"Who is that lout?" he demanded.

That lout was Pallio, a disreputable scoundrel of fifty odd in tattered tight candy-stripe pantaloons, a blue military coat, and curiously enough, an immaculately frilled and well-starched shirt front with jeweled studs.

"He says he can keep order," said Emma proudly.

"He does not look as though he could keep the Sabbath."

"But everybody knows Pallio. He's head of the

lazzaroni. He says he has ninety thousand men. All they need is arms."

"Why can't he come in the daytime, like anybody else?"

"He sleeps in the daytime."

"Humph," said Nelson. "What do you say, Sir William?"

"He is head of the *lazzaroni*, certainly," said Sir William, who, if he would not condone needless slaughter, was not in the mood to prevent it.

As far as Nelson could see, a few less Neapolitans would do no harm, no matter what side they were on. Palermo had taught him to Sicilify his conscience. Either the fellow would maintain order, or by morning there would be fewer among whom it would have to be maintained. "I shall give the fellow his guns," said Nelson.

"As Lord Nelson is now telling Lady Hamilton what he wishes to say to the Queen, you will probably know from the Queen more than I do of Lord Nelson's intentions," said Sir William smoothly, writing to General Acton. The less they knew of each other's intentions the better, since they all intended, except for poor muddling Emma, the same thing.

Emma, half wakened by the sounds of shooting and a wail or two across the midnight water, at first alarmed, thought drowsily, It must be Pallio maintaining order, and went to sleep again. In the morning there was no one to tell her otherwise. We maintain order by telling others to do it. How they do it has nothing to do with the maintenance of order, any more than the maintenance has anything to do with order itself. And we, of course, are concerned with order only.

Next morning the Cardinal came aboard, dressed not in his robes—which he had left in the Cathedral vestry after having discovered that he had celebrated unnecessarily a Godgiven truce—but in a purple, which is to say a red, soutane, brown riding boots, and spurs. Nelson was annoyed. He did not like to have his decks scratched.

The man did not look like a proud prelate. What pride

he had arose from family, not faith. He looked like a soldier, sore tried, saddlesore and weary.

There were words.

However, since the Cardinal did not understand English, and Nelson could not understand the Cardinal's French, and the subject of their debate was Italian, Sir William hoped not so much to bring them together as to keep them apart, and needed all his phlegm to do it; odd though it is that that term which among the poor means only oysterhocking, in a gentleman—if not a by-product of that weather which we emigrate to avoid—denotes swallowing hard.

According to Galen, the faculties of the soul follow the temperaments of the body. Perhaps so. Sir William coped. Phlegm was as inbred in him as ennui is in a Frenchman, or *terribilità* in an Italian, qualities which gave the first jurisprudence, the second wit, and the third lawsuits. God not only tempers the wind to the shorn lamb, he shears the lamb.

So though the Cardinal left in a temper, to debate with his allies; and Pallio had torn down the Cardinal's edicts and eviscerated whom he pleased; and though the Queen had written to say that a general massacre would cause her no pain; even though men might be savages, there must be no Mohawks here. The consul at sunset, who has sacked whole provinces, must still maintain the Pax Romana. To do so is both his duty and the source of his year's wealth.

"He was insolent. He must be paid in his own coin," said Nelson.

Sir William thought not. "It is justice," he said. "For justice, one need pay only one's lawyer. Anything else is called a bribe and throws the case out of court. He said that even if it had been better not to capitulate, we were obliged to honor a treaty once made. Honor it we must. He is quite right. Our only choice is between the breech and the observance."

"It will pain the Queen."

"The Queen's capacity for pain is almost infinite. There

is always room for more. If it is not this, it is that. It is her pleasure," said Sir William.

Cardinal Ruffo was a gentleman and a Prince of the Church. Between the crucifix on one side of the bed and the gun on the other, they could not arrest him. He could raise whole armies from that bed, whichever side he rose on.

"Lords spiritual should not be allowed to fight," said Nelson primly. "Mariolatry has marred his manners."

"His patron is St. Anthony of Padua."

"What difference does it make? They all come from the same womb," snapped Nelson, to whom even Charles the Martyr smacked of popery, and sent a declaration—to be forwarded by the Cardinal—that the rebels should surrender to the royal mercy.

They might as well surrender to the sea kraken itself. The Cardinal refused to forward it, and clambered aboard again, talking a blue streak, of which Sir William dared to translate only every third and least blue word.

Nelson gave up. "An admiral is no match in talking with a cardinal," he said, and wrote a note of hand, to explain he would not compromise. Royalty does not compromise. Neither does an admiral. With his own principles, perhaps; with those of others, never. Every man has his limitations; those of Nelson were greatness. He did not propose either to be bilked or balked.

Ruffo went ashore and told the French to flee by land, but since he had beaten them, they did not trust him and would not go.

The whole world came aboard to pay its respects. Emma had petitions for mercy by the handful; Sir William, petitions for place. Like children after the pantry, the strongest manage to clamber on top of the others to get the honey, for without a general scrimmage, no man could reach so high. We all have to scramble on somebody else's shoulders in this world, to accomplish anything, and while they are beneath us, we may as well push them down. In peaceful times, this natural process is a mere decorous shuffle in felt slippers; in time of trouble, it is a kick in the ribs administered by iron boots. The success of any government may be determined by the length of the queue. When the ranks are broken, every man is doomed.

Sir William appealed to reputation. "Fall in, save honor, and you may safely leave revenge to the King," he said. It was a toss-up whether the Cardinal would be arrested or not, but the coin came down a medal, new minted, with Nelson's head on one side and the Goddess of Clemency on the other, Britannia cowering behind her shield.

"Nelson is resolved to do nothing to break the armistice," wrote Sir William.

The Cardinal sighed with relief and went off to the Church of the Carmine, to give thanks. "Different characters express themselves in different ways," he said in his thank-you note, repeating what Sir William had just written to him. And then, thinking over the singular perfection of this trite apothegm, and adding it to his own knowledge of the King and Queen, he prudently resigned, and so kept his honor intact.

With honor intact, they might now do as they pleased.

The King disavowed the capitulation.

"Finally, my dear Milady, I recommend Lord Nelson to treat Naples as if it were a rebellious city in Ireland which had behaved in such a manner," wrote the Queen, thus raising a purely British but inexorable ghost, and apparently ignorant that the Hydra grows new heads.

Caracciolo's must fall first.

Nothing loath, Nelson intercepted the fleeing rebels and clapped them in close confinement on *polaccas*, where they could await the King's pleasure like animals rounded up for a *grand battu*. It was a simple alternative of surrender and be hanged, or hang out and be shot, as far as he was concerned.

Caracciolo was not so much betrayed as sold by one of his own servants, who though loyal, had needed the money, and was brought aboard the *Foudroyant* at nine in the morning. He had disguised himself as a peasant, an unwise choice, for though a uniform stays violence, a peasant provokes it. There could be no question of his guilt. He had changed sides and chosen the losing one; what else is guilt? It was a clear-cut case in a most indistinct country.

The court-martial sat at ten, and the man had been condemned by noon and was to be executed the next day, which, since the naval day began at noon, gave him five hours to live.

"But you cannot hang him," said Emma. "We *know* him."

"It is out of my hands," said Nelson, which was true enough, for he had just signed and dispatched the death warrant.

The female mind does not believe that any act is ever final. That is what makes Christians of them; they believe in reprieve. She begged again.

"He has had his trial, and has been a trial to many," said Nelson.

"There is mercy."

"His death will no doubt be a mercy, and is in itself merciful," said Sir William.

"He is a Catholic. Cannot he at least have a priest? He will want the comfort of Confession."

"Why bother to confess what cannot be denied?" asked Nelson, who had found the Cardinal quite enough priest for one day.

"Emma," said Sir William, "I think you had best go to your cabin. These things must be done, therefore they cannot be undone."

Emma went. She did not understand men.

"It is a bad business, all the same," said Sir William.

"He was a bad man," said Nelson, pulling out his watch.

Caracciolo was transferred to his former flagship, *La Minerva,* and hanged at five for his unwisdom; the body was weighted and cut down to fall in the sea.

Nelson and the Hamiltons were entertaining Lord Northwick to dinner. At the foot of the table was a roast pig. As the head was cut off they heard the cannon boom from the *Minerva*. Emma fainted.

"Ah women," said Nelson, "they are such delicate creatures," though this one was uncommonly heavy to lift. Sir William helped him. This opinion, and for that matter this woman, they held in common.

She revived. Now it was over it was not so bad. She ate.

Once Caracciolo was out of the way, the King was to arrive, but the Queen was not.

"Nobody wants me there," she said, and sent her black lists along. She recommended that the women be treated as were the men. She proposed to enlarge the scope of war. She wished to have Eleonora Pimentel's head.

To give the sailors diversion, Emma had installed a harp on the deck of the *Foudroyant* and gave concerts in the evening.

She sang odes to Nelson mostly, which went down very well. She helped abolish the silence, and among them, only Sir William had the reserve to find nothing objectionable in the voices of silence, which can be heard across that bay, although the dead are dumb.

"The King arrived on the tenth, so now we have nothing political to think of," said Sir William. His Britannic Majesty's government was forced to entertain royalty, not always an easy thing to do, since there is so little, on the whole, that entertains it. Ferdinand, however, was easily amused by being allowed to shoot seabirds from the deck when not busy ordering executions and rewarding the faithful. He was stern, he was the father of his people, and the Lord giveth and the Lord taketh away, as he never tired of saying.

He was quite himself again. He had not learned a thing. Nor, in his opinion, had he a thing to learn. He was quite jaunty. But he would not go ashore. Since the Hamiltons and Nelson did all the work, he had nothing to do but nothing, which not only took up most of his time, but suited him.

The last group of rebels surrendered on the 3rd of Messidor.

"What day is that?" asked Nelson.

"The ninth of August."

If we cannot be sure of the calendar, what can we believe?

Since he had disobeyed orders in order to stay at Naples, there was a good deal of talk. He did not listen. We cannot do the world's work and listen to its chatter as well. He had not the time.

A fisherman came aboard to say that Caracciolo was swimming toward Naples. Man not the guns only, but also the churches. He had risen from the dead.

From the King's cabin came something between a bellow and a scream. When they burst in, they found him down on his knees, blubbering for a priest, beating his scapular against the floor and pointing out the window.

It had sounded like a yarn. It was not. There was Caracciolo, sure enough, walking across the water rapidly, but bobbling like a buoy.

"You had better not look," said Nelson, but of course Emma looked. The entire fleet looked.

His body had become sufficiently inflated by gas to counterbalance the weights which had been tied to his feet, but the weights kept him erect, so that, borne on a small surface current, he was indeed rapidly approaching, his arms flapping dissynchronously, his head tolling like a bell. Where not bloated, the body had gone slimy, and of course the eyes were gone. He made the worst possible kind of fetch.

The King crossed himself into a corner. "We must flee! We must flee!" he yelled. He called on St. Ferdinand. He called on both St. Anthonies. He called on St. Januarius. He called on the Blessed Virgin. He had a long list.

"I am damned!" he screamed. "Damned!"

They sent for the chaplain.

The body bumped against the hull, as though knocking to come in.

"They come back," yowled the King. "They come back!" Poor soul, he was in torment.

Sir William looked at Nelson. Nelson looked at Emma. Emma looked at Sir William. They could none of them look at the King, who was hunching himself up toward an invisible altar, in a most unregal manner, and would next demand the Pope.

"He has only come to ask a pardon and a Christian burial," said Sir William.

"Yes," said the priest, who had not been able to think of anything himself.

The improvement was immediate. "You think so?" asked the King.

They thought so.

Ferdinand scrambled to his feet, dried his tears, and looked about him joyously. "Very well," he said. "I pardon him. Have the body towed to Santa Lucia, to the church there. But I pardon nobody else. And see the others are buried properly!" And glaring at them like a boar from a thicket, he turned and went snuffling off, leaning on the priest's arm.

"Probably some ships will soon be sent home from Palermo, and Emma and I shall profit of one. Every captain wishes to serve us, and no one is, I believe, more popular in the navy at this moment than Emma and I," wrote Sir William. Except for Josiah Nisbet of course, who had come back to disapprove. "We have had the glory of stepping between the King and his subjects, to the utility of both."

"I am going ashore," said Emma. "Will you not come?"

"No, my dear, I think not."

"It would do you good."

"No, it would only do me harm," said Sir William. "But go if you must."

She did not understand why not, so she went.

Though it had not burned, the city was still smoking. It had a cordite smell. People did not seem to wish to stir about, and though shutters were open at most windows, they were not folded back.

In an empty street she came most unexpectedly across Mr. Lock, the British Consul, sitting on a cart piled high with furniture. When she spoke to him, he did not answer very civilly.

As why should he? He had come to Naples to buy up furniture cheap from the Jacobin plunder, but had been denied first passage by Sir William and Nelson, and so had missed the best bargains, and all because of this superficial, grasping and vulgar-minded woman.

And what was the furniture for?

"If one is underpaid and denied the proper privileges of one's office, one cannot sleep on a bed of one's own choosing," he snapped.

"Still, you seem to have chosen a good variety," she said, peering into the cart, and went on.

She did not go far. She could see that the Palazzo Sesso had been despoiled, the Villa Emma plundered, and Sir William's private apartment bombed. She had no heart to see more.

"Of course it was," said Sir William. "It was because I was so popular. One can always depend upon the goodwill of the populace, for they do as they like, and then afterward they make amends. But only if they have done you some damage first; after all, they are only human."

Alas, a war kills not so much the living as the world they lived in. Sir William had been right. She should not have gone ashore. To have seen it swept away utterly would have been one thing; to see it in ruins, was worse.

"I saw little Mr. Lock, too. He was quite rude. I don't know why. He was buying up furniture."

"He is cousin by marriage to Charles James Fox, who looms large. We must have him to dinner, I suppose."

But he could not come to dinner. He was writing a letter to certain persons about certain persons, whom he would not name, but his father could be counted upon to show the letter around.

"I have settled matters between the nobility and Her Majesty. She is not to see on her arrival any of her former evil counsellors, nor the women of fashion, alltho' Ladies of the Bed-Chamber, formerly her friends and companions, who did her dishonour by their disolute life. *All, all* is changed. She has been very *unfortunate;* but she is a good woman, and has sense enough to profit by her *past unhappiness,* and will make for the future *amende honorable* for the past," wrote Emma, sending to Greville practically the letter he had once sent Sir William about her, and with much the same attitude. She could not know that, for her own attitudes had changed. She felt secure.

"It would be charity to send me some things, for in saving all for my royal & dear friend I lost my little all," she added. "Never mind."

The 1st of August was the anniversary of the Battle of the Nile. The centerpiece of the celebration was to be a barge fitted up as a Roman galley.

"And the sailors want me to sit in it, what shall I be?" asked Emma.

Sir William considered. Cleopatra would be inappropriate; Dido, for the same reasons, seemed far from wise; no one knew the name of Pompey's wife; and Bellona seemed uncalled-for, Britannia an anachronism. "I am afraid there is not much left but Calypso. You must do the best you can."

"What did she feel?"

"The barge will be forty yards away at least. Feel what you like, it will not be visible," said Sir William kindly, following the myth, and so encountering Penelope, a prudish young woman with a taste for tapestry. She came from Nevis. "Be something classical. It does not matter."

She was something classical. It did not matter.

There was a twenty-one-gun salute from all the ships at anchor, a general illumination, and the barge went by with lamps fixed on the oars, a rostral column, and two angels at the stern to hold Nelson's portrait up. Looking through his telescope, Nelson saw dear Emma; he had wondered where she was.

Feeling the eyes of the world upon her, Emma impudently waved. An orchestra sang his praises.

"I relate this more from gratitude than vanity," he said, writing to his wife, which was only the truth. Vanity was assuaged. It was now only gratitude that ached.

In his second draft, he thought it wiser not to mention Emma. "The beauty of the whole," he added, "was beyond description."

Having condemned 105 to death, 200 to life imprisonment, 322 to shorter terms, 288 to deportation and 67 to exile, the King made ready to depart. He was constitutionally timid. Confront him with a *fait accompli,* and he merely looked around for the accomplices. He would be glad to get back to Palermo.

Conditions were still savage in the streets. You could see the glitter of eyes just beyond the clearing made by torchlight. The tyranny of the minority will always perish; the tyranny of the mob survives.

In the Cathedral, the Cardinal was up to the end of his oration:

> . . . as though one brought back from the past the thing itself, all bloody, fresh killed and steaming, and held it up to the present and said, see what you have done. If you have not done it, you will come to it soon enough. And then the harpy throws the human rag away, and laughs.
>
> Oh God, in past time, when life was pleasant, they saw their past and future pleasant, and all history was one continuous meadow. But now, because of the way we live now, all the traps are opened up, the gunwales are awash, the slaves are chained to the anchor, for there must be no evidence, and we have bloodied all history with what we have done, and left the meadow reeking. There is no place where we can go, and as for the future, we shall not live to see it. Pray that it be not furnished forth our way. And let us die.

"The King is in great spirits, and he calls me his *grande maitresse,*" said Emma. *"Mais il est bonne d'être chez le Roi, mais mieux d'être chez soit."*

So off they sailed, with everything done and nothing

settled, back to Palermo again, for Naples, like Ireland, was now no place for pleasure or recreation.

"The wind," said Nelson, "is rising."

But justice was done; that left only injustice, surely, to be dealt with.

In Weimar, Goethe, who upon his return from Italy, emboldened by the looser morals of warmer climes, had taken a woman of the people as his mistress, was drawing up a will in favor of Christiane Vulpius, so she should be provided for in case the French came. She was no Emma. She was a *Kinder, Küche,* and *Kirche* sort of woman. But she satisfied him and presented no fewer social problems than did Sir William's excellent living gallery of sculptures. If the French came too close, he was even prepared to marry her, as the banker Récamier had married his illegitimate daughter to provide for her and then, since he had not been guillotined, had been forced to live with her rather than acknowledge her irregular birth, get an annulment, and so besmirch his name.

He was not, however, prepared to marry her just yet.

VIII

It seemed to them odd—they had always thought to go home to Naples, their stay in Palermo had been temporary, but now they had seen their houses in ruins, they had that home-coming feeling about Palermo instead. Once they reached Palermo, everything would be all right. It could certainly not be all wrong. The King, who in Naples had stayed in his cabin as much as possible, here walked about quite confidently on deck.

The ships processed into warmer air, scented with limes and oranges. It was siesta. Sir William gave himself up to a happy contemplation of melons, peaches, grapes, *prosciutto con fighi*, and other emblems of maturity. Nelson wrote letters. Emma, admirably posed, admired the view.

"I've told Lady Nelson all about you," said Nelson, startling her. He seemed these days to approach her each time from a different direction and always rapidly.

"All?" she asked blankly, with an inner thump. "But you do not know all."

"I mean I sang your praises."

"Oh those," said Emma, who knew all of them, for when nervous she sometimes sang them to herself. She was relieved.

Platonic as ever, he gave her hand a grateful squeeze. He was incorrigible.

"The Queen has prepared a fete in our honor," she told him.

At noon they dropped anchor in Palermo Harbor and the Queen came aboard, embraced Emma and clapped a necklace around her neck—the royal portrait surrounded by diamonds, suspended by a chain—stepped back to admire the effect, trod in the scupper and went wet-soled to dinner. Sir William received a similarly mounted portrait of the King. The Queen, who was sentimental about everything, gushed.

"It is a false bottom," said Sir William. "Take it out, and you can see the solid bedrock of indifference underneath," but only to Nelson. He was polite as other men are skeptical—that is, from habit rather than from any lack of conviction. He did not wish to spoil Emma's triumph.

They went ashore at a gilded stucco stage, emblematical of everything and nothing, where the local senators awaited them, robes flapping in the breeze. The city was drunk but not disorderly. The *Te Deum* sung in the Cathedral was long but uplifting. In the evening there was not one pyrotechnic display, but several.

"Pinchbeck," said Sir William, fingering his royal medallion, "but neatly mounted, all the same."

Nelson's gift was to be a title, a thing not only to be prized above diamonds, but considerably less costly to have made up, though an estate was included with it, as was also a diamond sword. The sword he accepted. About the title, he was wary, for titles, he had learned, are apt to become an expense.

Emma implored him to accept. Where else would he be offered a dukedom? "You consider your honor too much," she said, "if you persist in refusing what the King and Queen consider theirs."

"Lord Nelson," said the King, his tone elevated, his manner not, "do you wish that your name alone should pass with honor to posterity, and that I, Ferdinand Bourbon, should appear ungrateful?"

"Of course not," said Nelson brusquely, deeply moved. "I shall accept."

Glad to get rid of it, for it had gone begging, the King embraced him.

"Where the devil is it?" asked Nelson afterward.

"At the foot of Mount Etna, near Syracuse. The name Bronte means thunderer."

"The Queen has sent me two carriage loads of dresses!" shouted Emma, bursting in with the most splendiferous a hasty rummage could provide. "If I have fagged, I am more than repaid."

As the Austrian Ambassador said, no one but his master was forgotten here.

"He has done nothing worth remembering," snapped the King, who had hoped the Holy Roman Emperor would send a few troops.

"We are dying with the heat, and the feast of Santa Rosalia begins this day. How shall we get through it?" demanded Nelson. "Even our dear Lady Hamilton has been unwell."

It was the excitement; it did fair do her in.

Santa Rosalia was made of more durable stuff. A cave-dwelling ascetic, she had been so intent upon her devotions as not to notice that the stalactites dripped calcium and had solidified in the act of turning the penultimate page of a volume of the Church Fathers. God, in this case, had offered not bread, but a stone, and her handsomely chiseled features were trotted about yearly, carried aloft in procession by sturdy peasants with the biceps to manage her.

Between popery and propinquity, Charles Lock was not happy.

"That infamous woman," he wrote home, "is at the bottom of all the mischief which has rendered my stay so uncomfortable for the last six months. We have in Lady Hamilton the bitterest enemy you can imagine." He had no doubt of it; he had been seated incorrectly at dinner, according to his precedence as British Consul rather than his presumption as the husband of a relative of Lord Fitzgerald. It rankled.

What he complained of was true. Emma was without malice, and so, unsuited to the polite usages of society. As the Duchess of Devonshire had discovered years ago, though respectable enough in other ways, she had no small talk. Lock complained to Sir William.

"The Court has the impression you are a Jacobin," said Sir William. "You must be on your guard."

"She has insinuated my wife's principles are Republican," said Mr. Lock. This was quite untrue: as everybody knew, his wife had no principles.

"The Queen says that our not going about in society more shows we condemn it. But how can we go, if we are not asked?"

"I shall have Emma put you down on the list," said Sir William.

"No doubt Your Excellency means well, but what can you do, when there is a *person* so able and so bent upon counteracting you?" said Lock, forced to speak plainly.

"You will have the goodness to refer to my wife by her correct title," said Sir William. "She is not from Porlock. I do not haul you out of your own mire for the joy of being besplattered by it. You may go." He was not a man who reacted favorably to the use of force.

"She has poisoned his mind against me," wrote Lock. "His health is very much broken and his frame is so feeble that even a slight attack of bile, to severe fits of which he has lately been subject, may carry him off. With all this malice, her Ladyship maintains every appearance of civility with expressions of goodwill to us both." He had no patience with appearances, which was odd, since he had so much difficulty in keeping his own up that surely he might be expected to realize that others did not always find their maintenance easy.

"Public opinion should be formed, but never followed," said Sir William wearily, telling Emma about Lock. "But since it is our duty to others to do the former, and to ourselves, to avoid the latter, could you not be more discreet?"

"But I am discreet," wailed Emma, in some bewilderment, for in her lexicon—since she had compiled it from oral evidence—this word had a merely sexual meaning. She then went off with Nelson to play faro. They would have gone all three, but Sir William these days had to retire by ten.

Nelson's brother William had been baying after succession to the title, and now there were two would bay twice as loud. "Ambition, pride, and a selfish disposition are among the various passions which torment him," wrote Fanny, who knew nothing of Palermo, where even the heat was passionate. She added that Lord Minto's eldest son was deaf.

Nelson was not. Nor did he care for the high moral tone to which Admiralty correspondence seemed recently to have risen. "Do not, my dear Lord," he asked Lord Spencer, "let the Admiralty write harshly to me—my generous soul cannot bear it."

With that indifference to sensibility which is the chief characteristic of states sensible of the proprieties, the Admiralty wrote harshly anyway, and as he had warned, he could not bear it. He was accused of dalliance.

He scarcely knew what to do. He had had a sound Christian upbringing, which tells us what we shouldn't do, not what we should. Smiting the heathen is always allowable, but what does one do when one is smitten? For the Song of Solomon, as we know—for we have been told, if the subject must be brought up—is a purely allegorical work. It describes the soul's union with God. It settles for less.

And though universal applause can drown out the hypercritical, it cannot, alas, drown them outright. When the applause dies down, they become once more audible, like crickets at evening—like Consul Lock.

On the 3rd of September, the Queen concluded the display of her gratitude with a *fête champêtre*, the palace, the city, the gardens illuminated, and a counterfeit of the French flagship *Orient* blown up in fireworks and then allowed to sink through the black waters of the sky, still one more allusion to the Battle of the Nile.

Emma, disguised as the Genius of Taste, but she had risen above mere taste and that showed, led the party forward across the lawn toward a Temple of Fame, on the roof of which squatted Fame herself, blowing a trumpet. Inside the temple stood three wax statues, Nelson in the middle, with Lady Hamilton on one side of him and Sir William on the other. Prince Leopold, a boy of nine, dressed as a midshipman, mounted a stepladder behind the middle statue and placed on its brow a crown of laurel, the dew on its leaves counterfeited in diamonds.

Nelson then embraced the Prince. "You are the guardian angel of our papa and my dominions," said Leopold, who had been rehearsed, but not enough.

Since wax dissolves in warm weather, the statues were then removed to a lumber room.

"Entre nous, I fear their Sicilian Majesties will not follow our advice, which is to return immediately to Naples," said Sir William. Certainly the King had no mind to. What with venery and Venus, the palace and piscator, and the theatre in the evening as well, he found nothing lacking. Like Charles II—but with the advantage of one more kingdom, if far less brains—he did not propose to go upon his travels again.

"I have wrote you lately but short letters," Nelson explained to his wife, and it was quite true they got no longer, "for my time is fully occupied that I never set my foot out of the writing room, except now and then in the evening with Sir William and Lady Hamilton to the palace."

That there was a large state bed in the writing room nagged at him. These palaces, though sumptuous, were apt to be furnished in harum-scarum taste. The bed had been too large to move. It stood at the far end of the writing room, on a dais, and neither had been nor would be occupied.

He had been disappointed in Bronte, for though he

had not seen it, he had hoped to see some ready money from it. Expenses had been heavy.

"In Sicily, money is never ready," explained Sir William. "And if it is, there is a hand there all the sooner to take it."

Nelson had been informed that though His Sicilian Majesty's Government would be delighted to clear the title, this would cost £1000.

"The Lord giveth and the Lord taketh away," Sir William piously consoled. "They are a literal-minded people, being devout."

Once, when alone in the room, Nelson had been unable to resist the impulse to look under the embroidered coverlet of the bed, to see if it had sheets and blankets upon it. It had not.

"I have one piece of news to tell you which causes a few is it possible?" reported Fanny. "Admiral Dickson is going to marry a girl of 18 years, surely he has lost his senses. All true, the Admiral saw Miss Willings (a daughter of one of the minor canons at Norwich) not quite three weeks at Yarmouth. He fell desperately in love, gave balls on board ship, then on shore, in short was quite desperate . . . I heard Admiral and Mrs. Nugent have separated, a difference of temper she says is the cause . . . Miss Susanna I took to the concert last Thursday. We were entertained by seeing an old nabob make love to a very rich porter brewer's daughter . . . she must marry one of the most unpleasant-looking men in the world for the sake of driving four horses."

"Oh God," said Nelson. There was a ball to be given on ship that night. The arrangements he had left to Emma.

"Emma who looks as well and as blooming as ever talks of death every day," wrote Sir William to Lord Minto, with complacency and amusement. "I believe it is the heat and sirocco winds that depress us all for Lord Nelson complains too."

"I think you had better ask, in strict confidence, that Lord Elgin stop on his way out to Constantinople and investigate," said Lord Minto to Lord Grenville. "It seems there is something in the wind."

"Fox has shown me some most odd letters," said Lord Grenville to Lord Minto, "from a young relative of his by marriage, a Mr. Charles Lock, who is our Consul at Palermo."

Mr. Lock's dandiacal addiction to facial hair had resulted in an incident. The King could not abide facial hair, and in particular not side whiskers, which he associated with the Jacobin.

Despite a warning, Lock attended a court ball disguised as a Thames fisherman, though changing the red bonnet for a blue, for fear of giving offense.

"The King says your dress is indecent," said Sir William, in a flap out of nowhere. "You had better retire, put on a domino, and return."

Offended, Lock drew himself up to his little height, an acrobatic feat akin to the exertions of a macaw beaking its way back onto its perch.

"I have only to observe to Your Excellency that I wore this identical dress at a masquerade when several of *our* royal family were present; it could therefore never enter my head that it would be offensive here. If the character of my costume *is* economical, I have spared no expense in that of my wife, so it cannot be supposed that I intended any disrespect to this Court thereby." Mr. Lock was a typical member of the new middle classes and exhibited their morality in the same sense that a bitch in heat would have exhibited herself. "My wife," he added, "is the Peruvian over there. The one with the fruit on her head."

"Il n'était pas nécessaire que Monsieur Lock vint ici nous braver dans un costume sans culottes pour demontrer ses principes!" roared the Queen, though French is not a gusty language and she always shook like an old bridge when she clattered across it.

"Turn him out. Turn him out! Or I will turn him out myself," squealed the King, standing above the rising floods upon a bench, and glowering with the glum resignation of a Cnut.

Lock waited upon Sir William next day with a handwritten memorial of the incident.

"It is unfortunate," said Sir William, *and made no apology.*

Emma came in to say she had talked the Queen around, but since she was as clumsy to move as a barge, it had taken two hours.

"Lock," said Sir William, "that you should be agreeable perhaps transcends reason, but could you not confine yourself to common sense? The King trounced a whiskered Portuguese officer out of the theatre pit only last night. Unfortunately his fellow officers rose, pointed to their own whiskers, and burst into a horse laugh. As a result, His Majesty smarts. The punishment for side whiskers is three months' imprisonment. So shave."

Sobbing with indignation, Lock shaved. "So well does this artful woman know how to create herself a merit by this ostentation of what she terms doing *good for evil,*" he wrote home, after Emma had once more gotten him received at Court.

"I always heard she was a harmless creature, boisterous perhaps, but not bad," said Fox. "What's wrong with her?"

"She's there."

"Well, so's my cousin by marriage or whatever you call 'im. I must say he does not write a pretty letter."

"But he writes often," said Lord Grenville. "Where is Elgin now?"

"In Vienna."

Not only would the King not return to Naples, he would no longer listen to the advice of the Queen. He said he preferred to die where he was, and that not soon, rather than go where she proposed to send him.

"I have always foreseen that as I grew older my power would diminish," said the Queen. "If I knew where to find the River Lethe, I would travel there on foot in order to drink its water." Lethe's exact whereabouts being unknown, she toyed instead with the idea of a trip to

Vienna, which has always been on the Danube, a chartable stream. "I shall ask for a few months' leave to distract my mind, restore my health and marry my daughters," she told Emma. If she had not an army, she had daughters, and there are more ways than one of getting aboard a throne.

The King had commissioned Canova to do an heroic portrait, which loomed larger in Naples, where it was set up, than ever it did in the master's *oeuvre*.

"He allowed himself to be scaled the wrong way," said Sir William. "Nothing taller than eight feet has any aesthetic merits whatsoever. It is the same with any microcosm; multiply the field of vision, and you can see the flaws."

Lord and Lady Elgin arrived in October, he sending home the male, or serious, recommendations; Lady Elgin, being a woman, preferring to report upon the unforgivable, and hence irremediable, flaws.

Nelson was seen with Emma everywhere, most often drowsing beside her at the gaming table, and the public display of devotion must ever be an offense against the well-regulated decorums of society.

"Captain Morris went to Sir William to deliver some dispatches he had for Lord N. He read them and then called Lady Hamilton out of the room. When she came back, she said, 'Sir William, we shall not go to the country today; you must dress yourself and go to Court after breakfast.' 'Why?' asked Sir William. 'Oh, I will tell you presently,' said Lady Hamilton, flounced her head, and went on talking. Is it not a pity a man who had gained so much credit should fling himself away in this shameful manner?"

Lady Elgin was indignant. No matter who she was now, they all remembered what Lady Hamilton had been. And Nelson, to speak plain, had not come from a background much better, though Lady Nelson was understood to be, whatever her other faults, quite respectable.

Lord Elgin recommended that Sir William be recalled. Emma had grown too high-flown. If tampering with His Majesty's Navy was, on a low sensual level, explicable, tampering with His Majesty's Mail Pouch was beyond excuse.

"She runs everything," said Lock.

Having made their several reports, the Elgins went off to Athens: he to play marbles; she to entertain.

On October 5th, Nelson was forced to sail to the blockade of Minorca, with nothing to entertain him on the voyage but some letters from Fanny.

Brother William was still snuffling after the possible succession to Bronte. He was plump for a trufflehound. Josiah had sent home a description of the estate, and so —like Lord Falmouth in greater extremity—had given "last first proof that he had brains." "The dampness occasioned by the constant rain was beyond description." And worse than that, beef was 9/4 the stone. She was to go and brace her nerves in Devonshire.

In Palermo, they could not brace their nerves at all. "I wish it could be pointed out to the King that there should be an amnesty," said a courtier, "but who could do so?" He had already caused so much, that there was no one willing to risk his further displeasure.

Nelson returned from Minorca.

On the 9th of November, which was called the 19th Brumaire, there was a *coup d'état* in France. The Directory fell. Napoleon was in, and therefore the revolutionary calendar was out. He had better things to do than rename streets and confuse poesy with politics. In Germany, Goethe—as benign and mechanical as ever —saluted the dawn of a new age, but had no desire to beckon to it; a salute should suffice. In Palermo, Emma, who knew nothing of Cardano on Cards or the medieval versions of Fortuna, went gambling to celebrate. Her favorite game was faro. The word means lighthouse, specifically that beacon built in Ptolemy's day to guide the mariner home. Nelson dozed beside her. When his eyes were open, she dazzled him with a glance. When his eyes were shut, she wondered why he dazzled her. They were a noticeable couple, for both had been born egregious, a quality which cannot be concealed and so naturally provokes the ill-will of those who have everything to conceal themselves, mostly their own mediocrity.

> Pardon me, my Lord [wrote Troubridge]. It is my sincere esteem for you that makes me mention it. I know you can have no pleasure sitting up all night at cards; why, then, sacrifice your health, comfort, purse, ease, everything, to the customs of a country where your stay cannot be long? Your Lordship is stranger to half that happens, or the talk it occasions; if you knew what your friends feel for you, I am sure you would cut all the nocturnal parties. Lady H's character will suffer, nothing can prevent people from talking. A gambling lady, in the eye of an Englishman, is lost.

Nelson was a little man neither to his followers nor his friends. It was only his superiors who diminished him, as best they were able. He forgave the admonition, for gambling did not bore him.

"Why do you interest yourself in such things?" he asked.

"I don't. They interest me," said Emma, and shoved another pile of ducats down. "Besides, it is the fashion," she explained, lost, and paid up—with his money.

She paid up with a good deal of it, and there were other drains upon his pocket, which in optimum case was not so deep as a well but more like a cistern, being replenished from above when he rained money into it, rather from below by the cool crystal springs of a private income. Graffer, having no English garden to play with any more, Nelson sent him off to Bronte to organize an English farm as an example to the Sicilians of the singular excellence of nonvinous agriculture.

"I hope the news of the Dukedom," wrote Fanny, "is true, if you have money given to support the rank." Since he had not, he planted seven hundred acres to corn and watched Emma gamble.

"They have everything in common," said Damas, a

damned Frenchman, "money, faults, vanities, wrong-doing of every kind."

"Her rage is play, and Sir William says when he dies she will be a beggar," reported Lady Minto.

For New Year's there were fetes, but it was New Year's of 1800, and a century is more solemn than a year, for it is a kind of swivel which allows us to whirl either way, forward or back. A number of attitudes were permissible, so long as they were neither shown nor voiced and so long as they were not Emma's.

A little solemnly, like guests at a ball, waiting for the doors to the supper room to be folded back, perspiring from the crush of their exertions, they watched to see what would be given them as room and reward. For they expected empty rooms, prepared for them to enter. They would saunter in at the proper time:

—and, a little solemnly, having defended themselves stubbornly thus far, they prepared to fall back upon the ultimate room, the chamber in which they would die;

—or, securely, from boxes of rank and station, they waited, like grandparents, to see the new child, who might or might not be worth a christening mug;

—or, anyhow, the guns in the harbor fired a salute, the churches, despite the snows, were warm inside—the glass in their windows steamy—and there were midnight masses as well as singing in the streets.

A yellow rocket arched, sprang into bloom, and with the century it died. A cold wind blew through the gardens, like change, and roused thereby a whirl of snow and dead leaves, a sort of fetch.

Clocks chimed. There was a pause. The doors to the supper room were folded back. But there was no change, and, a little stiff, Miss Knight, who had been asked to the party, shook out her skirt and let out her breath and said "Well!"

It was over with. The world was still there. The millennialist must change his plans. And yet his defeat did not make them that more the festive. The night was cloudy and dark, the rockets now seemed to explode anticlimactically, and the Hamiltons and Nelson went home early.

At the rear of the Palazzo Palagonia, a terrace overlooked the sea, which was black but empty except for the flare of a single fishing boat rocking up and down not far out.

"Well, what will it bring?" asked Nelson as they stood there peering toward the horizon, each looking ahead from a different age, a different altitude; each having climbed a different height in time.

"Oh all sorts of good things, I expect," said Emma. "Doesn't it always?" She was thirty-five and now faced life head on, for now neither profile was the better one; they had both aged, so she favored neither side.

"I meant what will it be like?" said Nelson, taking her hand. He was forty-two, little had been granted him in the human way as yet, and New Year's is a lonely time. He felt cold.

Emma, who had an impulse to turn back, and who was besides both compassionate and sorry, took one of Sir William's hands in her free one and squeezed it confidingly.

But Sir William, who was seventy and could see farther than either of them and had taken Nelson's question seriously, looked out over the sea and said, "Whatever else it will be, it will be vulgar." New children are always vulgar, for if they are not vulgar, they are not children—and an old man will put up with much for the pleasure of congenial company—and besides, it would not be for long.

Emma, who had felt the sudden chill, asked to withdraw indoors.

"Take her," said Sir William. "I would like to remain outdoors a while." For though the society of others enhances our knowledge of them, if we would know ourselves, we must isolate the beast and contemplate him, enlarged, at our leisure.

He stood respectfully before the view, his hands folded, his legs apart, at rest, and realized—as soon as his thoughts had roiled up into some temporary identity before scattering again—that he had been remembering that in Apollonius of Tyana, and other authors, we may read that sometime in the late spring, the beginning of the old Pagan year, a voice had been heard across these waters, crying, "Great Pan is dead," and that the sound of that lament had lingered over the sea for a long time. Indeed, he could hear it now; and that when Anthony was at last put down by Octavian's favorite, there was heard in the streets of Alexandria the ghostly music, the sistrums and the tambours and syrinxes of the old gods, deserting him.

Yes, it would be a vulgar century.

Nelson, who had been gone for no little time, came out to join him. Sir William had thought he would. Poor man, no doubt he was puzzled, for he needed them both, a quite natural thing but not to the morality of a clergyman's son, for to the clergy, nothing is natural.

Since Nelson did not speak, it occurred to Sir William to wonder what he saw out there. Not Great Pan or the gods of Alexandria leaving, certainly. But he might very well be catching a glimpse of the glitter of the fairies moving off down the trod, for he was a Norfolk man, and Norfolk folk were often fey.

Sir William did not know whether it was the irreality or the reality of the world which pleased him more, but since the two alternate so rapidly as to form what seems a continuous image, perhaps it did not matter. He was by no means dissatisfied. We admire the whole, accept both, and pick our own way to our own death, though it is possible to wave to each other through the trees. It is an autumn ramble. The leaves are marvelous colors. The air is bracing. So why hurry?

But a glass of brandy at three in the morning would, on this occasion, do no harm.

New Year's, it is worse than a birthday, thought Emma. One does not *always* wish to sleep alone.

"Would you ever," said Mrs. Cadogan, "and I thought it was to be only a sketch." She was pleased as punch and just as jocular. She had attained to the quality;

she had had her portrait done, proper, in a miniature.

It was Sir William's New Year's gift. He had had all four of them done: Nelson in profile, plump, hideous, in the Sicilian taste; Emma all Sir Peter Lely—for it was a provincial place, Palermo, and the old styles die hard—with blue skin, breasts like honeydews, pretty in the face, and fashionably tousled hair; himself, well—"Ah yes," said Mrs. Cadogan, "that's himself"—a face which in Reynolds' day had been thrifty but dreaming and sad, was now sad but certain. It was odd. Mrs. Cadogan and he, they were dissimilar, but they both had the same look. They had both been watchers.

"Ma, you do look a perfect badger," said Emma.

The badger is a neat and tidy animal, and what is past is past. "It was my best dress," said Mrs. Cadogan. It had been her best mobcap, too.

The thing they had in common, Emma saw, was that they could both outstare you. She became evasive. "Nelson looks shocking, and I look a fright," she said. "Would packed ice help, do you suppose?"

"Silly girl, where would you get ice here?" Mrs. Cadogan took her own miniature and said good night, put the miniature away, took it out, went to bed, blew the candle out and went to sleep assuaged. Sir William, when he thought of it, always did the right thing, which was more than she could say for some she knew, even if sometimes it did take him twenty years.

Unfortunately the future is soon enough that imaginary time, the present, which is neither here nor there, but painted on the fore edge, and so, unless you know the trick, invisible. The present is only a riptide between two seas, a consequence of the past, dangerous, given to froth, or else invisible. The present looks placid, but has the strength to drag us down.

Sir William was in a jitter about finances. No sense could be made of Greville, and since teeth cannot be extracted at a distance, it was necessary to return to England to procure cash. But that was a voluntary excursion. This was worse.

"I have been recalled," said Sir William bleakly; he could face ingratitude, but not impertinence. "How can they? I have been here for thirty-six years."

He had not only become Italianized, but *italicized*. And now, to be dismissed with bad spelling, without so much as a *nota bene*.

"I shall protest to the dear Queen," said Emma, who felt herself suddenly cast out again, a feeling she had forgotten for years.

"My dear, I am still a British subject. I can be subjected to any indignity my government pleases. That is all the term means."

"But we could stay on here."

"We are people of position. What sort of people do you suppose we would become, if position we had none? We should not exist. We should be nonentities."

Emma went to the Queen. "She is half dead with grief," she said, when she came back.

"How unlike her. She so seldom does anything by halves."

"She says she will try to persuade the King to write to England on our behalf. Who are they sending out?"

"A young man named Paget. He is the son of Lord Uxbridge."

"It is Lock, depend upon it," said Emma. "He has been our undoing. I should never have caught him with all that furniture, and he should never have grown side whiskers."

The King, however, would do anything to thwart his wife, and so did nothing to help. Sir William did not come to hunt often enough these days, and when he did he was such a shambles there was no fun in him any more.

"Yesterday, on your departure," wrote the Queen, "I endured a scene of frenzy, shouts, and shrieks, threats to kill you, throw you out the window, call your husband to complain you had turned your back. I am extremely unhappy, and with so many troubles I have only two alternatives, either to go away or die of sorrow. The accursed Paget is in Vienna."

It was where Lord Elgin had paused earlier; it seemed to be where the devil stopped to change horses. Maria Carolina had even tried the kid gloves, but to no avail. Sir William was old. He did not shoot with a steady arm. He must go. And besides, Lady Hamilton had turned her back on His Majesty as recently as the last time he had pinched her, which was eight years ago.

"Furthermore," said Ferdinand, "I am no longer moved by white kid gloves," and flung them in her face.

"Den Dank, Dame, begehr' ich nicht!" For of course he knew the literature of his fetish and had been saving this for years. At last he had spoken German to her. He was not deceived. Sir William was used up, that woman now ran everything, and what was worse, was a friend of the Queen. So let her leave. It was one of those periods when Ferdinand's affections for his wife were in their waning phase.

"Und verläßt sie zur selben Stunde," said the Queen, her worst fears realized.

Sir William was not surprised. The last three *battu* had been held without him.

"But what are we to do?" wailed Emma.

"Why, make the best of things," said Sir William. "We were going home for a visit anyway; and perhaps when the fishing season comes around again, so will he, for I can still fish."

He had no desire to show his chagrin, which was scarcely in a fit state to be shown. It is so with all our emotions: when we feel them is not the time to show them, for they are not then at their best. They are then as useless as a shriveled balloon. It is only inflation makes them presentable.

"We will return," he said, with absolute certainty, since he did not believe they would. "Do not fret. And as for that, we are not yet gone. But I wish Nelson were not at Malta."

So did Nelson. He applied for leave to return to Palermo. His health demanded it, he said. Troubridge called him a fool direct. Ball wrote to Emma. But go he must. If it was not his health, it was the Goddess Hygeia, demanded him back.

"All I shall say is to express my extreme regret that your health should be such as to oblige you to quit your station off Malta," said Keith, his superior, who knew all about the Goddess Hygeia and did not like her. Health, to a well-bred Englishman, is always an unwholesome thing.

"She sits at the councils and rules everybody and everything," reported Lady Minto.

Lord Spencer, the Admiralty Lord, was plainer. "Having observed that you have been under the necessity of quitting your station off Malta on account of your health —which I am persuaded you could not have thought of doing without such necessity—it appeared to me much more advisable for you to come home at once than to be obliged to remain inactive at Palermo. I am joined in the opinion by all your friends here that you will be more likely to recover your health and strength in England than in an inactive situation at a foreign court, however pleasing the respect and gratitude shown to you for your services may be."

"It does not seem clear whether he will go home," said Lord Minto. "He does not seem at all conscious of the sort of discredit he has fallen into, or the cause of it, for he still writes, not wisely, about Lady H. and all that. But it is hard to condemn and use ill a hero, as he is in his own element, for being foolish about a woman who has art enough to make fools of many wiser than an admiral."

"Gossip makes the same ripples, no matter what the stone," wrote Fanny to her son Josiah, who had written to her about Nelson.

Josiah should be beaten with his own broomstick, on his own behind. Could none of them understand *friendship*?

Apparently not.

"Our private characters are to be stabbed in the dark," said Emma, denying everything, and besides, nothing had happened yet. She had been given the Cross of Malta and was now a Chanoiness of that order. Nelson had arranged it, and the Queen was having the order itself set in diamonds for her.

"Mr. Paget is to come by land," wrote Fanny. "I have seen some of his plate, which is fine, but there is not much of it."

"Give my love to Lady Minto and kiss the children for your sincere and attached Emma," wrote Emma, to Lord Minto.

"Indeed you shall not," said Lady Minto, who had a horror of disease. "She is a hussy. It would not be safe. Who knows whose lips those lips have touched? It would be better to burn the infected thing."

Minto smiled and filed the letter away.

"Is it a letter from your wife?" asked Emma. "What does she say?"

"That everyone is ill," Nelson told her, with a grimace. "It is what she always says. She is a born nurse. She haunts the wards. Lord St. Vincent has the stone; Susannah has fever in the bowels. My father is not well. Captain Pearson has died on his way home from Honduras, of yellow fever; and she has even been to Admiral Bligh, who says that yellow fever is indeed dreadful. He is the breadfruit tree man. She writes these notes to cheer me."

"One would expect her to dwell upon the cheerful side of things."

Nelson should not have spoken so of his wife, but he felt bitter. "Oh, she dwells there, all right, but her visits are paid to the other side of the house. It is about her visits she writes principally."

"I believe Mrs. Walpole will give me up for being too humdrum," wrote Fanny. It was damnable. To love another man's wife is, in the proper circles, customary; to love one's best friend's wife reduces her to Bathsheba at once. Why did Emma have to look at him that way?

She was only idly wondering. She could not be called scheming, ever. It was merely that, a starfish, she had been born with an instinct as to which rock to cling to and in which storm, so as not to be overwhelmed. A spume of indignation might flare forty feet into the air, but still, there she was, clinging, snug and safe. In calmer seas she swam pleasantly, involuntarily, with the tide, which drew her on.

She dropped her eyes. She had been worrying about whether or not Sir William could survive an English winter. If he could not, what then?

"Do you realize," she said, "that Acton has married his thirteen-year-old niece, during Carnival. Why on earth would he do that? He is sixty-four."

"Why, to save appearances, I expect," said Sir William luxuriously. "He had been a bachelor too long, a phenomenon imperfectly understood in this country, but finally tumbled to. No doubt people were beginning to talk." To be twice Emma's age was bad enough; to be five times as old as one's wife could scarcely admit of comment.

"He says he wishes to retire with her to England."

"Now whyever would he do that?" asked Sir William, genuinely surprised, "when he can quite easily go into hiding here until the girl is of age and the whole thing looks respectable?"

"It will make the Queen feel her age."

"No doubt it makes Sir John feel his," said Sir William, speaking from certainty. "Paget has arrived in Naples and wants my house here. I told him he could not have it, as I meant to return next winter."

"Then where will he stay?"

"For all I care, he can stay with Lock, and they can with profit extract the wax from each other's ears—the better to enjoy the mutual din," said Sir William, who did not mean to be unfair, merely unkind.

Nelson, who wished to help, without a word to anyone gave orders to detach two line-of-battle ships from the investment of Malta—for he was given to these sneaky streaks of kindness—so that at least the Hamiltons might leave Palermo in appropriate state. A cruise was what they needed to take their minds off the terrors of departure.

Sir Alexander Ball bade Emma make herself free of Malta. "We could make up a snug whist party every evening for Sir William, but we should fall very short in our attempts to amuse you, when we consider the multiplicity of engagements and amusements you have every day at Palermo," he wrote.

So it was arranged. Nelson had only one favor to ask. Could they not leave Miss Knight behind this time? There was no harm in her, but she had a habit to spring out at you from unexpected places, tablet in hand, to add to her memoirs.

Paget arrived at Lock's. Whatever there might or might not be for supper (Mrs. L. was a frightful housekeeper), you could always count on at least an earful there.

There was no direct communication between the Embassy and the Consulate. Lock had grown his side whiskers again. Apart from that, he was good for nothing but to curry favor and stamp passports.

"And even at that, he is not frank."

Paget, entrusted with an errand upon the successful outcome of which his future depended (to see Ferdinand bullied back to Naples, where he belonged), was eager to take up the reins of office, in order to put the horse before the cart. He would not, Sir William thought, be popular for long, if this was the line he meant to fish with, for the King preferred to stay where he was. One must always distinguish between the man and the office, however, and Sir William was almost prepared to do so.

"The Queen calls him 'the fatal Paget,' " said Emma.

"No, not fatal. Merely terminal," said Sir William. "But even the condemned have yet some time to live between the order and its execution, and I do not intend to be carried out the Appian Gate in a litter. I shall await the boat at Ostia instead." He proposed to hem and haw until the *Foudroyant* arrived and he could make his departure with some pomp. Paget should not get in until he was assured of getting out.

"Sir William cannot help adding that his sincere attachment to Their Majesties, their royal family and their Kingdom is such," he wrote to Acton, "that if he was not fully persuaded that in a very few months he may have the satisfaction of returning again, he should at this moment be in the utmost despair."

Persuaded, but not convinced.

"Lady Hamilton is busy crying you up as a Jacobin," said Lock. "It is the line she hews to." And he eyed Paget's lack of side whiskers. "It is what she calls all of us, so if that is what we are, we gain no distinction thereby. She could not endure to remain at Palermo shorn of her rays in the capacity of a private individual."

"Lady Hamilton is none of your damn business," said Nelson, who had been asked to intercede.

"I am sorry to say that Lord Nelson has given more or less in to all this nonsense. His Lordship's health is I fear sadly impaired [he had noticed a bloodshot eye], and I am assured that his fortune is fallen into the same state in consequence of great losses which both his Lordship and Lady Hamilton have sustained at faro and other games of hazard," Paget wrote home. Paget did not believe in games of hazard. He believed only in a sure thing, except of course for politics, where no money is involved—at least above the table—so it is a game of skill only.

"I merely wish to present my credentials, in order to proceed upon the business with which I was charged," he told Sir William.

"I shall present them when it is convenient."

"Your convenience or mine?"

"I fear you will have to wait upon mine, since I have no intention of waiting upon yours. I do not wish to remain here as a private individual. Unless you show me your instructions and there is something in them which obliges me to present my own letters of recall immediately, I do not intend to do so until the day before my departure. I cannot be guided by what you say *en l'air*."

"You have left me dangling *en l'air*. I can speak no other way," said Paget crossly.

"Ha! Wit!" said Sir William. "What you do with your life is your own affair, but I presume you have been given enough rope."

For the next two weeks the Hamiltons went to those parties the Pagets did not and to none of those parties to which the Pagets did, which is to say, parties at Lock's. However, Lock had time to explain his pet project—the raising of beef cattle on the island in order to improve the local agriculture.

"But where would you sell the meat?"

"Oh I wouldn't dream of selling it," said Lock, with some horror. "It is an experiment, merely."

"A pity. Our garrison on the island must miss their beef, not to mention the Navy," said Paget.

"My dear, we have failed in patriotism," said Lock to his wife. "Upon my soul, I had not thought of *their* need."

On the 21st, the *Foudroyant* entered harbor, all gun ports open, and flying Lord Nelson's flag.

"It is not exactly a yacht," he said apologetically as they stared up at the massive bulk of His Britannic Majesty's Second-Best Battleship. "But then, these are not precisely peaceful times."

Paget presented his credentials.

"Paget," said the Queen, "who replaces the kind, devoted Hamiltons, has made a bad beginning, advising us in a hard, abrupt manner and almost enforcing the King's prompt return to Naples. The King was offended."

"These people are so insensitive to all principles of honour and loyalty," wrote Paget to the Foreign Office, "I am of opinion that nothing useful or good can be effected but by the introduction and direct interference of Foreigners."

"*Io ne devo rispondere,*" said the King. "*Io sono Re, Padrone.*"

On the 22nd, Sir William presented his letters of recall.

"I shall abdicate," said the King, "rather than return to Naples with the Queen."

"I shall go to Vienna," said the Queen, "with my dear Lord Nelson, rather than remain alone with the King."

They were a compatible couple. They had much the same feelings about everything.

"I shall abdicate and leave the throne to Paget, and *he* can return to Naples," said the King.

"His Serene Majesty *has a very proper sense of Danger*," reported Paget. "In other words, he is a sad poltroon. With Acton, I am on the best of terms, save that we quarrel and spar nearly every time we meet. The Queen of Naples is certainly going to Vienna."

That was simply not true. He was not sad. He was on the whole very happy here. The climate suited him.

The *Foudroyant* sailed on the 23rd. The sails billowed out. The brass shone. The woodwork creaked. Sir William stood on deck, watching himself being pulled away from the harbor, like a broken toy on a frayed string. The sailor boys were all up in the rigging, to catch a glimpse of Emma.

"Is there anything I can do to make you more comfortable, sir?" asked an orderly.

"Why yes. If you would, it would be civil if you would tell the gun crew to pepper Palermo before we go."

"You are not to be taken seriously, sir," said the orderly, halfway between a joke and doubt.

"So it appears," said Sir William, and went below. Paget would make a hash of things, which was perhaps not his fault, he had ingredients for nothing else, but Sir William did not happen to care for hash. He did not, at that moment, care for much of anything.

However, the breeze freshened, the ship had an amiable roll, everything about a boat is so busy you cannot help but be caught up into the rhythm of it, and by the time they had reached Syracuse, Sir William had resigned himself and was eager to enjoy the freedoms of being out of office for a while.

Syracuse cheered him: we go back to the Greek to refresh ourselves. It quite revives us. There will therefore always be Greek revivals; though Bonaparte had brought back from Egypt with him a momentary fashion for everything from furniture to frills *"à l'Egyptienne,"* or at any rate, had made the Sphinx quite popular, which took brass (particularly on the furniture).

"Do you never tire of being Greek?" asked Emma, who was tired of it.

"We never tire of aping them. It is because our politics are Roman, I suspect," said Sir William, who, like the sibyl, used his knowledge to confound the suppliant, and as a diplomat, had often to maintain his reputation by providing riddles. He felt perky.

At Segesta, he asked to go ashore, if possible, alone. He wanted, he said, to make one last pilgrimage.

From the rail they watched the white longboat head for the beach, a parley for a donkey, and then a small figure bouncing up to the tableland.

"Do you suppose he will be all right?" asked Emma.

"He may well be all wrong, but he can take care of himself," said Nelson. The weather was warm. They went into the Captain's cabin, alone, for Mrs. Cadogan had been left behind at Palermo, to supervise the final packing.

"I can no longer contain myself," said Nelson, and fell upon her like a thunderbolt.

Emma felt reassured. She had been wondering now for some time how infinite was his capacity. She was an Armida, a Dido, a Santa Monica, and mostly Nike, in a windblown dress, with pleasure at the prow. But though his men adored him, this was scarcely time for interlopers at the shrine.

"Dear, dear Horatio," she said, rumpling what was left of his hair, "but we had far far better bolt the door," and leaned an arm around to do so.

Sir William strolled idly through a field brittle with flowers and dusty with pollen, the donkey and the guide behind him. The air was crystalline as high as the nearest lark, who merely scratched, but did not break, the silence. Piranesi had been here before him, but no one else. Like a small figure in a Piranesi, he raised the astonished arm to point the view, though his thoughts were less of a deeply bitten shadow than of a fresco, new found at Herculaneum, of a well-bred woman, wandering to gather flowers in an Elysian Field—his own view of what the underworld should be. Though the Greeks had chthonic deities, they wasted no time on the basement, but—sure it was solid—let the column soar.

Before him on a knoll stood the temple. It had never been finished. The pediments lacked sculpture; the cella stood, but lacked a roof. The pillars were unfluted and perhaps too plump in the miniscus. He went into the cella as into the shrine of a god familiar but unknown, the god who is always there because he is not there. His place is ready but we could not wait for him.

Weeds swooped out from the walls high up, like sconces, quivering with the candle flames of green fire. Lichen mottled the rocks, the oldest living thing, tenacious, colored rust and cadmium and *verde antico*. It was cooler within than without. A drum rested in a bunch of poppies, where it had fallen, and the air, though drowsy, had the freshness of a pleasing dream. New winds might be blowing, but they could not move stone, carry the spring seed everywhere though they might. A piece of fecund fuzz, dried already by the sun, took off in flight and hovered not far away from his nose.

He stood in the portico and looked out over the warm fields which sloped down to the sea, full not of ghosts, but of a decorous crowd which was quite alive—only not now—and which would always be alive—though not now. Over the fields rippled the crosscurrents and streams of the wind's direction, a little shudder, like that of flesh when you touched it first; and over the sea, the same.

"*Il faut que la raison rie et non se fâche.* We can at least smile. *Quand Neptune veut calmer les tempêtes, ce n'est pas aux flots, mais aux vents, qu'il s'adresse.*" It was something worth remembering, he thought, as he gazed out toward the ship. Emma must be discreet.

But the only rumor here was of quite different things. It is as well, he thought, that in my century religion came under the heading of philosophy, for in my age it did indeed make one philosophical, which is as good a reason as any for not venturing too far out into this century; whatever the powers of philosophy, still it does not encourage us to walk upon the waves.

And, placing his hand carefully against a column, he felt the stone so warm, so soft, so golden beneath his hand, and so cold and immutable within, that it refreshed one on the hottest day; it cooled the passions while it moved beneath the affections of the hand, more resilient than could be any flesh. He had done well to put his faith in marble, for faith had made him marble in return, warmed by the sun, like honey, and grateful to the fingertips. He rested his cheek for a moment against the cool stone, and then, warmed, went away. Could he have crumbled to an ash right then, ambition slaked, he would have done so. But since it is given unto all men to die, not crumble, back to the boat he must go. There had been only a moment of blancmange. The stone is by its nature discipline.

And yet: good-bye. I am a very old man and I love you very much. I find you moving. When I was young, I knew that that would be so, in the end. So now that, too, must have its end. *Ed è subito sera.*

Had there been an altar, he would have burned salt and wine and oil. As there was not, he went down through the fields again, with no need to look back, for he knew the temple stood firmly behind him, while in the fields ahead of him a woman wandered, gathering flowers.

It was her first experience of a physical man; her first, at any rate, in years. It was, to tell the truth—bar a Negress or two—his first experience of being one. He had married for respectability, and respectability does not encourage the male.

His body was that correct British color which, in jade, the Chinese call mutton fat—translucent and mottled as an oyster.

So this was love, she thought. Like hate, it was a most sustaining emotion. It buoyed you up.

"My God," sobbed Nelson, who wanted both his pleasure and to be punished for having it, too. "I have betrayed my best friend."

For the life of her, Emma could not see how. "Don't be silly. If he knew he'd be pleased. He's very fond of you, you know. We both are."

Nelson groaned.

"I shall tell him all."

"What! And cause your best friend pain?" asked Emma, not only shocked but alarmed.

"It is true that I should hate to cause him pain."

"Should you tell him, that would of course mean giving up both of us," said Emma evenly.

Nelson held his head in his hand. He felt all at sea, which is not surprising, since that was where he was.

"Besides," she consoled, "everyone thinks this happened ages ago, and so, I am sure, does he. So why distress him by acquainting him with the delayed date of a fact to which he has already had the time to grow accustomed through rumor?"

"I cannot live with it," said Nelson simply.

"Then you had far better live with us. On the whole, under the circumstances, I think perhaps that would be the best thing to do."

"But how *can* I live with my conscience?"

"It would be far better, in that case, if you were to separate," said Emma, who had been thinking about Lady Nelson and wondering what to do about *that*.

Nelson sulked. Without the rosy glow of possible damnation, he felt both naked and cold. What is the use of enjoying yourself, if there is no harm in it? He had been raised a Puritan.

"If I was not *sure*—if we were both not *sure*—that you were his true friend," Emma said, reasoning with a child, "I assure you I would never have permitted it."

"But what do we do?"

"Why, the same things over and over again, like everybody else. What else is there *to* do?"

Nevertheless, conversation at dinner seemed a little forced.

Oh well, I suppose she has fallen in love, thought Sir William, noticing the sudden improvement in her complexion. She has already abandoned one child, and now I suppose she wishes to abandon herself to a second. But it is too bad. I am afraid Nelson will take it very hard. And this is one instance in which I am impotent to help him. But then, the spectator is always impotent; he is no longer the victim of himself, and can therefore be kind without expecting kindness.

She was still there—they were both still there—so a few days of grumpiness, and everything would be all right, he supposed, though Emma's transports might be tiring.

So he ate with appetite, unhindered by made conversation; it is true, we dine unless the blow comes very near the heart indeed. It sounds French, though neither Rochefoucauld nor Vauvenargues could be called a glutton, and Rivarol died so young, it is hard to believe he had the time to eat at all. Unless, of course, it was Chamfort. Chamfort may not have lived very long either, but somehow one does have the impression that for as long as he could, he lived well.

There is much to be said for living well.

"What most afflicts a Noble Mind
Is manly Resignation,"

Emma sang, at the piano, which had been hauled aboard.

"For shou'd the maiden prove Unkind,
There's always ad-mir-ashun."

"Emma," said Sir William. "Don't bang."
"It is only a popular ballad."
"Yes, *I know*."
"Oh," said Emma, and thought that over. "Well, if you like, I shall play something else."
"It is necessary only to pay lip service to both sides of the repertoire," said Sir William. "I shall go fetch my flute."

So over the evening water there soon floated a flute sonata by Karl Philipp Emanuel Bach, a little sad, a little gay, for that is the nature of the flute. The Gods were not leaving Alexandria. The Gods were going, a little wistful, home.

"My God!" shouted Nelson, reading his mail. "Do you know how many people I am obliged to support in a station to which they have become accustomed only because I raised them to it? They queue up for the succession and then inquire anxiously about my health. It is not kind. I am surrounded by pilot fish, and Brother William sucks the strongest. Only my sister Matcham is agreeable."

At Malta, the island not being entirely subdued, they came in too close to shore, and were raked by shot.

"Get below!" shouted Nelson.

"I shall not get below. It is exciting!" shouted Emma.

"I said, get below."

"I shall *not*," said Emma, all patroness of the fleet, and every sailor's eye upon her.

Nelson pulled her away, while she laughed at him. The sailors cheered.

"Emma will have her own way," said Nelson later, "or kick up the devil of a dust."

Since it was warm weather, the dust must be laid. No doubt it had been, for they had both remained below for some time. Sir William felt sorry for her. A role is not the same thing as an attitude. An attitude is the matter of a moment, whereas a role once taken up has to be played through. It cannot be dropped if it does not suit you or if you tire of it. So, inevitably, it lacks the vivacity of an attitude.

Their last night at Malta was also the last reunion of Nelson and his old officers. Being British, his officers were amateurs in the best sense, unlike the French, who were professionals in the worst. No doubt Nelson would miss them, for now he had finally had his experience of women, naturally he would prefer male company, and after tonight, his male cronies would scatter, despite a similar preference, to homes of their own. Your amateur is rewarded with medals, titles and modest estates; your professional yearns for a throne, and so must play musical chairs with all Europe. But both of them long to be left in peace.

"I am sorry to find that Lord Nelson was thinking of returning to Palermo. I shall be afraid, if he does, that his *health* will grow worse and he will be obliged to come home," wrote Lord Spencer to Lord Keith. "We have therefore left a discretionary power to your Lordship to permit him so to do, if he should for that cause think it necessary..."

"Double talk," said Lord Keith, "but quite plain."

"When Lord Nelson was here, I shewed him your Lordship's letter, but I believe some arrangement with the Court of Naples to carry her Majesty to Leghorn has induced Lord Nelson to keep the *Foudroyant* and to take the *Alexander* with him," wrote Sir Thomas Troubridge to Lord Keith.

"Damn," said Lord Keith. "She shall not travel in my bottoms."

"I have applied for sick leave. I am going back with you," said Nelson.

Sir William looked relieved. It would be better so. Emma agreed. If she was not quite as sure of her own reception as she appeared to be, she was quite sure of Nelson's, and both she and Sir William could shelter under that.

At Palermo, where they stopped to take aboard the Queen and their own household goods, nothing had changed. The King would not budge; the Queen was aching to go; and Paget could not disguise his contempt, so he would not last long. Emma made one final arrangement before departure, to settle her half-forgotten daughter here.

"I think I can situate the person you mention about the Court, as a Camerist to some of the R.F—y, if her education *is good*. It is a comfortable situation *for life*.

The Queen has promised me. Let this remain *entre nous*," she wrote to Greville. Also, let her not come until Emma was safely gone.

There was a week of banquets, and the King proclaimed an amnesty, now there was no one left to hang.

"Ah well, it is nothing to worry about," said Sir William. "There is a little greatness even in the best of us, and now he has gotten it out of his system at last, no doubt he feels purified."

They set sail on June 10th, the King saying good-bye to them not at all like a sad poltroon, but with the satisfied air of a farmer who has finally seen the rooks dislodge themselves from the golden corn. He had weathered the storm. He might stay where he was. Indeed, since Napoleon had crossed the Alps, he might much better stay. So time had proved his statesmanship, even if he had not.

The Queen was gone. It was not only freedom, it was vindication.

IX

IT WAS NOT A JOURNEY HOME, it was a raree show, dragged around like Pompey's triumph, or Bajazet in chains, to please Zenocrate, a most unfilial thing, for Emma babbled unrestrained. Concupiscence had quite uncorked her.

"Livorno! Livorno!" shouted the Queen when the ships dropped anchor there. "Thank God, for having given me the firmness to leave. I am no longer contradicted, tormented and threatened. This is a great boon, and I am happy and content."

"I am no longer contradicted, tormented and threatened. It is a great boon. I am happy and content," said the King to Acton, in Sicily, and in his solemn way, winked.

"It is not time for the Queen to be making visits and retarding public service," snapped Lord Keith, and sent the *Foudroyant* to Minorca for repairs rather than allow her to travel on it. "Lady Hamilton has had command of the fleet long enough."

"I am desperate!" shrieked the Queen. "I only aspire to repose. I shall go overland."

"I hope it will not be long before Nelson arrives in this part of the world," wrote Lord Spencer from the Admiralty. "His further stay in the Mediterranean cannot,

I am sure, contribute either to the public advantage or his own."

Nelson decided to make the journey overland. He could not desert the Queen in her hour of greatest need, which was, as usual, now. Napoleon's troops were about. Their passage would not be easy.

"Sir William says he shall die by the way, and he looks so ill I should not be surprised if he did," wrote Miss Knight, who was of course with them. "And Lady Hamilton wishes to visit the different courts of Germany."

At Arezzo, the coach broke down and Mrs. Cadogan and Miss Knight stayed behind with it while the others posted ahead.

Miss Knight was neither good nor bad, but merely that very 19th-century thing, a lady. She had adapted to the times and would move with them. She took the desertion in good part, but tapped her feet.

Mrs. Cadogan, who did not move with the times and was unmoved by them, took the striped cloth off a picnic hamper and began to gnaw a chicken leg, which was no more than plain common sense.

There was a silence, Miss Knight, *who had seen enough,* observing, when the offer was made, that she felt no appetite.

"The way I look at it, it's now or never," said Mrs. Cadogan, "and though I cooked it myself, it's not bad."

This statement struck Miss Knight as being ungenteel, but quite rightly perceiving that to say so would be ungracious, she complained instead of a slight headache, and thus, having the excuse of illness, allowed herself to be consoled with a jar of meat jelly, delicately served, and some bread and butter, sliced *very* thin, while the postillion, under Mrs. Cadogan's direction, boiled water for tea.

Social distinctions being thus properly upheld, they proceeded, morally reenforced, but short on troops, under the guard of some passing Austrian cavalry to Ancona, where Miss Knight went to her room, locked herself in, and fell upon a roast duck ravenously, her headache miraculously cleared.

"Poor dear, she does feel it so," said Mrs. Cadogan obscurely.

"Feels what?"

"Faulty teeth," said Mrs. Cadogan. "She cannot munch, you know."

"You can form no idea of the *helplessness* of the party," said Miss Knight.

If it was not one misfortune, it was another, but on they went, with gossip always a good league ahead of them, like a cloud of midges. No matter how fast they rode, they could not catch up.

The Adriatic was stormy, Trieste was indifferent, and the trip to Vienna an anticlimax, not because it fell below the standard of discomfort maintained during the rest of the trip, but because they could feel no more. Vienna itself was better. Nelson was received by all ranks with the admiration which his great actions deserved, notwithstanding—as Lord Minto said—the disadvantage under which he presented himself to the public eye.

He did not present himself to the public eye. The public eye presented itself to him, as to the keyhole of a bedroom door. He had been caught napping.

He wrote to Fanny to say they would arrive in England on October 2nd, and was delighted to hear from Sir William that this would not be possible. He believed in putting off the evil day. Alas, women do not believe in evil; having been the cause of so much of it, they know it is a matter of fact, not belief. They have no illusions.

"You must expect to find me a worn-out old man," he added, and indeed recently there had been much to age him. He knew not how to act. His conscience had collapsed. He could only stagger up from his own ruins, a free man, to look upon his former chains. How had they held him for so long? He could but wonder.

"I don't think him altered in the least," said Lady Minto to her husband. "He has the same shock head and the same honest, simple manners. But why must he talk of Lady Hamilton as of an angel? She leads him about like a keeper with a bear. It is disgusting. Why must she sit by him at dinner to cut up his meat? Why must he carry her pocket handkerchief?"

Lord Minto shrugged. "Perhaps it is a form of *tic douloureux.*"

"He is a gig from ribands, orders and stars, but he is just the same with us as ever he was. If only it were not for *her.*"

"She is not so bad," said Lord Minto tolerantly, to conceal that secretly he liked her. "It is just that she has been rubbed a little, so naturally the original superficiality shines through."

On the contrary, she was in a bad way.

"My God," she said, when the door was locked, "I am with child!"

"It would be better, dear, not to name the father," said Mrs. Cadogan, who liked Nelson well enough but preferred a prosperous obscurity, and besides, how could it last?

"I could say much, but it would only distress me and be useless," wrote Nelson to Fanny, having heard the news, which made him giddy. He had always wanted a child, though according to Fanny they already had a son, Josiah Nisbet: hers.

"My God!" he snapped. "I have only cuckolded the man thrice, and here already is the egg. I call that quick work indeed."

He was unhinged, but proud. What did it matter now?

"At least now I am plump, it will not show," said Emma, and burst into tears, just as she had finally burst her casing of refinement—the way a sausage splits when it is boiled. A kit-cat minx is no kitten when she weighs ten stone. If we come not from a good bloodline, die we must, or blood will tell. Alas, it tolled daily in the tocsin numbers of that trumpet voice. Emma had repossessed her native vowels.

In the next room, Sir William, resting in bed, put down his book. It should have lasted him the afternoon, but the closing chapters of any life read very rapidly, for we read them the faster, wanting to be in at the kill. The book was the letters of Horace Walpole, dead now, too, though never an intimate; none to him, a few to Minto. Though sometimes on trifling subjects, they were never dull. He preferred letters to biography these days, for he had caught himself in the tattletale habits of slowing before the ultimate death scene and computing their ages from their dates: those who had lived less long than he into one pile; those who would live longer, into another.

He had heard Emma's shriek, though not its subject. It was true, she was wildly out of hand these days. Ah well, let her flaunt if flaunt she must, he thought, for once in England and she would be back in her cage for good, with a cloth over her. In England, brightly colored plumage is not admired.

"He must not know, for it would kill him," said Emma.

"I should think the cause of it would have done that, if anything could," said Mrs. Cadogan tartly.

"He shall not die. I need them *both*," sobbed Emma. "I feel so soiled."

"Ah ducks, now don't take on. At least this time you have the consolation that it was your own dirt."

"I'm fat and ugly and hold and 'orrible," said Emma, in hysterics. "And look at my neck."

"What's wrong with your neck?"

"It's *wrinkling!*" cried Emma. "I shall have to wear high collars or gorgetted net. Why did I not stay thin? Why must we all grow old?"

"At least it will help us fool the old man, if he wants to be fooled," said Mrs. Cadogan, who had divided loyalties. "Besides, you are not old. It is just that you are not young any more, either."

"Then I am neither one thing nor the other."

"Well, you are thirty-five. Enjoy it while you can. And watch your vowels."

"Oh poor, poor Sir William," cried Emma.

"Nonsense, there's nothing wrong with him. He's in the next room, the nice old gentleman, taking his siesta with a book, as so should you be," said Mrs. Cadogan, allowing the Viennese curtains to descend. "And as for the end of the world, it's a long way off. We shall none of us live to see it in our time, and that I can assure you for a fact. As for what happens to others, that's their own affair."

The Esterhazys gave a concert with—since Emma was known to be fond of music—old Haydn to play some of his own settings of the incomparable poetry composed by Miss Knight, all in praise of Nelson, all sung to his face while he stood there and beamed.

"In many points he is a really great man; in others a baby," said Minto, applauding when the screech was done.

Emma forgot to pretend to listen, for she had seen a faro table. Since he was not only a great musician but had been in the service of their family for almost fifty years, the Esterhazys took this ill. She had affronted the best-loved servant in Vienna.

At the faro table, she won £300 by laying out Nelson's cards for him. It was one of her better evenings.

Lord Fitzharris (who lost the same amount) could not disguise his feelings, and joined in the general abuse of her. Society will forgive you for having been a chambermaid if in return it feels free to refer to the fact in your presence from time to time. If you persist in but one eccentricity, eventually it will be granted you. But if you add to the first a second, that strains the cartilaginous exoskeleton of mutual tolerance to breaking, and down their gullets you go, boiled like a lobster, cracked like a crab and torn to shreds.

The Queen, surrounded by *gemütlichheit,* if tortured by piles, was in a better mood, for she had learned that His Majesty had requested Paget's recall.

"I repeat, that at all times and places and under all circumstances, Emma, dear Emma, shall be my friend and sister, and this sentiment will remain unchanged," she wrote in a farewell note, and then forgot all about her. The parting had been affecting, in the best Kotzebue style.

Sir William was better and evinced an interest in

Prague. To Emma, the charms of that town seemed merely architectural, but if it pleased the old man, why not? So off to Prague they went, Napoleon crossing Europe in one direction, and they in another.

The next considerable halt was at Dresden, in Saxony, which was said to be quite a pretty little court, for a place so northern and obscure.

But to malice there is no end, it is a round robin, for people write to their friends, and then their friends write to us. From being a profitable commission for painters, Emma had swelled to become a set piece for female letter writers, all of them ajostle to get their adjectives in first. Besides, it is a truth universally acknowledged that we may most flatteringly light up the corners of our own rooms by burning down a neighbor's house.

The Hamiltons would not care for Dresden, wrote Mrs. Elliot, whose husband was British Consul there, and so would be expected to put them up. The Court was closed down (it had shut upon receipt of the morning's mail, for rather than receive *that woman,* the Electress would receive no one), so there would not be much amusement.

The Hamiltons engaged to provide their own amusement.

"Damn," said Mrs. Elliot. "They are coming anyway."

"Well, if you will put them up, I will put up with them," said Mr. Elliot. "It will give Mrs. St. George employment for her pen."

"I caught her sharpening quills this very morning," said Mrs. Elliot, "and all her geese are bare."

There were no people in Dresden not acquainted with Mrs. St. George's pen, and few who had not received a little note. Her jaw was taut. Her eyes flashed. Her prose was firm.

"Sturgeon, dear Emma?" asked Nelson, at the buffet.
"Oh yes," said Emma.
"Chicken Marengo?"
"Oh yes. And gobs of cream."
"It is plain," wrote Mrs. St. George, "that Lord Nel-

son thinks of nothing but Lady Hamilton, who is totally preoccupied by the same object. She is bold, forward, coarse, assuming and vain."

"Russian salad?" asked Nelson.

"I can reach it," said Emma, bending over the jellies an enormous bosom, and digging in with a spoon.

"No thank you," said Sir William. "These days I do not eat. The only pleasure I have at table is in watching Lady Hamilton ah . . . er . . . feed."

Sir William is old, infirm, and all admiration of his wife, and never spoke today but to applaud her, thought Mrs. St. George, framing a phrase.

"Who is that damned woman with the inky stare?" demanded Sir William.

"I shall now give you the pleasure," said Emma, putting her plate on the piano forte, "of hearing one of little Miss Knight's songs," and plopped down on a chair.

"Cheer up, cheer up, Fair Emma, forget all thy grief,
"For thy shipmates are brave, and a hero's their chief,"

Emma rattled away while the plate, by sympathetic vibration, seemed about to tip its remaining Russian salad into the Black Sea of the rug.

Her figure, thought Mrs. St. George, is colossal, but, excepting her feet—which are hideous—well shaped. Her bones are large, and she is exceedingly *embonpoint*. She resembles a bust of Ariadne. The shape of her features is fine, as is the form of her head, and particularly her ears; her teeth are a little irregular, but tolerably white; her eyes light blue with a brown spot in one, which, though a defect, takes nothing away from her beauty and expression; her eyebrows and hair are dark and her complexion coarse; her expression is strongly marked, variable and interesting; her movements in common life, ungraceful.

Emma's voice triumphed over the clatter, for the plate had finally fallen to the floor. The others watched it settle.

"Her voice loud, yet not disagreeable."

Nelson picked it up.

"He is a little man, without any dignity."

Perceiving the evening to have turned squelchy, Sir William skated in graceful, distant, improvised curves around its incipient hole.

"Though the words are by our Miss Knight, the music, as you may have recognized, is by the incomparable Haydn," he said.

Nelson shut his eyes. The warmth of the candles, no doubt, had rendered him faint. He could not, however, conceal a slight twitch of the nostrils.

She puffs the incense in his face, but he receives it with pleasure and snuffs it up very cordially, concluded Mrs. St. George. It was good enough to copy into her journal.

The party rose to retire.

Miss Cornelia Knight, added Mrs. St. George, shaking her hand, seems the decided flatterer of the two, and never opens her mouth but to shew forth their praise; and Mrs. Cadogan, she added, with a frigid bow, Lady Hamilton's mother, is what one might expect.

Looking around to see if she had forgotten anybody, she saw that as usual she had not, and with quite a grateful smile went home to her writing desk and warmed to her task, though the night was chill, delighted to have a subject so worthy of her pen.

"She was framing phrases," said Mrs. Elliot.

"One begins to see how she does it," said her husband. "Or, at any rate, when."

"It almost makes one wish one lived in another town," said Mrs. Elliot wistfully. "To read them, you know."

"If they are quotable, they will be quoted. One has but to wait," Mr. Elliot assured her, and went to bed. Mrs. St. George, though unavoidable, was frequently fatiguing. He had toyed once with the thought of applying for a transfer to Magdeburg, despite the lesser stipend, but had discovered that she had cousins there and sometimes visited. So it could not be helped.

* * *

On the 4th, they all went to the opera, where the cast sang very badly and Emma all too well. On the 5th, Mrs. St. George was invited to inspect Lord Nelson in Court costume. If he could not go there, he could at least dress as though he could. She found him stuck all over with everything, like a galantine—diamonds, stars, decorations and chelengkh awhirr. On the 6th, there was a concert (instrumental only), and on the 7th, the Attitudes were displayed.

Emma showed signs of friendship at first sight. "Which I always think more extraordinary than love of the same kind," said Mrs. St. George. "She does not gain upon me [few people ever did; Mrs. St. George was ever in the van]. I find her bold, daring, vain even to folly, and stamped with the manners of her first situation. She shows a great avidity for presents, and has actually obtained some at Dresden by the common artifice of admiring and longing."

And, with some irritation, Mrs. St. George paused to dip her pen in a plain glass cube which must serve until the large allegorical work depicting Mors and Thanatos bearing Eurydice back to the Cave of Night (the inkwell), which had stood there until recently, had been replaced.

The Attitudes had been admirable, however. "Several Indian shawls, a chair, some antique vases, a wreath of roses, a tambourine and a few children are her whole apparatus. Each representation lasts about ten minutes. She represented in succession the best statues and paintings extant. The chief of her imitations are from the antique, but her waist is absolutely between her shoulders. It is remarkable that, though coarse and ungraceful in common life, she becomes highly graceful and even beautiful during this performance. But she *acts* her songs, and she is frequently out of tune."

It was vexing. There was actually something the woman did well.

On the 8th, there was an argument.

"I am sorry," said Mr. Elliot. "The Electress will not receive Lady Hamilton because of her former dissolute life, her . . . ah, origins . . . so to speak. That is why there was no Court Sunday. And I understand there will be no Court while she stays."

Nelson, who since the news of the child had begun to regard Emma as his true wife, was stung to the quick. "Sir, if there is any difficulty of that sort, Lady Hamilton will knock the Elector down, and damn me, I'll knock him down, too."

"Lord Nelson, you forget yourself. I should add that the Elector is a rather large man."

"Lady Hamilton is a rather great woman."

"The difficulty," said Mr. Elliot despairingly, "is his wife."

"A pumpkin eater, eh?" roared Lord Nelson, and charged from the room.

By the 9th, the Elliots had rallied sufficiently to give a farewell dinner, a thought inspiring in itself, though never before had they sat down to dine in a bear garden. Mrs. Elliot suggested exposing the other guests only to the Attitudes, thus to save the Hamiltons from further exposure and keep the bear garden for the bears. So this was done, except that Mrs. St. George, being a precursor of the press, could not be kept away; and unfortunately the bears got drunk.

"I am passionately devoted to champagne," said Emma, holding her second bottle by the neck. The velocity of her Attitudes had left her thirsty. "But where are the people? Sir William and I never seat less than sixty to dine."

"We thought," said Mrs. Elliot, "that this would be more intimate, and since we are about to lose you . . ."

"Lost," said Emma, lifting her glass. "All lost. A toast to absent-minded friends."

"Emma," cautioned Nelson. "Perhaps tonight we should not drink quite so much."

"Why not? We have a great many absent friends,"

said Emma. "They went away half an hour ago, all sixty of them, home to their frugal suppers. They would be better nourished boiling a glass egg. It is like one of Greville's imaginary meals." And she surveyed the table with some bitterness, for in truth there was not much food to be seen. "The bottle's empty."

"Indeed," said Nelson, "it is an empty bottle."

"To think that she is a *Chanoiness*," said Mrs. Elliot sotto voce. "It makes one doubt the probity of the Cloth. Though it was Lord Nelson, so I am told, who prevailed upon the Tsar to make her one."

"Tsar Paul," said Mrs. St. George, "though *a very religious man,* is not always in his right mind."

Emma, having put down her bottle, was enacting Nina, with a tambourine, and doing it intolerably ill.

"Mrs. Siddons need not worry," said Mrs. St. George.

"Mrs. Siddons be damned!" shouted Nelson, swept up into the meaning of the piece, though meaning it had none.

It was quite probable; she was a Catholic, so rumor had it.

"She will captivate the Prince of Wales," said Mrs. St. George, following this line of thought to its inevitable terminus, "whose mind is as vulgar as her own, and play a great part in England."

"I do not see," said Mrs. Elliot, "how the part she is now playing could possibly be enhanced."

Mr. Elliot was watching Nelson. "What is a pumpkin?" he asked.

"An American vegetable," said Mrs. St. George, who knew everything, "but the seeds are edible. It looks rather like a hassock, and is orange. There are some in the Botanical Garden here."

"Ah, that explains it," said Mr. Elliot, "but how the devil did *he* know?"

"I want to be presented at Court," said Emma, beginning to dance a tarantella.

"I assure you it would not amuse you. The Elector gives neither dinners nor suppers," said Mrs. Elliot.

"What!" shouted Emma, astonished. "No guttling?" To judge by the dinner they had just eaten, it seemed a poor shaky vegetable sort of place. There was a marmoreal crash. The goddess had fallen, and sat upon the floor, let the chips fall where they may. The tambourine sailed through the silence and landed, quivering, in Mrs. Elliot's lap.

"Good food constitutes the whole happiness of human nature," said Emma. "I have slipped upon the damned Jacobinical rug." And she giggled. "If the Queen is hoity-toity and will not receive me either, I care little about it. I had much sooner she settle half Sir William's pension on me."

And, astonishingly, she began to weep for her debts to society, though not quite for the same ones as her guests would have had her do. Her concept of society differed from theirs.

"Oh dear," said Mrs. Elliot, and drew her feet together, one neat-shod little ankle against the other, with her hands in her lap. "Oh dear."

Mrs. St. George herself had far outflown the raptures of mere composition. "When I called her colossal," she said carefully, "I strove for the exact epithet. For she is not gross. She has swollen in proportion so that the effect is that of an heroic statue towering over the terrain. It is this which produces the toppled and horrendous effect, now that she has fallen down."

"The exact epithet," said Mrs. Elliot, from behind closed eyes (her fan was pierced ivory, it concealed the spectator, but not the spectacle), "eludes me."

"Ah better so," said Mrs. St. George. "It is not your *métier*."

When Mrs. Elliot opened her eyes, it distinctly seemed to her that Sir William—his specific gravity shifted downward by desperation and postprandial port—was hopping around the room on his backbone, stars, ribbons, arms and legs all flying about in the air, while Emma, immense as Bona Dea, led him in that lascivious Viennese novelty, a peasant *ländler*.

It could not be true, however, for when she looked

again, he was lying on a sofa, quite exhausted.

The floorboards sagged. The candles guttered. It was time to retire.

"Oh, Horatio, Horatio," sobbed Emma. "I am so frightened." And turning to look over her shoulder, she said, "Sir William, pray attend me."

All three went down the darkened bedroom corridor, where Virtue called Oblivion to her aid.

She could not live within her allowance, so no one wanted her. If there is not room for one, how can there be room for two?

On the 10th, they departed by barge for Hamburg, which they would reach by drifting down the Elbe. The fine arts, the attitudes, the acting, the dancing and the singing were over.

"Where is Quasheebaw?" demanded Emma, missing her Negro maid, "I cannot possibly leave without her. She has a sentimental value. She was the first thing dear Lord Nelson ever gave me."

Quasheebaw was on the barge, knackering in French about a parcel forgot. Feeling the pangs of hunger, Emma yowled for an Irish stew, while Mrs. Cadogan sat on deck with a pail, to peel potatoes for it.

To Mrs. St. George, it was exactly like that print by Hogarth, of "Actresses Dressing in a Barn." They were on tour. They would guttle where they would.

How do you form the second person indicative of to guttle? wondered Mrs. St. George irrationally, gave it up as a quaint provincial verb, and went back to congratulate the Elliots on their deliverance, of which she found them very sensible.

There was a brief halt at Magdeburg, a small unrewarding place, and then ten days to rest at Hamburg, where the poet Klopstock, author of an ode to lost youth, admired the Attitudes. From Hamburg, they sailed across the North, or German, Sea to Norfolk.

Fanny had written to offer them a free bed.

"She does not mean it," said Emma. "No woman could."

"She meant to be civil, at any rate," said Nelson, who had begun to see that, yes, there would be difficulties.

"Have you told her yet?"

"Told her what?"

"Tales out of school," said Emma sadly. She did not like the thought of them.

The coast was looming up, if anything so flat as Norfolk can be said to loom. Sir William joined them at the rail.

"Isn't it exciting?" said Emma, sure it would be. The sea voyage had quite restored her, for she was always at her best in an emergency.

"If you have lived to see it, yes," said Sir William, who had been seasick again, and did not greatly care.

X

SIR WILLIAM HUDDLED into his lovat greatcoat, if anyone so tall, if slightly stooped, can be said to huddle, and stood on the balcony of the Wrestlers Arms at Yarmouth, behind Emma and Nelson. The weather was not good. At Palermo, the snow fell on oranges; here it fell on offal. Naples had left him with a distaste for balconies; he had always had a distaste for crowds. In his view, crowds come when they are bidden, as to the hustings. When they come unbidden, we may do well to feel that we have lost our grip. This enthusiasm for Nelson was no more than hysteria, and the balance of hysteria is uncertain: it is mounted on a swivel; it can turn either way. If we are to understand politics, we must regard the emotions of men as natural phenomena, like the weather. So at any rate Spinoza advises us, and we would do well to take his advice. A mob is like a natural catastrophe, a flood or a storm, the one a flood of water, the other, a brainstorm, though without a brain. Each blows over us, to do the same irrational damage, and can be predicted only after it has appeared, which is usually too late. These cheering people had a *lazzaroni* look. But no doubt Emma was pleased.

She was delighted. She need not have worried. They had done the right thing by traveling together, for whatever her reception might have been had they returned in a private station, Nelson was a public figure, so the return was a triumph. It was delightful to be the known inspiration of so great a man, share and share alike.

Their reception was a parade, but where does a parade go once it has passed the reviewing stand? It breaks up in the back streets, and she had not returned to England in order to return to its back streets. Therefore the parade must continue.

In London, Fanny was perhaps at last aware of the ultimate inconveniences of a marriage of convenience, and prepared to despond. If Nelson did not write, and he did not, the newspapers did. An unintelligent woman whose attention wandered easily, she had always read between the lines by preference, but she preferred those spaces blank. They were not blank now. They caught the highlights of innuendo. They shimmered nastily.

Nelson informed the Admiralty that his health was now reestablished and that he wished to serve immediately. It was true. Flattery had put new roses in his cheeks.

"Oh dear," said Lord Spencer to Lord Grenville, "it is that woman." Captain Hardy threatened to go fetch Nelson at once.

"It is evident," said Lord St. Vincent, "from Lord Nelson's letter to you, that he is doubtful of the propriety of his conduct. I have no doubt he is pledged to getting Lady Hamilton received at St. James' and everywhere, and that he will get into much *brouillerie* about it."

He had no doubts about his conduct. He was sensible always of an inner rectitude. Therefore whatever he did, he could not be wrong, so what others said of his conduct *must* be. That would have to be set right. He saw no reason why Fanny should not present Emma at Court, though the devil he knew how to ask her to do so. Fanny was sometimes difficult of approach. Her graciousness was circumscribed, it embraced only the sick, and seldom other women, of whom she was habitually shy.

However, Emma had the art to put a dromedary at its ease, let alone a drudge.

It was ridiculous to take this low moral view; the freedom of cities is not presented to the criminous, and this they had received not only at Yarmouth, but at every hamlet along the way, for everyone was out to see the man who had bottled up Old Boney, and who, though he had also let him escape, would assuredly soon have him corked again, for there was no one else to do it, which was both his own opinion (based upon experience) and theirs (soundly grounded upon terror). He foresaw no difficulty.

At Ipswich (flags, bunting, contentious yeomen, the apple-cheeked poor, the mayor, the syndics of the city, a rostral column, and dear Emma; also, Yorkshire pudding, elastic as a Rhodian sponge, soaked in bitumen gravy and surrounded by beef half raw and turnip mash half cooked; they were home; in what other country but one's own would a badly boiled onion be considered a *personal* attention from the host? It is not true to say the English eat only to survive; on the contrary, they survive what they eat, an altogether different thing, which builds character. Only the Prince of Wales, ulcerous and greedy, had added to his boyish vices the essentially adult peccadillo of a *French* chef, as Sir William pointed out), Nelson could stand the strain no more. Round Hill was not far away, and forgetting—he had sent so many and those so contradictory—his instructions, but remembering that Fanny had offered them all a bed, if not the same one, he decided with exasperation to put his head upon the block, confront the two women with each other, and get it over with.

Besides, since he had none, he wanted to show the Hamiltons that he, too, had a home.

But Round Hill was closed. The servants had to let them in. The rooms were bare, the ceilings too low, and everything was tricked out with that total absence of the esthetic which is what the genteel mean by taste: the furniture respectable, the wallpaper discreet, the rugs reserved, and nothing vivid anywhere except perhaps in the pantry—the vibrant colors of possets and jellies put up to be carried to the sick. The rooms were chilly. His stump hurt. The £2,000 the estate had cost would not have sufficed to furnish Sir William one room, and Norfolk has no Herculaneum, merely barrows.

The house reeked of rain water in a stone crock, a patchouli jar of moldy rose petals, rubbed gillyflowers, lavender in sachets, the odor of benzoin against the cough, and the burnt stench of mutual misunderstanding. For Fanny was willing always to be understanding, given only she never be put to the effort of actually having to understand. In short, the world had shrunk. Round Hill was too small for him. He did not belong here.

Sir William, who had no objection to small rooms if there was anyone in them he wished to see, was politely admirative. But Emma looked affronted that the parlor ceiling was so low (it was twelve feet), hesitated, and then made her way to the small desk in the window, the sort of useless escritoire at which a woman perches when she wishes to scramble her domestic accounts.

"So this is where you sat when you made your great, great plans, before you came out to us," she said.

Glad somebody had said something, Nelson joined her. Watching them from the doorway (of course she had to touch him: it was his wife's house), Sir William, who had read Rochester upon Nothing, as well as Longinus on the Sublime (in Boileau), found himself repeating to himself:

> Kiss me, thou curious miniature of man,
> How odd thou art, how pretty, how Japan!

The memory sometimes presents us with some mighty curious labels for some even more peculiar jars.

"So this," said Miss Knight, with the unerring accuracy of the truly insensitive, "was *his* home." She had to say something; it was the penance exacted for participation.

There was nothing for it. Fanny was in London. They must proceed.

She was with the Reverend Edmund, Nelson's father, at Nerot's Hotel in King Street, clothed in those two suits of flannel it was her custom to wear in the winter, and not feeling, as she had hoped, any the better for it. Even the dear Reverend Edmund had suggested titivation, in his clumsy, unworldly way, but at forty-two that was plain nonsense.

From time to time she was brought news of Nelson's advance, but did not feel in the least like a general. She was not campaigning. She had neither strategy nor tactics. What she did have was rights. She had done her duty. She had come to town. Her cause was just. That sufficed.

And though she would have liked to have been pleasant, though she would have liked to appear spontaneous, that would not have been seemly at her age (earlier it had merely been impossible or gauche or unbecoming or, for that matter, buried with her first husband where it had died); and a brief flutter of hope, arising from anticipation as from a dovecote, had turned soon enough to exasperation and the proper bearing suitable to her new station in life, with every day—and now with every hour—that he did not come.

A step in the corridor, laughter, subdued suddenly, the turn of a doorknob, a man in hotel livery to announce him, and the little man stepped into the room at last. At first all she noticed was that, as she had feared, he was overdressed. Fanny was restricted to the phenomenal. She saw only a man, tired and worn, who had been naughty, but that need not be mentioned. As for the nimbus of greatness, she did not perceive it. It was not phenomenal. It was merely irrelevant and would die down soon enough, thank goodness, if they ignored it.

"My dear boy," said the Reverend Edmund, choked up, and was embraced. Naturally the old man was affected, for he was very old—it was a miracle he had lived long enough to see his son—and as naturally he was gratified, for Nelson had undoubtedly been *most* successful. Though the emotion was perhaps excessive, it helped to smooth the transition to quieter, more matter-of-fact joys.

"Good morning, Fanny," said Nelson.

"Good day, Nelson. It is a pleasure to see you so well."

And they both stopped where they were, tingling as though pulled erect by invisible wires.

"You look well."

"I cannot complain."

Would it were so, thought Nelson, wondering what to say next.

Fanny was wondering what not to say. Though seldom at a loss for a phrase, when it came to fitting them together, she was quite hopeless. Usually she kept them in a drawer, against the arrival of some clever person.

"No doubt you will want to rest after your fatiguing journey [he did look peaked]." Fanny for want of anything else to do, plumped up a goosedown pillow on the divan.

"I have brought you some lace trim from Hamburg," said Nelson, bringing the package out.

She took it and went with it to the window. The Reverend Edmund said, tactfully, that he would withdraw.

"That is not necessary," said Fanny. She had nothing to say he could not hear her say. "Father, you must rest. You must remember your age [Gaudy stuff. What on earth was one to do with it? *Her* taste, probably]."

Nelson, who was forthright to the point of being either quarrelsome or affectionate, depending upon the situation, could have screamed. One always hopes to find them changed. They never are. He watched the clock.

"We have taken you a separate room," said Fanny. "Does your arm pain you?"

It did, but the woman's ruthless solicitude was too much like being stripped by a Fury. Five minutes, and there they were piled up around you, your teeth (bad or missing), your eye (missing or bloodshot or *strained*), your arm (missing), your cheeks (quite sunk in), your life's blood (thin, it was winter), your temper (apt to lose it anyway), your all and everything defective, found wanting, and just the way she wanted it. The damned woman had never seen a spring.

"Admiral Parker," said Fanny, in her thin resolute voice, clearly *making* conversation, "fell downstairs again last week. Apparently he is *very* bad."

"He was never good," said Nelson, who could not stand the man, "but I am sorry it had to come out on the stairs." Why did women have this passion for shrinking everyone to merely normal stature (that is, smaller than themselves)? No wonder one wanted to escape, always. He found Fanny confining.

The clock struck. He could go away.

After a short hesitation, the result of a prolonged inner debate, Fanny stretched her neck out, head to one side, to be pecked, looking mighty like a mole that has blinked in the light. It was one of her concessions. It would please his father.

Nelson kissed the proffered cheek and left, and *damn, damn, damn, damn* down the corridor.

"A most affecting meeting," said the Reverend Edmund. "He has gone to see his friends settled in, I suppose."

"Most affecting," agreed Fanny, and meant it. It had been all her nerves—which was to say, her emotions —could bear. They were not up to much, but they had risen to the surface, all the same. Now, with a *plonk*, they darted back to safety. Yes, vulgar stuff, the lace, and what was worse, *like him*.

"You can see he has no one to take care of him," she said. "He used to be so careful in his dress, and now he looks gaudy."

"Ah well, he's a famous man now, Fanny," explained the Reverend Edmund happily, warmed by his son's appearance, but like a man toasting before a fire, feeling a cold blast on his shins from the other side. "He must dress the part, you know."

Fanny did not know. Position she could understand, even if the uncertainties of her present exalted one (though the Herberts of Nevis were of *very good* family) fretted her; but fame was vulgar.

"He *has* changed," she said.

"I did not find him so. He was always the genius of the family."

"Genius, fiddlesticks!" snapped Fanny. "He has behaved most ill."

The Reverend Edmund decided not to press. It was one of her indispositions, he supposed. When a bad-tempered woman persists in never showing it, naturally from time to time she will be indisposed, to ease the strain. She was a good woman. One had to bear with her. She could not find all this agreeable. All the same, he would have been grateful for a little more ease and a little less care. But since he needed the care, he would try to help her.

Lord Nelson [*The Morning Herald* informed its readers], the gallant hero of the Nile, on his arrival in town, was met by his venerable father and his amiable lady. The scene which took place was of the most graceful description, and is more easily to be conceived than described.

"Ah!" said the Reverend Edmund, "just as I thought," and passed the paper to Fanny to comfort her.

"You wanted to see *me*," said Miss Cornelia Knight (a person of no importance: Miss Cornelia Knight, *the* poetess). "I am so flattered." This was her way to put him at his ease.

Sir Thomas Troubridge was not put at his ease. It was not the poetess he had come to see, but the daughter of Admiral Sir Joseph Knight, for the Navy looks after not only its own, but their own as well. This is called tradition. Though badly wounded, Troubridge was a handsome man, still youthful in manner. He wished he were anywhere else but here. There was not only loyalty to Nelson to be thought of, but also loyalty to a naval widow's child.

"I do not know how to put the matter delicately," he said.

"Then put it as best you can!" snapped Miss Knight, who knew what was coming, for she had eyes in her head even if she had learned to close them. "Though living a sheltered existence, I have been much upon the Continent. I may be offended, but I shall not be shocked."

Her little game was about up. Though a resident in this household in all innocence, she could hardly stay on once she had been offered a bite of the apple. She would have to move out, and what then of the autobiography? She would be no better informed than any other informer.

"Surely you have heard some rumor of what goes on in this house," said Troubridge unhappily.

"Sir, I am too grateful to Sir William and Lady Hamilton to lend credence to rumor," said Cornelia, in her haughty manner.

"Well," countered Troubridge, still more unhappily, eyeing a bowl of apples on the sideboard. They were Gravensteins, he noticed. "One does not have to lend credence to fact. It is just there. Whether you believe in it or not."

"Oh!" gasped Cornelia. It was quite a fine little gasp. It was followed by an equally fine little silence, devised to simulate startled enlightenment. "It is true that things have become *very* unpleasant." Emma had caught her sighing over poor Lady Nelson, about whom it really was too bad.

"I am sure you would not wish to lend your support to the, so to speak, insupportable," said Troubridge, not wanting to come right out and say the thing.

"Oh no," said Cornelia, who had been housed, fed and feted for a twelvemonth now, and felt suddenly the need of support herself.

"I think it would be better that you move out at once. After all, we do not want you *smirched*," Troubridge said heartily.

There was a pause.

"The Nepeans have suggested that, until you can find some otherwhere, perhaps you would like to take refuge with them. Your retreat could be disguised as a visit."

Cornelia brightened. The Nepeans were not only rich but well connected; they were quite respectable.

"I shall pack my few things," she said. "This cannot be easy for you. I know your loyalty to our dear Lord Nelson, who is a fine man, no matter what people say. I am much in your debt."

Once she had packed, Troubridge showed her to her carriage, shut the door on her, and waved her solemnly away. And that, he thought, makes one gossip the less. Though Nelson might be an excellent strategist, at tactics Troubridge was not bad; so off rode the dickeybird, weight eight stone, and would that there were two of her, *clack, clack, clack.*

As Vice-Chamberlain, Greville had chambers for nothing at St. James, which was fortunate, for freehold grew more expensive every day; Edgware Row was built over; and if he could save on nothing else, he was always prepared to save on his own expenses. So he received them there, that red-brick relic of times past being as close to Court as Emma was ever to get.

Though by no means resembling that highly polished shiny pink object, the Banker Rogers, Greville had become equally octopoidal. His hair was now thin; in compensation, his manner had become more weighty; he had a small pink mouth adapted for sucking; he had a beak; and since he still minced upon his toes, he had a pouter pigeon look. In short, people found him charming, charming, charming—even sometimes when he was out of the room. The years of talking to Towneley had left their mark, and so had Taste. He was fifty-one (Towneley was well-nigh dead).

"How nice it will be to see him again," said Emma. "I am quite curious." And meant it. She expected to enjoy herself, and it was her suggestion that they go all three, *Tria juncta in uno,* for that she would enjoy even more.

His rooms, though paneled up in the best Regency (it was expected any day—the King was once more coasting down toward the dark winter ponds of insanity, on which the ice was again thin) style, were at the same time dark and damp, in the good old English tradition. They had an old-boy donnish air about them, down to the bowl of winter flowers which no woman could have arranged. Otherwise there was no change. The Honorable Emily Bertie, only a little cracked, and dirty-blue brown because of Sir Joshua's passion for asphaltum as a medium, her skin turned milk glass, her nose inalterable, balanced from one wall the Paulus Potter cow, the size of a Shetland pony, which still munched mellifluously above the mantelpiece on the other. There was a good old English sideboard, and two very bad new French chairs, neither of which Emma remembered, and a console with legs in the new Egyptian taste, sphinxes with brass faces, mahogany bodies, and below, slipping in and out beneath their petticoats, brass feet.

Charles himself, all hospitality, had half an empty tantalus out and four very small glasses, their glass thick and sparkling, their capacity, unlike Emma's (of which he had been warned), small.

Nor, though he had heard she had gained weight, had he expected to find her so huge. It was as if someone had moved in the Farnese Hercules and changed the sex. The floorboards creaked.

"Charles," she purred, "how very pleasant to see you again." And with every evidence of pleasure (all neatly labeled and laid out upon a table: it might not look like much, but it would hang him), she pumped his hand.

"My dear Emma," he shrilled, with *some* emotion. "What, no kiss for Greville?"

"Why no," she said, shaking her parasol. "Not now. Whatever would dear Lord Nelson think?"

What dear Lord Nelson was thinking was that Sir William merely played the flute; he did not sound like one. Why must these men of taste grow shrill with age? A capon, to Nelson, belonged where it belonged, upon a plate.

Greville, casting a roguish eye upon the company,

clinked stopper against tantalus and proposed a small drink.

"It is so long," he said, "since we have *all* been together. My goodness, it has been nine years." And he regarded Emma critically. "If you were younger, I could say, My, how you've grown. But as it is, I know not what to say."

"Good," said Emma.

"The sherry is indeed excellent," pronounced Nelson, venturing out into the silence first, warily, but with his best foot forward.

Greville giggled. "It is one of my little economies," he said. "Number 452. You will not get it any other where, but Figgis is a reliable man."

"Figgis?"

"My wine man."

(He knows not what he does.)

"Ah, then you like it?"

("No.")

"You are to be complimented, Charles."

"A most tastefully appointed room," said Nelson, who hated everything in it down to the last *famille verte* vase and Dutch Delft ginger jar. It was a clutter. It was too hushed. He had never before drunk sherry in chapel. The décor would have profited for being dusted by a poltergeist. He wanted air.

"Well," said Emma, "I don't mind if I do."

Greville looked as though he had been struck.

"Don't fuss, Charles," said Sir William. Immediately Charles modulated to a manly tone, sincere, concerned, responsible—even considerate—and poured Emma some more. The upper registers for art, the lower for commerce, and in between a calm and level purr.

Sir William felt at his ease, for there were tidbits here from his own collections as well as the Correggio, the barterable bargain of a lifetime which had turned out to be a Cambiasi, though Mr. Vandergucht had offered *half*. To date, the Correggio had been his only error. In short, they were all so delighted to see each other again that they felt quite uncomfortable.

* * *

"That man is a scoundrel," said Nelson to Emma privately. "He would want to talk, but I put a stop to the damned gabble, gabble, gabble. We are used to speak our mind of kings and beggars and not fear being betrayed, but Judas himself was never such a tattletale. He is too old to be a piglet any longer. I hope Sir William feeds him turnip tops." But later, as he usually did, he cooled down. Though he wasted no oil, Greville understood to perfection the fine art of water smoothing, and was down on his knees with a trowel instantly, a fellow Mason, the better to cement (the metaphor is mixed—so were his motives) relations.

"What is this story she spreads about, about a previous secret marriage?" asked Greville of Sir William. "It will accomplish nothing. It did not take place. And if it did, the rules of society are never retroactive. She cannot be received at Court." He was in a temper.

"I believe she has some hopes of creeping in under Lady Nelson's pinfeathers," said Sir William, amused by all this, though sadly so.

"Lady Nelson is nothing but an elevated commoner. There is a limit to the number of people you can pull up by your own boot strings." Having no children of his own, Greville was much taken up these days with genealogies, as is the way with disappointed men.

It was not Sir William's. No, he is not at all like me, he thought, and felt a warm glow of self-gratulation and also a twinge of neuralgia, a complaint he had for years forgot.

"Pray tell me, Charles, in what month do you finally bring yourself to light a fire?"

"January," said Charles, without thinking.

"Good," said Sir William gravely, rising to his feet to ease the stiffness in his joints. "I shall return."

On Sunday the 9th, Nelson paid his respects to the Admiralty Board, and afterward was so amiable as to show himself to the people. When the curiosity of his grateful countrymen became inconvenient, he ducked into Somerset House, was smuggled out a back way, and that evening entertained the Hamiltons at Nerot's Hotel, which gave the two ladies a chance to make comparisons, if not conversation. On Monday, Nelson moved to a house in Dover Street; the Hamiltons to Beckford's house in Grosvenor Square, for the house they had taken in Piccadilly would not be ready until New Year's. On the 12th, Nelson and Sir William were presented at Court, where they got a cool reception. His Majesty merely asked if Nelson had recovered his health, and did not wait for a reply. This rudeness was not the result of moral indignation—the Queen looked after morals—but of etiquette, Nelson having used his Sicilian title without asking English permission. He must mind his manners, apply for permission, and mend his signature. Nelson had not known. In Palermo, there had been no end to personal display; but England is a limited monarchy. He put in his petition and signed himself Nelson and Bronte from then on.

That same day he and Lady Nelson went alone to Lord and Lady Spencer's.

Across the table, Fanny, who had talked both left and right until she was dizzy, drew to herself some walnuts, peeled them, put them in a glass and offered them to Nelson, who was sitting opposite her. The gesture would prove to all that they were not estranged by anything more serious than a healthy, natural reserve.

Nelson swept the glass aside so roughly, for he was a little in wine, that it shattered against a set dish, and glass and walnuts flew everywhere.

Fanny was startled into tears. Lady Spencer rose and suggested that the ladies retire. And then, since she was hostess and so had first grab, descended majestically upon Fanny, so that with one thing and another, in three hours—once the gentlemen had come upstairs and the ladies had gone downstairs and the last carriage had departed through streets spread with invisible straw—it was possible for her to burst into her husband's dressing room with her dramatic announcement.

"She has told me how she is situated. She now knows all."

"Well, now she has seen what she says; no doubt she knows what she thinks," said Spencer, unhelpfully. "But I wish she did not."

"The poor thing had to talk to someone or burst."

"I should say her bubble was burst already. It is a damned shame. The man is too indispensable to be dispensed with. Why could he not remain a bachelor beyond Gibraltar, like the rest of them, and leave his reputation intact? What else do we have brothels for?"

"Spencer, that is a *man's* view."

"Well, now it seems it is a woman's business," said Spencer with a reminiscent sigh, for he had not himself been abroad for some time. "But what is to be done?"

"Why, send him off to be a bachelor," said Lady Spencer, "and when he returns they will both be that much the older." For she knew by experience that though a marriage can survive a long separation, passion cannot.

"*Ummm*," said Lord Spencer. "*Ummmm*."

"I cannot live without you," said Nelson, who was, alas, sincere.

"You silly boy, you do not have to," said Emma, who was, alas, now not. "We can all four visit back and forth." It was still her hope that Fanny might be induced to sponsor her at Court.

"For a woman who says nothing, she kicks up the devil of a row," said Nelson. "How I long to embrace you. Has Sir William returned?"

"Ah so do I," Emma agreed hastily. "No, he went out, but will be back shortly."

"I must return to her."

"Nelson," enjoined Emma, who thought Fanny a frail stick of a woman, but one never knew. "Be true unto yourself. Do nothing *vile*." For a woman eight months pregnant, she did not show it. She looked a virgin still.

"I shall not. Besides, she is in her flannels."

"In her *what?*"

"Pink. Two suits. She feels the cold."

Well, let her, thought Emma, as so do I, despite a fire smoking green in the chimney, with cord wood 2/6 the basket, wet. It is a characteristic of the English winter that so few of the trees seem to have been felled in time.

"My own dear wife," said Nelson, who had figured out this way of regularizing both their union and their child, for he meant the thing to be legitimate, no matter how. "If only it were not for *her*."

He found the situation trying.

On the 13th, Fanny was presented at Court, in the presence of Nelson, to the Queen, who gave him a cursory nod and Fanny a most warmhearted, but at the same time shrewd, smile; for not since Soemias had so many women gathered together in one room to legislate so much upon a subject so severe. She had been got at.

All of which Greville reported to Sir William with a wealth of, to himself, gratifying detail. Aristotle informs us that justice is wisdom without desire; but if there is to be justice in this world, there must also be tit for tat, and Greville was not one to forgive easily anyone who had used him as a ladder up. Now she should have a ladder down, and moreover, it should be the same ladder, but better placed.

The Morning Herald, though cautious of the libel laws, presented its readers with a sketch of Lady Hamilton's character which left her none.

"The lady of Sir William Hamilton, K.B., who with her husband has lately accompanied Lord Nelson to England . . . in her 49th year . . . figure . . . now on the wane . . . *conversaziones* are at least sprightly and *unceasing* . . . the chief curiosity with which that celebrated antiquarian Sir William Hamilton has returned to his native country . . ."

"William, I am not a curiosity," said Emma, at her most wrathful. "Sue."

"What about, my dear?"

"I am *not* forty-nine."

"If it is not a misprint, you most certainly would be by the time the case was settled, in or out of court," said Sir William. "It is only a newspaper."

"But it is *read*."

"Only by the quasiliterate," said Sir William. "Do not distress yourself. The better part of the world has yet to learn to spell."

His favorite niece, Mary Dickenson, had paid him a visit.

"William, she is an enormity."

"Large, Mary, merely large."

"Uncle, we call because we are fond of you, not because we wish to hear your wit. I own I feel responsible, for I condoned the match. But she must not be seen with this man."

"This man is my close friend, Mary."

"Then so much the more reason he should see her less."

"We will not talk about it."

"Then ours will be the only silent tongues in London," said Mrs. Dickenson, gathering up her gloves. "I am truly sorry. Come to see us when you can, but do not bring *her*." And out she swept.

Though the visit had made him angry, he discovered that Mary's advice, when followed, gave him such peaceful moments as were permitted him. As usual, it was sound. So when he went to visit her, he did not bring Emma.

"If we are to go to Ranelagh, I insist that Greville come, too," said Emma.

"But, my dear child, why?"

"Because he does not get out enough. Besides, it is Bannister's benefit."

"But if she wants you to come, why not?" asked Sir William, bewildered.

Charles was indignant. "Very well, if we must go through this dumb show, why we will."

So to Ranelagh they went and promenaded themselves in the approved manner and were gawked at and heard Nelson praised; and with a little coaxing from the audience, Emma was prevailed upon to sing, which she did most affectingly, a ballad about Nelson, of course. Once the song was ended, she seemed content to go home, and Greville equally eager to hand her into the carriage.

"You have the memory of an elephant," snapped Greville, which was only half of what he wished to say, a perfectly balanced phrase, but he dared not complete it.

"Yes," said Emma. "I am so glad you could come with us after all. Good night, dear Greville."

There was nothing he could do. He must bide his time.

On the 18th, both couples went to Covent Garden, as an example of solidarity. The applause was deafening. Nelson bowed, as to a sea surge, which considering what the sea had washed his way, was only courtesy. The Reverend Edmund burst into tears. The orchestra played "Rule Britannia," with Miss Knight's extra verses sung by all.

Everyone then sat down: Lady Hamilton on Nelson's right, Lady Nelson on his left, so that he was wedged between them; and the two older men behind. The performance was that last new comedy called *Life*. Lady Nelson wore white, with a violet satin headdress (the color of mourning), and Lady Hamilton a blue satin gown with black plumes on her head (to adorn the coach).

* * *

At night, now, Nelson often walked the streets, in that winter weather both an eccentric and an eerie occupation. Sometimes he would get as far toward the haunts of Tyburn Hill as Shepherds' Market, there to sip grog at midnight among ruffians and go unrecognized. Sometimes he went into Hyde Park and let the snow whirl around him, as though he were inside one of those glass balls they give to children which, when overturned, produce a flurried flocculence around a central figure, though the flakes settle in time and must be shaken up again. Putting his hands in his pockets, he trudged on, a small, compact rage, intensely cold.

It was a nightmare, and as in a nightmare, these white expanses were sometimes crossed by fugitive and curious shapes. He did not notice. By this time in his walk, he had entered the immense silences of Grosvenor Square, to stare up at a few dimly lighted windows in Beckford's house, at number 22. Since he could not enter this door at this hour, back to Dover Street he went. He did not look well.

On the 25th, they went, all of them, to see the play *Pizarro*, with Kemble, who had never been better. The animals go in two by two, but stop at four. The heat was so great that Lady Nelson fainted, had to be carried from the box, and was therefore applauded when she rallied sufficiently to be supported back into it again. She returned the applause with a bow, and sat down.

Lady Hamilton, who had not fainted, but who felt the heat, also bowed.

Nelson was leading too social a life. Lord St. Vincent wrote to warn him of its dangers, for there was much risk of illness in going out of a smoking hot room into the damp, putrid air of London streets. Nonetheless, out he went, for he could not abide to stay in. Lady Nelson was debarring him from his station, if not at the side of his child, at least at the side about to produce it.

"The reason *why* Lady Hamilton has not been presented at Court," explained *The Morning Herald,* in its mendacious way, "is her not having received any answer from Her Majesty to the letter of recommendation of which her Ladyship was the bearer from the Queen of Naples."

"We are going to Beckford for Christmas," said Emma. "Would you like to come along?"

It was one of those evenings when Nelson had come in out of the snow.

"Yes, I should."

"Do you mean you are going there without your wife?" demanded Fanny.

"Sir William is a very old man and a very close friend. He may not see many more Christmases."

"I dare say not."

"It is useless to argue. I am going."

Beaten brass is one thing; beaten putty quite another. Neither was wax in the other's fingers, but the process is called *cire perdu*. It is impossible to argue with a public monument. He went.

They stayed at Salisbury overnight, in order to observe the prospect first by day, for though Beckford had called Horace Walpole's Twickenham a Gothic mousetrap, his own folly towered like a Gothic guillotine and was accounted thereby a considerable spectacle.

And there it was, all 276 feet of it, casting a sundial shadow through the light sprinkling snow, a sight for sore eyes, and those rubbed in disbelief.

"*O tu severi religio loci,*" said Nelson (for he had had Latin as a boy). "By God, the thing is real."

"On the contrary, it is principally plaster of Paris," corrected Sir William. "But that, I grant you, of an inspiring cast."

Getting out of the carriage between two rows of remarkably handsome footmen, all carrying candelabra in broad daylight, they ascended a flood of stairs if not into the warmth of the nave, at least toward the source of warmth, for the draft of frozen air which swept down the hall had some heat caught on its fore edge, like fluff on a broom. The footmen advanced ahead of them, to illumine the Gothic gloom.

"My goodness, where does he find them all, and all so alike?" said Emma, whom Aprile had taught tolerance, and since she was that rare thing, a sexually satisfied woman (her only passion was guttling), she did not mean it ill.

Behind them clanged (it had taken four months and two acoustic tinkers to produce that clang) the immense, authentic but copied doors.

"Welcome, welcome, welcome," piped a small still voice a hundred feet away, "to the Halls of Vathek."

Unfortunately the building shook in the slightest breeze and snow on the roof was always a problem. The floor was stone. It was not Emma who set the hall in motion with majestic tread.

For the last sixty feet of the hall, they were entertained by a medley of "O God Our Help in Ages Past," "Green Grow'th the Holly" and "The Hero of the Nile," pealed from the bells in the belfry, though by the time they reached the crossing, this had modulated reassuringly into "Hearts Stout as Oak," and the weather was warmer.

Here a butler met them and led them around a statue of Antinoüs and a sleepy immovable St. Bernard called, to judge by the cellaret around her neck, Lucy, toward the parlor. Beckford was waiting to meet them—surrounded by a few friends, all glittering, all young—himself garbed in Court costume, a Turkish pelisse bound with fur, and a velvet smoking cap.

They found there an assembly of all that was best in the worlds of title, rank and glory, which is to say, people like themselves, who were not acceptable to the proper cadres of polite society, and therefore had to accept each other; who instead of discussing dogs, the public schools, their children, the weather and each other, prattled about Kant, Kemble, Coutts, and the intimate, archly delineated lives of people they had met perhaps once and would never know. Always by first name and of course knowingly, with that simper to be found nowhere but in a chafing dish—the soft simper of a freshly coddled egg. Take away the daily duchess of which each *cognoscente* has but one, and he would dwindle at once, without a head to stand on.

"Molly . . ." "Fred . . ." "Old Q . . ." "The most divine . . ." ". . . the sidling, effeminate nonesuch came ogling across the lawn, and poor Paddy was in a dither, not knowing how to address him . . ." "Grant her at least the wit to choose a good banker." (The future Duchess of St. Albans had just come up for the last time.) "Such an ordinary little man." "Overdressed." "The last bagwig in London." ". . . Lady Conyngham." "Of course, absolutely impossible." "Dicky said . . ." "A fetishist. Largest collection of Delft wig stands in Cumberland . . . Bald as an egg and likes her to paint his pate with Chinoiserie designs in robin's-egg blue." "Which was wicked of him, really . . ." ". . . is a clergyman's son, I suppose she appeals to his sense of sin, which as you can see, is *enormous*." "Then the wig is lowered and that's all there is to it. She takes her guinea and goes. Most odd." ". . . but ten years ago, when she could not only reach the note to which she now aspires, but swung there like a monkey . . ." "His mother is furious of course, because the property is entailed, and who could beget a child upon a wig stand?" "Very sad." ". . . so I said, call him Mr. It is a courtesy title merely."

"Who's Molly?" asked Nelson.

There was a short scurrying whirr back into the wainscot. He was an outsider. He came from where the world's work is done. "Who's Molly?" they asked blankly, unwilling to face the implications of such a question. For who was Molly when you came right down to it? A mere nobody who had been so fortunate as to marry, some thirty years ago, the second son of Lord Ipswich, who had then no possible pretensions to the title . . .

"You must remember that the world, according to the Brahmins and Warren Hastings, is supported by an elephant which stands on a tortoise. If you have not eyes in your head, neither is this the time to explain the exquisite symbolism of the device. But you have only to look to see which one is which . . ." "Of course genuine. Angerstein almost bought it, though true, how would *he* know . . ."

With that unerring instinct for hindering the actual performance of the sexual act which women do have, Emma sat down between two young Honorables who had been looking at each other speculatively, and did not get up again until one of them had seen, hopelessly, the other drift away.

"Such a nice quaint old man. A perfect period piece." "A museum of the tastes of yesterday." "Related to everybody." "Well, I can quite see they hold her up. But what does the tortoise stand on?" "Water, you silly thing. So you see, it all works out." "Schlüter, in his work on Claude, cites it nowhere, but of course the index is bad."

"Emma!" cried Beckford, whose sincerity was apt to be intense, led her forward, as though on a string, and presented her to the company. "You superior being. You Madonna della Gloria. You unique and marvelous creation. So glad you could come, for a few days repose, uncontaminated by the sight or prattle of drawing-room parasites."

(Not at all delicate, ill-bred, often very affected, a devil in temper when set on edge. She affected sensibility, but felt none—was artful—he wrote in his memoirs.) And casting over her a beady eye, he made her welcome. He was a *true* friend.

Emma enjoyed herself. Christmas is a dour time for the childless, but they were all quite jolly, though the only mistletoe discoverable hung in the butler's pantry, and the guests had a habit suddenly to disappear in ambiguous pairs.

As for Fanny, who was on both their minds, let her go sailing to sea in a bedpan, since that was all she understood. Nonetheless, Nelson looked forlorn and proved difficult to cheer.

On Christmas Eve, Emma did the Attitudes, "not the ruin of their former glory," as Master Godfrey (one of the more anomalous guests, but a most talented boy soprano) said, "but the *tumulus*," and was rewarded with a ravished glance. He had found a variation on a joke grown thin. He had earned, if not their gratitude, at least a moment of their attention. He promised well.

Since it was not prudent at this late date to move about, she did Agrippina with the Ashes of Germanicus, with the assistance of a chair. In a dim light, she was most affecting and most applauded.

"Master Godfrey," said Beckford. "Show us your soprano."

So Master Godfrey did.

"So artless," said Emma. "So wonderful."

Afterward they were compelled to admire the Claude, all £4,000 of it, and since it was neatly labeled, found it admirable.

"And these?" asked Sir William, glancing at some views of the house framed nearby.

"A young man called Turner, but Sir Francis Beaumont swears by him," said Beckford. "Lovely, ain't they?" At 40 guineas each they seemed poor value, but he was a coming man, so one had to have them. "Angerstein has one."

"They are all new people," said Sir William. "But since I am not vain, I shall let the young admire them, and pass on. Since whatever you do, once you are old, will be considered old fashioned, you need no longer make the effort to keep up. Which is, in any case, futile. You cannot conceive how restful I find it to be at last out of date. It has taken years off my age. Indeed I find it makes me feel quite contemporary again."

Mrs. Cadogan heard someone snuffling down the Gothic corridor, and when she opened the door there was Nelson. A natural love of intrigue had conquered an acquired moral sense, but not the display of it. Tight-lipped and mendacious, Mrs. Cadogan let him in.

Nelson was not in a good mood.

"And do you like these people?" he asked Emma.

"What people?"

"Beckford's friends."

"They are not friends. They come to gawk."

"And gabble," he said. "You should not have done the Attitudes. You might lose the child."

"Well, I haven't lost it yet," said Emma, who was fed up with carrying the thing, and wondered which he would miss the more, the child or her.

"We are never alone."

Ah, that was better.

"These people tell you all about your own business, and could not sail a paper boat on Round Pond," he said bitterly. "I assure you it is no rest."

"They mean well."

"They mean *nothing*. Why the devil are we here?"

Emma's voice dropped to a reverent conspiratorial hush. "Business," she said.

"What, to hawk bibelots?"

"Not exactly."

"Ye Gods! Then what is going on behind my back?"

Emma examined his back. It was too narrow. There would never have been enough room, and had the matter not been so serious, she would have giggled.

"If you won't tell a soul, Beckford wants a peerage, and we need money, and he *is* William's cousin, so he said that if William could get one, because he couldn't himself you know—there was a scandal, it was hushed up, but of course everybody knows about it—and be able to give the reversion to Beckford, well . . ."

"Well what?"

"Well, I should have five hundred pounds for life, and William two thousand. And we do need the money."

"You need not worry. I shall not tell it to a soul, for no one here has a soul to tell it to," said Nelson. To him, it sounded a sordid, stupid business. "A peerage is either the recognition of merit or the inheritance of favor," he added, thinking about his own.

"Don't be so stuffy. What did your brother William ever do? And yet he is bound and determined to have yours, and what is more, he will."

"That's an intolerable thing to say."

"I don't say he isn't very nice," said Emma, explaining patiently, as to a child. "But if it weren't for that, we'd not see hide nor hair of him, and that's the way the world is."

"It's not the way I am."

"Oh well, it's easy for you. You're different. But when most people know each other, it's for a reason." And with the busy look of an apprentice who has just involuntarily let slip a guild secret, Emma began industriously to buff her nails. "Besides, he has a very nice house, and it's not everybody who's asked here, you know." For people may talk about principles all they please, but who has the moral force to refuse an invitation? Men are so silly.

"Damn," said Nelson, who wanted his fury dampened by romance.

"Patience," said Emma gaily. "Patience." Though she was worried herself, what with one thing and another, and the furniture not yet in the Piccadilly house.

"My little wife is tired," said Nelson, gurgling with emotion, though even to him that phrase sounded cottagey and absurd in these surroundings.

"You mustn't brood," soothed Emma, who wanted her plots to hatch, though nothing would incubate in this cold. "Besides, it's only for a day or two more."

On the 29th of December they returned to London.

On the 1st, Emma and Sir William moved into their new house at 23 Piccadilly, with the bow windows overlooking Green Park, which was quite pretty, the mound of the icehouse picturesque as an old Gothic barrow among the trees.

"I have had a wine bill this day," said Sir William, shuddering, "for four hundred pounds." She had the Midas touch. Whatever she put to her lips, she drank money.

"I don't understand it." Emma frowned. "We have had no more to dinner than usual, though of course in Italy the wine is a little cheaper. Besides, I don't drink wine. The men do that, when we go upstairs." So it wasn't her fault. She was *not* extravagant.

"If you could be a little more careful, my dear."

"I sold my diamonds to pay for the furniture, didn't I?" demanded Emma, who had indeed done her part. "William, what are we to do, for the dining room won't seat more than forty, and with old Q and someone for him to goggle at, the list comes to forty-two?" And she looked around at the furniture, the deed to which reposed snugly in a dresser drawer upstairs. Not only had she made her sacrifice, but even worse, one of the snuffboxes had turned out to be paste brilliants only. What was the use of living if you could not do it properly?

Lord Nelson was announced.

Today, thought Emma, who could not live without him—but sometimes men have to be led—I will be *cold*, and primped a little.

"On this day His Majesty was conducted from the Presence Chamber to the Throne in the House of Lords by the noble Admirals Nelson and Hood," reported *The Morning Herald*.

Taking his seat among his peers, Nelson could not but realize for the first time and with some sense of shocked enlightenment, that one's peers are, of course, *men*. How many of them, he wondered, have my problems to conceal?

"I shall call her Tom Tit," said Emma, watching from the window Lady Nelson leaving after having paid her first, last, and as it was to turn out, only call. "For she walks like a tomtit, hopping and jerking about, one shoulder higher than the other, out into the snow, and pecking away all the time at a vast invisible lump of suet dangling before her nose."

"Emma, that's quite enough," said Mrs. Cadogan, though peering over her shoulder, she saw the resemblance, too.

It had not been a cordial meeting. *Tria juncta in uno* cannot be four. The Knighthood of the Bath is an exactly limited order and cannot be added to until one of its members dies.

On the 1st of January, Nelson had been promoted

Vice-Admiral of the Blue; Lord Spencer having taken Lady Spencer's advice. On the 2nd, the Nelsons had breakfast with William Haslewood, their solicitor, for there was always someone there these days. Lady Nelson preferred witnesses.

"Lady Hamilton," said Nelson, with that irresistible impulse to fit the name of one's beloved into the conversation of those who do not happen to share one's affection, "was most gratified with your call, and I am glad you brought yourself to make it. You will find her, as I have found her, an affectionate friend, a true compan—"

Lady Nelson soared from the breakfast table. "I am sick of hearing of dear Lady Hamilton this and dear Lady Hamilton that and Lady Hamilton the devil knows what, and I am resolved that you shall give up either her or me!" she snapped. She had no doubt of the decision, and had her marriage bond to prove it.

Ah, at last, thought Nelson, she has forced the choice upon me, and with calm—since it was her fault—said, "Take care, Fanny, what you say. I love you sincerely, but I cannot forget my obligations to Lady Hamilton or speak of her otherwise than with affection and admiration."

"Apparently not. If you cannot, others can. And what is more, do," said Fanny. And turning to Mr. Haslewood, for she never forgot her social obligations, she added, "Mr. Haslewood, I bid you good day, good-bye and short shrift," and galloped from the room, leaving the enemy in the field, but able to call her soul her own and every inch of her intact, in fighting trim.

"Ha!" said Nelson. "A rift. Haslewood, no matter what has passed in this room, I would assure you that Lady Nelson has always my esteem." He sounded much as though he had just left her his second-best bed.

The front door slammed. A carriage clattered off. They waited until the sound had died away.

"I must be going, myself," said Nelson. "I am due at twenty-three Piccadilly. May I drop you on the way?"

"Ah well, if we're all going," said Haslewood, who had

not the pleasure of Lady Hamilton's company, but knew the address. "Why not?"

"William," asked Emma, gazing out at Green Park, "what do swans mean?"

"Twins," said Sir William succinctly.

Emma, who had been about to say "How pretty," averted her gaze.

"Leda, and Castor and Pollux, and Helen and Clytemnestra, you know, because Jupiter, as Lemprière so felicitously puts it, availed himself of his situation," Sir William explained kindly. "In some versions, however, it is Nemesis, not Leda, who spawns the brats."

"I have been told to hoist my colors at Plymouth," said Nelson. "We must devise a code."

"Can you not put your departure off?"

"It is Duty," said Nelson, not altogether vexed to be at sea and have firm ground beneath his feet again and know where he stood, that is, on deck, and no women anywhere. "I shall never desert you, of that you may be sure." He was eager to be off. William was waiting downstairs, at his favorite game of estimating what the plate would fetch if there should be a sale, and could the initials be shaved. It was curious how seldom you came across a used teaspoon on the cheap, monogrammed N. Though now, with a B in the offing, the chances would be doubled, which cheered him up.

Nelson was a boy. It was years since he had devised a code, not since he had been courting Fanny and made up one so elaborate that she had had to use a code book. For an instant he saw the bay at English Harbour and felt once more the vast relief of leaving, for the last time, her Uncle Herbert's house.

"It is necessary," he explained, "that when we correspond, you shall be the protectress of a Mrs. Thompson, who is about to have a baby, and Mr. Thompson will be one of my seamen." He warmed to his tale. It was romantical.

"Nelson," said Brother William, materializing in his

307

shapeless, ectoplasmic way, "we shall be late to Lord St. Vincent's for luncheon." Lord St. Vincent had influence, and where better to pass the long wait than in a choir stall at some not too provincial cathedral, and then hoist up to the peerage from there?

William got his luncheon; Emma was left in the lurch; and Nelson's flag was hoisted at Plymouth to the plaudits of the multitude and to his own vast annoyance, for Lady Nelson had taken a liberty permissible in a mistress, but unforgivable in a wife, and packed his things all wrong.

"If I want a piece of pickle, it must be put in a saucer, and I have six silver bottle stands but not one decanter to fit them," he snarled. "I could have done all in ten minutes and for a tenth part of the expense." To Emma, he added, "I long to get to Bronte, for believe me this England is a shocking place. A walk under the chestnut trees, although you may be shot by *banditti*, is better than to have our reputations stabbed in this country." As for his wife: "She is a great fool and thank God you are not the least like her."

Emma would have thought little fool the more appropriate description, but otherwise had no objection to the letter, particularly as it enclosed provision for the child, in the draft of his will.

"Emma," said Mrs. Cadogan, "is indisposed."

"More than usual?" asked Sir William, with instant sympathy.

"It's her stomach," said Mrs. Cadogan. "She will stuff herself, you know."

"Yes," said Sir William—he was finding it quite a useful phrase these days—"I know." For truly there is no end to learning; it can occupy a man a lifetime. One may not know everything, but one ends by knowing all.

Yet it was pleasant to have the downstairs' rooms to oneself and no more than six to dinner. That saved the walk to one's club, which in January, in town, was no small saving.

This sky, always the color of dirty, dusty, sleazy prolapsed silk on the ceiling of a deserted ballroom, was getting on his nerves. One always forgets while one is away that the little discomforts of home are the loathsome unendurable ones, for anyone can lump it on campaign, but who can bear to rough it in his own drawing room? His fingers ached. His eyes smarted. He had a chilblain. He felt like Louis XV, dying panicstricken but resigned at Versailles, for how can you get to the top of the hill when the road you are on leads down? He meant to survive this winter, but to the old, winter is a siege. Open the window, and the drawing room choked with vast gray monsters made of sea-coal soot. Four old ladies, six cows and two Barbary apes had coughed to death in the late fog, said *The Morning Herald*. In St. James Park, an elderly female petitioner had been hit in the stomach by a disoriented, low-flying and agitated duck, fallen, and broken her hip. At Palermo, no matter what the weather, at least it had been possible to see your way about, whereas here, candles made the world the darker and you could hear the thing snuffling in the wainscoting at night, while the fire in the bedroom grate got lower and lower, and the consolations offered us by Cicero and Seneca did not help.

> I shall go quietly,
>   merely shutting my eyes:
> I am beyond surprise,
>   but not beyond feeling.
>
> Art is only a sigh
>   a few are remembered by.
> Joy is a thing felt once.
> I am a fool. I am a dunce,
>   but not beyond feeling:
>
> I shall go quietly,
>   merely shutting my eyes.

But not this winter. But not just yet.

"Ah, Mrs. Cadogan, how extremely kind of you," he said, not noticing what she had brought, but she was the only visitor he had had that day. A thoroughly respectable little person, Mrs. Cadogan, no fool, but she knew her place.

"Would you like me to stoke the fire up for you?"

"It doesn't matter."

"It never does any harm to drowse in a cosy room," said Mrs. Cadogan, and vigorously stoked it up.

"I put another log on," she said, surveying the bed and the old man in it in his stocking cap, and his face still the color of bronze. At the door she paused with her hand on the handle, peering through the shadows anxiously. "Good night, Sir William," she said, with almost a smile, and left.

It was not until then that he realized he had been waiting for her to come in. She sometimes did at this hour, these days. The stuff she had brought was tea, a sovereign remedy, so they said, for snow blindness.

"Ah well," he said, rather touched on the whole, and picking up his Seneca again, plowed firmly through the night, whose lapping about the bed no longer bothered him. Once past midnight, and he was safe for another day, and the maid would be in soon enough, to draw the curtains and exchange the tea for fresh.

The permutations of the affections are peculiar, devious, reassuring and odd, Sir Harry Featherstonehaugh had married his housekeeper, and not a peep out of him since.

"Sir William's feeling poorly."

"Who is not?" demanded Emma, surveying, between spasms, a bowl of hot water, some towels, pillows stuffed against the crack under the door, and other signs of imminence.

"It's a good thing for you I was the victim of a diverse youth," said Mrs. Cadogan grimly. "Here it comes, so push!"

"Curious," said Sir William, "it is well past Christmas

Eve, and yet methought I heard one crying 'Child.'"
But since it was cold and he was not really awake, he went back to sleep again.

Over the mantel was a mirror for company, but not being awake, he could scarcely look for the reassurance of seeing himself in it. So the room was completely empty. He had decided to lie low.

Nelson, who had known him for years, found that he knew very little about Mr. Thompson, really, except that since he had had a child, then he must indeed be married, and a fig for Josiah. Poor Fanny had written to say that the only offense she could imagine herself guilty of was pushing Josiah forward, and very well, if that was what had come between them, Josiah was of age now to fend for himself, so she would cast him adrift if Nelson would but return. That she should make so scandalous a proposal merely showed her for the monster that she was; as Mrs. Thompson said, What mother, no matter what the provocation, would desert her own child?

> I believe poor dear Mrs. Thompson's friend will go mad with joy. He cries, prays and performs all tricks, yet does not show all or any of his feelings, but he has only me to consult with. I cannot write, I am so agitated by the young man at my elbow. I love, I never did love anyone else. I never had a dear pledge of love till you gave me one, and you, thank my God, never gave one to anybody else. I would steal white bread sooner than my godchild should want.

> "And white bread is the best bread,
> For the English poor eat rye,"

Nelson chanted to himself as he capered around the cabin.

"And what's all that about?" asked a swobber.

"He has his moods, but it looks to me like an extra round of rum, though who Thompson is, I'm damned if I know."

For the Vice-Admiral of the Blue was dancing a lopsided jig before a portrait on the cabin wall and singing himself hoarse with:

> "Mr. Thompson had a child,
>   ee-aye-ee-aye-oh.
> And to this child he gave estates,
>   ee-aye-ee-aye-oh.

Which put him in mind at once of cryptograms, anagrams and peacock pie.

Its name will be Horatia, daughter of Johem and Morata Etnorb [he scribbled]. If you read the surname backward and take the letters of the other names, it will make, very extraordinary, the names of your real and affectionate friends, Lady Hamilton and myself. Give the nurse an extra guinea, and Mrs. Cadogan shall have a small pension, but my man of business says you are grown thinner.

By eight and a half pounds.
A child. A child. "Oh, you are kind and good to an old friend with one arm, a broken head and no teeth," he said. Since Horatia could not be recognized as his in England, she should have the revenues of Bronte instead, if not—in time—somehow, the title too. She had been begotten in the South. Bronte was hers by natural right.

"Never before," said Sir William, encountering Emma and Mrs. Cadogan on the stairs, "have I known you to return a bonnet." For Mrs. Cadogan had by the strap a brown leather traveling hatbox, bearing the Hamilton crest, and punched on the lid, oddly enough, with a series of small holes.

"Never before," said Emma, "have I been put to the necessity of doing so," and out she swept into the snow, toward a town hack which had been summoned for her, apparently.

Sir William was relieved. He had had no desire to add

a Hamiltonian to the Harleian miscellany, and applauded the discretion, while deploring the need for it.

"They say," said Greville, "that the King is about to go to the Pagoda again."

In his set, the King's infirmity was referred to in this way, its being well known, though never to be publicly mentioned, that when George III was about to go mad, the Chinese Pagoda at Kew fascinated him so much that he was apt to behave in such unseemly ways—from the ground floor to the top, and in the sight of all—that the doors had to be barred against him.

"They have been locked," said Greville, "for a week." Sir William, who had once diverted the Society of Dilettantes with a description of Priapian worship fifty miles from Naples, was prudent not to draw a parallel.

"If the Prince of Wales is made Regent, perhaps he can be persuaded to do something about Milford Haven," Greville persisted. "And since he likes his women plump, and Emma is now plump, why should he not be charmed into it?"

It was worth considering.

When Sir William got home, he found Emma just returned, with the hatbox open beside her, trying on a bonnet before the mirror.

"There," she said. "Is that not much better?"

"I cannot judge. I do not know for what it is a substitute," said Sir William, and in passing, got a whiff either of starched muslin, newly ironed, or of baby, the two smells being similar. "I wonder if we could not have the Prince of Wales to dine, for he has always wanted to hear you sing duets with the Banti creature."

Emma gave him what is commonly called a long look, but since it is well known that the best way a woman may put a devoted lover at his ease is to make him jealous, wrote off to Nelson at once, to announce the event.

"Sir William," came the answer right back, "should say to the Prince, that situated as you are, it would be highly improper for you to admit H.R.H. I know his aim is to have you for a mistress. The thought so agitates me that I cannot write." Which is what we always say when we are about to write ten pages.

A thoroughly accomplished woman, Emma went on to the next reassuring gesture, which is to accuse the dotard of infidelity.

"Suppose I did say," he snarled back, "that the West Country women wore black stockings, what is it more than if you was to say what puppies all the present young men are? Sir William ought to know his views *are dishonorable*." He longed for the day when, her "uncle" dead, he and Emma might retire to Bronte. "My longings for you, both person and conversation, you may readily imagine. What must be my sensations at the idea of sleeping with you."

In the next day's post, he felt horrible.

"All your pictures are before me [they had a low cunning dishonest look]. What will Mrs. Denis say, and what will she sing [the Banti had not been available, Mrs. Denis was the next best thing]—Be calm, be Gentle, the Wind has changed? Do you go to the opera tonight? They tell me he sings well." He threatened to drop her unless she dropped H.R.H.

Well, that had gone exceedingly well, thought Emma, and as the third step is reassurance by *indirection*, wrote off to Mrs. William Nelson to say she was so ill that she could not have His Royal Highness to dinner on Sunday, which would not vex her.

"I glory in your conduct," said Nelson. "As to letting him hear you sing, I only hope he will be struck deaf and you dumb, sooner than such a thing should happen." He made two enclosures, the one the draft of his will, providing handsomely for Horatia (it was a second draft); the other the news that "that person has her separate maintenance, let us be happy, that is in our power; for mine is a heart susceptible and true."

All of which was all very well, but as everyone knows, even the most susceptible heart has to be tuned occasionally; to screw it up to concert pitch requires some effort, and an aptitude for female arts was never known to work any woman ill.

"My God," thought Emma, with that emotion unique to the born artist who finds that something he has done easily for the first time has at the same time been done exceeding well, *"I am professional."* She might now look out upon the female creation with a scorn that hitherto had been limited to their lips, not hers. "I may do what I will."

Alas, money was still a problem, for the fine never pay so well as the fashionable arts, which in their turn are the more expensive. But never mind, she was a woman, and if getting and spending, we lay waste our powers, why then it was only just that the labor should be evenly divided—the one half to the one sex, the other to the other. And any woman who has just lost eight and a half pounds, why of course she must have new dresses; it is a saving really, for they cost only a little more new than the price of altering the old ones. Frills, furbelows and bows do more to rock the human heart than vases.

Vases, however, steady it.
Sir William wrote:

> I have represented the injustice of that, after my having had the King's promise of not being removed from Naples but at my own request and having only empowered Lord Grenville to remove me on securing to me a net income of £2,000 per annum. I have fully demonstrated to Lord Grenville and Treasury that £8,000 is absolutely necessary for the clearing off my unfunded debt without making up my losses. Upon the whole then I do not expect to get more than the net annuity above mentioned and the £8,000; but unless that is granted, I shall indeed have been very ill used. But I hope in my next to be able to inform your Lordship that all has been finally settled. I am busy putting in order the remains of my vases and pictures that you so kindly saved for me on board the *Foudroyant* and

the sale of them will enable me to go on more at my ease and not leave a debt unpaid—but unfortunately there have been too many picture sales this year and mine will come late.

The first-floor library was a litter of bits and pieces ripped from the walls of the Palazzo Sesso, and vases everywhere, a few fresh barnacled, that Greville had managed to salvage from the wreck in the Scilly Roads, so it was only civil not to notice in Greville's bedroom a small, late-Roman bronze that had been packed, he was sure, in the *Colossus* cargo. Just as civilly, Greville did not mention it either. However, better there than gathering water weeds in twenty fathoms, and he had been honest about the vases, anyhow. Not one of a wet provenance had come recently upon the market.

One was only in England temporarily, to visit friends, but all the same, Sir William was aware that that walk through the weeds at Segesta had been the last one, though there were signs of hope, for the snow in Green Park was thawing into slush, and the sun did not set now until as late as 4:30 in the afternoon.

On a vase the color of chicken bone, a piper played pan pipes, a woman danced, and in an invisible meadow, flowers bloomed.

Nelson arrived suddenly, on leave of absence. He wanted to see the child.

"But it is quite safe. It is with a wet nurse in Marylebone," said Emma, puzzled. "And since you have only three days . . ."

"I wish to go there now."

"But I can't go now. Sir William will need me when he comes in."

"Damn Sir William. What is the woman's name?"

"Gibson," said Emma. "Oh how my heart cries out to see it! But as you see, I cannot come." And she began to do her hair.

It was a small, mean, respectable house with a worn

scrap of drugget on the parlor floor. He would sit on the floor and play with the child by the hour, or rather, since the toys he had bought were too big for it, he would play with the toys while he watched the child. When it began to howl, he was dismayed.

"You must forgive me," he said. "I have never before been alone with a baby."

"And what is the mother like?"

"The mother like?" He blinked. "Oh, Mrs. Thompson. She is dead, poor lady. She died of joy."

Mrs. Gibson accepted this without a quiver. "Well, I'll say this for the dead, they do pay regular," she said. "And Mr. Thompson?"

"Oh he's a shabby fellow," said Nelson happily, experimenting with small fingers soft as seed pearls.

Mrs. Gibson, who had been found by Mrs. Cadogan, liked no-nonsense better than fine words, and tips on top of salary best of all, but now she had seen both bottles, so to speak, curiosity was gratified; she was willing to keep mum.

"It is such a pretty child," said Nelson, utterly confounded.

It was in truth a healthy, tugging, fat-rolled, simpering brat, a little solemn and given to crying, But then, we always enjoy the sound of children crying, so long as they don't keep it up long enough to annoy; their grief, though genuine, is transient and therefore meaningless. We like to hear that grief is so.

Mrs. Gibson picked it up fondly. It was worth three guineas a week to her.

It was worth a good deal more than that to him.

And as Emma Hamilton, the wife of the right Honorable Sir William Hamilton, K.B. has been the great cause of my performing those services which have gained me honours and rewards, I give unto her in case of the failure of male heirs, as directed by my will, the entire rental of the Bronte estate for her particular use and benefit, and in case of her death before she may come into the possession of the estate of Bronte she is to have the full power of naming any child she may have in or out of wedlock or any child male or female which she, the said Emma Hamilton . . . may choose to adopt and call her child . . . diamonds . . . snuffbox . . . sword to be delivered on her coming to the estate . . . and as Emma Hamilton is the only person who knows the parents of this female child . . . and to this female child I give and bequeath all the money I shall be worth above the sum of twenty thousand pounds, the interest of it to be received by Lady Hamilton for the maintenance and education of this female child . . .

"I shall now begin and save a fortune for the little one . . ."

Love letters, even from our lovers, do not make agreeable reading. The emotion imbalances the understanding, so that we cannot describe, we can merely show, our symptoms. Such letters may be scanned to make a prognosis, that is all. Whereas, in his better moods, he was not only capable of an amusing turn of phrase, but also made sound sense. Only think, all that just for a child.

"Josiah is to have another ship and go abroad if the *Thalia* cannot soon be got ready." "Lady Nelson is to be allowed £2,000 a year subject to the income tax, which I will pay." "Lord Nelson gives Lady Nelson the principal of the £4,000 mentioned above to be at her disposal by will [it was her dowry]." When the followers of Mahomet put off a wife for barrenness, the dowry is returned.

"We must manage till we can quit this country or your uncle dies." "Now, my own dear wife, for such you are in my eyes and in the face of Heaven, I can give full scope to my feelings. We are one heart in three bodies."

"I suppose they share it around," said Captain Hardy, an honorable man, but a partisan of Lady Nelson and so an indefatigable reader of blotting paper, "when they feel the need of one. I wonder who has it now?"

On March 4th, Nelson wrote his letter of dismissal to his wife. "My only wish is to be left to myself, and wishing you every happiness, believe I am your affectionate, Nelson and Bronte." A draft was sent to Emma.

She had won.

* * *

"Well, William?" asked Mrs. William Nelson, having shown him the following note:

> I wish you would take a post chaise and go to London and be near and as much as possible with our dear Lady Hamilton, who loves and esteems you very much. I will tell my brother that you are gone, therefore he shall either meet you in London or go round by Hillborough and arrange his church duty.
>
> In doing this favour you shall be at no expense, and you will most truly oblige your sincere and affectionate friend,
>
> NELSON AND BRONTE.

Brother William, slipping into the better of his two public roles, gave a clerical cough.

"Well, which way does the cat jump?" demanded Mrs. William, who, as a future Countess, deferred in everything to her husband, the future Earl.

William gazed at the ceiling for guidance, but saw only the lath distinctly showing through the plaster, like ribs.

"I do not propose to go mousing for the pleasure of it," said Mrs. William. "Where is duty?"

Abandoning the Cloth as inappropriate, William descended to his other role, that of doting brother.

"I think, considering the circumstances—and I have considered them that I must enjoin you to comply with my dear brother's wishes. He has always been a kind and generous friend, within his limited comprehension of those terms, and although, even indeed because, his conduct is beyond human understanding, we must ever strive to be humane. Though not quite a lady, she is none the less bereft. It is our Christian duty to console." And with a bland, forgiving, understanding smile (Nelson had warned him not to see the Hamiltons too often himself, as they found him a bore), all glow and no heat, he added: "At least she is not an uppity woman. Lady Nelson *was*. If we cannot condone irregularity, it is our duty to overlook it. All the same we must not lend it color, so I shall leave my clerical collar at home."

Indeed not: they had no color to spare. But it had been a moral struggle, which is always a physical strain, so William looked extremely pale.

On the 12th of March, Nelson sailed for Denmark under the command of Sir Hyde Parker, to blockade Copenhagen.

"It is your sex that makes us go forth; and seems to tell us—'None but the brave deserve the fair'! And, if we fall, we still live in the hearts of those females who are dear to us. It is your sex that rewards us; it is your sex who cherish our memories."

Which was only true. There was not a woman in England who would not wave her husband good-bye, to see her nation defended, though when it came to sons, the matter was more serious. After that, war was a simple matter of waiting to Applaud the Hero and Hail the Conquering Brave. We are not amazons, but parades are exciting. A woman likes things uniform.

"I feel sorry for Sir Hyde," said Lady Malmesbury, "but no wise man would ever have gone with Nelson, or over him, as he was sure to be in the background in every case."

"Sir Hyde Parker had run his pen through all that could do me credit or give me support; but never mind, Nelson will be first if he lives, and you shall partake of all his glory. I hate your pen-and-ink men: a fleet of British ships of war are the best negotiators in Europe," wrote Nelson to Emma.

Greville, whose life had been ho-hum and chagrin, had quite by chance stumbled upon ah-ha and laughter, for he had bought for a penny Gillray's new cartoon of "Dido in Despair." On a window seat lay open *Academic Attitudes* and a dirty stocking. On the floor lay a ribbon and a book of antiquities. On the dressing table, a pincushion and a bottle of Geneva. In the middle sat an Emma with elephantiasis, roaring pudgy with despair, and through the window the British Fleet could be seen retreating.

> Ah where & ah where is my gallant Sailor Gone?
> He's gone to Fight the Frenchman for George upon the Throne.
> He's gone to fight ye French, an, t'loose t'other Arm & Eye ...

"And left me with the old Antique to lay me down and Cry," he read, memorized it—which was not difficult—and then, being an unselfish man, decided to share his pleasure in the work of so eminent an English draftsman by the common device of mailing Emma a copy of it, in a wrapper, plain.

"Whether Emma will be able to write to you today or not is a question, as she has got one of her terrible sick headaches," wrote Sir William.

But Greville was in a whistling mood, for if you cannot pay the piper just yet, you can at least hum the tune.

Not all the family followed Brother William over to the winning side at once. "I hope in God one day I shall have the pleasure of seeing you together as happy as ever. He certainly, as far as I hear, is not a happy man," wrote Sister Bolton to Lady Nelson. And the Reverend Edmund asked if he could contribute anything to the further increase of her comfort.

On April 2nd, Nelson won the battle of Copenhagen, as usual, by disobeying orders, since battles are as often won that way as lost. News of the victory reached England on the 15th.

"It will mean advancement to a viscountcy at the least, I expect," said Brother William, rejoicing—with his usual universal sympathy—in the welfare of another. "We must monogram the sheets."

This was done, and very handsome they would look when eventually it proved possible to bring them out for an airing.

In London, the news went down less well and there was unusual emphasis upon the casualty lists. Public illuminations were forbidden, the money for them given to the bereaved, for preventive war prevents nothing and obliterates more than it saves. To fight Napoleon was one thing—for everyone dreams of being Napoleon, and yet has no desire to be one of his dreams—but to fight the Danes to help bottle up Napoleon was not popular.

However, 23 Piccadilly burned with lights. Old Q was there, Brother William danced the tarantella with Emma, a simple innocent dance in which a satyr chases a nymph rather than a title. But Sir William, at seventy-one, had been obliged to drop out.

"Your brother was more extraordinary than ever," wrote Sir William to Nelson. "I have lived too long to have ecstasies, but with calm reflection I felt for my friend having got to the very summit of glory. God bless you and send you soon home to your friends." He meant what he said, for women and what they do need not impinge upon what we are among ourselves; and if one has retired from the competition, one cannot very well feel defeated by a mere movement backstairs.

Emma, having exhausted William, the Duke of Noia, her own maid and finally Quasheebaw, was forced to dance alone.

"It would be difficult to convey any adequate idea of this dance, but it is certainly not of a nature to be performed, except before a select company," said Wraxall, the historian, who had looked in and then as promptly popped out again. "The screams, attitudes, starts and embraces with which it is intermingled give it a peculiar character."

In July, Nelson came home.

"I have sometimes a hope of receiving you once more surrounded not with public honors alone, but what must add pleasure to every other gratification, a return to domestic joys, the most durable and solid of all others. Be it so O God," wrote the Reverend Edmund.

"You will at a proper time, and before my arrival in England, signify to Lady Nelson that I expect—and for which I have made such a very liberal allowance to her—to be left to myself, and without any inquiries from her; for sooner than live the unhappy life I did when I last came to England, I would stay abroad forever," wrote Nelson to his man of business; since he was in the wrong, he intended to act with firmness from now on.

On the 27th, as Earl Nelson, he landed at Great Yarmouth, and he and the Hamiltons went to Staines, to fish.

"Would that he had the command over himself which he exerts over others," said Lord Spencer. "And if Lady Nelson were half the woman Lady Hamilton is . . ."

"Lady Nelson is not a woman, but a reputation, though it is marvelous how she keeps up. She wishes to save her good name much more than she wishes to save him," said Lady Spencer impatiently. "And since to her that name is Herbert of Nevis, not Nelson, there is nothing to be done either for or with her. She must go be glum at some provincial watering place, as she prefers." Happy the woman who has at last found her grievance.

"But it is irregular, and the crowd loves him all the same," said Spencer.

"If he were sent to sea again, the irregularities would be less and the public would love him the more," said Lady Spencer, who had given the same advice before, for she was dependable. "You have only to move him about a bit."

So that was settled; all that was needed was a new emergency.

Unfortunately the crowd loves an irregular liaison, given it may read about it in the papers rather than be scandalized by it next door. For what are the great for, if not to do the same as we, if we but dared?

At Staines, they stayed at the Bush Inn, the whole lot of them: William Nelson to guzzle and grope for favor; Emma to guttle; William's wife, to be company; their daughter Charlotte, to clack; and Sir William and Nelson to fish at Shepperton, nearby.

It is pleasant to fish.

They were in one of those ideal landscapes which the English achieve by their usual combination of weeding and leaving well enough alone. The view had aplomb. Water spilled over a stone shelf into a still pool, and from there rippled clear and cool over small stones. The sky was blue, but flocculent with clouds, so that the light alternated, varied, and then came out again. The grass was green and sappy. Under a boulder grew a nibbled crop of violet flags. The nearest sound was a cowbell two fields over. The trees did not stir. It was one of those landscapes which transcend themselves—so exactly the symbol of what they are, that they enter the mind forever; eternal moments, every one of them.

In this dingle, he was far from wishing his uncle dead, for Uncle had disappeared, as so had he. They were merely two men fishing—Sir William, the older; and Horatio, the favorite and favored friend.

In the evening they were together at the inn, which had a garden down to the Thames. Since it was a benevolent summer that year, this meant that they had supper outdoors in the long northern twilight, with lanterns in the shadows and such a scent from the bushes as would make you believe yourself in some better, well-managed, genteel Italy. Other men have wives who shut you out. Sir William, who had only Emma, let you in. Nelson found the party congenial. Brother William might be a timeserver, his wife a rattle, and their daughter a clack, but at least they were all together, which they would not have been had Fanny been there, for Fanny would never have countenanced the informality of supper on the lawn of a public inn, and was both too shy and too proud to put guests at their ease until she left them, while the port went around. With Sir William as a counterweight, the world regulated itself.

And yet Nelson felt sad. It was the twilight, perhaps. Or the fact that they did not live here; that it was only an inn; that there was not much time left—for he felt this these days; that life passes like that white swan out there, floating along the river, in this dim light no more than a blur and a beak. A thought more suitable to Sir William than to him.

I would rather be nibbled by sharks than by time, he thought. Had Emma not persisted to go at such a gallop, they could have jogged along quite well.

He was ordered to Deal, to prepare against the rumored French invasion being mounted at Boulogne. It was the worst scare the English had had since the Dutch sailed up the Medway a hundred and fifty years before, though he suspected it was no more than a ruse whereby Troubridge, Hardy and the rest of the Admiralty Board planned to keep him away from Emma. Well-wishers have no private lives; that is what makes them so concerned for the public good.

"I came on board," he wrote, "but no Emma. I have 4 pictures, but I have lost the original. Will you come down? It might grieve me to see Sir William without you, but if you approve, I will ask. Send to some good wine merchant for three dozen of the very best champagne and order to the Downs by waggon, or I shall have nothing to give you."

It was an inducement. Sir William and Emma went. But what was the use of that, if the old man was always there?

"Emma," said Nelson, "I want you to find me a house. Any house."

"But what about Sir William?" asked Emma, alarmed and astonished, and just as everything was going so smoothly, too.

"You and Sir William will, of course, come on visits. We will always have a room for him. But I want nothing of his in the house except him. For this is to be *our* house."

"But we are going away!" wailed Emma. "Sir William with Greville, and I to the seashore."

Nelson had not been told. "Very well, then, when you return."

"Recollecting that Sir William and Lady Hamilton seemed to be gratified by the flavour of a cream cheese, I have taken the liberty of sending 2 or 3 of Bath manufacture," wrote the Reverend Edmund.

"I have a letter from Troubridge, recommending me to wear flannel shirts. Does he care for me? *No*."

"Here we are, my dear Emma, after a pleasant day's journey. No extraordinary occurrence. Our chaise is good and would have held the famous *Tria juncta in uno* very well, but we must submit to the circumstances of the times!"

"Sir Joseph Banks we found in bed with gout and last night his hothouse was robbed of its choicest fruit, peaches and nectarines . . ."

And that exhausted the day's letter bag, thought Emma, who while Sir William went to Wales, had come to Margate with Horatia, and now sat upon the sands, or rather in a wicker bath chair, sheltered from the wind, in quite her old Ariadne attitude—the one Romney had drawn, though styles in hats had changed. Emma Carew was settled for life, thank goodness, and besides, Emma herself was here by choice. Horatia was a favored child, so it was safe to encourage her. Her parentage held no ambiguities, she was an adopted daughter, the child of the poor defunct Thompsons. And on the whole it was warm; the day was fine. If I cannot hold him, the child can; it is all over, so no more scheming, and so I can at last be myself again.

Getting up somewhat heavily, Emma laughed like a girl and turned her face, cast her eyes down in quite the old Romney manner—even if nowadays the loose flesh on her neck made wrinkles—and skipped a stone across the surface of the sea, secure to play the mother now, since it was only play.

Horatia was such a pretty child, flaxen haired, well dressed, and very like a pet rabbit with a pink nose. Emma looked down at her fondly, and then, sensing something, rose to her feet.

"Winklewoman, go away!" she snapped.

But there was nobody there. It was just that sometimes, in the twilight, things hover so.

"I do not understand it," said Sir Joseph, very decrepit, very gouty, his foot done up in bandages and propped upon a gout stool, but delighted to see a friend still portable. "My exotica do well enough in the winter, in the glasshouse, but they do not seem able to grow accustomed to the summers here. They seldom bud."

The servant finished fussing with the grate and retired. They heard her pause to listen outside the door and then, discouraged that she had been detected, squeak across the hall floorboards and so away.

"William, I am concerned," said Sir Joseph. "The Jerboa has swelled to Jeroboam size."

"I beg your pardon?"

"I speak only as a friend. A Jerboa is a sort of little rat that gets along by leaps and bounds. Do you understand me? Not only is your family concerned, families are always concerned with what does not concern them, but your friends take it very much to heart."

Unfortunately Sir Joseph really was a friend; he would have to have an explication.

"I have the consolation," said Sir William, "that those invisible horns you are at this moment endeavoring not to admire as they sprout from my forehead, though inevitable, were at least placed there by a friend. They are the laurels I look to."

"A curious sort of friend."

"Yes, quite curious. I will grant that that he has seduced my wife does not altogether seduce me. But he is a fine fellow, it is not his fault, and at seventy-two one gets a little lonely, particularly if one prefers the company of the young."

"Yes," said Sir Joseph, "I know."

"It is the very phrase I use myself," agreed Sir William. "And since we both so clearly mean the same thing by it, then since we both know, discussion is unnecessary."

"But—"

"No but. The things that make us happy at one age are not the same as those which make us happy at another. If she makes him happy—which I doubt, for he seems in the torments half the time, poor fellow—then I feel he is amply repaid for so far forgetting himself as to be affectionate toward and considerate of the feelings of a very old man. He is to be pitied, not censured; it seems he can still feel passion."

"Seventy-two is not so old as all that. That's merely seasoned timber," said Sir Joseph, and added an *ouch!* for he himself had remained flesh.

"Perhaps, but I need glue."

"And Charles?"

"My nephew can always be depended upon to look after his own, whether it is his yet or not," said Sir William shortly.

Two days later he was at Milford Haven, sailing a boat on the bay, as he had done in his youth, and listening to Charles' eternal explanations about money and the lack of it and his own poverty; and how, though there was no income, yet in time there would be some, of that he was sure, but at the moment not, for he was out of pocket himself.

" 'Great worth, by poverty oppressed, is slow to rise,' "

said Sir William, who greatly enjoyed to tease Charles. "As Johnson says. But could you not try?"

"I am trying."

"You must remember, my body is not dead yet," said Sir William impersonally. "No doubt you will succeed in time, but I have not much time." And since this was true, he dragged Charles off to the Newmarket races, and enjoyed himself hugely, borrowing fifty pounds from the boy and losing it rapidly.

Though an admirer of horseflesh and pretty women, as became his station, Greville did not gamble.

Emma thought Nelson's unexpected suggestion of a house, though it had taken a hint here and there, an excellent idea, for who knew where she would live if Sir William were to die? He could not leave her much, and what woman of the world would want to sit on an obscure chicken farm, for so she had heard Bronte described, out of favor at court (the dear Queen had never written), out of office, and one's sole companion a retired one-armed Admiral? Besides, Nelson must have some place to entertain his friends.

After some hunting about, she found Merton, "Paradise Merton" as she called it, a small estate in Surrey, an hour's drive from the Piccadilly house, for of course that could not be given up. It was too important to Sir William to retain a house in town. The house and all its contents, said Nelson, were to be hers by deed of gift. So truly, with a light heart, she could set about to make *him* a home.

Sir William, of course, would be equally welcome there. "I assure you every study of mine shall be to make you happy in it. I shall buy fish out of the Thames to stock the water, but I bar barbel. I shall never forget the one you cooked at Staines."

Emma and Sir William were about to go down to Merton for the first time.

"What is that plant doing in the hall?" demanded Sir William.

"Lilac," said Emma, who was excited. "I thought it would look pretty peeping over the wall, and I like the scent so. Both white and mauve."

But though she fussed over it and watered it and even asked the gardener what to do, the lilac was one of her failures. It would not grow.

Sir Joseph sent *exotica*, the zinnias from Mexico in particular successful, though a little strange. It was a plant the Bishop of Derry (released from French captivity at last, thank goodness) had once admired.

The house and grounds had been a bargain at £9,000, complete with furnishings and a private stream. The duck close and field needed to complete the prospect could be bought later. Nelson was helping support some fifteen people, what with Charlotte's singing lessons, Fanny's allowance, pin money for Emma, a loan to Sir William, an annuity to his brother Maurice's widow, another to Graffer's widow in Italy, Josiah to look after, his sister Bolton's children in need of a boost up, and a few more. Duck Close would have to wait.

As so would he, for he could not come ashore just yet. "You will make us rich with your economy," he wrote Emma. As so she would, but there were initial expenses of course. It was necessary to have the carpenters in.

The house was actually two cottages side by side, joined Siamese-twin fashion in the middle. A new eating room and a kitchen had to be added; the south wing had to be revamped for the accommodation of the servants (with a pleasant big bow-windowed downstairs sitting room for Mrs. Cadogan, who would be housekeeper).

When the alterations were complete, the result was a pleasant two-storied red brick house with a white woodwork entrance capped by urns—of the sort that Anthony Devis had enjoyed to paint fifty years earlier—with bedrooms in each wing, a gallery between, and auxiliary staircases so that everyone could be private.

As Beckford—who had dropped by, for gossip must be gathered if it is to be dispensed—had said, it had five bedrooms, most conveniently arranged, a strong room, a dining room for guttling. In short, it was like the Halls of Eblis, cottage-ornée style; "there was a room for *every* vice." Vanity and pride were scattered indiscriminately throughout in the form of portraits of Emma interspersed with Nelson's souvenirs and trophies. The house was to be a shrine, not only to the Hero of the Nile, but also to his *inspiratrix*, his presiding genius, his goddess, she—as he said these days himself—who made his victories possible. The Angelica Kauffmann went in the eating room, the Vigée-Lebrun in the withdrawing room, the Romney of "The Ambassadress" in the front hall—as was only proper—and in the breakfast room, sketches only, but twenty or thirty of those. It was a pity Sir William had never had her sculpted, for a few busts in Nelson's library would have done no harm. However, a Sophocles, a George III, a Homer, a Voltaire and a Burke did quite well. Since perhaps women do not belong in a library—except for an "Alope with Child," by Romney (a graceful allusion to Horatia) to balance the Hoppner of Nelson wearing everything—she left the library alone. Sloth was represented by a sofa, elegantly upholstered in gold and white sateen.

"To be sure, we shall employ the tradespeople of our village in preference to any others in what we want for common use, and give them every encouragement to be kind and attentive to us," advised Nelson. "I expect that all animals will increase where you are." She was a Circe, too. "Have we a nice church at Merton? We will set an example of goodness to the under-parishioners." He thought to have Horatia christened there, but gave the idea up, since the rector would want the parents' names for the register, which would be awkward.

"You are to be Lady Paramount of all the territories and waters of Merton, and we are all to be your guests and to obey all lawful commands." He wanted all his family and naval friends made welcome. It was to be a home. He dreamed of it incessantly.

Lady Paramount was building a chicken coop.

Sir William sat in a wicker chair on the lawn, a rug across his knees, steeped in that autumn tea called sun, and marveled. He was also faintly shocked, for of course one does nothing with one's own hands. One orders it done. This reversion to type at the age of thirty-seven appalled him. She was a daughter of the people after all.

But Emma, with Mrs. Cadogan, was happy, oblivious and full of laughter. She was having a lark.

A white hen flew up into a tree, and Emma was after it, calling "Cupidy, Cupidy," and shaking her skirts. It was certainly droll, he had to admit that. A cock stalked the gravel path. And when Emma and Mrs. Cadogan lined up along the canal and gravely took two mallards and three mandarin ducks out of squawking baskets—their orange feet folded up under them, held them out and dumped them in, whereupon they righted themselves self-righteously and paddled about, reassured if mystified, with the hauteur of animals recently picked up but now themselves again—he had to admit he was amused. He laughed outright. It is true: as we get old, we return to simple things and take comfort from the very shrubs; and if we are just waiting, it is pleasanter to sit on the lawn in the pale sun to wait, than to lurk indoors.

He wrote to Nelson that night, on a smooth-polished mahogany table, while the crickets cracked away outside in purely aural constellations,

> We have now inhabited your Lordship's premises some days & can now speak with some certainty. I have lived with our dear Emma several years. I know her merit, have a great opinion of the head & heart that God Almighty has been pleased to give her; but a seaman alone could have given a fine woman power to chuse & fit up a residence without seeing it himself . . . You have nothing but to come and enjoy immediately; you have a good mile of pleasant dry walk around your own farm [beyond lay the cow pastures]. Your plan as to stocking the Canal with fish is exactly mine. I will answer for that in a few months time you may command a good dish of fish at a moment's notice.

When the purveyor arrived, he was as good as his word and even peered into the baskets while the man dumped the minnows into the canal, a slithery, silvery mass.

"Probably the child will be lodged at Merton, at least in the spring when she can have the benefit of our walks. It will make the poor mother happy I am sure," said Nelson, and sent off for his father, who was still seeing *that woman*, to ask him to pay a visit. On October 23rd, he arrived himself, at dusk, the cold air pungent as the odor of apples in winter store, and paused outside the gate, as overwhelmed, as frightened and as delighted as a child at its first pantomime.

There was the house; there was the steeple; open them out, and there were the people; though he had requested privacy and not to be annoyed by visitors or strangers, for it was retirement with his friends he wished for.

A low autumnal mist hung over the river, and from the invisible garden came the smell of leafmold and compost heaps. Light from the windows shimmered on the mist; and then there he was, ringing at his own door like any beggar, for there being no carriage drive, he had walked up the path—as Sir William would have said, had the season been later and so appropriate to such a remark—to view the Presèpio.

It was Sir William, tall and gracious, who opened the door.

"My dear Nelson," he said, like a father with a marriageable daughter, who quite approved the match but knew why the guest had called, "Emma will be down directly." We need an intermediary to our joys. Sir William was a male confidant through whom it was possible to explain the offstage action and yet keep the unities intact.

It was a charade; and if it lacked an Italian *opera-buffa* passion, well, this was England, which was jollier. In England, we do the same things, in our own way, but we give them different names, for if the wasp is missing, so is the sting.

On the wall of the entryway, "The Ambassadress" held Romney's dog in her lap. Things dragged about for years now stood on tables or hung from walls which did not creak in a high gale. The chandeliers did not sway. Everything had come to rest.

And when Sir William bowed himself upstairs at 10:30 and Emma, devoted as ever, followed him, Nelson had a final tipple at the port while listening to Sir William walk to the south wing, where his bedroom was, while Emma's lighter tread returned to the north one.

Although he had no acquaintance among those of the upper gentry the next moral stage over—who were always careful to ask Y when Lady X came, and Z because otherwise Lord W. wouldn't, and so did not recognize his feelings for what they were—his emotion on hearing the creaking in the corridors above was much the same as theirs. He had seen to everything. The weekend would go.

* * *

In the housekeeper's room, Mrs. Cadogan, who had heard the same sounds, listened to Sir William mutter his way to bed, and thought that though no doubt some folk found it all very odd—and indeed she found it so herself—being snug and warm inside an anomalous situation was by no means as bad as the way it looked when you were outside looking in; in fact, once you had caught your breath, it was only natural. She also considered that Merton (and this snug little room with the Lowestoft plate, locked trunk, pottery bust of George II, and Sir William's gift miniature in a velvet frame on the dresser) suited her. It was all very well for dear Emma to write of her in Palermo that "she has adopted a mode of living that is charming, lives with us, dines &c, &c, onely when she does not like it, for example, great dinners, she herself refuses & as allways a friend to dine with her & La Signora Madre dell' Ambasciatrice is known all over Palermo," but it was agreeable not to have to refuse great dinners and not to have to speak Eyetalian.

Tomorrow she was looking forward to that excellent lifetime game of *keeping the tradespeople in their place*, and *"Of course in Cheshire we never heard the likes of that, well I never!"*; and in other words (her Eyetalian was nothing much, but her French was fair) *la vie commence demain.*

In her room, Emma, who had had almost twenty years to learn that desires once satisfied do not have to be satisfied too often—though what *do* men get out of it, that makes them like it so?—was primped, primed and waiting, and so not at all surprised (though she affected it) to see the handle of her door turn.

But the next day was better. She was a little girl. She wore white.

They went for a tour of the grounds, both the mile of dry path and the streams which crossed the property.

"It is our Nile," said Nelson to Emma.

"It is the Canal," said Sir William, with familiar memories of Stowe.

It was in truth the Wandle, a minor tributary of the Thames. A wattled fence prevented the escape of the fish, but one of the royal swans had hopped over from the other side and now sailed about, to the vast annoyance of the ducks, who were commoners.

Brother William had arrived with his daughter Charlotte. He was always cordial to Emma. She could have no legal children, and for so long as Nelson lived with her, neither could Fanny. He was a loving brother.

When Sir William went fishing, Charlotte tagged along. She had taken a fancy to the old gentleman, even if he did bark at her when all she had done was to upset his creel, shout a bit, and throw rocks in the Wandle.

> He has been *very, very happy* since he arrived, and Charlotte *has* been very attentive to him. Indeed we *all* make it our constant business to make him *happy* [wrote Emma to Mrs. William]. Sir William is fonder than ever, and we manage very

well in regard to our establishment, pay share and share alike, so it comes easy to both parties [of course when they were in town, Sir William paid the expenses. Twenty-three Piccadilly was *his* house] . . . Sir William and Charlotte caught 3 large pike. She helps him and Milord on with their *great coats;* so now I have nothing to do."

"Child, I do not propose to stoop to the height of a dwarf at my age. You must let me mind my own coat," said Sir William tautly, trying to grab it away from her. But the sly child was not only a great clack, she had hooks for hands, and if she fancied herself injured, put up an enormous fuss.

"Dammit!" he snapped. "Give it back."

So off she went, wailing, toward the kitchen quarters.

"But she *likes* you," said Emma, bewildered.

"She is a self-centered, willful, murderous, cacophonous monomaniac," said Sir William. "And, moreover, I am pleased to say, no relative of mine."

"Her mother doesn't know how to dress her, poor thing, that's all; her armpits bind," said Emma.

"Nonetheless, if she is not discouraged from screaming along the canal, I shall strike her with the next pike I strike," said Sir William, and took himself upstairs.

"Charlotte," said Emma, "I am afraid, child, that fishing is something men do."

"Daddy doesn't."

"Daddy is not . . ." began Emma, and paused to consider. "Daddy is a clergyman," she decided finally, but it had been a close thing.

Next day it was she who had to interrupt him. She had been gardening, for though women have no hobbies beyond meddling, marrying off and needlework, when they get past the childbearing age and begin to ape the Graiae, they turn either to gardening or public works. Gardens have no menopause; there is always the hope of something new; one can bully a bulb as well as a baby. As for public works, they are only a form of the higher meddling, and so gratifying in the extreme.

"William," she said, "will you fetch Charlotte from her music lesson for me?"

"No," said Sir William, who so far today had not caught a thing.

"But I can't go. My hands are too dirty."

"Indeed they are, my dear."

"Now don't make a scene," she coaxed. "Someone has to fetch her; she can't trill away all night."

"Why not? There would then be hope that by the morrow she might trill no more," snapped Sir William, but he fetched her.

However, even Charlotte went home in time, all eagerness and adenoids, and life flowed on, or would have had not Emma followed her usual custom of silting up the time with guests, to form some diversion in this backwater.

"The whole establishment and way of life are such as to make me angry as well as melancholy," said Lord Minto after a visit. "The house is covered with nothing but pictures of her and him, and the love she makes to Nelson is not only ridiculous but disgusting. To make his own house a mere looking glass to view himself all day, is bad taste."

"The complaint my dear son has felt," said the Reverend Edmund, "is, I know, very painful. He must not venture without a thick covering, both head and feet, even to admire your parterres of snowdrops which now appear in all their splendor. The white robe which *January* wears, bespangled with ice, is handsome to look at, but we must not approach too near *her*." He, too, had been brought around, though he had pangs about deserting Fanny.

"Let everything be buried in oblivion; it will pass away like a dream," wrote that lady, making her final effort to overcome the inevitable.

But Nelson had found oblivion elsewhere.

Sir William had not. The chickens squawked. The rooster crowed. And Charlotte had come back for a visit.

"It is but reasonable," he wrote to Greville, "after having fagged all my life, that my last days should pass off comfortably and quietly." He was beginning to discover that a paying guest has no home. He minded the infidelity far less than the noise, the disturbance, the drinking, and Emma more Wild Polly of Portsmouth than still and perfect as a vase, unraveling her Attitudes at Portici.

Also, there were the almost quarrels.

"My man of business says you told him to tell me not to send you any more advice about seeing company," wrote Nelson to Emma, having escaped to town.

"Nothing at present disturbs me but my debt and the nonsense I am obliged to submit to here to avoid coming to an explosion," wrote Sir William to Greville, "which wou'd be attended with many disagreeable effects, and would totally destroy the comfort of the best man and the best friend I have in the world. However I am determined that my quiet shall not be disturbed, let the nonsensical world go on as it will."

* * *

"Has she been working on you?"
"Working on me? What about?"
"About the will," said Greville.

"No, of course not," said Sir William, realizing he must look as ill as he felt, which would never do. But he managed to sound thoroughly shocked—convincingly, too, for of course she had been. Since they had done nothing to earn it, naturally his relatives would feel they had a right to his money. Not that there would be much.

Greville came neither to 23 Piccadilly nor to Merton these days. It would be indelicate of him to do so, he said, by which he meant that the situation there was too indelicate for him to stomach. "And as Vice-Chamberlain to His Majesty, I could not allow it even to be suggested—as my presence would suggest—that Their Majesties lent color to . . . ah . . . um . . . em . . . well, *any* irregularity."

"But I am his wife. Why should Greville have everything?" demanded Emma. She was indignant.

"What signifies the dirty acres to you?" shouted Nelson right back. "You've not even seen them."

"I haven't seen the income either," said Emma. "Nor has Sir William. And you yourself said Greville was a scoundrel."

"Then there is no need to keep him company."

"But I don't *like* Greville!" wailed Emma. It was always so difficult to make men understand that a woman has so little to fight with, to protect her little all, that a scrupulous choice of implements is seldom in her power.

"My partiality to you, and the thorough confidence I have in you, despite of any attempts that have been made to disturb them, remains, and will, I am confident, to my last moment, in full force," wrote Sir William to Greville. "My visit to Milford last year convinced me of the propriety of all your operations there, which may still operate in my favour during the short time I can expect to live, but must be attended with immense profit to my heirs hereafter...."

Emma was a Hamilton by marriage, not by character, and there is an entail of the heart as well as of land. There was, perhaps fortunately, only one of her. But there were many Hamiltons, and that they be provided for was no more than Roman piety. In each generation, the same couple play out the same inevitable drama—it is only the circumstantial details that change—and for this they will need the family costumes, props and properties.

"I admit she is sometimes difficult," said Nelson.

"Always admit what cannot be denied," agreed Sir William, "but only to yourself; never to others. That way you save both the appearance and the reality."

He was not bitter. Nonetheless, he knew that an old man must never ask for anything he cannot pay for; so much for candles, so much for wine, and a lien against the estate in order to bribe a proper funeral and an affectionate regard.

Alone in the house at 23 Piccadilly, he found himself trying to remember when emotion in him had died. It was difficult to detect the exact moment, since he had been a dutiful son, an affectionate husband, a fond uncle, a passionate connoisseur of the antique, a kindly lover, an obliging husband the second time, a warm friend upon occasion; there was no chink anywhere, therefore it must have been at some other time—when he was a child perhaps. He had thus come equipped to maturity, for it is true, the absence of consideration allows us to be considerate; the death of loving, to be affectionate; the irrelevance of hope, to be cheerful; death by slow social strangulation, to be sociable; and if we can hold our liquor, so much the better—we shall be clubbable fellows to the end. So we become the fetches of ourselves, always beckoning, but no one comes, because we are not there. We are only an appearance. We have become realists.

Dear me, this won't do at all, said Sir William to himself, rather hoping Mrs. Cadogan would appear with one of her loathsome cups of beef broth, but she was at Merton. It is my body is depressed, not I.

Though he had been sensible of its inevitability, even as a young man, Sir William had seldom pondered the decline itself. There are only two forms of decay available to us: either one dies surrounded by one's loved ones, or else one goes off to the graveyard in a weary rage, like a bull elephant, all by oneself. Which is to say, the cleaning woman finds you the next morning dead, with a book fallen off the coverlet and the candle snuffer never used. All of which was unavoidable and therefore could be accepted. What he could not accept, and had never envisioned, was that one should sit dying surrounded by loved ones who not only paid you no heed whatsoever, but screamed their heads off besides.

The ancient Romans, when simulating that civilization to which they aspired but for which they would make no effort beyond the borrowing, were saved from the horrors of decay—if eminent enough—by the social discipline, legal benefits and imperial sanction of suicide. When they could not kill each other, they calmly (we are told calmly) killed themselves. But that was before

Christianity imposed dalliance upon even the post-Augustan mind and went fishing for souls with the sky hook of salvation, jerking us ashore whether we wished to be landed or not.

The next best thing, I suppose, thought Sir William, since I am about to leave England for the last time, is to pay the obligatory round of courtesy calls and farewell visits. And indeed it will be agreeable to do so, for people are always at their pleasantest just before you leave. And since I do not like this house empty, back to Merton Place I suppose it must be.

Nelson had bought two cows, two calves, the back pasture and the duck close, too. He proposed a farm.

"Emma, do you like what you have become?" asked Sir William, thinking of Greville's Paulus Potter and perhaps of his Honorable Emily Bertie, too.

"Become?" she asked, astonished. "Why, I am what I have always been." She went on feeding the chickens.

That was perhaps true, yet for a brief moment fifteen years ago she had given promise of becoming somebody else. It seemed to him curious that Nelson should like her for what he thought to be her polish, whereas he—who had supplied the polish—had liked her best for something polish can never give.

If only it were not for the noise, thought Sir William, who was beginning to find the bosom of a family as bumpy as that of Diana of Ephesus (whom, indeed, in other ways, Emma was coming to resemble).

It was spring. Charlotte came and went, an adolescent timeserver, like her father. The apple trees were in early bloom and there was now a beehive. Emma turned around and around in the kitchen garden, like an old winklewoman, to choose an icebox lettuce which, since there was still frost at night, had the feel of a pickled brain in an anatomy school. Charlotte, all ink and vivacity, was translating one of Madame Sevigné's letters, not well. The Reverend Edmund was to arrive and would be company, or at any rate, a coeval.

Sir William, who could not bear it, went up to town.

When he returned, it was to find still another child there. Horatia was now over two.

"She is the daughter of one of my cadets, a man named Thompson," said Nelson. "I propose to adopt her, and Emma has kindly offered to assist."

A great deal of his time was spent sitting on the grass with the child. Emma, in her best little-girl manner, also played with it. It was a docile child. Sir William had no complaints to make of it, but the whole household now seemed organized around it. You caught glimpses of it being dandled somewhat every time you went for a walk or tried to use the library. Even Mrs. Cadogan had taken to hovering.

The apple blossoms came wandering down, cast loose by an afternoon shower.

"And the *dish*," said Emma, with a glance at Nelson, "ran away with the spoon," playing with Horatia's toes.

"Fork," said Nelson.

"Not in this case." Emma gave him one of her more dazzling smiles. It was their love pledge, was it not?

Sir William, who had gone to the orchard for a stroll, turned back and did not know why he was so angry, except that the child so clearly had the Nelson nose.

Was Greville to be disinherited to the benefit of that? He was not ravished by the appearance of little Miss Thompson. And if he wished to take the carriage to town, why should he not do so? It was his carriage.

> I have passed the last 40 years of my life in the hurry and bustle that must necessarily be attendant on a public character [he wrote angrily]. I am arrived at the age when some repose is really necessary, and I promise myself a quiet home, and altho' I was sensible, and said so when I married, that I shou'd be superannuated when my wife wou'd be in her full beauty and vigour of youth. That time is arrived, and we must make the best of it for the comfort of both parties. Unfortunately our tastes as to the manner of living are very different. I by no means wish to live in solitary retreat, but to

have seldom less than 12 or 14 at table, and those varying continually, is coming back to what was become so irksome to me in Italy during the latter years of my residence in that country. I have no connections out of my family. I have no complaint to make, but I feel that the whole attention of my wife is given to Ld. N. and his interest at Merton. I well know the purity of Ld. N.'s friendship for Emma and me, and I know how very uncomfortable it wou'd make his Lp., our best friend, if a separation shou'd take place, and am therefore determined to do all in my power to prevent such an extremity, which wou'd be *essentially detrimental* to all parties, but wou'd be more sensibly felt by our dear friend than us. Provided that our expences in housekeeping do not encrease beyond measure (of which I must own I see some danger), I am willing to go on upon our present footing; but as I cannot expect to live many years, every moment to me is precious, and I hope I may be allow'd sometimes to be my own master, and pass my time according to my own inclination, either by my fishing parties on the Thames or by going to London to attend the Museum, R. Society, the Tuesday Club, and Auctions of pictures. I mean to have a light chariot or post chaise by the month, that I may make use of it in London and run backwards and forwards to Merton or to Shepperton, etc. This is my plan, and we might go on very well, but I am fully determined not to have more of the very silly altercations that happen but too often between us and embitter the present moments exceedingly. If really one cannot live comfortably together, a *wise* and well *concerted separation* is preferable; but I think, considering the probability of my not troubling any party long in this world, the best for us all wou'd be to bear those ills we have rather than flie to those we know not of. I have fairly stated what I have on my mind. There is no time for nonsense or trifling. I know and admire your talents and many excellent qualities; but I am not blind to your defects, and confess having many myself; therefore let us bear and forbear for God's sake.

If it was querulous, he could not help it. Rage without either the will or power to punish is always querulous.

Of this even-tempered epistle, Emma caught only the next to last phrase.

"Horatio, he knows about the child!" she yowled. She was both indignant and frightened.

Nelson took the letter, read it, and became solemn. He did not reassure her.

"It is his way to hint. He says he is not blind to my defects." She could think of no others.

"He is right. There is no call to shout at him. He is not in his grave yet, you know," said Nelson soberly.

"*I* shout at Sir William?" She was outraged.

"Up and down the stairs again."

"But he's so difficult sometimes."

"He is an old man. And though you are not, thank goodness, his wife, he is your husband. And for mention of that, I do not like these incessant dinner parties either."

"I only ask your friends."

"What friends? Does Troubridge come? Does Hardy come?"

"But we cannot afford two carriages, and the one is always in use. Charlotte uses it. Your brother William uses it. All the Nelsons use it. And something must be available if Horatia is to be fetched. Besides, it is not my fault. They have been asked."

"Let the old man have his chariot," said Nelson. "And let him also have his evening quietly till it be out."

She did not understand. She was deeply hurt. He did not seem to sympathize.

With Mrs. Cadogan she fared no better.

"But why? Indeed I am not conscious of any fault. What have I done?" she demanded, and threw a scene and roared like a lion, who in times past would have shivered like a mouse.

Mrs. Cadogan folded her hands. "You've been yourself and it won't do," she said. "If you tumble him down, you will tumble right after him. Sir William means exactly what he says."

Emma pouted, a thing she had never done when young, when misfortune had slimmed her down and made her acceptable. But being at bottom a good-tempered creature with no malice in her—only a little necessary tendency to plot—she said,

"Very well, he shall have his chariot if he wants one. I suppose we can economize somewhere."

And off she went to Sir William's room, to say she was sorry; and sat on the floor and rested her head against the arm of his chair and confessed that, yes, she had been bad, though this twenty years later, she did not cry, but watched a branch sway outside the window instead.

"Oh, William, do forgive me, do," she said. "It is all so difficult to manage."

"It is too late in the evening for Greek Attitudes," said Sir William. "It is not a matter of forgiving or forgetting either. It is simply a matter of learning how to control yourself. Now go to bed. I am tired."

So Emma gave him a filial kiss on the forehead, and since contrition had made her hungry, went downstairs and ate two slices off a saddle of mutton in the larder, and a bunch of haws; puzzled, while cracking them, with the feeling that she had done all this before.

But she would *try*. If he wanted to go up to town, very well, they would all go up. It was some time since they had had a week in town.

In April, Nelson's father died at Bath, on the 26th, which was Emma's birthday. Nelson was himself too ill to attend the funeral.

"My poor, poor Horatio," said Emma, compassionately. She was still his little wife. But Nelson had had a wife before.

"I should like to sit a while with Sir William," he said. "Alone."

Emma went off, just as relieved as not. She did not understand silent grief. In Cheshire, one held a wake and beat the walls. She could remember that from childhood. For one must do something, and there is nothing to say. They are just dead, that's all.

Whereas as far as she could overhear, Nelson and Sir William sat in the library and said nothing whatsoever; she was relieved when at last she heard the stopper to a tantalus chink.

Nelson was standing at the window, looking out at a gray day.

"I tried to make her sensible," he said, "that she must modify her ways, since she cannot mend them. She has a loving heart. It is merely that it takes these overexuberant forms."

Sir William said nothing. There was nothing to be said. If they could not share the same wife in the same ways, it was nonetheless evident that they had come to share the same burden.

"She has many virtues," said Nelson doggedly.

"Yes, many," said Sir William, also loyal.

The devil of it was, they were both fond of her.

"I am glad you are here," said Nelson. "Which is odd, for I have been jealous sometimes."

Sir William refilled their glasses. "Strong brandy never did any man ill," he said. "And you, too, I think, feel often much alone."

"He was a nice old man toward the end. He did his best, according to his lights."

"Yes, he was," agreed Sir William. But the property should go to Greville, all the same.

"The dear Queen has returned to Naples," said Emma, reading *The Morning Herald*. "I wonder why she does not write."

"Ah yes," said Sir William equanimously. "I wonder."

"And she pledged eternal friendship," said Emma scornfully.

"And so did you, my dear," said Sir William, who had heard that Maria Carolina now made much of a Countess Razoumovski, a perfect unique friend, and like the Russian lady on the boat, no doubt all sensibility.

"Well, I can't write letters to everyone," said Emma, but she looked put out, all the same. However, that was in the past, and as for the present, they were off for a journey to Wales tomorrow and she was looking forward to that, for things had been dull at Merton recently, with so few guests; she had felt constrained.

The trip was a triumph, barring a temper tantrum and an incident along the way.

Oxford bestowed its freedom on Nelson and made both him and Sir William Honorary Doctors at Civil Law. From there they went to Woodstock Manor and up to Blenheim, a damp and soggy pile, admirable for the connoisseur of pictures, since the landscape combined Salvator's wildness, Claude's enlivening grace, and cascades and lakes as good as anything in Ruisdael.

Unfortunately the Duke would not receive them, though they might survey the grounds if they so wished.

"Nelson," shouted Emma, as they left, "shall have a monument to which Blenheim shall be but a pigsty!" She was outraged.

At Gloucester, they met the tailor and ate the cheese while the crowd cheered and church bells rang, which was more as things should be. And at Tenby, their reception was equally exhilarating.

"I was yesterday witness to an exhibition which, though greatly ridiculous, was not wholly so, for it was likewise pitiable, and this was in the persons of two individuals who have lately occupied much public attention," said Mr. Gore of that town to his family. "I mean the Duke of Bronte, Lord Nelson, and Emma, Lady Hamilton. The whole town was at their heels as they walked together. The lady is grown immensely fat and equally coarse, while her 'companion in arms' has taken to the other extreme—thin, shrunken, and to my impression, in bad health. They were evidently vain of each other, as though the one would have said 'This is Horatio of the Nile,' and the other, 'This is the Emma of Sir William.' Poor Sir William, wretched but not abashed, he followed at a short distance, bearing in his arms a *cucciolo* and other emblems of combined folly."

The *cucciolo* was a recent acquisition. It was a little dog, the progress from overeating to dramming to little dogs being not unknown among women bigger than they used to be.

The small company went up the street and Mr. Gore went home, not unsympathetically, for since Sir William was an old man—among a people noted for their almost Chinese reverence for age per se—public censure had decided merely to pity him; to feel for Nelson (he was a Hero but had been much abroad where life was notoriously unhealthy, so no doubt he had caught the Passion there. But then, our health is not our own fault); and to loathe her.

The fourth anniversary of the Battle of the Nile was spent with Greville at Milford Haven. There was a Welsh fair, a rowing match, a cattle show and a banquet. Nelson, struck by the possibilities of the harbor, recommended to the Admiralty that a dockyard be established there. So, thought Greville, he is a fine fellow led by the nose, that's all.

At Hereford, the Duke of Norfolk bestowed the city's freedom in an applewood box and afterward gave them cider. Unfortunately Sir William insisted she smile at the crowds when they laughed at her and that he be allowed to fish, when what she wanted was that he come with her, to lend her support. Afraid to speak out in her own defense, she left a note on his pillow instead and retired to her room with audible groans.

> As I see it is a pain to you to remain here, let me beg of you to fix your time for going. Weather I dye in Piccadilly or any other spot in England, 'tis the same to me; but I remember the time when you wish'd for tranquility, but now all visiting and bustle is your liking. However, I will do what you

please, being ever your affectionate and obedient,
E.H.

"Emma," said Sir William, "get up."
"I will not attend the dinner. I have one of my sick headaches."
"If you persist in parading about like small German royalty, you must learn the discipline and smile until they stop booing," said Sir William. "Now come along and do not spoil our banquet. As for my desire to fish, it is an excellent stream, I shall not see it again, and I propose therefore to fish it."
"Fish and be damned. I will not go."
He fished, and what was more, presented the catch to the innkeeper, who served up a small fry for dinner, with a most excellent salmon as the centerpiece.
Bah.

But on a good day she was still agreeable, and at Downton, where Richard Payne Knight entertained them, consented to impersonate a few antique coins—in short, more Attitudes, but this time from the neck up only.

At Worcester, the freedom of the city came in a porcelain vase rather than an applewood box, and Nelson ordered a dessert service with his arms all over it. At Birmingham, fittingly enough, there was a performance of *The Merry Wives of Windsor*. At Warwick, as usual, the Earl talked too much, and at Althorp, they stayed with Lord and Lady Spencer.

"It still goes on," said Lady Spencer.
"Most clocks do until they run down," said Lord Spencer, who had been shocked by Nelson's appearance. "We must get him to sea again. I do hope war breaks out before it is too late. If not, some other pretext must serve."
Fortunately war, like Emma's elbows, was always breaking out, and if she found sea bathing efficacious, so would the fleet, no doubt. It was only a matter of time. All that was necessary, was that Bonaparte go

first, to break the ice. This time, however, Bonaparte seemed a little slow to commence, sensing it, perhaps, to be thin.

By September, they were back at Merton. "We have had a most charming tour which will Burst *some* of THEM," said Emma. "So let all enemies of the GREATEST man alive perish. And bless his friends."

In November, Romney died. "Why fancy that!" said Emma. "I wondered what had become of him. And I was going to write a letter to him, too." Which was true enough. She had been meaning to write it now for the past ten years. And looking at "The Ambassadress" with a wistful expression, she added, "Poor George."

And then it was winter again.

Once more Sir William looked out into the garden at that parterre of snowdrops—lovely, nodding, insubstantial things which the Reverend Nelson had not lived to see again, but had admired. He looked at them from a rapidly increasing distance. He had tired of life, as one does of everything in time, unless it tire of us first. It is but civil to make the first move. One must put the world at its ease. But the snowdrops merely nodded good-bye affably, or else they were shaky on their pale green sappy stalks. Like them, he had pulled through, and yet it could not be too long now. For though the snows had half melted and the woods were full of floral processions—all moving off, all circling back, all fugitive, all part of faërie—it was time for him also to say good-bye.

He turned to the fire in the grate, and watched water bubbles hiss at the end of a log, with the peristaltic movement of a centipede.

Well, what have I done? he thought. I have published some excellent engravings after the antique. I have detected Vesuvius in an eruption. I have forced the British Museum to pay handsomely—a thing not easily done. I have finally unloaded a spurious Correggio; and I have undergone Emma.

I shall be remembered, I suppose, for that. Alas, I

can deal only with the esthetic; the inesthetic is beyond me. So since there is nothing I can do about it, all I can do is to sit still in the midst of it, looking at an old volume of landfalls, of almost identical coasts, wistfully. Indeed it is a blessing to be a little deaf.

"Nuncle," said Horatia, who had been brought in to visit him.

"No," said Sir William; but yes, she was a docile creature, and it was not Nelson's fault.

As Sarah Churchill had said when old—that first best and worst of the Marlboroughs, but the woman showed shrewd sense—in this life there is nothing to be done but to make the best of what cannot be helped; to act with reason oneself and with good conscience toward others. And though that may not give all the joys some people might wish for, yet it is sufficient to make one very quiet.

In March, he went up to town for the second time that year, to present to the Society of Antiquaries a mutilated stone head bearing traces of gilding on its coronet, a piece of the ancient walls of Merton Abbey. It was, he hoped, the last piece. Then, not caring to cause distress, he had himself moved from Merton to 23 Piccadilly. Not caring to cause him any, Emma and Nelson came along.

"He is very very bad. He can't, in my opinion, get over it, and I think it will happen very soon," said Nelson. "You will imagine Lady Hamilton's and my feelings on the occasion. Indeed, all London is interested in the fate of such a character."

Though willing to be obedient, his sister Bolton could not imagine them, quite.

On the 6th of April he died, with Nelson to hold one hand and Emma the other. For dying is very like giving birth: in either event, one has to brace one's self.

"Gone?" asked Emma.

"Gone," said Nelson, looking down at that face which had always been a mask but now had nobody to look out through it any more. He closed the eyes.

Straightening up like conspirators once the act is done,

they caught in each other's eyes an expression which said both too little and too much. It disconcerted both of them. The body lay between.

"Our dear Sir William died at ten minutes past ten this morning," said Nelson, and careful of the proprieties, moved in with Greville for the time being; and then, even more carefully, out.

"Unhappy day for the forlorn Emma. Ten minutes past ten dear blessed Sir William left me," wrote Emma. She was finding the air a little thin, but had taken a house in Clarges Street, for she had to have some place in town. Greville had evicted her from 23 Piccadilly at once.

"Sir William Hamilton died on Sunday afternoon, and was quite sensible to the last," said Captain Hardy. "How Her Ladyship will manage to live with the Hero of the Nile now, I am at a loss to know—at least in an honorable way."

The body was taken off for burial in Wales, and Emma was left alone with Mrs. Cadogan. "They have taken away something that belonged to me," she said. Which was true; they had.

"Are you my mummy?" asked Horatia, who was three now, and like the other one, precocious.

"Your mother is a woman Too Great to be Named," said Emma, and began to weep.

The will was not read until the beginning of May.

To his dearest loyal and truly brave friend Nelson, a copy of Madame Lebrun's picture of Emma in enamel, by Bone. "God bless him and shame fall on those who do not say amen."

To Emma, £300 in cash and an annuity of £800— £100 of it to go to Mrs. Cadogan during her lifetime.

The rest to Greville, who was also to administer the estate.

"My dear Emma," said Greville, with a small smile he had been saving now for twenty years and could at last let out. "I shall see to everything."

And charged her interest, fee and tax.

"Eight hundred pounds a year. It is not enough money to throw at a cat," said Emma. Her expenses had risen. Her standards had changed. It was a worry.

She spoke to everyone. She petitioned for a pension.

"She talked very freely," said Lord Minto, "of her situation with Nelson, but protested that their attachment had been perfectly pure, which I declare I can believe, though I am sure it is of no consequence whether it is so or not. The shocking injury done to Lady Nelson is not made less or greater by anything that may or may not have occurred between him and Lady Hamilton."

So pension she got none.

Nelson, who had been ordered to the Mediterranean, allowed her £100 a month housekeeping money. He made no bones about going. "If the devil stands at the door, the *Victory* shall sail tomorrow forenoon," he wrote to St. Vincent. But neither did he make any bones about his intention to come back.

"That dear domestic happiness," said Codrington fondly, "never abstracted his attention." Their hero was himself again. "He has sighted Gibraltar. He will be a bachelor beyond it."

So it was all not quite the way Emma had imagined it would be, though she might have Horatia at Merton as much as she pleased, and see Old Q in town, and of course the Matchams were coming on Thursday and the William Nelsons for the weekend, and there were always some of Nelson's naval friends to entertain; they were good boisterous boys, there was no harm in them. Something was always happening. And so . . . And so . . .

Madame Vigée-Lebrun was in London, so Emma went calling, in a black dress, a black cloak, black gloves, a black bonnet. Since she must wear mourning for a year, it was well that black suited her. Her hair was done in the new fashionable Titus cut.

Time had not altered the Great Refugee, but she was running out of royalties to paint, and since she shrank from the thought of penciling a parvenu, was here to do the peerage.

The two women consoled each other.

"In Sir William I lost both a friend and a father," wailed Emma, noble in grief, like Adrienne Le Couvreur, but showing no signs of having swallowed poison. "And how do you find England?"

"*Eh bien,*" said Madame Lebrun—with a philosophical shrug—in that engaging way which so endears her countrymen to all. "*C'est curieux. En Angleterre, l'esprit public est plus sain; en France, l'esprit particulier vaut mieux; de sorte qu'en Angleterre vous trouverez plutôt un meilleur peuple, et en France, un meilleur homme. Mais,*" she added graciously, if without conviction, "*c'est toute la même chose.*"

Commissions were not going well.

Through the window, Emma glimpsed a white lilac nodding beyond the glass. Wishing to smell it, she went to the window to let the fragrance in, to refresh her. Unfortunately the window would not budge.

"It sticks," said Madame Lebrun in flawless but contemptuous English. It was a word she had learned recently.

Emma was baffled. Was she supposed to weep again? she wondered.

She is playing a part, thought Madame Lebrun, beady-eyed as ever. The English *always* play a part.

"I too have lost my little all," she said. "The house in Paris, you know. Confiscated." Not a bacchante, she thought, a veritable Bacchus, like that horrid Italian one in the Boboli Gardens. Or is that a Silenus? However, she managed to look sympathetic. She wished to hear more.

"I can never be consoled," said Emma experimentally.

"*Évidemment,*" said Madame Lebrun, watching Emma's hands from force of habit as that so sad lady wandered around the room. Lady Hamilton she might be, but Madame Lebrun did not care for commoners.

At the piano, Emma's eye was caught by a sheet of music, Richard Bloomfield's "A Visit to Ranelagh."

"'As performed,'" she read, "'by Miss Randles, aged three and a half, the Wonderful Musical Welsh Child.'"

"Whatever is this?" she asked, curious.

"Something a friend brought to amuse me," said Madame Lebrun, and added kindly, "I have not heard it. *C'est épatant, elle dit, mais ce n'est pas le tonnerre.*" She had the Gallic weakness for linguistic bead stringing, if not the ability. Her black little eyes clicked like an abacus.

But Emma sat down at the piano and rattled away.

"To Ranelagh once in my life,
  By good-natur'd force I was driv'n;
The nations had ceas'd their long strife,
  And PEACE beam'd her radiance from Heav'n.
What wonders were there to be found
  That a clown might enjoy or disdain?
First we trac'd the gay ring all around,
  Ay—and then we went round it again.
                                        It was jolly.

" 'Tis not wisdom to love without reason,
  Or to censure without knowing why:
I had witness'd no crime, nor no treason,
  'O life, 'tis thy picture,' said I.
'Tis just thus we saunter along,
  Months and years bring their pleasure or pain,
We sigh midst the RIGHT and the WRONG;
  —And then WE GO ROUND THEM AGAIN!"

"Oh I *like* it," she said. And forgetting her costume, she was radiant and smiling.

Madame Lebrun was not impressed. *"On ne gagne pas plus à ennuyer un Francais qu'à divertir un Anglais,"* she said in her shrewd, kindly way, totaling up her mental sum.

"Oh but I *do* like it," said Emma, for it had a cheerful ducking and bobbing rhythm. It had quite put her in spirits again. "May I have it?"

"Of course, dear child. Why not? If it suits you, take it," said Madame Lebrun, who had never heard such a vulgar low song in her life; so typically English, and besides, now curiosity was satisfied, it would be well to get rid of her. They are *canaille*.

So out Emma sailed with it, into the bright, fresh, crisp spring air—feeling ever so much better for having done her duty and paid her respects—humming the tune happily, with an occasional glance at the words, and delighted, considering what the recent past had been, to be out in the present tense again, where the sun still shines. It was a lovely, lovely day, and off she drove, beguiled and beguiling.

Life is a dream.

Cranbrook—Paris—Walnut Creek
June—November 1962